LET GO MY HAND

Also by Edward Docx

THE CALLIGRAPHER

SELF HELP

THE DEVIL'S GARDEN

EDWARD DOCX

LET GO MY HAND

PICADOR

First published 2017 by Picador
an imprint of Pan Macmillan
20 New Wharf Road, London N1 9RR
Associated companies throughout the world
www.panmacmillan.com

ISBN 978-0-3304-6352-2 HB
ISBN 978-1-5098-5102-7 TPB

1 3 5 7 9 8 6 4 2

A CIP catalogue record for this book is available from the British Library.

Printed and bound by CPI Group (UK) Ltd, Croydon, CR0 4YY

Visit **www.picador.com** to read more about all our books
and to buy them. You will also find features, author interviews and
news of any author events, and you can sign up for e-newsletters
so that you're always first to hear about our new releases.

For O, S, W & R

who taught me the meaning of love.

Act 4, Scene 6: On the Dover Cliffs.

GLOUCESTER   Let go my hand.
    Here, friend, 's another purse; in it a jewel
    Well worth a poor man's taking: fairies and gods
    Prosper it with thee! Go thou farther off;
    Bid me farewell, and let me hear thee going.
EDGAR Now fare you well, good sir?

Shakespeare, from *King Lear*

'First we've got to clear the ground.'

Ivan Turgenev, from *Fathers and Sons*

'Oh God said to Abraham, "Kill me a son"
Abe says, "Man, you must be puttin' me on"
God say, "No." Abe say, "What?"
God say, "You can do what you want Abe, but
The next time you see me comin' you better run"
Well Abe says, "Where do you want this killin' done?"
God says, "Out on Highway 61"'

Bob Dylan, from 'Highway 61 Revisited'

PART ONE

PORTRAIT OF A FATHER

DOVER

I should never have agreed to any of this. But I only start to feel the reality when we arrive in Dover and pull into the ferry terminal. I wind down the window for border control and the cold air blusters in – all sea salt, diesel and ship rust – and I can hear gulls screaming like there's been a murder.

I hand over the passports.

'Holiday?' the border guard asks.

And I hoist myself a grin: 'Yes.'

She glances over at Dad and I lean back so that she can see past me and decide if we're the kind of people who might want to blow up the ferry for some insane reason not to do with anything that matters. We're in the ragged old camper van because we don't have a car. Dad has fallen asleep in the passenger seat, which is all wrong, given that we used to do this every summer with him at the wheel, long after my older brothers didn't want to come with us and it was only me and Mum and Dad.

Back come the passports. I stow Dad's with mine in the little compartment under the wheel as if I'm the one who's in charge. Then I take a self-conscious breath of that sea air again, making out to myself that it's a big surprise, which it always is, and I roll us gently up to the next booth, where a guy from the ferry company hands me one of those oblong pieces of paper with the number of the lane in which you're meant to queue for the boat. Ours says '76', which is five years older than Dad. I hang it from the rear-view mirror and head towards the lanes of eager cars waiting to board. And all of a sudden, my emotions rise and I don't know where to look or how to be.

The thing is that right about now, when I was a little boy, Dad would pull up and jump out of the driver's seat to make the tea, racing with himself, like he was one of those Grand Prix mechanics. And because in those days the van was packed too full to get to the hob when we were travelling, and probably because he didn't want to disturb Ralph and Jack because they could be such difficult bastards, he'd hunker on the tarmac and light the little camping stove. And I'd be right there crouching down beside him, watching the tiny blue flame roar and stretch in the blustery wind, hands on the knees of my best summer-holiday jeans, five years old but acting as if I was working for Ferrari, too. And all the while in the van, my brothers would be reading, and Mum would have her window down and she'd be hanging her arm out and craftily smoking her Luckies and hoping that the line didn't get called before the water was boiled because she knew that once he had started, Dad wouldn't give it up until he'd had his 'cuppa', as she liked to say in her best British accent.

So next I need to work out whether Dad and I are going to have some tea while we wait, which I will have to make, since his 'capacity for fine movement will continually diminish', as they say in one of the eight hundred PDFs I've read about 'what to expect' and 'how to prepare'. And this seems like another impossible thing that we have to decide.

A man in a high-visibility jacket waves us into 'lane 76'

4

with the other vans and four-by-fours. I pull up and the handbrake clicks like some old watch wound to the end of its spring. And because I don't want to speak to Dad with this emotional surge going on, I open my door and climb out all in one movement – as if I am the one who gets cramps in his legs.

But straight away I wish I had stayed in the damn van. Because now I'm standing in the car park looking at the darkened windows of this off-road estate car with all these kayaks on the roof and bikes on the back and the father of the family is getting out and saying, 'I got it – two caps and a latte,' and he's shooting me a look across the hood like he's this big leader of men or something and don't I just know he's a great father and he'd probably be a great warrior, too, if he had to be, which he doesn't. And I'm shaking like maybe I *am* going to blow up the ferry. And so I turn round and next thing I'm sliding open the noisy rear door of the van, which needs oiling, but when are we going to do that?

'How you feeling, Dad?' I ask.

'I'm fine.' Dad smiles, looking back from the passenger seat up front. He is wearing terrible clothes as usual – his custard-yellow fleece, his beige over-washed chinos, his lightweight walking boots of which he is unaccountably proud. 'Thinking about a jog,' he says.

I nod slowly. We row back and forth between jokes and sarcasm these days like we're scared of landfall.

'Just had one,' I say. 'You were asleep.'

'Another half-marathon?'

'Yep – and a couple of klicks sea-kayaking.'

He looks at me and sucks his teeth. We hate a word like 'klick'.

'Actually,' he says, 'I might do some of that aggressive yoga.'

'It's very spiritual out there, Dad.'

He surveys the massed ranks of SUVs silently laying waste to whatever future humanity might yet sneak. His jaw spasms from time to time and he yawns a lot.

That sea air has slipped in around my shoulders and cooled me down. I climb up and Dad starts loosening the catch on his seat so that he can swivel it to face backwards. I start filling up the kettle from the water carrier. It looks like we're going all the way on tea. So I set up the grey plastic table in the back at which we have had so many convivial meals. Dad bought the van in 1989, just before I was born; it's a metallic blue, boxy, unfashionable 1980s-style VW and you wouldn't want it – even if you inherited it strife-free. But – for us at least – it's got soul. Which counts. Or which *should* count.

From the edge of my eye, I can see that Dad is struggling to get the passenger seat swivelled round. When you're not having trouble with your legs, you can press your feet into the floor and turn it that way. But Dad gets this feeling of pins and needles a lot, he says; he's got what they call 'lower limb onset'. All the same, I don't want to be doing everything for him – and I'm not sure what is tactful – here, now, ever. So I leave him to it and fire up the stove.

Part of me is thinking that Ralph better show up. But another part is thinking that maybe we're better off without him and that we should keep it to just the two of us – me and Dad – for as long as possible because Ralph has got some kind of metaphysical rabies. Yet another part of me is wondering how Jack can do and say what he is doing and saying. How can he now refuse to come? At what point does he concede Dad might be for real? And surely Jack is worse than Ralph because if his behaviour isn't passive-aggressive then I don't know what is. At least with Ralph you get straightforward aggressive.

Ralph and Jack are actually my half-brothers – twins; Ralph the thin one, Jack less so. They have a whole other view of Dad. Like he is more or less a different man to them. My mother used to say that they were 'psychologically impacted' by him. But who knows – maybe it's the genes? I read somewhere that genes are like the ingredients and your family environment is analogous to how you cook them up.

I glance across. Now Dad is kneeling down in the front footwell, pushing the seat round with his arms and shoulders. He raises his head so that we're looking at each other properly for the first time since he woke up – or pretended to wake up. Then he comes right out and asks me the same thing I asked him: 'And how are you doing, Louis?'

'Been better,' I say.

He nods. 'Well, just so you know, Lou – and to answer your question – I'm feeling happy right now. Really happy.'

I don't know how to be with this so I say: 'Maybe you should have spent more time in the footwells of clapped-out vans, Dad.'

And then he smiles at me properly – like he smiles all the time now – really sad-but-happy, really sorry-but-glad, like we've sorted everything out between us. These new smiles don't help and I wonder sometimes if they're a side effect of the drugs. I'm here for him. But it's not like that makes it fine for him to be smiling at me like this every five minutes. And it's not like I *agree*. Or not any more, I don't. Not now we're actually doing it.

So I go and stand in the narrow galley at the stove in the back and make like I'm extra busy spooning the leaves into the pot.

He's turned the seat, which he's pleased about. He levers himself through the gap from the front – his arms are still good – and he sits down with a theatrical sigh of satisfaction.

'How long do we have?' He nods in the direction of the sea.

And this is pretty much the worst question he could have asked but it takes him a half-second to realize it.

'I mean how long do we have before the ferry sails?'

'We're early,' I say.

And this is the worst answer. We've had this problem for the last eighteen months, of course: half of what we say now sounds too significant and the other half sounds so vacuous that I don't know why we waste our time saying it at all. Maybe that's why we jump into jokes all the time. Maybe that's why we have always jumped into jokes. But we're trying to live in the present – whatever that means. And what else can we do? We have to go on talking. We are a talking family. Talking – language – is what made us the most successful of the hominids; that's what Dad would say. Does say. Often.

'You must have had your foot down, Lou.'

'Not really,' I say. 'The roads were empty.'

'Lucky we didn't come in the Aston or the Maserati.'

'Yeah – or we'd probably be there by now.'

Dad weighs this a second, like maybe we should segue into serious. But then he says: 'Slow driving – do you think there's a new movement in that?'

'What? You mean like Slow Food and Slow Cities?'

'Yes.' He is animated now; ideas seem to make the muscles in his face come back to life again. 'You can pretend that Slow Driving is a whole new philosophy and get paid to give lectures to people with too much time on their hands. I can see the book now.' Dad nods and holds up finger and thumb as though describing the quotation on the back cover: '"The crushingly obvious repackaged again – for people who missed it the first three times." Chuck in a smattering of quotes from the Greeks off the Internet and you'll be away, Lou.'

Dad is big on the Greeks. He calls Christianity 'the great hijack'.

'I thought the Greeks were mainly pre-car, Dad, pre-driving.'

'I mean Greek quotes about *life*. Turn it round.'

'Turn what round?'

'Your argument.'

'I'm not making one.'

'Yes you are. What you're saying is that the Greeks were able to examine life more deeply *because* they drove so much slower than we do.'

'I'm not saying anything.'

'All their philosophy, the plays, the democracy, the sculpture, the Olympics . . . it was all because the Greeks were the original Slow Drivers.' He draws a professorial breath and makes as if to address the midweek Life Coachers' get-together in Notting Hill. 'Ladies and gentlemen . . . we all know for a fact that everybody was so much happier before today. But the question is why?'

'The question is why.'

'Let me tell you.'

'Wait . . . Charge us first. Then tell us.'

'Take, for example, Ancient Greece. We stopped being happy . . .' He pauses in mock profundity. 'We stopped being *centred* when we stopped Slow Driving.'

I shake my head. Dad and I have a whole list of words and phrases we just don't like. 'Centred' is right up there with 'klicks' and words like 'legend' and 'eclectic' and 'curated'. We don't know why exactly – but not liking particular points of vocabulary unites us in some secret back-channel way; flashlights we shine across the misty swamp of everything that lies between us.

And now the kettle is steaming the window where Dad has drawn back the crappy little curtain and we're feeling good again.

'Did you bring those croissants?' he asks.

Croissants, devilled kidneys and oysters: my dad's three favourite foods.

'Oh yeah. Six.'

'Well, get them out then, Lou, what are you waiting for?'

I ease the croissants from the top of the blue cool box that always travels with us and then I get the milk out and the two surprise-hit metal mugs that I bought one time when we were in New York together for Christmas with my American-Russian grandparents. And then I pour the teas in the way I've seen Dad do it a thousand times – holding the pot high as he thrusts the water down the spout, trying to make it hit the leaves hard on the way out so as to compensate for the fact that we're pouring too early, which we always do. And now there's the taste of tea and croissants and the sound of the sea on a pebbled shore someplace close by and an apricot morning light that is streaming in and showing up all the marks on the windscreen from all the thousands of miles we've done together.

But we're only about three way-too-hot sips into the Darjeeling when everyone around us in their off-road cars decides to start their off-road engines as if there is a sudden danger that the ferry might fuck right off without them and disappear for ever, taking France with it. And I'm shaking my head at Dad – like this always happens – and we're both finding it pretty funny.

So now we've got to gulp down the tea, burning our throats through to our lungs, so that we can get a stronger top-up from the pot, because really the second cup is what it's always been about. And we're cramming our croissants as if we're three years old like my nephews. And the next line along is already moving.

'We better get weaving,' he says.

That's one of his favourite words.

And for a moment it feels like we are going on holiday after all.

My father was born in Yorkshire in the last hours of Churchill's wartime ministry; but he drank his first milk under Clement Atlee. So he likes to say. And every once in a while, despite the decades in London, you can still hear a previous England in his voice – the old timbers creaking beneath the rebuilds, the extensions, the facades.

He was an only child. His father was from Yorkshire and owned a famous stonemason's yard. He was locally renowned for his lettering but made most of his money overseeing the rebuilding of thousands of miles of dry-stone wall. My grandmother was a dressmaker from Lancaster. She, too, worked all her life and had a lucrative sideline, this time in making curtains. So the two of them were financially much better off than they ever pretended – especially by the end. But after Dad left his first wife for my mum, they cut him off and refused to speak to him.

Thus my grandmother died estranged from her son. No time to change things or understand. I sometimes think about that. All of their life together, all of those hours raising a child and then suddenly a feud; then silence; not another word; for ever. I think my grandfather attempted some kind of a reconciliation with Dad, but he got Alzheimer's and the end was messy and fraught and gruelling.

I never met my father's parents. Ralph and Jack remember them quite well though. They would go and play in the stoneyard beside their old house on the outskirts of Halifax. Ralph's take is that they were absurdly proud, covertly cruel, small-hearted people – grudge-bearers, secretly miserable and afraid. Jack's is that they were decent, determined, hard-working, law-abiding, scrupulously fair folk who found a way to get on and had no time for those who did not. I can't be sure – I've seen pictures of them in the 1950s and their world is unimaginable to me; the way they stand – awkward with the camera and unable to smile because (so they seem to want to say) a smile has to be *earned*. When I was little and Dad was teaching me things – the planets, the map of the world, the history of Europe – he used to make out that he was the last living embodiment of the Wars of the Roses. But now he says that even those echoes are fading and that Britain is a story that people no longer know how to write.

Before he met my mother, my grandparents' pride in my

father was as deep and resonant as it was unspoken. Dad was one of those Catholic-school boys, who somehow dodged the paedophile priests and allied endless hard work to a formidable intelligence. He excelled in every exam he ever sat. All the way up. And up. Until, eventually, he became the Director of Studies in English Literature at University College London. (Hence his three sons tending that way.) He still believes the English language to be our greatest gift to the world. Not modern democracy, nor the railways, nor the Web, nor Newton, nor Keynes, nor Darwin, nor the NHS, or whatever else some people think England is, was, made, invented – but the language itself; its reach, its subtlety, its poetry. He would go farther and say that literature, because it uses language, provides us with the raw material with which to think – as the other non-linguistic arts do not. Many a long motorway haul, he would find an opportunity to remind me that language is 'the defining, the redeeming and the pre-eminent characteristic of human beings'. And he'll tell you straight: the English language is the greatest language of all.

Now I'm not totally sure how many other languages he actually knows – some bad German, some good French – but you never met a man more committed to his credo. We used to trek all over the country so that he could give talks on the 'nature of deception' in Shakespeare or the 'nature of constancy' in John Donne. Or he'd drive me to these muddy-assed literary festivals to judge poetry prizes. I've never tried it, but if we were to say to him, 'Dad, nobody gives a shit' – then he'd say straight back, 'I do.'

Our house is near enough a private library. You won't see that in a few years' time, I suppose. Physical books, I mean. Shelves. Spines. Dad himself has written several books –

including his career-defining one on literary theory. Not that anyone reads that kind of stuff any more – except maybe students – although I didn't notice any of my friends bothering when I was at college. In fact, maybe I'm the only person who has read Dad's 'big' book in the last ten years and I didn't really get into it that much; I was just taking in the words like one of those whales that swallows the entire sea and then spits it all out again and hopes that something nutritious got stuck in the baleen. Apart from Mum, I should say, who read it again before she died – underlining sentences with a pen. So that's two of us. I don't know about Ralph or Jack – it's a good question. The only one of Dad's books I could say that I ever enjoyed is his one on the Shakespeare sonnets – which I can pick up and put down and then pick up again without getting lost, or confused, or feeling like I need to check into a monastery in order to focus on it properly. Then again, like everybody else these days, I'm suffering from acute mental eczema and I can't concentrate on anything for more than twenty seconds.

To tell the truth, there's not a subject on Earth that Dad *isn't* interested in. Everything from the Higgs boson to the forgotten stations on the Tube, via J. S. Bach, J. M. W. Turner and what happened to the Neanderthals; he's read about it, thought about it, got a view. Mum once said it's his curiosity that she married. And she was right. It kind of rubs off on you. You feel like everything is interesting whenever you are with him because he's more or less into everything – except golf, any kind of reality TV and religious people. Mum used to say that he was a 'one-man testament to education and self-reliance'. (She always called him Laurence.) And that's true too: besides or beneath the self-importance and the vanity, Dad has something powerful and honest in him – a streak of something that you know can never be bought or sold or traduced. And I think it cost him a few times in his life. He never got to be a professor, for example. But here's the strange thing. Whatever this quality is, I've noticed Dad finds it almost impossible to deploy with his own family. Sure, he can be Mr Disarmingly Direct and Open with almost everyone . . . *except* his children, *except* the two women he has loved.

Most of all, Dad is hard to disagree with. He has this moral intensity that makes you feel like you're not just wrong but bad. Which is not to say he doesn't like to debate. In other ways, he's the most engaged guy you are ever going to meet. He wants to have a conversation – all the time, with everyone and anyone, about anything and everything. Maybe that's the main thing about him: he vehemently wants to have a conversation.

Something rare though: my father genuinely loved my mother. Mad about her. Not always the case with marriages, I've noticed. He doesn't talk about it now because those were the years of trauma with Ralph and Jack but once – when Mum was dying and I was being devious with Dad – I asked him how they met. And he said he was in New York for some off-the-scale pointless academic conference and he went out one night on his own 'to listen to the new literature' and 'to get away from all these frauds talking about Jane Austen and Post bloody Modernism'. He said that he saw her doing a poetry reading and that he just knew: that it was as sudden as it was certain. That's what he *said*.

—

We came to the decision to drive some time back in the falter-ing spring, one Saturday lunchtime, at a cafe called Clowns in a forgotten square in south London not so far from the river. We were too early. And the place was empty save for an old guy behind the counter wearing an apron and reading the sport in Italian with the expression of a man who had yet to come across anything that might suggest a fundamental rethink. The walls were covered with these huge pictures and drawings of clown faces – sinister, joking, garish. There were clown postcards pinned up by the till. A clown mirror in which to better establish your own reflection. Clown mugs. The whole thing caught me off guard. And I remember sitting down at this table at the back while all around these death-white eyes in black heart-shaped patches looked on aghast and these livid red mouths silently laughed at us.

Ten minutes later, I was trying to eat an unlikely pasty with a side order of shredded carrots while Dad carved his way through this goat's cheese quiche, oblivious; he always eats one-handed, cutting with the edge of his fork when he's not waving it around to make his many points.

'How many times have I flown?'

'I don't know, Dad. About five hundred.'

'But not once more than I had to. I hate it, Lou.'

'I know you hate it. I was there for quite a few of those flights. You were very clear about hating it.'

'It's not the flying.'

I've noticed that when people say 'it's not the', it usually means 'it *is* the'. I kept on trying to eat and thought a bit about the difference between grating and shredding.

'It's just – I hate the attitude of the security people.'

'That's mainly JFK, Dad. And it's understandable.'

'They remind me of the Nazis.'

'How many Nazis have you known?'

Dad separated another section of the base of his quiche with the fork. The strange thing is he doesn't do anything with the left hand that he's freed up by not using his knife. Instead, he holds the edge of the table tightly like he's expecting an earthquake or something.

'You put thick people in uniform and that's what you get – revenge. The revenge of the conceitedly thick.'

'The conceitedly thick?'

'Yes. It's as if they're trying to tell you that "a-ha!" being thick might have appeared to be embarrassing when we were all at school and they were still coming bottom of every test the government could devise to mask the truth – but actually thickness has its privileges, its benefits, its long game, and *now* who's laughing?'

'The Nazis.'

'Don't pretend you like them, Lou. I'm telling you: they think they're some kind of thick master race – and, no, they don't see that as a paradox.'

'Are we Jewish now?'

'They think they're saving the Fatherland from disaster every time they say: "Sorry, sir, no liquids."'

'Don't go through with liquids.'

He pointed with his fork. 'I tell you what, Lou – the terrorists have won. That's what I think every time I go to an airport. Imagine the billions of human hours that they've stolen from the rest of us. Billions and billions of hours of *our* lives – now devoted to getting undressed in front of overweight security monsters just so that they can have a rummage of your tackle.'

'So I guess we can't fly . . .'

He ate some of his quiche. Now we were coming to it.

'I'm going to drive. I want to drive.'

'But you can't drive any more, Dad.'

'That's why Doug is going to drive me.'

'Dad.'

'He has agreed.'

'Dad, Doug—'

'What *about* Doug?'

'You've only known him for . . . like, five years or whatever.'

'Don't say "like".'

'Doug is a mechanic.'

'That's your objection?'

'Of course it's not my objection. I'm just saying Doug is . . . Doug is a guy you met on a Roman dig or whatever—'

'Lower Palaeolithic dig, Lou, long, *long* before the Romans.'

'Right. But because he happens to live a couple of streets away and he's fixed the house and whatever, doesn't mean—'

'Doug comes round a lot. We've been to three or four digs together.'

'So just because he's driven you to look at some early hominid rubbish dumps – he's the man to drive you to Dignitas?'

'The point is that I'm used to being driven by him. He knows me well.'

'Dad, don't deliberately not understand what I'm saying.'

'Sorry. Whatever I'm doing, Lou, it is not deliberate.'

'Subconsciously.'

'You can't be subconsciously deliberate.'

'You're still doing it.'

I breathed in. I breathed out.

'I'm not saying Doug isn't a good person. But I can't let Doug drive you.' I looked up and forced myself to face him. 'I have to do it.'

He paused. 'And I can't ask you to do that.'

'I know you can't. And I'm not going to do it because you're asking. I'm going to drive you there because I *want* to do it.'

'But I don't want to put you through it, Lou.'

'You're not putting me through it. The situation is. The disease is. But let's not pretend that Doug is a good option.'

'I'm not pretending anything. I can't—'

'Dad. Think. What am I supposed to do? Wave you off and then just shut the door and sit down for a beer in front of the match in an empty house – the same house that I've lived in all my life with you and Mum?'

That struck home.

'Jack is going to say goodbye in London,' Dad said. 'That's what he wants.'

'You know that's not true. Jack doesn't want you to do this at all. He's totally against it. You know that. Jesus.'

Dad went still.

'Let's try to stay with what is real,' I said. 'Jack is refusing to come because he doesn't want to encourage even the idea. And he doesn't think you're serious and he doesn't think—'

'I *am* serious.'

'I know that, for Christ's sake. But Jack . . . Whatever. Anyway, let's not pretend Jack wants to "say goodbye" in London. Christ, I hate that phrase.'

'I suppose I'd thought you could meet me in Zurich. Synchronize your flights with Ralph.'

'Synchronize my flights with *Ralph*?'

'As in get there at—'

'But Ralph is the least reliable human being of all time. I mean we can't even—'

'Meet him at the hotel.'

'Dad, for fuck's sake.'

'Lou.'

'Sorry – I'm sorry – but the flight-times and the meetings are really not the issue here. This is going to be the worst day of my life whatever.'

'No it's not. No.' His eyes began to glass. He is always at his weakest and most vulnerable whenever I put him in my shoes. All his certainty and his will to live – *his will to die* – seems to leave him and whatever pain and tremor the disease brings rush forward into his face. For this reason, I try not to do it to him. But the thing is that our feeling for one another is continually creating this insane reversal: whenever I think of being him, I want to assert his absolute right to die; whenever he thinks of being me, he wants to carry on living.

'Lou. We've talked about this. And if you—'

'We have. Over and over and over. Intellectually, we have reasoned our way to a standstill.'

'Not a standstill – a decision.'

'Dad.'

'And every step – *every* step – we can change our minds. Right until I'm in that room . . . I never want to be doing anything – for even a second – that you don't agree with . . . The minute you're not—'

'Dad, I don't want to talk about it all again now. Not here.' There was suddenly nowhere to look but at a room full of clowns. 'I'm just saying you can't fly. Doug is not driving you

– he'll probably be charged with murder apart from anything else . . .' I bit my lip. 'We're preparing everything. Isn't that the whole deal? That we can plan. That we're as ready as we can be? That we control the thing?' I fought myself a moment; my voice is always wanting to rise on me. 'I'm saying someone has to drive you and—'

'Doug.'

'—given that Mum is dead and it's not going to be Ralph or Jack, then it has to be me.' I made myself smile. 'I *want* to drive you. Doug is no part of this. I'll be fine.'

Now there was water in his eyes that he couldn't blink back. 'I can't ask you to do that.'

'I know you can't. And I know you're not. I'm doing it because I want to do it.'

Two of the side effects are what the PDFs call 'Watery Eyes' and 'Emotional Lability'. The former is due to 'slack-ness in the muscles of the face that may result in the normal lubrication of the eyes overflowing'. And the latter is a term they use to describe the problem of 'emotional responses being affected, leading to laughing or crying involuntarily'; though 'it is important to remember that these behavioural changes have a physical cause'.

'Then Jack has to come,' Dad says, quietly.

'Yes, Dad. Jack has to come.'

But Jack had said he wasn't going to come. Because Jack was in some kind of monumental and principled denial roughly equivalent to my father's monumental and principled avowal. And because Jack did not think my father was serious. And neither, in his way, did Ralph. They suspected him of manipulating the situation – manipulating them. I told them, of course, that his seriousness was as serious as the illness, which was as serious as it was possible to be. But they always came back: yes – but do you think he's actually going to go through with it – do you?

'I'll speak to Jack again,' I said. 'Of course he has to come.'

EVERYTHING AFFECTS EVERYONE

On the ferry, I'm queuing for fuck knows what. I look across the lounge at Dad. He is sat in an uncomfortable chair reading by the window. We've travelled all over Europe – Dad and I – and, sure, maybe his 'special relationship' (Mum's phrase) with me *is* because of the animosity with Ralph and Jack but all the same . . . All the same, looking at him over there – reading, always reading – it's as though I can feel my heart's fist uncurling and reaching out towards him like those Michelangelo fingers he took me to see one time in the Vatican when I was too young to care or notice and only wanted ice cream. Now, though, I wish that he'd turn round – I don't know why – just so that we can look at each other. I want him to do that expression he did when I was a boy and we were watching TV and some politician was serving up the shit – the way that he'd turn from the screen and look over with his eyes as if to say, 'What the bloody hell is happening here, Lou, and what are these people *talking* about?'

'The queue is too long,' I say.

Dad looks up. He's been engrossed and hasn't seen me walk back to him.

'It's making me suicidal,' I add.

He winces like he's long suspected I am out where the buses don't run and shuts the book he has been reading.

'Do you want to stay here?' I ask.

Squalls of consumption are gathering around us. He almost answers me – why not? – but maybe he senses that I'm suffering and so instead he says: 'No, let's go on deck and get some air.'

'It's back that way I think – past Duty Free.'

'OK. We'll take our time.' He eases himself up. 'I thought Duty Free had been abolished.'

'It's not really Duty Free any more, Dad. They only call it that – to make people carry on doing whatever they were doing before.'

He's on his feet with his stick and ready to go. 'But without the freedom from duty?'

'Yep.'

'Great. Well, we can stock up on essential fragrances on the way past.'

I've been looking forward to this – and dreading it. We always head out on deck; it's another of our summer-holiday rituals – maybe some kind of parody of being sailors that only we find funny. Or something to do with fresh air and a way of physically marking the distance a holiday opens up on your regular life. There goes the familiar coast. Here comes the unknown. But now I'm worried about Dad walking because the boat is starting to roll a little.

And, sure enough, by the time we get to the Duty Free, I can sense that he is anxious – though he isn't showing it. His left foot is dragging. But it's not as bad as it has been. Or maybe he's somehow forcing control back. There's a plastic wall with a rail that he's using. He's actually smiling but underneath I can tell it's killing him – the effort of this walk and the fact that walking itself should have come to this. I don't know whether to go towards him or keep going on my own.

The announcer comes on – too loud: 'Our on-board store is now open. We offer substantial savings on high-street brand names – such as Kokorico, the new masculine body fragrance by Jean Paul Gaultier.' And now I'm feeling extra nausea because I've forgotten to take my travel tablets and the problem is that some children have stopped on their way past and they are standing there staring at Dad like only kids can stare. But Dad keeps on going. And that's when it suddenly occurs to me that he's doing this walk for me; that I want him out there on deck; but that he's not really up to it; and that this is precisely the kind of thing he wants not to have to undertake, to do, to be, for the next nine months or however long it is before his respiratory muscles become so weak that his body won't breathe for itself. Whatever it is that I need from him is the exact same thing that humiliates him. More than this, I now see: he doesn't want to get worse in front of me – specifically *me*. If it were someone else who had to witness his degeneration – Doug, for example – then he might go on.

I clench my jaw and run my tongue back and forth across my teeth. I'm hoping the children don't start mimicking his walking. I don't know what to do – whether to let him be his own man or go back myself and reach out and physically support him. So I just stand there, not knowing, with my heart somehow bobbing up in my throat like it's trying to choke me. And that's when I get that surge of feelings again. I don't know how to describe it exactly, other than that it's physical – like a kind of poisoning or the opposite of being in love – and that it swells up inside until there's no part of me unaffected; and yet I can't be sick, I can't be rid of it, so that when it comes – I'm left taut, brim-full, feeling like I'm drowning – but from the inside out.

The kids run off. I make a big effort to relax my jaw and force myself to watch Dad; it is unbelievable how hard it has become for me to look at him. He is at the point of needing a wheelchair. At the MND clinic in Oxford, they describe four stages: onset, walking with sticks, wheelchair, bed. There is a fifth stage, of course, which they don't mention.

We go past this half-doughnut of Belgian truckers slumped around a slot machine and thumbing in their coins like it's still 1983 or something – but I could kiss their fat floury faces for how little they care. And, yes, I'm thinking, it will all be OK. We will take our time. And I know we'll get out on deck because I never met anyone more determined than Dad – he says he's going to do a thing, and he does it. I rearrange my coat over my arm and I'm glad I have remembered to bring Dad's windcheater, too, because it's always much colder on deck than you think it's going to be.

And we're so nearly there – almost through the lounge and within sight of the white door that takes us outside – when there's an extra big roll and the ferry lurches a little and my dad grabs at a seat to steady himself and maybe knocks at the back of this guy's head – though hardly at all – causing him to jerk forward and spill less than one sip of his coffee.

'What the bloody hell?' The guy twists around, all self-righteous, like we've just launched a drone strike on his e-reader. 'What the hell are you doing?'

'I'm so sorry.'

'For Christ's sake.'

There's a smear of coffee on his screen. And he's making a

huge deal of flapping for a napkin, then turning round in his chair again and looking back over his shoulder at Dad. I can feel embarrassment tunnelling in the bones of my face.

'What are you *doing*?' The guy is fifty-five, I guess, and he's got these expensive glasses that have the brand name on the stems like we're all supposed to care. His wife is opposite, dressed in clothes too young for her, and she looks at Dad with these narrow eyes which are meant to burn with outrage on behalf of her husband but which I can tell are full of something she can't quite disguise, some kind of glee that another bad thing has happened to the man with whom she has chosen to drain down her existence.

'I'm sorry,' Dad says, calmly. 'It was an accident. Not got my sea legs yet.' Dad is looking at the screen. I can tell he's checking out what the guy is reading. 'Is your device OK?'

'I don't know. I can't tell. It's misting up . . .'

'I'm sorry,' my father says again. 'If it's damaged, then I will gladly buy you a new one.' Dad gives him one his of smiles of affirmation-despite.

But the guy is looking up at Dad like his whole experience of the world has long been reduced to the single feeling of irritation and this is exactly why. For a moment, time refuses to move on and we are all of us bobbing about, seasick and desperate, on the empty black ocean of eternity because this guy can't work out Dad's problem or see Dad's stick; and, of course, Dad looks pretty normal when he's not moving and so why is he just standing there, holding on to the back of this guy's seat, smiling slack-lipped, and why doesn't he offer to get some more napkins or another coffee or something? Most of all why doesn't he let go of the chair?

I can tell that actually Dad is afraid – not of the man, but of trying to walk any further – because the ship has really started rolling like one of those coin-slot hippos my nephews like to ride outside the newsagents.

The man's wife looks at Dad, loyal now that there's a chance to vent some hostility. 'Is it working?' she asks.

And suddenly, I'm there.

'Let's keep going, Dad,' I say. 'I want to ring Ralph before I lose the UK signal – tell him we've left.'

'Seems to be,' the man is saying.

'Here's my name and number,' Dad says, taking out one of these old-style embossed business cards he carries with him for occasions such as this. 'Get in touch this afternoon – straight away – if it packs up. We'll order you another one.' He pauses as if some new thought – or attitude – is declaring itself. 'Let me recommend something I recently read.'

'No. Don't.'

Dad ignores him and starts to write on the card, leaning on the back of the guy's chair.

'Come on, Dad.' I say, offering my arm. 'Let's get weaving.'

But Dad carries on writing and points in the direction of the e-reader. 'The great thing about these devices is that nothing is ever going to be out of print again. Got to be good for humanity – right? There you go. Give it a chance and I promise you will enjoy it.'

The guy is now refusing to acknowledge my father is even alive so Dad comes out from behind the chair and leans down to pass his card to the man's wife. Dad has moved into some new mode – not angry but somewhere between resolute and reproving – teacherly.

The woman looks up. She wants to be even more hostile

but she's unsure and Dad's got this powerful front-of-the-class way of projecting himself.

'Well,' Dad straightens on his stick, 'have a good holiday. And don't stay together unless you really want to.'

'I beg your pardon,' she says.

But that's it – off we go – and, for the first time since all this started, our arms are bound across each other's shoulders like we're two soldiers limping away from the front line with all the bombs and guns and explosions booming out behind us and cracking the sky apart. And I am thinking that it feels so strange and alien and intimate and close all at the same time – to have the fact of Dad's real living body leaning on me, to feel his breath, his weight, his pulse and the pressure on my arm caused by the rhythm of his shuffle, which is both the rhythm of his disease and the rhythm of his being.

My mum's real name was the Russian form, Yuliya, but everyone called her Julia. And probably another of the reasons that my father got into her so fast was that her parents were originally Russian, and she had this whole I-can-speak-the-language-Commie-chic going on. That, and because she was a famous poet for about ten minutes when she was young. And also because she had these turquoise eyes and this killer scruffy copper-coloured hair that you couldn't fake and that pretty much wiped out all the other women. My dad always says that he read somewhere that a good-looking woman who is happy without having to work at either being good-looking or happy drives *everyone* crazy – all the men, sure, but all the other women, too.

My mother died four years ago – predictably – from her

cigarettes – after we both nursed her – mainly Dad. She was from New York. We went out there at least once a year because it was free – since we could always stay with my grandparents or my aunt Natasha – though later Natasha moved to Yonkers on account of a sandy-haired loss-adjuster called Andrew who didn't work out, which I thought was pretty funny but couldn't say. Anyway, yep, cancer aside – I was lucky with my mum and New York.

For a long time I even pretended to be flat-out American until Dad said – 'Hey, Lou, you don't need to pretend – you *are* half-American.' So I guess you could say that America is my second home. Actually, I'm hoping it will be my first home soon. There's not going to be much for me to stay in London for – except Jack and his children.

My take is that Mum saved Dad from what he used to be.

And now that she's gone, Dad is . . . reverting, re-emerging.

One time, when I was twelve or so, I read the note Dad had written in the front of the copy of his book on the sonnets, which he must have given to Mum back in the early days: 'When something is missing in love, you know neither its nature nor its exact shape until you meet it – and then you will know it for ever.'

It is a massive relief to be out on deck. The wind is gusting and the clouds are hurrying by like a parade of crazy haircuts for much older men. We're at the back of the boat and straight away I can see the foam and churn of the wake that stretches out behind us towards England: thick and white, then stringy, then soapy, then streaked, then disappearing until there's nothing but the same grey-green swell of the sea all around and it's like the whole ferry was never there. I don't know why, but it starts to be important to me that the wake doesn't disappear and so I'm straining my eyes to see if I can make out a slight difference in the waves beyond after all – something that endures a while longer.

Dad and I head towards one of the plastic tables that they bolt down onto the deck. We're still locked together. Dad is taking big deep breaths, like he's counting them, and I'm still staring at the sea when these hippy students come out and sit down at the end of the table. They're smoking roll-ups and making like they grew up in some Brazilian favela, where they only narrowly escaped being shot by writing really meaning-ful songs, before they hitchhiked across two continents to get here. I hear one of the boys saying that he's 'open to totally any kind of experience' and I figure that enough is enough. And so that's how come Dad and I start off down the side of the ferry and end up where there is this white chain saying 'private' with all these lifeboats hung above our heads.

The wind tugs a little harder down here. I put on my coat and hand Dad his. I'm trying not to look up and think about lifeboats and that maybe there will be a cure that can rescue Dad and what if it is discovered next year – or next fucking week?

So then I just come right out with it: 'If Mum was alive would we still be doing this?'

My dad looks over at me from zipping up his wind-cheater. 'No,' he says. 'No we wouldn't.'

'I thought not.'

'But you know why?'

'I'm not sure I do.'

'Lou.'

He has these steady blue eyes like quartz beneath the grey crag of his brow. And he's looking at me as if to ask – do I want to go through it all again? And I know if I say I do, he will. The problem is I want to go through it all for ever.

So instead I say: 'I've started this new reading group at work.'

Which is a massive lie. And straight away, I feel terrible. But of course he's not going to know. And this makes me feel worse.

But then he says: 'Can I have one of your cigarettes?'

And if fifteen dolphins had leapt out of the sea with harmonicas and guitars and all started singing 'Mr Fucking Tambourine Man' I wouldn't have been more surprised.

'You don't smoke, Dad.'

'I'm taking it up again, Lou. Been waiting nearly thirty-five years to get stuck back in.'

I hesitate. I didn't know that he was aware that I smoked. We're such hypocrites, the pair of us – and Mum and Ralph and Jack. My whole family might as well carry round a big sign saying: 'Everything we do and say, we mean the total opposite.'

'It's OK,' he smiles. 'You have to do what your dad tells you, remember.'

I fumble in my coat for where I've hidden them. 'Why?'

'I used to hate that question, Lou.'

'Not as much as I used to hate your answer.' I pull out a cigarette from my battered packet. For all the obvious reasons, I loathe smoking; I only do it to piss myself off even more. I hand one over.

Dad holds it cocked at arm's length and asks: 'What answer did I give you?'

'Just because. That's all you ever used to say to me, Dad. Just because. Just because. Not particularly helpful. And not particularly clever.'

'If ever you have children of your own, you'll come round to it.' He raises a hand to stop me interrupting. 'You will. Believe me – you will. We *have* to do things for our fathers – and our mothers – just because. I can't light this with my teeth, Lou.'

I pass my Zippo across. I'm not going to actually do it for him. There are limits.

But there's a petulant wind now that won't let up. So next thing, we're hunkering down, our two heads right close together, with these two cigarettes sticking out that we're trying to get lit. And he unzips again and makes a tent with his windcheater but it's not enough until I do the same with mine and we've got both sides covered. And so now there's only the two of us in there, and I can sense the movement of his lashes, and the blood in his ears and feel the warmth of his breath.

The smoke gets in his eyes and so when we stand up and turn back to the rail it looks like he's crying so I say: 'You *used* to smoke? When was that?'

He's blinking and squinting and embarrassed but it does the trick because he says, 'I used to smoke when I was your age. I gave it up in 1978 before your brothers were born. Believe it or not, I was hoping to set an example.' He gives this low laugh that he's got – like the universe is such an immense mystery that all we can do is stand back in amusement and awe. 'And look what happened. You've been smoking like a rent boy for the last few days.'

'It's been quite stressful, Dad.'

'Imagine the stress of watching your son doing the exact same thing that killed his mother.'

'I'm going to stop.'

'Well . . . maybe if I start again, you will.' He glances over. 'Reverse psychology – it works on your brothers, Lou. Not sure what works on you. Bribery? Or – what's the opposite of reverse psychology?'

'That would be encouragement, I think, Dad.'

'Right. Well, I *encourage* you to stop smoking even though I am taking it up again as of today. Will you promise me?'

'I will,' I say. 'I will. I hate it.'

The ferry does one of these big structural shudders that ferries do.

'What reading group – what did you start?'

'Actually, it's a Slow Reading group.'

'No.' Dad looks across at me like he wants to believe. 'Really?'

It's such a lie that I have to be totally serious: 'Yes – first Monday of every month. There's about ten of us so far. We all read the same thing – a poem – or a few pages from a serious novel – and then we talk about it. The idea is we concentrate – on the writing.' I can feel my soul turning to ash so I say the only thing that I know will divert us into something else. 'I started it with Eva – we get people from her office to come, too.'

This time Dad has to stop himself looking across. We never ever talk about girlfriends. I know for sure that he wants to have some kind of a man-to-man conversation but I'm pretty skilled at never letting the subject get started because he's so old-fashioned and clumsy about 'women' that it makes me cringe – so just by saying her name I'm opening the door. Which he knows. Which is why he doesn't want to look over – in case I see him edging through and close it fast. But, of course, now I have to leave it open all the way to punish myself for being such a liar, which I feel terrible about – on top of everything else I feel terrible about, which is everything.

'Remind me,' Dad says, sideways, 'is Eva the one who is pushing you forward or the one who is holding you back?'

'Dad.'

'I got the impression last year was fairly . . . hectic.'

'Don't say "hectic".'

'Busy. Engaging.'

'That was before.'

'Where is she from?'

'Tufnell Park.'

'Ah, a Londoner.'

'Her dad is from Yeovil. Her mum is Eritrean.'

'How does she feel about going out with someone from Stockwell?'

'She has an airport security scanner outside her room.'

'Must be awkward.'

I am about to make a joke about body searches and already having my belt off when I get through the door – but it feels wrong, so I say: 'Her dad used to run this stubbornly unsuccessful late-night tapas bar and her mum part-owns an Ethiopian restaurant in Tufnell Park. That's how they met. Eva says it was the worst marriage of all time.'

'That's a busy category, Lou.'

'No – they're definitely contenders. Eva says that one Christmas her mum dressed up as Santa and snuck into her room when she was pretending to be asleep and left her a bunch of presents. But then, five minutes later, her dad came in and took them all out again – also dressed as Santa.'

'Interesting.'

'And then her dad came back in again, ten minutes after that, and put all the presents back – but with these little white labels stuck over where her mum had written.'

'Bloody hell.'

'So then her mum comes back in – still dressed as Santa – and starts looking at the presents like she couldn't believe what her dad has just done. At which point her dad comes back in to check what her mum is up to – and they start arguing with each other – louder and louder – until Eva is lying there wide awake while these two Santas are yelling at each other through their wispy white beards at the end of her bed – all on Christmas Eve.'

'Has it affected her?'

'Everything affects everyone,' I say.

Dad looks at me. I look back at him.

'What's she doing now?'

'Same as me.'

He can't hide his disparagement: 'She's a database manager?'

'No, she's a solicitor. I meant the same as me as in . . . drifting aimlessly in the shallow seas of futility and false purpose.'

His brow furrows; he really doesn't like it when I joke about my job and I want to keep the good vibe going so quickly I ask about the book that he's still carrying: 'What are *you* reading?'

'The sonnets. Seventy-four. "But be contented".'

'Do you know it off by heart?'

'Yes – that I do.'

'Say it then.'

'No.'

'A line?'

'But be contented when that fell arrest . . . Without all bail shall carry me away . . . My life hath in this line some interest.' The wind blows in his hair. I can see he feels better out here. And that makes me feel better. He finishes the verse: 'Which for memorial with thee shall stay.'

'I wish I knew some poetry by heart,' I say, because it is true and because I love Dad talking about what he loves.

'You have the Internet on your phone, Lou. You don't have to learn anything. In my day, we had to commit things to memory – so that we would be able to use them again. Otherwise it was a trip to the bloody library on a bus every time you wanted to check anything up. Unimaginable now. Are there even any libraries left? There can't have been a bigger generation gap in history than between yours and mine.'

Dad looks for somewhere to put out his cigarette. There's a bucket of sand behind us. He waits for the wave, pivots on his stick, takes a step and dips down to drop the cigarette and then shuffles back, reaching for the rail.

'You think that it was better before though, don't you?'

'I do.'

'Why?'

'Because when you learn something, when you commit it to memory, then the words are in you – physically – or chemically – or however the brain works.'

'Neurons.'

'Exactly. In a way, the words exist inside you – in the neurons themselves. And so they're available to other neurons. So when your thoughts fire through your mind – there's all this Shakespeare in there for them to fire across. And that's got to be good – for the subtlety of your thoughts – for your ability to express yourself.'

Out on the Channel, some guy in one of those little yachts is more or less mountaineering across the waves and – not so far off – another ferry is pummelling back the other way.

'It's like a part of you *is* Shakespeare, Lou. And that part is available to all the other parts that are not.'

'I'm going to learn some.'

'You should. Not for me. But for yourself.' Dad shifts his weight. 'The more words you know, the better you can say whatever it is that needs to be said. Language is thought. Thought is language.'

'You always say that.'

'It's worth saying again. Put good things in here and there's a chance good things will come out.' He raises a finger and taps it on the side of his head. 'You know, even if I had tens of millions of pounds, I'd never buy a boat.'

'I just don't think we're seafarers, Dad.'

'What would you buy?'

I put out my cigarette in the same bucket.

'An apartment in Rome,' I say. 'Some place good-looking.'

'Do it. Sell the house.'

'Dad, don't.'

We fall silent, leaning on the rail, and I get this strange feeling – as if I am able to see my father clearly at last, as a man, without the binding twine of all those billion bonds of our DNA or the thousands of hours we have spent together; but also as if those same bonds have never been so tight and true. And now we're staring at the sea together like I guess a lot of dads have done with their sons – except not like *this* – and the waves are dipping and swelling and starting to shine all mackerel-backed in this shard of light that's sparkling all the way back to whatever Britain might yet be before it fades and is gone for ever.

RALPH

My brothers and I have always been close. Which is surprising – since I am also the living embodiment of all their trouble with Dad, and, indeed, all the trouble that has happened between everyone. Now I think about it, I suppose the gap between us is so big – eleven years – that maybe it goes all the way past mattering and comes back around to not mattering again. They used to pretend that I was a musketeer, the same as them. And they'd say, 'All for one and one for all, Lou' – mainly to make me feel I was 'big' when I was 'little', but also because we were 'in it together'. I now see that – subconsciously – what we meant by 'it' was our father.

When I was born, my brothers were living with Dad because of their mother's alcohol-related issues – the screaming and the subsequent solicitor-related stuff. So I've never known it any other way: they've always been my full brothers. And what with all the toddler-sitting they had to do when my mum and dad were out – which was a lot – they fell into the habit of looking after me, stopping me choking and falling down the stairs and playing with kebab skewers – all of that.

They did a lot of teaching me, too, whenever they came back from college; taking me out on my bike, showing me how to light fires, introducing me to real music. And, over time, I guess I developed this strange way of doing things with them – for them. Especially Ralph. Not in terms of what was happening in our lives day to day. But more in the way that whenever he wanted to kick back or show off or stretch his personality, he knew I'd be right there – the world's most eager audience, devoted, amazed, without any other judgement but admiration. Likewise, whenever I did anything – a clever message straight back to some girl, learning how to do bar chords on the guitar – I would have him in my mind, giving me the nod with a big brother's nice-one-Lou expression, keep going.

There was this one time, I remember: I was fourteen and he was in his middle twenties – busy being an out-of-work actor – and he had come over for my dad's sixtieth with some Sami-Swedish fashion student who he was dating and who had everyone secretly crying into their hands on account of her ludicrous beauty. This was before Mum even knew she was ill and the house was full of Dad's Labour Party we're-the-coolest-government-ever people (whom he 'joked' about as 'betrayers') and all these folk that Mum always knew – un-recordable singer-songwriters, un-producible screenwriters, un-readable poets – everyone in London who never made it, she would say, and who are never *gonna* make it, Lou, due to 'the climate'. And I was supposed to be reading this poem that Mum wrote for Dad but I'd left it upstairs and so I went up to fetch it in order to practise because I was feeling secretly frantic with nerves. But just as I got to the door at the end of our narrow attic corridor, I heard a woman's voice saying, 'Don't stop, don't stop, don't stop' – and since this was my first time hearing this stuff live, I hesitated; and tuned in. The problem was that the floorboards in our house groan and creak. And two seconds later I knew I was busted because the room had gone silent. And *that* forced me into having to pretend that I'd only just come running up through the house and that I hadn't been eavesdropping at all. So the only thing to do next was to knock on the door – nice and loud and rat-a-tat-tat.

'Ralph, I need to get something,' I shouted. 'And you need to come down . . . I'm doing my mum's poem and Dad is giving a speech.'

Sounds of stalled exertion.

'Ralph?'

Nothing.

'Ralph – I know you're in there.'

'Well, fuck off then.'

'Sorry. I need to get the poem. And you're supposed to come down. Dad wants to say something. He doesn't want you to miss his speech. It's important. Come on, man.'

'So is this. I am having sex.' Sounds of the bed sighing. 'And I'm not alone.'

Ralph was then – as now – incapable of embarrassment; an actor for ever devoted to his audience whomsoever it might be. Even in his early twenties, though, he freely admitted that, by any reasonable standard he was an awful human being. It's true: I am a total penis, Lou, he would say – candidly, shaking his head and sucking his teeth as if admitting liability at the scene of a minor car accident. I accept that, you accept that, we all accept that. There's nothing to be done about it. But at least . . . at least I *do* accept it. Which is more than can be said for everyone else around here. At which juncture he would raise his eyebrows and look invitingly at me.

I re-addressed myself to the crack between door and frame: 'Jesus, Ralph. Can you just give me the poem? Then you can get right back to it.'

'Lou – go away. I've got a huge erection and you're my brother. It's not right.'

Sounds of suppressed female laughter.

'Ralph, I'm being serious.'

'So am I. Never more so.'

But there was no chance now that I was going to spend twenty minutes running up and down the stairs waiting for everyone to orgasm. And I could tell Ralph was in some kind of perverse protest mode. I had no choice, therefore, but to entrench my position: 'Give me the poem and I'll go, Ralph. I can't go down without it. I've got to read it to everyone. I think it's on the desk.'

'Nope.'

'Please.'

'No man should ever get out of bed with a woman in order to placate another man, Lou, especially not his little brother. Oscar Wilde said that.'

'Oscar Wilde was gay, you idiot.'

'He said it before he came out.'

'OK, fine. But just so you know: I'm going to get the poem now because I don't want to let Dad down . . . And I don't believe you'll get the job done in time.'

More laughter from inside.

I guess this was the kind of thing I meant about always being one another's favourite audience – because the truth is that some part of him wanted me to come into that room and see him there; and some part of me wanted to go into that room and have him witness how cool I was with the whole sex thing.

'I'm coming in.'

'Lou, don't – whatever you do – come in here.'

'I'm coming in.'

'For your own sake, Lou. It's horrible. I'm telling you: there's spunk everywhere.'

'I'm counting to three and then I'm coming in. One, two . . .'

And so, shielding my eyes, I opened the door and walked head down into the room. The bedside lamp had either fallen or been knocked to the floor so that shadows reared on the walls. Ralph sat up. Never was there a man more at ease with the emotional discomfort of others. His girlfriend had pulled the covers over her head and was clearly intent on not being in the room at all. Somewhat piously in order to mask the crimson of my own shame, I crossed straight to the desk.

'So . . . this is interesting,' Ralph said, placing a pillow behind his head. 'My weekend finally takes off.'

I lowered my shield and frowned, trying not to look in his direction, searching through the mess on the desk for my printout of the poem while he lit a cigarette with the noisiest and most protracted rasp that any man ever made in the striking of a single match.

'Don't smoke, Ralph, you bell end,' I said. 'I've got to sleep in that bed. Jesus.'

'I should have warned you, Kristen,' he said. 'Since I left home, my little brother has launched a one-man jihad on joy.' Ralph waved the flame ostentatiously dead. 'We're going to have to watch out for him. By day, he patrols the house forbidding all human pleasure. By night he sleeps with burka and cilice. Feverishly masturbating, no doubt.' Ralph was talking to the duvet, but really he was still talking to me. 'What the fuck is happening with your haircut, Lou?'

The covers shifted. He sent an idle smoke ring ceiling-wards in search of a hook on which to hang around a while.

'Have you joined the Young Conservatives?'

'At least my whole life is not a massive embarrassing failure, Ralph.'

'Yet.'

I glanced across at him and met his familiar half-smile. Ralph was always fair skinned but his tousled auburn hair was longer then and fell easily over his eyes which have always been set deep, like our father's, though lighter – the pale blue of robin's eggs. Dad once said that he looked like a secretly gay Indian maharaja's dream of England's opening bowler – which pretty much sums my brother up.

I was more or less dying now – and I couldn't find the poem and I was afraid that I'd put it down somewhere and would have to rush to print it out again on our juddering grain-thresher of a printer.

'Sorry, I don't know what's going on. I'm sure it was on this desk. Maybe it's downstairs.'

'It's here.' Ralph eased it out from beneath the mug he was using as an ashtray on the bedside table. He knew he'd transgressed.

'Jesus, Ralph.'

'It's very good,' he softened.

'You are such a—

'Nightmare. I know, I know. But I read it because I was interested, Lou. She may not write much, your mum, but she's . . . she's a great poet. Don't let anyone ever tell you different.'

Ralph studied English and got the highest marks ever awarded to a mortal at a university; and as far as I was then concerned, this meant he was not only the most sophisticated human being I knew, but also the most sophisticated human being *possible*. The fact that he chose not to become an academic was somehow an unspoken joke at our father's expense.

'It's anapaestic tetrameter,' he said. A sun-burnished knee was now visible thanks to some new arrangement of the duvet. 'So you should read it with a lilting-rolling rhythm.' His hands danced slowly as he spoke. 'Like Byron's . . . "The Assyrian came *down* like the *wolf* on the *fold*".'

He passed the poem over. Now the duvet was drifting up the very faint blonde down of her thigh. His cigarette fizzed where he dropped it into the cold tea.

'For fuck's sake, Ralph.'

He pretended to apologize: 'All the other rooms had lodgers or children in them, Lou. It came down to a choice between my dad's bed or my little brother's. I'm agnostic – as you know – but this seemed marginally less disturbing for everyone else.'

'Deep-level issues.' I shook my head. 'Deep level. Seriously, Ralph – try psychotherapy. Pay someone to pretend to be your friend and listen to your problems.'

He smiled a Mephistophelean smile. 'Surely we can discuss all this later, Lou. At the moment, you're just standing next to my bed watching me, your older brother, in a sexual situation. And that's way weirder than anything I'm doing.'

'*My* bed,' I retorted.

She moved. I glimpsed her pubic hair. Then the revealed leg clamped the edge of the duvet and drifted no more.

'You should come down and hear Dad speak,' I said. 'Come on. There's no point being here otherwise.'

'Why, I wonder, does Dad feel the need always to be giving speeches?'

'Not always. It's his sixtieth birthday, for Christ's sake. Come down.'

'Maybe it's going to be about the whole child-abuse thing we've wiped from our minds, Lou. At *last* we get it all out in the open. The alcopops. The hazy parties. The perma-tanned television presenters. The half-familiar MPs.'

'You guys . . . you are sick.' The duvet spoke quietly but vehemently at the wall. 'What is *wrong* with you British people? Even the Swedes . . . we don't say these kind of things.'

'It's Lou – I told you – he's got big issues.'

'Come down, Ralph.'

'But I can't stand any of the people down there, Lou. They make me want to stand naked on the stairs and spear heroin into my eyeballs.'

'He would want you to be there.' I was heading for the door. 'And I'm sleeping in here tonight. Just so you know. *Not* on the floor, either.'

He called after me: 'Lou, just so you know: you're the opposite of an aphrodisiac. Every time you talk, you push orgasm further down the agenda for the rest of humanity.'

'Fuck off.'

'Shut the door.'

'Fuck off again.'

I pulled the door behind me. And then went tharn as I heard the familiar step on the attic stairs. Half a run. Purposeful. Demanding. Invasive. I didn't know whether to go back into my bedroom or start down. But I felt this sudden certainty that I had to protect my brother from my father and my father from going into that room. Looking back, I can see now that so much of Ralph's behaviour was a sexual rebuke to Dad . . . As if he were saying: you were secretly sleeping with someone else on my tenth birthday; now I am sleeping with someone else on your sixtieth; you broke the family with sex; you made infidelity OK; then you canonized it; so live with the consequences, old man, because every woman I will ever meet is more important to me than you; and every time you want me to pay you attention, every time you need me, I won't be there. I'm not sure Ralph saw it that way himself – or not explicitly; but that's what he did, that's what he was always doing; he took the specific and he made it general; every new girlfriend was a way of mocking Dad, reproaching him. The lessons that the son takes to heart turn out to be those the father never realized he was teaching.

Dad was at the top of the stairs. 'Hello there, Louis,' he said. 'We've been looking for you. Ten minutes. Is that OK? Are you all right?'

'Just been to get this.' I held up the paper and hoped that he wouldn't guess it was a poem that Mum had written for him since I didn't want to spoil the surprise of what I was going to read.

He was hesitating – uneasy, a little drunk.

'Have you seen your brothers?'

'No. Maybe in the garden?'

He was looking at me with a concern that lived next door to suspicion.

So I made it about my nerves. 'I'll be down in a sec. I want to read this through again. Can you give me five?'

I turned to go back into my room, hoping he would go back down the stairs.

'Well, can't wait to hear it, Lou, whatever it is.' He hesitated again. 'If you see them, will you tell them it would be nice if they appeared for the speeches?'

'Yep.'

He started down.

I half pushed open the door and hovered, holding my mother's poem, neither in nor out of my own bedroom.

'Hello, Louis,' Ralph said. 'Back for more? We were just about to start enjoying ourselves again. Who was that?'

'Jack,' I lied. 'Ralph – please come down. I'm fucking nervous. I don't know anyone here and I feel like a right cock doing this reading.'

'We are coming.' Kristen sat up suddenly, clinging to the duvet. 'No question, Ralph. We go for your brother. Come on.'

'It seems we are heading down, bro, especially for you.' Ralph sighed and slowly put his hand on the edge of the duvet. 'Well . . . turn away, Lou, or face me naked.'

'You say that every night.'

'And yet still you don't turn away.'

Kristen looked from one to the other of us and shook her

head: 'Let's try to be normal human beings – just for a few hours – OK?'

I smiled my thanks and went out to sit on the stairs to practise my poem while they got dressed.

We have been to some odd places together over the years, the two of us. And Ralph is still the only person I know who really *gets* it. But now . . . I don't know how he's going to be. When he arrives, I mean, from Berlin – where he lives and works as a successful puppeteer.

If he arrives.

L'AUTOROUTE DES ANGLAIS

'No, but listen to that, Lou . . . Almost silent. What we doing?'

'Close to sixty-five, Dad.'

'Exactly. Almost silent . . . that's the beauty of rear-wheel drive.'

'And what beauty it is.'

So now we're driving along the French motorway – the A26 – and it's turning out to be one of those days where the sun keeps on coming and going between the clouds like they're testing the system in heaven. Meanwhile, we're passing by signs to the Somme and Dad's got the map open unnecessarily on his lap because he hates 'satnavs' and, of course, we can't put any music on because it would affect us too much. So instead we're talking about engine noise.

Dad ignores my sarcasm and rams right on: 'And that's why I didn't get a new one . . . Because after eighty-nine, they moved the engine to the front – diesel – and they make a racket. That's the problem with four-wheel drive.'

'What's the problem?'

'The *noise*.'

But I also ignore him because I know that when Dad says 'noise' like this, he wants to talk about 'noise' as a major issue in 'the modern world'. By which he means – initially – non-classical music, particularly as played in shopping centres, pubs, restaurants and so on. But by which he really means 'noise' as a symptom or signifier of 'inanity', which he considers is forever on the verge of taking over our public life, culture, civilization. Behind even that, though, lurk some angry feelings about the people involved in the making and consumption of the 'noise'. And I can feel my jaw tensing because (on some deep level I don't fully understand) this anger of his makes me angry, too. But now is not the time; now is not the time.

Another sign pops up and says 'Reims 254 kilometres'. The kilometres are going so much faster than miles. All the same (and even though it is off the scale insane), we're in a slight hurry because I have booked us into this Champagne chateau for the night – it seemed like the right thing to do – and we have to be there for six because that's when the pre-dinner tasting starts. So I accelerate a little to pass a convoy of lorries that have appeared ahead.

'They had to do it, though,' Dad says.

He is nodding like he's pretty pleased to have got the inside on this. Dad is big into his vans and roads and driving and cars and maps; it's a hangover from some old-school idea of masculinity from when he was a boy way back in the last century. He used to take me motor racing at weekends when we weren't at poetry festivals. Once a year, we would drive to the Belgian Grand Prix and camp. We still follow Formula One like other people follow football teams – Ralph and Jack, too. Dad's hero is Jim Clarke; Dad says Clarke was 'a great', which is the highest accolade Dad ever gives. Ralph's is Senna. Jack's is Prost. I refuse to have a hero – just to annoy them.

I can feel the exact half-second when Dad becomes conscious of my lack of overt attention to what he is saying – and how that hurts him. So I say: 'Who had to do what, Dad?'

'VW had to do it.'

'Why?'

'Because of builders.'

'Builders?'

'Yes. Builders all wanted flat-bed trucks so that they could load easily from the back. So they had to move the engine to the front. Which means from nineteen-ninety on, you're dealing with a front-situated engine and—'

My phone starts ringing inside the glove compartment. I've got this atrocious ring tone – 'Jelly on a Plate' – from when I was last playing with Jack's children because they find it hilarious – although nobody knows why – since they don't even eat jelly and they use plastic bowls. So now we're just two Englishmen on our way to commit suicide, glancing across at one another while racing in the wrong direction down a French motorway called L'Autoroute des Anglais and listening to a hysterically insistent 'Jelly on a Plate'.

Dad opens the glove compartment and answers it: 'Hello, Larry Lasker . . .'

He is grinning and doing this 'keep your eyes on the road' thing with little nods of his head.

'Oh hello, Eva,' he says. 'No I'm afraid you've got the wiser and more seasoned model.'

My father is actually winking at me.

'Lou is driving. Well . . . I *say* driving. He's not written the van off yet.'

'Dad.'

'A few close shaves coming out of London.'

I reach out. 'Dad – let me speak.'

'Had to remind him which side of the road to drive on – when we got off the ferry.'

'Dad!'

'Eyes on the road, Lou.' He holds up his hand and goes silent.

I try to imagine Eva – she's probably in her flat in Tufnell Park, standing on her mattress at her gable window to combat the strange reception issue.

Eva and I have only been together-together for ten months, but she knows what is happening because we share everything – coffee, money, shampoo, every shiver, every song. But I didn't tell Dad about her. Not in any detail. I don't know why. I keep secrets. Maybe because I was trying to give myself some place that I might make towards on the other side of this, some place that was nothing to do with my family. To involve her seemed wrong, presumptuous, since she wasn't bound up with them, only with me. And I didn't want them to have to deal with her being there; or her to have to deal with them dealing with her; or me to have to deal with all of it. Most of all, I wanted to shield her from their ravening.

Now, though, as I'm glancing over, I can feel that Dad is sieving what she's saying like only Dad can do. And I can't stand to think of Dad imagining her with me after he has gone. And suddenly, the whole idea of keeping my father and Eva separate feels like it was another big mistake. Among the many. I extend my hand for the phone. 'Dad – can I talk to her.'

He holds his finger to his lips. The side of his face is slipping into this slack expression of solemnity.

My eyes are burning. And it takes me a moment to realize

that it is because someone is flashing me in the rear-view mirror. Somehow, we've moved into the fast lane to go past this Citroën who, in turn, is passing the trucks. But this Citroën is only doing one mile an hour less than me. So it's taking for ever to get by and I can't pull out of the way.

'Thank you, Eva,' Dad is saying. 'That took courage.'

The flashing comes again. And this Mercedes is now so far up my ass that if I even touch the brakes, we will all die. So I put my foot all the way down on the gas and we are not Slow Driving now – no sir, we're racing to Zurich as fast as we can and the engine is making plenty of noise.

'I will,' he says. 'I will. I'll have him call you – as soon as we stop.'

We're past the Citroën. Dad is holding my phone up high to hide his face and he won't turn towards me.

'Thank you. Yep. Goodbye . . . Yes.' I can tell Dad wants to say something more, something that resonates, but he doesn't know if he should. 'Goodbye,' he says, again. 'And really good luck.'

The Mercedes is coming by and this Botox-beast in the passenger seat is looking up at me like I am the one who screwed up her surgery.

'Dad?'

'Sorry,' he says.

'Maybe we should stop.'

'OK. Yes. Let's pull over at the next lay-by.'

'OK . . .'

I don't know if he means stop *stop*; or just stop. I know that if I say we should stop and turn around, then he will. It is the one thing I am certain of: that my father will abide by my wishes. There's some kind of tectonic understanding between us that guarantees this. Beneath it all. That we do this willingly together or not at all. But in another way I can't have him saying he wants to stop *stop*. I can't have him doubting anything. Because then everything we have been through becomes meaningless and my brothers will have been right all along.

He's still not looking in my direction and I can't keep glancing over without making our embarrassment worse. He's suffering. Emotional lability. He's shaking almost imperceptibly. He looks so ill in this overcast light – so wan and wasting and weak. Like dying is an active, minute by minute, process that I can actually see. Which it is.

I don't know the best way to be.

'Sorry,' he says, hoarsely, 'I shouldn't have answered.' He places the phone back in the glove compartment and fiddles with the catch. The flickering light annoys him. The bulb is going.

'There was no name. It said number blocked. I don't understand these bloody phones.'

He does understand – he has had a phone for twenty years.

'Dad – don't worry about it.'

He rummages a second more then says: 'She sounds sparky.'

'Sparky' is not one of his words – and it makes me wither inside to hear him use it because it means he doesn't know how to talk to me about this. So because I know that Jack is the best distraction from Eva, I say: 'I thought it might be Jack.'

'Did Jack say he was going to call?'

'No. No, he didn't. But . . . you should call him.'

'I will . . . He knows we left?'

'Yes.' Now I'm hurting him even more. The fact that Jack is not coming is Dad's greatest sadness – or defeat. But at least it's something that I can hide behind while we crawl out of the moment.

'Look,' I say, 'there's an *aire de repos* – six kilometres. Do you want to stop there?'

'Yes . . . Yes.'

We sit in silence a while. Driving down the road. A horrible despair hovers between us. Like it's about to define our whole lives. I would rather have him at his most rancorous – raging, ranting; anything other than this. Anything that revivifies him. Black birds rise from the roadside like ashes scattered into the wind.

My father murdered my mother's poetry with his very presence. Oppression. Asphyxiation. He smothered her as surely as if he had lain down on top of her with a pillow.

A major side effect of the treatment that Zeus, Yahweh, Jesus, Allah and the gang have been dishing out to me for not believing in them is that I've had to think a lot about my parents. And – yes – once they got married, my mother never really made it as a poet – despite her talent. Ah, Lou, she would say, truly in headaches and in worry life vaguely leaks away. But she taught me a lot about the 'greats' as she would call them – and I feel a sort of responsibility to . . . I don't know . . . to keep poetry in my life. Whatever *that* means. Sometimes these bits and fractions and half-lines come into my head like 'the centre cannot hold' and I have no idea where they are from or who wrote them.

I should also say that Dad completely wrecked his first marriage – and probably the minds of Ralph and Jack – in order to marry my mum. Fifteen years, vows, wife, the emotional well-being of his children – straight down the pan. We're talking court orders. We're talking people standing outside windows screaming about love and hate. I said my father was 'honest' not 'good' – lots of people think they're the same thing and they're not – nothing much to do with each other if you ask me.

And yet I've never seen it the way my mother and father had it with any other couple – young or old. They flat-out loved each other – physically, mentally, spiritually. A lot of couples like to live with all these roses and vines wrapped around them – check out the scent of heaven; observe the fruits of paradise – and, sure, it all looks and smells beautiful; but behind the flowers and the fruit and the foliage, the columns are all chipped and dry and crumbling away to nothing. Whereas my mother and father could just stand there gleaming white, two pillars and a mighty arch: welcome to the temple of love, people.

My best shot is that it was to do with an absence of any *persuading* themselves about each other. Even the word 'commitment' doesn't quite cover what they had – because that suggests there was a struggle with something that had to be overcome so that the 'commitment' could be made. So what does this tell us? That it's fine – no matter how you behave – as long as it's in the name of true love? That good is blithely born of bad and vice versa? That a world of lies can give birth to a world of love? (The honesty was only ever a streak.) And where does that leave Carol – Ralph and Jack's mother? Living in that basement flat in Bayswater, listening to the radio and measuring out her life in those bottles of cheap white wine that she keeps shoulder to shoulder in her fridge door.

Sometimes I think that maybe grief is what is torturing my father most of all – grief, not the disease. Maybe that's why he's doing this – because he doesn't see any purpose in carrying on without my mum. All this . . . All this is an elaborate requiem for her.

I say the only thing I can think of to say: 'Why do the French call them *aires de repos?*'

He's still croaky. 'Not following you, Lou.'

'As opposed to service stations, I mean.'

'It's interesting,' he says.

Maybe the only upside of Mum's death was that it taught us how to pull ourselves together – how to find the false things to say that pass the time, that do the job of fending off reality until we are able to get back up and fully engage with the enemy ourselves.

'It's interesting the difference in the words that the two languages deploy, Lou. And what those words tell us about our national characteristics.'

'How do you gloss it?' I ask.

'Well, as you say: we call them service stations.'

'Yes . . . Meaning?'

'Meaning we tacitly consider that petrol and food are the same – fuels – with which we "service" ourselves.'

'Whereas?'

'Whereas the French term – *"aire de repos"* – suggests that they assume that their citizenry would like to take their time over eating and consider this activity distinct from the purchasing of petrol.' He starts to gesture at the windscreen again – remonstrating. That's what he likes to do, I'm thinking, remonstrate with the outside world. 'Meaning – second – that the French tacitly assume their fellows will be carrying better picnic food than any roadside chain of offal-bucketeers could serve up.'

'And third – I sense there's a third, Dad.'

'Meaning – third – that they also assume that their countrymen would like not to be corralled through some kind of soulless mall but, where possible, would like to eat and to rest beneath the splendour of the open sky.'

'Is that why you're a champagne socialist?'

'You're the one who booked us into a Champagne chateau.'

'I'm not a socialist.'

'We're very much back in fashion, Lou. What are you?'

'A person.'

'Don't be facetious.'

'A facetious person.'

Discussion and debating eases us, soothes us, heals us – 'The Socratic Method' as Dad calls it. Or 'arguing' as Mum used to call it. This is another problem we all share: that we need opposition to feel OK. Otherwise, maybe we don't exist.

'I am a socialist,' Dad declares, 'because I believe human beings can do better than to understand and organize themselves through the clumsy, grinding and *miserable* metaphor of the market.'

He is alive again.

'Witness the crash . . .'

'Nope.'

'. . . An eisteddfod of bailouts and bonuses and economic bunting for the very same banks – and bankers – who pillaged civilization in the first place. Bailouts funded, naturally, by taxpayers. By us. The people. What *is* that if not socialism? Your phone just beeped.'

'Pass it here. Straight away, Dad. I'm not fucking kidding. Sorry.'

'Wait a—'

'Right now.'

'Be careful, Lou. Keep your eyes on the road. This is the turn-off.'

I grab the phone, swap it into my other hand and hold up the screen. It's a text.

'Who is it?'

'It's Eva,' I lie.

Because, actually, it is Jack; and he's asking a question I don't know the answer to.

JACK

I edged the bathroom door open.

'Siobhan?'

'No, it's me.'

'Lou. Hello. Come in.'

I stepped inside. The bathroom was small – has always been small – which didn't help the situation. Jack has long needed a bigger house (such as Dad's, ours, mine).

He glanced up. 'Woah, Louis. What is going on with your hair?'

'Growing it.'

'Right.' Jack grinned. He was on his knees in his suit surrounded by nappies, towels, infant pyjamas and an array of bottom-related ointments, lotions, creams and gels. He was trying to remove Baby Percy (our nickname for his daughter, the youngest of his three children) from her clothes, an effort that she was resisting with an intense physical and psychological determination that belied her age – one. This struggle was further complicated by the fact that her own version of the tummy-trouble had managed to escape her nappy the better to reach up her back and disperse itself with some enthusiasm among the many layers of her winter clothes. Jack paused from grappling with her thousand buttons and gussets and flaps in order to tuck his tie into his shirt to prevent it dangling into the mess.

'*Careful.* Don't stand there. Those nappies are dirty. Everybody in here has got diarrhoea.'

'That's how I like it.'

'Can you find me some more wet wipes? There's another packet in here somewhere. Under the sink.'

In the bath, Billy and Jim, Jack's three-year-old twins, were pouring water on each other's heads, one with a sponge in his mouth, the other with a toothbrush.

'Don't drink the water, boys,' Jack cautioned, straightening up. He contorted his eyebrows at me in a can-you-believe-any-of-this expression not dissimilar to that of our father's when watching the news. Jack looks more like Dad than Ralph because he is robust and solid rather than being so guardedly thin, and because he keeps his auburn hair shorter and his blue eyes are shaded with grey. Most of all, because he has a stubble beard streaked here and there with white and gold, which makes him look older, and, well, fatherly.

'Hello, Littles,' I ventured. I am godfather to the boys. 'Is it bathtime?'

They greeted the fatuity of the question with that expressionless infant contempt that children reserve for such occasions and continued – with a fraction more concentration – to suck upon sponge and brush respectively.

'Say hello to Uncle Lou,' Jack urged.

They continued to suck but cut me a wave each. 'The taxi is here, Jack, by the way.'

I sometimes think my main job in the family is to play the tactful emissary between the irreconcilable and the insane. Apparently, I am the only person whom everybody likes. Or, at least, whom nobody *blames*. Which seems to be the same thing. So, gently, I add: 'We need to get weaving.'

'Not possible.' Jack looked up from the struggle. 'Percy, the boys and I have solemnly sworn to cover the house in shit before they go to bed. We won't sleep till it's done.' He glanced over at the twins. 'Don't *eat* the sponge, Billy. You both did your wee-wees in the bath – remember?'

Riotous laughter from the bath.

'Can I do anything?'

He made as if to lean aside from the excretal abyss: 'Here you go. All yours, Lou.'

Jack smiles a lot more easily than Ralph. He finds things funny-broad more than he finds things funny-deep.

'Should we just go? And you catch up?'

'No. How are Dad and Siobhan doing down there?'

'It's civil. Dad is being sarcastic about the television. Siobhan is deliberately not noticing.'

Jack peeled off Baby Percy's little pink tights. 'If I can get them all clean in the bath, you go down and tell Siobhan that it's job done and then get Zita – the babysitter – to come up. Say they want to say hello to her before we go out. I'll bribe her to get them out of the bath and then we're away.'

'I no like Zita,' said Billy.

'Wet wipes, Lou. Wet wipes. Wet wipes. Wet wipes.'

'I'm looking.'

The bathroom was knee-deep in towels as well as everything else.

'Should Dad come up?'

'No. You'll start a war.'

Jack was down to the last layer before the nappy itself –

some kind of Babygro covered in absurdly complicated press-studs. I handed him the wet wipes. If sex is Ralph's rebuke to my father, then Jack's reproach is his sleeves-rolled-up style of fatherhood. I'm not sure how conscious this is in his case either. But part of him definitely relished being late for Dad because he was too busy being a father.

Jack used to be a journalist. Now he is in public relations for a life-insurance company. It's an embarrassment (Jack), a defeat (Dad) and the abandonment of hope (Ralph). As a consequence and by way of compensation for all this humiliation and pointlessness, he is now paid five times more. I've noticed this seems to be the way of things white-collar-wise: the more tedious the job, the higher the pay. But there's another irony in that Jack used to be a communist. For real. He went to college in Edinburgh and he used to sell *Socialist Worker* and wear boots and have one of those high short-back-and-sides cuts that Leninists seemed to share with rockabilly kids long before any of it was cool. Don't ask me why: in search of fatherly approval, or calling fatherly bluff, take your pick. Maybe he even believed it; there's always that chance with Jack.

Jack frowned. 'Dad is serious about tonight?'

'Never more so,' I said.

'Christ, Percy, keep still for one minute.' I could feel Jack tensing. 'There is no point in even discussing it. Dad is never going to go to Switzerland.'

'Tell *him* that.'

'What is his problem?'

'Motor neurone disease.'

Jack looked over. 'Try not to be a complete penis, Lou.'

He has an unsettling way of being deadly earnest. Where Ralph makes you feel inelegant and wrong, Jack makes you feel frivolous and wrong.

'Well, that *is* his problem.'

'There are plenty of people who get motor neurone disease. Stephen Hawking.'

'Not at Dad's age. It's terminal. No exceptions. Absolute max: two years. That's what they're saying at the clinic.'

'Dad is just not a Dignitas man.'

'How would you characterize a Dignitas man?'

'We are not a Dignitas family.'

'How would you—'

'Percy! Keep *still!*' With the care of a bomb-disposal expert on the last operation of his tour, Jack was now removing the nappy itself. The smell of sour baby milk filled the close air of the room. 'Does he think we won't look after him when it gets worse?'

'I don't think it's the looking after him that he's worried about. It's the getting worse.'

The boys were splashing.

'There must be hundreds of care options,' Jack said.

'Not hundreds. And they all wind up in the same place.'

'He might at least discuss it.'

'That's why he's here, Jack.'

'No, he's here to *tell* us that this is what he is doing.'

'He definitely can't discuss it if you won't discuss it.'

'I mean . . . Switzerland? Really?'

'Maybe they'll change the law and he'll be able to do it in Shepherd's Bush. But until then . . . it's Zurich . . . or Albania or New Mexico.'

Naturally, I had gone behind Dad's back and relayed the progress of his thinking to Jack during the last few weeks. But Jack had decided not to tell Siobhan that Dad's new plan was what tonight was all about – partly, I guessed, because Jack had thought that up until now Dad was merely 'exploring' the idea, and partly because he wanted Dad to take the consequences of tabling the discussion vis-à-vis Siobhan.

Jack raised Percy's legs. 'He's being stubborn and truculent.'

'That's what he says about you.'

'But this involves all of us. We are the ones that have to go on living – with the consequences. In a way, this affects us more than it affects him.'

'Somehow, you're managing to be selfish about Dad's illness.'

'Plus he wants our approval. And I—'

'Why don't you put these excellent points to *him*?'

'We've been through all this.'

'You and me, Jack. Yep. Lots. But you and D—'

'Boys, will you *stop* splashing?'

Jim took an extra-large suck on the toothbrush and swallowed with melodramatic emphasis. And then – once he was sure he had the room's attention – he tipped the contents of his plastic cup over the edge of the bath.

'No,' Jack raised his voice. 'Jim. No. You do *not* pour water out of the bath.'

Billy started eating the soap.

'Billy!' Jack shouted.

At which increase of the volume from her father, Baby Percy decided she had taken as much as she was going to take and launched an assault on the entire house's hearing.

I must have looked anxious because Jack mouthed above the burgeoning racket: 'I've forgotten her milk. She likes milk at bathtime. Shut the bastard door.'

Baby Percy was now kicking and wriggling as if her tiny life depended on Jack never cleaning her bottom again. His tie had somehow slipped and swung down above the ever-spreading diarrhoea. He cursed. I was reaching down to pull it up for him when, suddenly, Billy appeared to detonate himself with the abrupt and terrible wail of a suicide-bomber. 'My eyes! My eyes!' he yelled.

'Shit! *Shit.*' Jack leapt up. 'He's got soap in his eyes.' He leant over and deployed a towel in Billy's direction.

Baby Percy redoubled her screams.

Then it started raining everywhere.

Icy, frozen, torrential rain filled the room.

Jack was bellowing: 'Turn it off. Turn it off. It's freezing!'

Somehow, Jim had turned on the shower.

'Turn it off, Lou. Turn it *off.*'

Billy screeched. Percy screamed. But they were as nothing to the high-pitched shrieking of Jim.

I jumped over Baby Percy and tried to lean into the shower taps without getting my clothes wet.

'Turn the bastard off, Lou. *What the hell are you doing?*'

The trebled cries seemed to fill every available register of the human ear – echoing and reverberating off the tiles about our bewildered heads. But it was impossible to quite reach the mixer without getting wet. I gave up and bent past Jim who was huddling uselessly against the deluge that was now soaking my clothes. The water stopped.

'Oh God.' Jack spun around, letting go of Billy, who slipped, howled and started to go under.

'Percy, come *back*. Lie down!' Jack picked up the still filthy-bottomed Percy and held her aloft without further plan.

I grabbed Billy, soaking myself again and accidentally knocking into Jim in the process, whose little face was astounded and then horrified.

Somehow, Percy had got into the boy's nappies as well as redistributing her own. There was infant excrement all over the floor. There was water everywhere. The children's pyjamas were sodden and the clean nappies were swollen from the flood. Percy moved up through the gears to hit full lung. Jack was now holding her above the sink and swearing that he couldn't find the plug. The water was too hot, too cold.

Billy started to choke on his sponge.

Jim was shivering from the cold of the shower and flat-out bellowing: 'Out! Out! Out! Out! No like it! No like it! Out! Out!'

Jack was yelling: 'Take my tie off, Lou. Take my fucking tie off. Find the plug. Turn the cold off. There's shit everywhere. My fucking tie. There's shit everywhere.'

At which moment Siobhan entered the room.

Ten minutes later we went out to discuss whether or not my dad should commit suicide.

AIRE DE REPOS

We're somewhere short of Arras. The *aire de repos* turns out to be one of those obligingly wooded lay-bys off the motorway that the Europeans seem to do so well – a clean, convivial, carefully planted copse that somehow cancels out the noise of the cars. A safe harbour. While I am standing listening to my dying father defecate, I text Eva, the woman with whom I make love, and I think about Freud and Jung, of whom I know nothing except that they are beloved of a certain sort of intelligent person – like, for example, Ralph.

Where *is* the bastard?

I text his German mobile. I text his UK mobile and copy it to email and send that, too. He said he would meet us en route. The sickening thought comes that maybe on some level – shallow or deep – he's decided not to communicate by way of stopping Dad: like Dad won't do it if he doesn't see Ralph first. Either my brothers are not taking this seriously; or they are taking it so seriously that they're going to stop the whole thing by not showing up.

'Success,' Dad says pretty loudly from within the cubicle.

This must be the first time we have been to the toilet together since I was three.

A man with a precise and somehow pompous goatee walks in.

'You OK?' I call to Dad through the cubicle door.

'Yep. Pleased to say, Lou, I can still wipe my own bottom.'

I glance across at Goatee; he gives me an arch look.

Dad speaks loudly from within: 'That's actually the main reason I want to do this now.'

I am both amazed and not at all surprised that my father is trying to start this conversation at this moment and in this manner. (My phone buzzes: a three-word text from Eva: 'I love you.' How the fuck did they manage before phones?) The only way to take my father on when he deploys his jokily-being-serious tone is to do the same right back. I'm not sure such exchanges get us anywhere. But since our destination is death, I'm not sure it matters that they don't.

I speak loudly through the door even though there is no need to do so: 'What are you talking about? What is the main reason you want to do *what*?'

'The fact that I can still wipe my own bottom is the main reason I want to make this trip.'

'You're saying that you want to kill yourself because you can still wipe your own bottom?'

The goatee guy can't figure out whether he is dealing with perverts or clowns. I need to speak to my brothers.

'Do you think that's a common feeling?'

'Actually, yes I do.'

Dad flushes the toilet. So I raise my voice even further.

'Life and death: it's all about the anus?'

'I think that the fear of decline, the fear of incapacity is really a fear of not being able to wipe one's own bottom.'

'Right.'

'I think that is what people really mean, Lou, that's the physical anxiety in their mind – when they say they want to die with dignity. OK, I'm ready for action: come on in.'

71

Goatee is buttoning up. He frowns. I push at the door and edge inside.

Dad is bent over, head down, as if he might fall forward any moment and knock himself out on the floor. His legs look scrawny and he's holding one with his hand because it's twitching.

He looks up. 'It's a threshold,' he says, quietly. 'A threshold we do not wish to cross, Lou.'

I reach forward and offer my arms and haul my father upright; it's the getting up and down that he finds so tough.

'On one side of the threshold you can clean your own bottom,' Dad says. 'And on the other – you can't.'

'And that's significant, Dad?' I help him pull up his trousers. He has his wrists on my shoulders.

'Yes. It is.'

We are face to face. Saliva spools from his mouth.

He lowers his voice. 'I don't want to have anyone else doing this for me. Least of all you, Lou.'

I drag up a smile and chain it to my lips. I can hear breath entering him and leaving him. He is looking at me. I can feel myself nodding slowly. I can feel the surge and churn of my emotions again: disgust, sadness, anger, pity, terror, despair, love; each vying in the same instant with its opposite. The last time I slept with Eva, I dreamt about the ground cracking apart beneath my feet: on one side what I felt, on the other what I said – and the fissure between them widening and widening so that I must surely fall into the roiling lava below.

I say: 'I'm glad it's me in here right now – not Doug, I mean. I really wouldn't want to miss this, Dad.'

'Yes, poor Doug though.' Dad smiles. 'The man loves a communal toilet. That's his archaeological speciality.'

72

'We should send him a picture. Is he on Snapchat?'

'What's that?'

'Doesn't matter.'

Out we come. We bind arms and shoulders – so that we're locked together again. Goatee is hammering the hand-drier as if it's responsible for all the slights he has ever suffered. He shoots us a disapproving squint that becomes a synthetic smile as he sees Dad's stick. But ever since the ferry, I've moved past all the what-other-people-think stuff – and so on we go, sanguine and shameless, shuffling towards the washbasins. There's a sparrow flown in through the open side of the building and for a moment it tilts its curious head to watch us – two men side by side washing their hands in water that only gushes or dribbles.

The beginning of love is the end of sleep. From the start, I was at a disadvantage because she was more intelligent but the whole Eva thing nearly cost me what was left of my shredded mind. Three months of completely incomprehensible confusion and uncertainty. Until, at last . . . We were standing in the darkness on the threshold of her flat.

'Sorry,' she said, ducking down and fumbling around beneath what I could just make out must be her desk. 'The main bulb is horrible.'

A sidelight flared and she crossed her rug. She has the blackest possible hair, which here and there escaped her tea-cosy hat that night and fell in long loose question-mark curls. It was impossible to tell whether her expression – her manner – was shy, or defiant, or both at the same time. And when she looked across, as now, her eyes were so dark that it seemed pupil and iris were one.

'Nice place,' I said, fatuously. Then to keep us both from dying: 'Maybe we should drink something. I'm feeling really sober. I mean it's fine to be sober but we—'

'Actually . . . drinks I *can* do,' she said. 'What would you like?'

'What have you got?'

She took off her hat and coat and slung them on the burial mound of clothes draped over her huge cracked-leather chair. By London standards, her flat was pretty big though much of the space was under the eaves. Her bed was a mattress half-unmade beneath the two beams that rose up into the gabled window; and, on either side, she had laid out her books in a long line where the ceiling sloped down to meet the wooden floorboards. There was an old kitchenette, her desk and a tiny fireplace with a single candle. Another door led off to what I guessed was her bathroom. Above the fireplace, a black-and-white picture showed old cars lined up behind a starting tape against a backdrop of crowds, palm trees and ancient buildings: 'Italian Racing in Eritrea' read the title.

'I've got everything,' she said.

'Everything?'

'Yes. Literally. Everything.' With a mock flourish, she threw open what I had assumed was some old wardrobe but I now saw was filled entirely, four shelves deep, with bottles of every colour, shape and provenance. 'Drinks,' she said.

'Jesus.' I drew the deeper breath of re-assessment. 'No wonder you don't come out much. You must be wasted most days.'

'Melted by breakfast.' She inclined her head, pretending rueful commitment to her cupboard. 'Not seen a Sunday in ten years.'

'Seriously though?'

'When Dad closed down the tapas bar, I got to keep the bottles.'

'Nice.'

'Not really.'

She had a way of not-exactly-contradicting me.

'Not really?'

She reached in at the shelves, raising the odd bottle as she spoke: 'Well, how much Van Der Hum tangerine liqueur or . . . or cucumber vodka is a girl going to drink? On her own?'

'Wait—'

'What?'

'Tangerine liqueur?'

'Yep.'

'I'll have a large. I drank it a lot when I was in New Orleans. Two ice.'

'That's the other problem.' She winced, looking towards the sink.

'What?'

'No ice, no mixers and . . .' she stepped over towards the kitchenette, 'no glasses.'

'I see plates though,' I said. There was a tiny drying rack by the butler sink.

She narrowed her eyes. 'Yes . . . plates we have.'

'Well, OK then, we pour the tangerine dream and the cucumber moonshine or whatever onto the plates and just lick.'

'Like thirsty werewolves?'

'Exactly.'

'What about disgusting mugs?' She stepped over to the messy desk. 'I have two of those.'

'Even better.'

She pulled a bottle out of the wardrobe on the way back. 'I sometimes drink Jägermeister – it's kind of tasty for about five sips and it feels like it's at home in a mug. When were you in New Orleans?'

'I wasn't. I was . . . I was joking.'

'Do you always make things up?'

'Constantly.'

She finished rinsing the mugs and then looked at me as she dried them with paper towels.

'Insecurity or boredom?' she asked.

'Both. Plus fear of loss.'

'You're blushing.'

She came over with the mugs and a book of matches. Then she lit the wide candle in the fireplace and we sat together on the floor amidst the cushions. I looked at the poster of the cars.

'Is that Mussolini's doing? Barging into Eritrea, I mean, with fast Italian cars.'

'Well, Eritrea was an Italian colony before the Fascists. But – yes. Good knowledge.' Her face took on a brace-brace expression. 'Are you one of those boys who knows a lot?'

'I know a lot about very little.'

'What are your specialist areas?'

'Fragments from the poets and early hominid refuse disposal. You?'

'Formula One and *patatas bravas*.'

'Shit, no.' My face must have betrayed my earnestness.

'Yes . . .'

'My dad loves Formula One,' I said. 'I've been to a dozen Grands Prix.'

'My dad, too. He's the one who bought me that poster.'

'Jesus,' I said, 'this really *is* a first.' I offered my mug and we chinked. 'Let's move to Rome and get married. Open a vegan cafe selling books. We could burn used Formula One tyres in a cosy little stove without telling anyone. Just to fuck the hipsters up.'

She looked at me directly and without blinking and said nothing and I felt the crimson tide rising again for having over-stepped some kind of mark.

But then she said: 'We could call it "Pit Stop". Or maybe "Box Box Box".'

And that was when I knew that it was going to be OK because, this once, luck was with me . . . The truth is that I had lied to my father about women. I did not, in fact, have any girls pushing me forward or holding me back. I was never 'busy', never 'hectic'. I have red hair. (From both father and mother.) And what this seems to mean is that I'm absolutely nowhere with ninety per cent of the world's señoritas. Nowhere. Not even a first look, never mind a second. As far as most girls are concerned, I might as well be a gay Belarusian abattoir owner with galloping nostril pubes and the blood of a thousand baby lambs on my hands. On the other hand, with the remaining ten per cent, I have always been everything they have ever dreamed of. Really. Some girls – not many – but this tiny determined faction – they just *love* me.

I had not known, but all along – astonishingly, astoundingly – Eva had numbered herself among that little band of the auburn-loving acolytes. Yes: she was one of the blessed ten per cent. To her, I was that most desirable of men: a pre-Raphaelite vampire. (Her words.) And our previous 'communication problems' (so it transpired) were all due to the fact that she had sadly (so very sadly) been in the long process of splitting up from her boyfriend – some thirty-two-year-old iguanodon of the civil service who had all but bored and bullied her into getting engaged, but whom, she knew now, she could never marry because of his fundamental inability to grasp how meaningfully to interrelate with actual human beings, not least Eva herself. (My words.) Our intermittent meetings in twilight autumnal cafes to share dungy carrot cake and sewagey green tea were (she later confessed) all that she felt she could manage until she was clear of the wreckage of his malignancy and tantrums. This had been the cause of the incomprehensible confusion.

That night, we lay together in her bed, naked and warm and close against the cold with the gleam of the moon in the frost on the glass of her window above.

THE MEANING GAP

My father and I shuffle down the path from the washrooms. The change is unspoken. But suddenly we are walking everywhere together with our arms round one another. He's worse, I think, than even a week ago. Or maybe he isn't. Maybe he's pretending to be worse because he thinks this will help me, because he thinks that the struggle of these steps will lodge in my memory, make it easier. Afterwards.

I can't accuse him of shamming, though. And in any case: what does it matter if his deterioration is real or faked? Because now that we're so tightly bound, with each and every step we feel easier, we feel like we're investing these minutes with due weight and import and significance. Maybe this is how to live: convince yourself of something and then repeat until fade; everyday human philosophy in action.

We're ignoring the Eva call. We just can't talk about it. Not now. One of the biggest problems we have is that if we start talking about one thing, then we get into another thing . . . and so to the *only* thing. Neither of us is ready for that again. Because what we are doing is like this massive exquisitely balanced equation that describes the universe – which is to say an equation that describes everything we have ever said to one another about what we're doing. And so to start saying even one tiny thing more would mean the equation would become unbalanced and we'd have to stop immediately and re-write the whole thing from the beginning to the end. And it's like – if we are going to attempt such a thing – then I have to save us for the right moment to take the universe on since you can't do that shit more than once or twice in your life.

Dr Twigge, the shrink we saw together a few times, says that it is natural to wish to make sense of things: that this is a very human urge, but that – in a way – there is no sense to be made. In return, my father said that this was what Camus was 'getting at' in *Le Mythe de Sisyphe* when he talked of the clash between the human need for meaning and the fact that meaning is not pre-inscribed in the world. 'This need – *that's* what Camus meant by the absurd, Lou, not that things are absurd themselves.' I remember Dad called it 'the meaning gap'. Then he and Twigge started enjoying themselves and talking to each other about a lot of stuff that was nothing much to do with why we were there.

Dad sees the other VW first – it's the same crappy box-shaped 1980s model as ours. There are these two guys fussing around the back: one crouching and then getting up again; the other just standing there with a plastic cup. The van is leaning like it's irreversibly sick of driving, of being a van. Only then do I clock that the tyre is flat. And immediately I'm wondering: what if *we* break down? What then? But obviously all I am able to think about is myself – and maybe this is another generational thing – since straight away, I realize that Dad must have been thinking the exact opposite because he's already heading us in their direction, past the picnic table, over the tarmac and under the trees. The sun is out and we're in good time, but still we're due at the Champagne chateau at six at the latest and I want to get there with a spare hour so we can relax into the whole damn thing.

'Puncture?' Dad shouts over, in English.

Here we come, two ragged messengers bearing news of incalculable defeats.

'*Ja*. Big problem.' The croucher looks over, seemingly too preoccupied to be surprised by our interest. He's one of those undeniably fat guys – pale skin luminescent with a light signature sweat, yellow 'Carlsberg' T-shirt straining with the effort of containment, taller than he seems, now that he stands up, and disconcertingly hairless.

'Big problem,' he says again. 'We have to get Dean to Denzlingen tonight.' He nods towards the other guy – as if we might well know him already. 'Dean – Dean he is playing three nights. We're *am arsch*.'

Dean takes a sip. He's a good deal shorter with furtive ferrety eyes and a face that slopes back from his nose on either side like he's fresh from two weeks' testing in a wind tunnel.

'Maybe I should start hitching, Malte,' he says, quietly. He is English.

'Is your spare gone as well?' asks Dad.

'That's the problem – right there.' Malte has that peculiarly German combination of earnestness and detachment. He tightens his big lips and then puffs out his heavy cheeks. 'We are not having the extra wheel.'

'No spare?' Dad winces.

And now we're all standing looking at the flat tyre. For a second, I think Dad is going to offer ours.

But then he asks: 'What happened to it?'

'I don't know.' Malte draws his head back into the ready pillow of his neck and raises his palms. 'It is supposed to be right here – yes – hanging on the back – or maybe hanging on the front side – but I drove this van since one year and I have never seen it.' He kicks ineffectually at the tyre. 'We are totally screwed just because the wheel is pumped down.'

'Flat,' says Dean, quietly.

'Exactly,' Malte acknowledges. 'No air. Pumped down.'

Dean takes another sip.

'We've got the same van,' I say. 'The Westfalia.'

'The T3,' Dad says, sagely, citing Volkswagen's internal nomenclature. 'The spare is at the front on these models – under the radiator.'

I glance across. Dad is doing his bemused face that he deploys whenever he's trying not to make fun of people.

'They're rear-wheel drive – the T3s,' Dad says. 'That's why they couldn't put the tyre at the back because there's no room.'

'Because of the engine,' I say, hoping to clarify and to include Dean.

'*Ernsthaft?*' Malte frowns and then grins. 'You are fucking me.'

'We're not fucking you,' I say.

'Well . . .' Dad makes to move. 'Let's see if you've got one, then.'

And so now all four of us are round at the front of the van where the shade is deeper under the trees.

'OK,' Malte offers, 'I'll look from down under.'

He lies on the tarmac and edges backwards beneath the front of the van while his T-shirt rides up revealing a startled white belly that slops this way and that uncertain as to how best to obey the rapidly changing geometries of gravity.

'*Ja!* The tyre is here!' Malte shouts up. 'It has been hiding itself underneath – all the time.'

'Is it useable?' Dad is leaning down, talking to the belly, holding on to the front of the van.

'I think so – *ja* – it's pumped full.'

'Pumped up,' Dean says and takes a sip.

'Well, you're in business then,' Dad says.

'Yes. This is clear.' There's a pause, then Malte's voice comes again – less sure. 'But how do we get it out of this little under-cupboard?'

'There's a catch at the front – and a restraining bolt. Then it's sitting on a tray. Have you got any tools?'

I look at Dean.

'*Nein*,' says the stomach. '*Schieße*.'

Dean swills his drink rapidly from cheek to cheek.

It turns out – after cursory consultation – that Malte and Dean don't have anything in their van that might in any way contribute towards expediting the matter in hand. So it then turns out that Dad and I are going to fetch *our* tools in order to help them change their wheel.

And of course, once we get back to our van, I start thinking that I should really ask Dad if he's sure he wants to do this – spend his time like this. We're committed but – in the circumstances – they can't really complain if we just drive away. And yet it seems to me (as we open the tailgate) that clearly Dad *does* want to do this. He carries tools – he has always carried tools. He prides himself on his resourcefulness. There might be nothing he loves more in the world than having the right tool for the situation. When it matters, he's ready. It's another generational thing. Men should be ready. This is what Dad has been saying – with his life – all his life. Fix things. Strip the engine. Deal with that bastard of a dishwasher once and for all. Take the inanimate world on and tame it. And when the time comes: be ready, not blank and hopeless. He wants to use the tools now. And it is his time, not mine. And what else would we be doing? What else *should* we be doing?

'Max twenty minutes,' Dad says, maybe sensing all these thoughts as we lope-and-stick our way back towards Malte and Dean.

It next turns out that Malte is beyond clumsy into some new territory of the physically self-cancelled; his limbs seem to be made of margarine.

Then it turns out that Dean can't do anything at all.

'He's a pianist,' Malte explains. 'That's why he can't use his hands – for anything – except for the piano playing. He's playing three nights through – he starts tomorrow. He really needs his fingers. Tonight we meet the sponsors. Rheinmetall. It's very important. The sponsors. Very important for the music.'

So that's why, finally, it turns out that it's *me* who is sitting on the tarmac, prising off the hubcaps and leaning into the spider spanner to loosen the wheel nuts.

'Anti-clockwise to undo, Lou,' Dad says, before I even start.

I know this of course and I have to stop myself reacting – now is not the time – so instead I say: 'Got it.'

'It's stiff?' Malte asks.

'Yes,' I say.

'What are you playing?' Dad asks Dean. They are standing in a semicircle around my ears while I struggle. There is heat in the September sun when it breaks through.

'Debussy,' offers Malte.

'Debussy?' Dad asks.

'The flute trios,' Dean says, in a voice that would prefer to go unheard. 'Some solo. Some Chopin, too. Part of the Denzlingen Festival – for Debussy and Gourmet Foods. It's . . . It's not very big.'

'Did Debussy spend a lot of time in Denzlingen?' Dad asks. 'What's the connection?'

'He stayed one night on the way somewhere else,' Dean grimaces. 'He is supposed to have eaten this Gourmet-Death menu at the place he stayed.'

'The famous Feinschmecker Hochgenuss dinner.' Malte grins.

'Afterwards,' Dean continues, 'he is supposed to have said that German cooking was better than French. Which is why there's this food and music festival. It's a bit of a joke really . . .'

'Dean is a super-famous guy,' Malte offers, proudly. 'You might know him if you like classic. Dean Swallow. He plays a lot of piano. I am his agent.' This last is delivered with the tone of a man announcing himself as the new ambassador at some great court. 'I drive him to the concerts. We take the money for the flights and the hotels but then we use the little van to travel and to sleep. We put the profits in the pockets. It's a good plan – *oder?*'

I look up. Dad is smiling. I am sweating but I have all five nuts loosened. I jack up the back of the van and ease the wheel off.

'Discs on the front. Drums on the rear,' Dad observes. 'Evens the weight on the axle.'

Malte is rolling the spare over in a parody of a mechanic. 'Hey you guys should have a drink. Dean – get them a drink. It is hotter now – *ja?*'

'What are you drinking, Dean?' Dad asks.

Malte laughs: 'The sponsor's dinner makes him more nervous than the piano.'

I look up. Dean is staring into his Styrofoam like he wishes he could stir himself right in there and be gone. 'It's amaretto and fresh lime,' he says.

'You want some?' Malte rolls me the spare and takes custody of the flat. 'We have ice.'

'I have to drive,' I say.

'Clockwise, Lou,' Dad says. 'I never heard of anyone drinking amaretto with lime.'

I tighten the wheel nuts one after another. Then I let the jack down and get to my feet so as to stand on the spider wrench and tighten them further.

'That'll do, Lou,' Dad says. 'It's quite a long leverage.'

'You think that's tight enough?'

'That's fine: you don't need to overdo it.'

I'm sweating. I straighten up. I realize I completely trust my father's competence on this and – it now strikes me – on everything. And I don't know what to do with this thought. I can hear the traffic on the road rushing by – and I'm thinking this is what madness sounds like – this moment. They're all rushing somewhere. Hundreds every minute. Not to die. But actually – yes – to die.

I pull out the jack. 'We should hit the road, Dad.'

But Malte is about as delighted as I have ever seen anyone and wants to reciprocate somehow: 'Guys, you have totally saved our eggs. Thank you! Thank you. Come on, have a drink: Dean, how much amaretto do we have in there?'

'We really can't,' I say.

'No, sure.' Malte nods. 'You're driving your father, I

understand. But what can we do for you? What about some *wurst*? We still have the special ones from Detmold, I think. Dean?'

Dad is leaning against the van while I pack up his tools. He looks at Dean and says: 'Do you have any CDs or anything – of your playing?'

Dean winces again. 'Yes, I've got one. But it's . . . it's quite obscure.'

'We'll take that.'

Dean shrugs and moves to go and fetch his CD.

Malte is putting the flat tyre in the van. He's way too lazy to fix it back up under the front.

And because I don't want that job to be mine, I say to Dad casually: 'The tasting starts at six.'

'Plenty of time, Lou,' Dad says.

Malte comes back with a business card which he tries to give to Dad. But Dad is watching Dean as he steps diffidently down from his van. So Malte gives it to me with a call-me-if-ever-you-need-vice wink.

Dean holds out the pale CD as if it were a slab of elderly feta cheese. His face is on the cover.

'We'll listen to this,' Dad says. 'And spread the word.'

Dean's blush starts at his nose and heads aerodynamically back towards his ears.

I know how he feels.

Dad stands up as straight as he can. 'Keep on going, Dean. Stick with it,' he says. 'Nobody else will ever play like you. Take delight in it, that's the trick. Where possible – take delight.'

—

There are three audio cassettes covering maybe two and a half hours in total. The first begins with an evil hissing and then nothing until you start to hear these odd shouted words and muffled crashes – like the sounds of people far away, crying out their wares at a market stall. And then you can hear something like the noise of someone hitting a metal bin lid but on the other side of a wall. The recording stays like that for about a minute and it is impossible to make out the words or understand the bangs.

Then a door opens and you can hear someone come into the room where the machine must be. They are breathing heavily – right there close to the microphone. And then the tape stops for a second.

When it comes back on, the volume of the recording has been turned right up and the hiss has become a louder analogue buzz. You hear the person walking away again and then you hear a quiet voice – clearer now, but still not quite audible.

And then you hear the sudden screaming.

The shock of it – so loud. A vicious torrent of words. Completely clear but for the distorting rage of the voice.

The violence of what is being said is terrifying.

Followed by the sound of something shattering.

And then another male voice saying, 'Don't. Don't do that. Don't. Don't. Don't do that.' Over and over again.

We were four days from Christmas and Eva was ill with a cold and she had the shivers but the world was ours and nothing really touched us. She came out of her shower room, her cinnamon skin the darker against the white of her towel, steam chasing her.

'How you feeling?' I asked.

'OK ... It might not be Ebola after all.'

I shrugged. 'Maybe the mild form.'

She looked around the room and noticed that I had tidied and made the bed fresh. She came over to where I was washing up our three dishes at the sink and put her hand round the back of my head and held our foreheads together. Then, with her face still close to mine, she said softly: 'You're a good little carer, aren't you?'

And I pulled away and she must have seen it in my expression.

'What?' she asked. 'What's wrong?'

So then I just started talking and it all came out impromptu ... And after I had told her everything, with the two of us standing by that sink, she asked simply: 'When did he find out?'

'Nine months ago.'

'You should have ... And what? He's already decided?'

'Yep. As soon as there is what he calls "serious deterioration". He's hoping probably next year. You have to start the process a long time before.'

'He's *hoping*, Lou?'

'His word.'

'Jesus.'

'There's no cure. Some people get two years, some people get four, but it's terminal and there's no real treatment. The average time from diagnosis is fourteen months. So we're way past halfway already.'

'I mean ... what? So you wake up and you can't move?'

'No, it's gradual – month to month – but it's relentless. He's lucky in a way. It's not affected his hands too badly – not yet. Or his speech. He . . . he says he doesn't want to let it get too late. He wants to be able to talk.'

'Lou . . . I'm so sorry.'

But I said to her not to be sorry because it was a relief that I had talked to someone outside the family at last. A mighty relief. But then I took a shower myself and immediately started to think that I had over-burdened us. That we were going to crash. That I shouldn't have spoken. That I had poisoned our infant relationship and the only pure happiness I had.

When I came out, though, she was dressed in her jogging bottoms and a T-shirt and sat in the big leather chair that I had freed of her mound of clothes, drying the ends of her hair with her towel, leaning her head this way and that as she did so.

And she said, simply: 'Is he *sure* he wants assisted suicide?'

And I loved her the more that she wasn't all false tones or fake emotions around death. I had feared that most of all – feared how it would have made me feel about her, the distance that it would have opened up. Instead, she looked at me steadily – but with so much intelligence and fellow-feeling in her expression that my heart rose and I felt myself physically lighten.

'Well, Dad would call it assisted dying not assisted suicide.'

'Is there a difference?'

'They say one replaces life with death while the other replaces a bad death with a good one.'

'Fair enough. And what . . . you just go to Dignitas and that's it?'

I shook my head. 'It's not as easy as people think. You have to become a member of Dignitas and then get all these different medical reports done here before they'll even consider you. Which, by the way, the British doctors don't want to do in case they get in the shit for murder. There's a ton of admin to get green-lit.'

'Green-lit – what the fuck?'

I told her about how people mistakenly thought that Dignitas was a clinic. But that really the whole operation was an administrative service that helped the terminally ill get through all the Swiss legal stuff. That they give the clinical bit to the medics that they hire in. And I told her about all the documentation that Dad had been required to get. And about how – when you get to Zurich – you have to go and meet one of their affiliated doctors and get the prescription. But that even then – you have to speak to them a second time before you can go to the blue Dignitas house.

'Only after all of that,' I said, 'do you get to drink the special poison.'

She puffed her cheeks out and exhaled slowly.

And it was a symptom of how far into the world of trauma I had already travelled that I misunderstood her and thought she was expressing consternation about the distance to Zurich rather than the nature of what we were doing.

'I know,' I said, 'I know. It's a disgrace that you can't choose to end your life in this fucking country. But we can't get into all that. Dad wants to campaign. Of course he does. But I don't.'

'What? You don't want him—'

'I don't want him on the TV and radio going on about his

right to die. It's bad enough as it is.' I looked over. Concern weighed in her eyes. I softened my voice: 'He used to be on a few radio shows – and he wrote reviews for the papers. He was one of those media dons. But we have a deal,' I said. 'That he doesn't do any shit about this that I can't handle. And that . . . that we can change our minds.'

'Who else have you talked to – apart from me?'

'We saw this shrink for a while. And we went to see this family . . . They did it back in 2008. And a couple of relatives.'

She swapped the towel to the other side of her hair and looked up at me sideways from beneath the tilt of her head. 'What did they say?'

'They said that . . . that after a few years pass, you're so pleased you did it because you keep looking at the calendar and thinking, "He'd be dead by now. And it would have been much worse."'

'So if you can go into the future and look backwards, it feels like a great idea – five years from now or whatever?'

'Yeah.'

'But that doesn't make it feel like a great idea now.'

'Nope.'

'Fuck.' She straightened her head and let the towel fall.

'But in another way,' I said, 'your mind races forward. I mean . . . straight away when he told me – I saw everything. I saw the deterioration, the wheelchair, the end. You see it all. You're kind of grieving ahead of yourself. Something like that . . . I don't know . . . Sometimes I can see his death like a presence in his living face.'

She got up and came over and raised her finger and thumb to my cheeks and drew me in. I could tell that she was momentarily hurt that I had not told her before – but that she was trying not let this feeling show because she didn't want to make it about her.

So I said: 'I should've told you before. But . . .'

'But what?'

'I didn't want this – us – to be burdened. Jesus, I hate that word. I wanted to get us over the line.'

'What line?'

'I wanted us to be – I don't know. I didn't want all this heaviness between us. I wanted you and me to be—'

'You don't know how much.' She spoke now in a whisper, her face close, her eyes dancing from one to the other of mine. 'You don't know how much you're in my mind. All the time. *All* the time.'

She has this twitch in her brow when she's being serious.

I was so brimmed full of feeling that to move would have been to fall.

LOST

We are late. We are lost. We are stressing.

'Go back up that way,' Dad says. 'That turn – there. It's got to be up there.'

'We came from the right,' I say. 'So it must be right.'

'No, it's left. Up there. *Must* be.'

'Can't be.'

'Must be.'

A vine-tractor is lumbering towards us. I pull away across the oncoming lane unnecessarily fast in front of it. I'm driving aggressively now. I can't be sure but I think I saw the van's temperature gauge rise when we were queuing on the motorway; it's as though the recent exertions have caused it to become introspective. And it may just be the irregular muffle and echo of the narrow country lanes but the engine sounds different, like it's complaining, like it wants to be treated with more dignity.

The first tasting is at six – in ten minutes. We paid for the whole package – much more than merely dinner and accommodation – and Dad thinks they'll do the best champagnes before the meal – 'you can't eat anything with good champagne, Lou.' So there's the additional angst of wasting our money. Not that it *matters*.

'Keep your eyes peeled,' Dad says, fractiously.

'I'm looking.'

'What's that? What can you see up there?'

'Cows.'

'No, up there.'

'A house.'

'A chateau?'

'No, that's not it. Dad. It's much bigger than that. And it's yellow.'

'That *is* yellow.'

'No, that's beige. The chateau is crazy yellow like custard. Like your fleece.'

'How do you know?'

'There were pictures on the Internet.'

'Oh, the *Internet*. Right. Well.' His scorn is bottomless.

The satnav breaks in: 'At the next junction, continue straight on.'

But there is no junction.

Dad lets out another told-you-so puff. 'It's not *real*, Lou, that's the problem.'

I keep driving. A frantic pheasant appears from the verge, veers into the road, feels the proximity of death and forces itself into cumbersome flight.

'What's not real? The Internet?'

'Satnavs!' He gestures at where the offending technology is suctioned to the windscreen then begins fumbling for his glasses in the glove compartment. The flickering light irritates him all over again.

I reach forward to turn the satnav volume down. I wish I'd just flown to Zurich a few hours before – checked into the hotel, popped over to the blue Dignitas house, got the job done, checked out and flown home.

'Maybe it was the wrong postcode,' I say.

'Chateaux don't have *post*codes, Lou.' Dad puts on his glasses. 'I knew I should have brought a proper regional map. You can't read anything on this. I've got it at home. This *exact* area. Never trust these wretched devices.'

We are very close but the satnav is confused or wrong or has not been updated. And somehow this is my fault. Dad has a way of transmuting such failures into evidence of the failure of the modern world and proof that progress is an illusion, that civilization has lost its way. Somehow, the satnav's failure is not just a technological failure, it is a *moral* failure. And it's like he wants to elbow this imaginary point into my ribs over and over – even though it's insane and he knows it, and I know it, and we're only getting more and more insane talking like this.

'Is that clock right?'

The clock says five. He knows we haven't changed it to French time.

'No, it's very nearly six now,' I say. 'But we can't be more than three miles from the place.'

'No, I mean is it precisely six? Or is it a bit fast. I think it's a bit fast isn't it?'

'I don't know,' I say. 'I haven't touched it.'

We can't talk about time or clocks. Of course not. But I want to make the point that if we hadn't stopped for forty-five minutes to change Malte's tyre then we wouldn't have this problem. I want to make the point that none of this matters. Instead, I am squashed again and again behind the heavy door of his told-you-sos, which he slams open and then slams shut on me. And then slams open to tell-me-so again. I feel like Jack must feel in Dad's company – a claustrophobic anger that makes me want to ward him off and escape his presence; the feeling – not that he's right or wrong, not that I want to argue with him – but that I don't care what he thinks about anything. Or maybe this is more how Ralph feels. I don't know. The thing is that sometimes I think Dad is *my* disease. And that he's virulent. But I want to be well. I want to be free. And what does that mean?

'Right. Stop here,' Dad says. 'Stop.'

Now there *is* a junction. But with a left and a right and no straight on. We cannot keep going. There are no signs. The empty sky doesn't know us. I stop the van. I wind down my window. There's no breeze but the smell of cut greenery somewhere.

'If I can get service on my mobile,' I say, 'I can get the website.'

'Turn that thing off.'

I do as I am told like a dutiful child.

'That thing is absolutely *useless*, Lou.'

'I can get the website on my phone.'

'For*get* websites.'

'The website has directions on it.'

'You should have written them down – on paper. What were you thinking?' He folds the map of France into the relevant section. 'Right, let's work out where we are – on this *actual* map. We need a village. Near here.'

'We passed through a place called Vignerons.'

'What would you say? Are we about twenty miles south-east of Troyes?'

'More or less. Hang on. I've got roaming.'

'Roaming,' he says with pure sarcasm that even I can't attain.

I ignore him. 'I've got Google.'

He ignores me. 'OK. Found it. Let's go back to Vignerons. Then we'll know where we are.'

'Yeah, but we still won't know where the chateau is.'

'One thing at a bloody time.'

My phone pulls up the page. 'Here we go. Directions. From Vignerons.'

'Right – pass them here. Let's go to Vignerons and proceed from there. I will *write* them *down*.'

And so I turn us around and we drive back the way we have come. Poplar trees march down a gradual slope to where white cows graze in a field dusted with buttercups; beyond, the gentle hills rise and the late September sun is slipping westward over the promising vines.

Low British skies of rag and bone. I was six. My dad had taken me to a motor race – some minor circuit somewhere half-hidden in a shallow, misty English valley. I remember that the rain stopped and started and the wind was blustery. And so the racing was treacherous and exciting. We watched together from a muddy man-made knoll by the side of the track which swept towards us, curved left, and then fell away further into a dell, tightening for the drivers as it did so. First the open-wheel Formula Fords and then the Touring cars and then the Minis, streaming by, side by side, spray from the tyres, probing for the limits of adhesion. We had spent a long time in the van on the way there debating which corner was likely to produce the most 'action'. This came down to a choice between two 'spots'. Usually we would spend half the day cursing our luck, wryly convinced that all the overtaking and crashing – all the daring – was happening at the other place. But on this day, we got it right.

I remember the feeling of shared excitement; when you know for sure that you're in exactly the same happy space as someone you care about; and the additional connection and delight of that consonance.

In the changing conditions, some of the drivers simply came in too fast and lost control – 'over-cooked it', as Dad would say. Others made the first part of the corner but their trajectory took them wide and onto the grass as the gradient and increasing acuity caught them out. Others again lost it when they got a wheel up onto the grip-less smooth white kerbs. I remember the sound – the desperate whine of the brakes followed by the near-silent swish as they travelled across wet grass and then the thwack of the impact as they thumped into the wall of tyres right in front of where we stood together.

But every now and then a driver would somehow hold it together – slither down the outside, and with supreme skill, his front wheels the only part of the car following the con-tour of the track, somehow overtake his competitors. And Dad would say something like, 'Number twenty-seven has really got "it".' And even though I couldn't tell you what 'it' was – I knew exactly what my father meant.

And it is still with me, this idea – really deep: that some people have got 'it'. And I've always wanted to be one of those people. I've always wanted to be like those drivers who can stay on the track in changing conditions when everyone else is crashing, retiring, out.

I remember that I wore khaki wellingtons that day and that I had a new cagoule with a hood and a string that drew up beneath my chin. My hands were cold and my father crouched down after the racing cars had passed, while we were waiting for them to go round the lap, so as to cup my hands inside the warmth of his own greater palms.

At lunchtime, we went to look around the pits. We walked together, eating hot doughnuts, which my mother would never have allowed – cinnamon and sugar. There were no safety restrictions in those days and so we wandered between the cars: some of them being prepared to go out; some of them covered in mud with torn bodywork. I remember the wide black racing tyres with tiny white stones embedded in the rubber. I remember the vegetal smell of the engine oil. I remember the growl and then the sudden bellow of the engines, which would start up at random here and there as the mechanics tested something. I remember seeing the drivers carrying their helmets with their arms hooked through their visors.

I remember that day most of all because I lost my father.

He was right there, holding my hand; and then he let go.

I remember precisely the moment of knowing that he was no longer standing beside me. I had my newly freed hand cupped to the window of a touring car so that I could see the dashboard inside. But when I stood back, I was alone. A six-year-old boy. I remember how panic came falling and roaring out of the sky. How the world changed – in that second – into a place full of strangers and fear and absence. I remember this sudden sense of myself – for the first time in my life – as separate to my father. As a person, a child, in the world. I remember how everything came at me all at once – how would I eat, stay warm, stay alive? I remember the physical surge of terror.

I ran up to a stranger, no more than waist-height. I told him my name and that I was lost. And the stranger took me somewhere – and I followed him – and we came to the place which must have been where the commentator worked. And someone made an announcement and I heard it on the tannoy – all around the circuit: 'Will Laurence Lasker please come to Race Control, we have your son, Louis. Will Laurence Lasker please come to Race Control, we have your son, Louis.'

And I remember seeing my father again and only then – only then – did I start to cry. And I remember that my father let me sit in the front of the van when we drove home, even though I was too small for the seat belt; and I remember that I never wanted to be without him again.

THEN TRY FOR UNDERSTANDING

The Internet might be able to show you the whole world but it can't tell you how you are going to feel when you get there. Château Chigny is one of those good-looking French mini-mansions – neither shabby nor smart, but creamy-yellow fronted and symmetrical, with pale-blue shutters thrown welcomingly open and tall thin chimneys rising elegantly from a steep-raked French roof flanked by two conical Norman-looking towers at the end of either wing. We sweep up the long curving plane-tree-flanked drive and my hopes rise a little. There's one of those high n-shaped vine-tractors that we saw before on the road. There's a rusty red Peugeot that collapsed years ago. There's a friendly brown-and-white dog barking and a skew-whiff old child's swing. The gravel crunches when I step down. The arrowed wooden sign says 'bienvenue'.

I run round to Dad's door to help him. I can smell honeysuckle and I can feel the faint heat from where the sun lately warmed the stone path that leads to the arched front door. I pick up Dad's stick and he holds my shoulders and steps out.

'Just the job,' he says, looking all around.

Dad and I, we might fight but we try not to sulk.

'Let's hope they can come up with the goods,' I chime in.

'It's a beautiful evening,' he continues. 'Hopefully we'll catch the last rays.' This is pure Dad-speak and I want to keep it going. Something eases in my spine. Another insane thing is that I spent about nine full days secretly researching everything about this journey. I wanted it to be the kind of trip my dad would plan for me – even though he wouldn't plan, we'd simply all go, camping someplace near the next thing we were hoping to see – a prehistoric cave, or the birthplace of Beethoven, or some castle crazed out of nowhere by Mad Ludwig the Moon King. So I've booked us places and cancelled and rebooked and researched and got into a screwed-up state about everything – the size of the rooms, the views, the food, the wine. Dad loves his wine. He had this teacher at his school when he was sixteen who taught him some of the basics, which he's trying to pass on to me. But I must have a palate like a squeegee mop or something because all I can ever taste is . . . well, wine.

We walk together up the path and push the heavy front door, which opens easily into the friendly gloom and the smell of French-polished wood.

A woman emerges and circles neatly round behind her narrow desk at the foot of the stairs. I guess she is in her early fifties. She has this dark brown bob that she has to hook behind her ears as she leans forward to pass us the old-school signing-in slip and I can tell Dad finds her attractive in that French severe-chic kind of a way. But she has the manner of someone who has been left with too much to do and she has a habit of holding on to her lower lip with her teeth as though she expects at any second to be called away to deal with whatever it is that has been bothering her all her life.

She speaks in French, which I half understand. It's no problem, she says. They are going to wait twenty minutes for us. The dinner can be delayed. Everything can be delayed.

Dad thanks her. He says something about the wine. She smiles distractedly and her eyes move quickly as she takes our passports – I sense that she has had enough of her guests for this year. He says something more about when the chateau might date from. And, for a moment, I see Ralph in my father; were it not for his Catholic guilt, or his Northern contrariness, or his being an austerity baby, or whatever it is that so bedevils, drives, consumes him, Dad might have had many girlfriends, many wives, many friends except . . . Except that he *does* suffer from all of these things and except that he has not got Ralph's easy and natural understanding of other people. Instead, Dad can't tell that the French woman's smile is indulgent and placatory. He has no sense of her independent reality as a person, as another human being with a million concerns nothing to do with us, him. He's running his old twentieth-century software; he misreads her and thinks that she is in some way flirting with him; and so he begins to talk more about chateaux and the history of France. Even the way he adjusts his stance on his stick and dips his head to speak is faintly embarrassing and inappropriate; but I also feel sad for him since actually there's a kind of innocence to his talk . . . Because, in another way, he thinks that everyone is fascinated by architecture and history and he can't imagine a world where this kind of chat is beside the point or of zero interest. He's never been able to see that his slice of the world is not the whole cake. Nowhere near. And yet, still . . . still he wants urgently to share it because he thinks that everyone else must therefore be starving hungry.

We're in a hurry so I change quickly in my room, fire Eva a text and then speed down the corridor to help my father. I'm wearing a jacket that Eva chose but it's out of place here:

too London, too something else. Wherever I am, I never look right.

The door is open in case something happens. So in I go. My dying father is lying on the bed semi-naked with his eyes shut; he's napping but he looks like a tranquillized wild animal that they've taken for tagging because of the dwindling numbers. His skin is deathly pale save for the red sunburn on his forearms and forehead. The hair on his legs is thinning. Without his animation, without his life force, his limbs seem spindly and ungainly – subsided, collapsed – he's a hide of bone and wasting muscle, no longer stalking, pouncing, roaring, no longer ferocious. He has managed to get most of his clothes off but not his socks or pants. I have the sense that he gave up.

'Dad,' I say. I feel nauseous.

He opens his eyes. And it is like a miracle to see their light, to watch them seek me. He starts to sit up. He's moving. And now it is me who is stuck still, motionless. When he speaks, his voice is almost too much for me. Soon, I won't be able to hear what he has to say – no matter what. I have to force myself to go around the bed and remove his socks. Then I help him to sit up. I can't look at him.

'Let me get the shower on,' I say.

'OK, standing by.'

I cut across to his bathroom and mess around with the shower taps to get the right temperature. And so . . . And so we're back in life again. And I'm thinking that you would have hoped that after all this time someone might invent a shower where fixing the right temperature would be easy. But it seems like yet another thing humanity can't figure out for itself. I need to speak to Jack or Ralph.

I come back in and Dad is leaning on the upright chair, drooling a little with his lopsided grin.

'Walnut desk,' he says. 'Second Empire. Guess the date.'

All my life, he's been teaching me this way.

'1750,' I say.

'Nope. Second Empire is 1852 to 1870, Lou. Napoleon the Third.'

'Napoleon's grandson?'

'Nephew.'

I scoot over and help him down with his underwear.

'People would pay a lot for this privilege, Louis.'

'I'm not saying I don't feel lucky, Dad.'

'Just don't start taking it for granted.'

'If ever there was a man who didn't take things for granted, Dad, it's me.'

'And don't waste your intelligence.'

We bind arms.

'What is that supposed to mean?'

I can feel my phone buzzing in my pocket as we three-leg our way back towards the bathroom. I am thinking that this is the first time I've walked my naked father anywhere.

'Don't let yourself get bogged down by the admin, Lou.'

'Dad, I'm a database manager; it's all admin.'

'A lot of people . . . a lot of people spend their entire lives on the admin. Take it from me: you're not going to feel any kind of satisfaction if you get to my stage in life and all you've got to show for yourself is a lifetime of administrative proficiency.'

'Should I tweet that?'

'Would anyone notice?'

'Does anyone notice anything?'

'You do, Lou.'

'And look where it's got me.'

The water is tepid. Dad climbs in anyway.

'Bloody hell, Lou. This is freezing. What are you trying to do to me?'

'OK, let's see if there's a little more hot in the tank.'

I ease the tap a millimetre at a time because I am scared it's going to scald him. But we get to something warmer that seems to hold. So I hand Dad the soap and he gets busy with one hand while he grips the soap tray with the other – the same way, I notice, that he holds the table when he is eating.

'It's expensive – to watch,' he says.

'Jesus, Dad.'

'Sorry. It's the disease.' He taps his head. 'Makes me free.'

I dive back into the room. I booked the biggest and the most beautiful for him. I don't really know about decor but maybe it's all Second Empire or belle époque or something – there's azure wallpaper striped with pale gold and dried flowers and a brass bedstead and dark wardrobes and everything you could want if you were like my father. My jacket is wet from the spray. I take it off and hang it on the back of the upright desk chair. I need to make the call and I'm thinking about lying down on the chaise longue but then I remember the balcony and so I open the windows and step out. Which immediately feels like the right move. The vines stretch away, rising and falling, in straight and serried files; there's a pale track leading to an ochre-roofed house in the distance – another farm; and a field of something blue on a hillside that might be lavender.

'Jack.'

'Lou, thank God. Where are you?'

'We're at this chateau in the middle of nowhere. Sorry, I couldn't call before. I was driving.'

'I'm coming.'

I've got my phone clamped to my face. But I'm watching some kind of hawk turn in the widening gyre.

'I'm coming,' he says again.

Relief is flooding my spirit like metaphysical morphine.

'I've told work that Dad is ill.'

'Understatement of the year.'

'I'm getting a flight. Where shall I fly? Where are you going to be?'

'Tomorrow, we're heading to this place near the Swiss border. It's a spa. Maybe fly to Basel.'

'Who flies to Basel?'

'Someone must. Try one of the expensive cheap airlines. Or try flying to Strasbourg.'

'OK, keep your phone on.'

I'm scared I might actually start to cry so I say nothing and watch the damn hawk.

Jack says: 'I don't know what I was thinking, bro. I'm sorry.'

I can't speak.

'I've been going mental all day, Lou,' he says.

'Not as mental as me.'

'What time did you set off?'

'Way too early this morning.'

'Are you OK?'

'Can't take another minute of my own existence.'

'Well, hang on a day. I'm coming. I'll talk to the bastard and then we'll ... we'll all go home. This is so insane. Is Ralph coming?'

'Supposed to be.'

'I've been calling him. His phones are all on voicemail,' Jack sighs. 'He's such a penis.'

'He said he would meet us. Tomorrow night – that's what he said. He knows all the places we're staying.'

'Is Dad being OK or is he being mad?'

'When he's OK, it's too weird. When he's being mad, it's even weirder. But you know – we're in Madsville pretty much all the time right now. *Centre Ville.*'

Now Jack falls silent.

'What should I say?' I ask.

'About what?'

'About you coming. He'll know. I mean, he'll know you're coming to stop him.'

'I don't care.'

'He'll think you're angry.'

'I'm way past angry. I'm something I don't even know what I am.'

'Welcome to my world.'

'What are you doing this evening?'

'Champagne-tasting.'

'Jesus.'

'What are we supposed to be doing?'

'I don't know. I don't know. OK: listen, definitely text me tomorrow so I know where you are.'

'Of course I will.'

'Don't leave France.'

'I won't.'

'Don't go anywhere *near* Switzerland.'

'I'm driving. We go where I want.'

'I'll try Ralph again. He's probably out of credit.'

'Shouldn't you phone Dad?'

'What's the point?'

'I don't know . . . You're his son?'

'I need to speak to him face to face.'

'I better go. He's in the shower.'

'OK. OK, I'm going to sort out a flight. I'll see you soon. Hang in there, Lou. Sorry I've been such a dick.'

'Don't worry about it. Runs in the family.'

Now the fields are golden and the sun is sinking like one of those Viking burial ships set aflame on the sea and the clouds are all under-lit in their evening colours of peach and rose and pale vermilion. I have this sudden feeling that making champagne – something the world definitely wants, treasures, celebrates and is willing to pay for – that must be a happy life; out in these French fields in all seasons, the science of viticulture, the art of wine-making, the history of it all, and the whole planet excited to visit. Or maybe two generations in, all you want to do is go to New York, rent some scratchy little hutch and pretend to be a filmmaker like every other bastard. I don't know.

Dr Twigge would say you sublimate your parents' insecurities and sabotages as a child and fashion them into a deep subconscious narrative of self-criticism – this is the voice that you come to hear as an internal commentary and, worse, to believe. This is the hostile, self-defeating, and self-destructive adviser who promotes anger and pessimism and cynicism. Every human being has one – euphemistically, they call it the 'inner critic'. The trick, they say, is to learn to recognize the problem and then tell it to fuck off. But what if it's your father you want to silence? Ah, well, say the shrinks, death is a great time to make peace with your parents. Bury the bad voices with their dead bodies. Heed only the good voices thereafter. Distinguish. Let love reign. And if you can't manage that – then try for understanding.

Ralph placed his cigarette in the ashtray and surveyed the menu. 'I wonder is it possible to have *un*seasonal greens. And *non*-heritage carrots?' he asked.

'I want pesticides,' Jack said. 'Pesticides and preservatives.'

Ralph nodded. 'Yeah – something processed and heavily packaged and with lots of air miles.'

'Ideally from somewhere with a bad human-rights record.'

Ralph picked up his cigarette again. 'Maybe they've got Chinese battery-chicken or some ocean-dredged crabsticks.'

'OK, Lou,' said Jack. 'What have you never eaten before?'

'Lobster. I've never eaten lobster,' I said, still trying desperately to impress them but secretly attracted to the 'and chips'.

When I was around nine, I remember that my brothers took me out to dinner. Ralph was at the beginning of his (not) working as an actor. He had picked me up from school because Mum and Dad were away for the weekend. Meanwhile, Jack was working (for free) for the *Fulham and Hammersmith Chronicle* – a paper that seemed to be so belligerently short-staffed that he already got to write about everything from NATO air strikes to restaurant reviews. In those days, Jack's hair was longer and he was thinner so that he and Ralph looked much more like identical twins when they were together: art fraudsters, maybe – Ralph the forger,

Jack the dealer. I felt like a god whenever I was with them. But then (as now) my brothers never came off the gas in the way they talked in my company – and they probably should have kept some stuff away from me when I was younger. I remember, for example, that when the food arrived, they got on to the subject of Carol.

'I went round there three days ago,' Jack said. 'And Christ, the atmosphere . . . It was . . . It was like one of those Soviet submarines that has got trapped at the bottom of the Arctic Sea.'

'What happened to that man she met up with once – what's his name – Arnold?'

Jack shook his head. 'They went to the cinema and had an argument about subtitles.'

Ralph nodded slowly.

'She's not as resilient as usual,' Jack continued. 'I would say she's depressed.'

'Which is the only intelligent response to the world,' Ralph replied.

'Don't be facetious.'

'Which is the second most intelligent response to the world.'

'Try engagement.'

'Try acceptance.' Ralph shrugged. 'I think she's proba-bly—'

I interrupted: 'Which bit of the lobster do you eat?'

'Start with the claws, Lou,' Ralph said.

Jack ventured: 'I'm saying maybe . . . maybe she needs to see us a bit more round there.'

'She is completely fine when she's out.' Ralph attempted

to cut his pan-fried veal with his fork. 'I went to a concert with her last month. Life and soul of the interval.'

'Yes. As long as you stay off the subject of Dad.'

'Obviously. But that's been the case for ages. Don't go anywhere near the subject of Dad and she's as ostensibly normal as everyone else is ostensibly normal.'

'What are the claws,' I interrupted, again. 'Are they these little bits?'

'No, the claws are the huge claw things at the front,' Jack said. 'I'm just saying . . . I'm just saying it's so *dark* in there. You need to have all the lights on in order to see your own hands.'

'She lives in a basement flat, Jack. It's bound to feel a bit submarine.'

'Maybe we should buy her a new place. She could move. We could help. Something airy and—'

'Jack, the problem is not her fucking living quarters.'

'I'm trying to be practical.'

'Superficial.'

'Maybe if we took care of some of the superficial stuff, then—'

'The problem . . . the *problem* . . . is that she's a functioning alcoholic.'

'Well, then – no, listen to me for a second – maybe we need to try and do something about that, too.'

'And the real problem behind the problem is that she has had her heart fractured into a thousand pieces by the man she loves.'

'Yes but—'

'As far as Mum is concerned, love is singular and it endures for life – or it isn't love.'

113

'I'm not—'

'The real thing cannot be rivalled or replaced. That's her definition of what love *is*, Jack. And who are we to argue? In order to cheer up, she'd have to bin the foundations of her entire belief system.'

'Let's tackle—'

'There is only one solution and you know it: Dad. And that is never ever going to happen. Not ever. They tortured one another past the point of permanent disfigurement and then Dad did something even worse: he got up and left the torture chamber, closing the door behind him.'

'Right.' Jack nodded sarcastically. 'So we – her kind and loving sons – leave her to her despair?'

'We leave her alone. The measure of her suffering is testimony to the measure of her love.'

'We callously abandon our own mother to her depression.'

'I keep telling you: she needs to be depressed in order to enact what she believes about her marriage – her life.' Ralph inclined his head and raised his palm in an offering of reasonableness. 'Maybe she *enjoys* being depressed in some way. People do. Take a look around. Stunned disbelief is taking widespread hold. Half the world cannot understand what the fuck the other half think they're doing.'

I cut in: 'How do I get the claws off?'

'Just pull them, like this.' Jack reached over and detached a lobster claw for me. 'I'm saying I think she needs us, Ralph. She seems to be turning inward. She doesn't have enough real-world input. And if not us . . .'

Ralph sighed. 'Why do I sense the word "duty" about to arrive in this conversation?'

114

'I think that we do have a *duty* . . . a duty to cheer her up at least.'

'As I say: let's take her out more.'

'That as well. But we also have to be there . . . To be there in a quiet and regular way. More often. No drama. Just having a glass of wine. Just making the dinner. Chopping carrots.'

'Chopping carrots – that's your solution?'

'We have to interact without melodrama.'

Ralph grimaced. 'Impossible.'

Jack met his eye. 'What I am saying is that it's about *being* there for her. She needs—'

'But *how* . . .' I cut in loudly this time. 'How do I eat the claws? They're really hard.'

'It's an exoskeleton, Lou,' Ralph said. 'In a way lobsters are really only huge insects. You eat the insides rather than the outsides.'

'I've never eaten an insect.'

'Seriously,' Ralph said, 'fuck going round there, Jack. She loves the theatre, she loves music. She needs to go *out* more.'

Jack had reached the end of his oxtail with the expression of a man wishing that there was somehow more of the ox to go. He sat back. 'I think – even though she would never say it – I think she's lonely. Isolated. She listens to the news all day—'

'Which is enough to make anyone suicidal.'

'We need to persuade her . . . To move flats. To get it together. To stop drinking. To live again. Engage. There could be thirty years ahead of her. Why not seize them?'

'As I say: maybe she wants to be left alone to suffer in peace and quiet. Have you thought about that?'

'You can't go through life decrying life. What kind of life is that?'

'A very popular one.'

'But *how* do I eat the insides?' I asked. 'The skin on this lobster is really hard.'

'It's a shell, not a skin,' Jack said. 'Crack it, Lou, crack it. I'm saying we must at least offer to help . . . it's for her own benefit, Ralph.'

Ralph sighed more deeply. 'Have you ever – have you ever in your whole life – managed to suggest one single thing to Mum that might be for her own benefit?'

'She likes talking and—'

'No, she's utterly impossible to talk to on a personal level. Everything is immediately taken as an insult.'

'She's very proud.'

'What do people actually mean when they say that?'

Now Jack sighed.

'They mean,' Ralph said, 'that a person is fearful and brittle. They mean that a person cannot allow any contention or openness of mind for fear that their entire world will shatter and they will be left without their certainties. They mean that a person is so fragile within that they have created this rigid carapace as a protection.' He indicated my lobster.

'You're wrong.' Jack shook his head. 'Everything you say is only ever partially true and yet you pretend that it's a complete explanation.'

'That's what we love to do here on planet Earth, Jack. Join us. Please.'

'She's got me and she's got you, Ralph. I'm a knob and you're a nightmare. But that's it. That's all she's got. We have to show some . . . some love.'

'OK – OK – OK.' Ralph softened. 'Fuck it, then: you win. Let's go round there now. Straight after dessert.'

Jack weighed the challenge. 'All right, let's do that,' he said.

'Lou, what's wrong?' Ralph looked at me. 'You haven't touched your lobster. No, don't *lick* it.'

And so we banked into the Bayswater basin just as the low London sun gave up again somewhere in the west.

'Looks like she's in,' Ralph said.

'Very seldom out,' Jack replied.

'My point exactly. Can you get this?'

Jack paid the driver through the window and we stood a moment, three brothers in the brief and uncertain dusk of a stuccoed London street.

Carol's building was the colour of exhausted white underwear; it was five storeys high and must once have been a grand place owned by somebody who did something that made money. Nowadays the old house had been divided and subdivided into more flats than the pillared portico had space for buzzers. On the second floor, there was an open window and inside a man in boxer shorts was hitting a punch bag. On a neighbouring stoop, a woman in a hijab was speaking animatedly into an entry-phone in a language I will never know. Meanwhile, in the great and on-going war, the gulls flapped and screamed the high vantage of the rooftops while the fat London pigeons patrolled the yellow lines of kerb and gutter, tick-tocking back and forth with news of territory held and skirmishes lost or won.

I remembered hearing my own mum say once that Bayswater was 'transitory'. I didn't know what she meant then. But my take is that few things are sadder than moving to a transitory part of town and staying put.

I crossed the street and followed my brothers around the black railings, past two reedy plants, down steep stairs, past the flaking security bars on the basement window – and so to a brown door with the appearance of being crushed beneath the stoop. Ralph pressed the bell which rattled rather than rung. Classical music was quieted. We stood listening to the sound of someone inserting a sequence of keys.

'Who is it?'

'Mum,' Ralph said. 'It's us.'

'Ralph!'

'No less.'

'Hello. Hello! One second.'

A bolt was shot.

'Who constitutes *us*?'

Ralph leant towards the door: 'Me and Jack and a surprise . . . a surprise visitor.'

'Jack! Why didn't you phone?'

'We did.'

'I didn't hear it.'

'You've got your Brahms on too loud again.'

'What a surprise. Oh, bloody hell. Wait a second.' The sound of a security chain and then, finally, Carol opened the door.

She was shorter than I had imagined – or maybe it was just that she seemed to have thickened from the angular younger woman of the photographs I had seen. She had silvery blonde hair now, though still in the same fringy cut – as though she had only agreed not to curtain herself from whatever was in view unwillingly. She wore this long grey skirt with a grey cardigan and there was something in her stance and bearing that suggested she had run out of people to be sardonic with and so had started on herself.

'Sorry for the short notice,' Ralph said. 'We were—'

'Who the . . . ?' Carol's expression travelled from delight to something frozen, hostile, involuntary. 'Who the hell is that?'

'This is—'

'Get him away!'

'Ma,' Jack said.

Her voice began to rise and thin. 'Get him away!'

'Ma. He's only a boy.'

Suddenly, she was shooing wildly with both hands. 'Get him . . . Get him . . . Get that *child* away from here!'

Ralph stepped into the space between us and shot a look at Jack. 'Mum, it's OK,' he said.

'Out of my sight! Don't ever!' And now her raised voice ricocheted round the basement well and tore upwards at the world above: 'Get him *away* from here!'

'Ma.' Ralph raised his hand to her elbow as if to calm a child. 'Ma.'

But she was coming out: 'Don't ever! Ever. *Ever.* Get that bloody child away!'

She was pushing past and my brothers were physically blocking her now, holding her.

'You! *You!* Look at me! Look at me, child.'

Over Ralph's shoulder, her face was contorted with her fury. I turned and ran back up the stairs behind me, slipping, smashing my knee. I ran on down the street, her shriek swirling and echoing as if trapped for ever in the shell of my ears. I ran until I had run too far and I was suddenly alone, on an unfriendly London pavement, tall houses pressing in with the gathering darkness, strangers passing by, hiding my tears in the crook of my arm.

ON THE ESCARPMENTS

There are two other British couples staying at the chateau. They already hate us because we're so late. I want to say, 'Relax, people – I already hate us, too.' But instead Dad and I struggle up past the old tractor and the crooked bench to the door of the cave – actually a barn – and receive their hellos with better grace than they are offered.

Inside, it is dark and cool and smells of sawdust and spilt wine. The French woman is our tasting hostess; she seems to be doing everything around the place. There are four champagne bottles on the big barrel by which she stands. There are these huge wooden wine racks down two of the walls. There's some strange gigantic spider-claw agricultural equipment that seems like it might easily double for torture duty were the Inquisition to pass by. We all stand around – except for Dad, who takes the only chair. As he settles himself, shifting his legs with his hands, he looks up and says something about *L'Assommoir*, which I don't quite understand except that it's funny. Our hostess smiles – not by way of reciprocity but as if at the persistence of a favourite pupil – and my father's easy French gives him the instant seniority of the room. Even the effortful way in which he moves does not make him an invalid to be pitied or patronized but somehow confers charisma and authority; centrality. I feel a new pulse of certainty. My father doesn't want to be in a wheelchair.

My father doesn't want saliva to leak from his slack lips as he slurs and slips on the surface of words that he once so commanded.

Our hostess starts in on her spiel in what I sense is a deliberately thickened French accent. We all stand and listen to her for about ten minutes – none of which we understand, except Dad, who asks questions like he's genuinely inter- ested, which of course he is. Soon enough, Dad and the French woman are just talking to each other and the rest of us are left out.

Meanwhile, it takes me a while to figure out what the low volume squeaks and squeals are that we all keep hearing. Finally, I realize that they're coming from a little white chunky speaker that one of the other men is holding: a baby monitor. Every so often, he ducks away from not listening to the French woman to hold it up to his ear in a move that is designed to be discreet-but-noticed.

One of the other women is making some kind of oblique play in my direction about how she is glad that she's *not* with the baby-monitor guy. She starts a conversation: I'm Leah, she says, and I have no choice but to join in. Soon we're all swapping stories about who we are and what we think and where we're heading. I say stories because there's no way I am telling anybody the truth. But then, I don't think the others are telling the truth either; only the stuff they like to hear themselves say in public. Dad would argue that life is the story we tell ourselves about ourselves; that it's all stories for *Homo sapiens*; narrative. Ralph says that he is 'with Sartre' and that our lives are really only the collection of stories by which we misunderstand ourselves. Jack says, 'It feels pretty fucking real to me.'

I want to tell the other couples that it isn't their fault; that I can't respond or interact at the moment; that it's just that I'm on the way to killing my father; and that its making me dislike people who are inattentively alive. That they could have been anyone because I'm only dealing in the tectonics these days and everything else feels like bad acting. But I don't say any of this. Oh no. I join in like the weasel little pleaser that I am.

Which is how I find out that Leah and her husband are ad-agency millionaires and that the other couple, Neil and Beth-Marie, have had two children and are the first people on planet Earth to do so. The ad-agency millionaire doesn't say much and he looks a bit like I imagine Richard the Third must have looked; tall but a little hunchbacked and twisted with prominent wrist bones and eyes that speak of an intelligence that he knows he has deployed in the wrong direction. He can't smile but his mouth sort of twitches every so often. I figure he's my only chance at dinner.

I stage a phone call. And I go and stand outside.

The sky is bruised from dealing with a mighty sunset – maroons and purples and a low streak of bloodiest red.

I stand there for a while saying 'yes' 'no' 'yes' 'no' 'yes' 'no' – to nobody on my phone. Yes, the world is ancient. No I don't want to ever go home. Yes. No. Yes. No. Yes. No. I don't know.

The landscape eases me. I share this with my father. Something to do with its lack of concern for human paltriness. And I start thinking about all those prehistoric people, fathers and sons, way back before there were any homes, squatting on their escarpments and watching out for danger in the dusk. Yes. No. Yes. No. Yes. No. Eros. Thanatos. Creation.

Destruction. All the way back to the dawn of time. And before that? And *why*? My mother got into Buddhist teachings and read a lot of mystical stuff – maybe to get back at Dad in some way; maybe to chase the fleeing ghosts of her poetry. And once she told me that she'd read in the Kabbalah that Life was the means by which the Universe was trying to understand itself – and that maybe humanity was its best effort so far. I like that idea.

'Lou?' Dad is standing behind me holding on to the barn door with his stick. 'Who was it?'

'Eva,' I lie.

'All OK?' he asks. His eyes are bright.

'She says it was good to talk to you.'

'Well . . . it was good to talk to her.'

Luckily, Richard the Third appears with two glasses.

'Here you go, guys,' he says.

'Hang on – we're going to sit on that bench,' Dad says. 'What's the verdict?'

I help Dad across while Richard the Third hovers. I think he suspects me of faking the call. Which elevates him further in my estimation.

'Not dry enough for me,' he says. 'I like my champagne dry. How about you?'

'Wet,' I say.

Richard the Third's mouth twitches into the suggestion of a smile, many smiles. He passes the glasses. 'I'll bring out the next one as soon as we're live.'

Dad and I hold the wine up to the mighty sky and peer at it as if we might divine the future in the random rising of the bubbles. There are few things that make my father happier than tasting wine. I have this feeling that I have done the right thing again. I've seen him taste so many times – the whole ritual, a joke, a game, but neither. And suddenly I'm happy because he is happy. Just the two of us out here somewhere in the gloaming of an unknown planet with the whole universe wrapped around our lives.

We swallow the first mouthful. And Dad has his nose straight back inside the flute.

'Straw, straw to begin, Lou. But then . . .'

'Biscuits,' I say.

'Biscuits, yes, but also tart. Oh, it's very good.'

'Cooking apples?' I suggest.

'Apple crumble.'

'Almond.'

'More complex.' Dad hesitates. 'Apple pips?'

'Cyanide,' I say.

He takes another sip. 'Oh wait, I'm getting minerals, Lou. On the nose.'

'I told you. Cyanide and tin.'

'Smokier,' he says.

We're both drinking freely now.

'Oh, this is a *serious* wine,' Dad says, vehemently.

'Smoked mussels,' I offer. 'No – hang on – a tin of smoked mussels.'

'Left open,' says Dad.

I nod. 'Smoked mussels left open in the tin.'

'Oh, but hang on; hang on, Lou. *Big* fruit again on the finish.'

'Big something.'

'Floral notes.'

'Whispers of spice.'

'Basil,' he says, as if he's got it.

'No – bergamot,' I counter.
'Dandelion.'
'Deeper, Dad: molasses.'
'Prune?'
'Damson.'
'Lighter, Lou: elderflower.'
'*Grapes*,' I say. 'Grapes.'

I talk to Twigge in my own mind. I don't know why. (Like other people pray, I guess.) This kind of behaviour is exactly the sort of thing you should tell a psychologist. But of course it's exactly the sort of thing you can't tell a psychologist. Or not one that you've only met a few times. He was a friend of a friend of my father's. They had 'shared a platform' at the Cheltenham arts festival years ago – for no reason as far as anyone could tell. We went to consult with him because Dad thought it might be 'good for us' (by which he meant me) and because he wanted us to 'talk to someone intelligent and respected in the field'.

I only ever got to see him once on my own. But I wanted to ask Twigge: is it normal to love the *idea* of people more than their actuality? Because I've noticed that – when they're talking about their children, when they're talking about their parents – people seem to fill up with feelings much more if the children and parents in question are *not* there. Get them in the same room, though, and they can't stand the sight of each other. What does that mean, Doctor?

But the closest Twigge ever came to speaking directly to the issues of 'your circumstances' was when he pointed out (actually to the bookcase) that – no matter who or what you become – you remain the child of the same mother and father. If you're lucky enough to know them, this will be the most fundamental relationship of your life, the most formative and the most unique. The likelihood (he went on expansively to say to the window) is that one will be affected by, and involved in, their deaths. ('One' – his word.) Indeed, this 'involvement' turns out to be one of the duties of being a child – often the main duty. (So he has come to think.) There are exceptions, of course. Millions choose to have nothing to do with their parents. What's the Auden, he asked? Your father says you're a budding poet.

I hate the word 'budding'.

'Larkin,' I said. 'They fuck you up, your mum and dad.'

And probably because he got the wrong poet, Twigge then had to talk even more despite the obvious discomfort that saying anything caused him. So that's when he finally said something interesting. He started to talk about the 'ponds' that people come from. (His word again.) He said that in some ponds the innocent are fed lies. And thus they learn to croak.

I wanted to ask him more about this but then he started off about 'choice' and 'choice architecture'. He said he shared Jung's view that there is always a choice. Sure, I said. But there's no *good* choice. And can you tell me this: what is the right thing to do in a world where there is no right thing to do?

That shut everything down again. Impasse.

But I took three things from our solo session. All of which I did not say. One. Death is what intensifies love. The subconscious (which knows that it has got to end) feeds the conscious (which knows that it has not done so yet). Two.

Life is about coming to terms with an ever-lengthening list of our losses. Three. Knowing things intellectually makes very little difference to how you feel.

FOR WHICH RELIEF MUCH THANKS

Dinner is to be served at this long table just inside the big open French windows looking out down a long path, which is lit with ankle-high solar lamps so it looks like a runway for errant nocturnal poultry. The room is beautiful in the way you'd hope a dining room to be beautiful in an old French chateau – tall ceilings, a pale-blue stripe in the walls, elegant dark-wood furniture that dimly shines with the lustre of exotic suns entombed. There are tall candles and the table-cloth is ivory white like it was made long before the Revolution and hasn't blushed since.

A girl brings things in and out with way more effort than interest – she's fifteen, I'd say – tall, with freckles and this quick transactional smile that makes me want to go outside and have a cigarette with her in order to get to the bottom of whatever her problems might be.

We are sitting down and nobody dares to touch the bottle in the ice bucket because it feels somehow wrong to go on drinking champagne regardless.

Baby-monitor Neil is talking like he has established this great reputation with himself for wit: 'I've heard rumours that it's monkfish,' he says. 'Which is a result. I love monkfish cheeks.'

Straight away, though, it's war. Because Leah isn't buying it, or him, or anything: 'I hope they're not farmed,' she says.

Which brings Beth-Marie: 'Can you even farm monkfish? Aren't they more like sharks?'

Which causes Neil's phone to appear.

Dad and I are facing one another. I'm thinking that I may be the only person in the world who doesn't actually like the taste of champagne.

'What has the Twitterverse got to say on the subject?' asks Richard the Third. His real name is Christopher Turnkey, which he half whispers in the manner of a sports commentator during a tense moment in play.

'Hang on,' Neil says. 'I'm on Wikipedia.'

'And?' Christopher prompts. He hoists the champagne from the bucket and offers it round.

Neil reads: 'Monkfish is the English name of a number of types of fish in the north-west Atlantic, most notably the anglerfish genus *Lophius* and – ah, yes! – the angel*shark* genus *Squatina.*'

'I thought so,' says Beth-Marie, 'some kind of shark. Well, distantly related!'

'Does it say anything about farming?' Leah asks.

'Nothing here.'

'Maybe they only farm the cheeks,' I say.

The girl comes in with a basket of different loaves. Beth-Marie tries to reinstate herself as the most wholesome of our party by making out that she doesn't mind which bread she has; for some reason it's getting more and more important to her that she comes across as happy-go-lucky in direct proportion to the actuality of her unhappy-go-planned. Leah doesn't eat bread of any sort. Neil has a bread-maker. Christopher is on the UK Food Council, which has recently recommended to parliament that we institute a stronger regime for more detailed bread labelling.

'So where are you guys heading tomorrow?' Leah asks.

And that's it.

'We're going to kill ourselves,' I say.

'Lou,' Dad says.

'Sorry,' I say. 'Just Dad. I'm going to give it a few more months.'

Once we started going steady – in that impossible phrase – Eva became the still point of my turning world. We lived mainly at her flat because it was so much nicer and she had no flatmates and we sat together on her cushions and drank terrible ad-hoc cocktails made from cunning old liqueurs – Frangelico, Bénédictine. We told each other about our lives before we met, which seemed now to have been carefully choreographed to lead up to this point. And that poster above the candle in her fireplace became like some kind of totem or a portal into another, wider, more exciting world that knew nothing of uneasy Britain. We talked about our work and what we wanted to do in the future. I encouraged her in her plan of going to Asmara in Eritrea where her grandmother was from and setting up an office. She encouraged me in my writing. I said that if she moved there, I'd go with her. Turn my back on database management. I said that we should travel together. Buy flights. Afterwards.

And that led us back to Dad.

She put down her iPad and said that she'd been reading about how 'the impact' on the 'family-carer' was massive. The carer is the one doing all the worrying, Lou, she explained.

And nobody can care better than the family-carer because nobody knows the patient so well. That's the problem. And it gets so that only a family-carer will do because – as the disease worsens – the patient needs the intimacy of life-long rapport. They need someone who knows what the blinks really mean. The carer watches the patient decline and – day by day – the carer also becomes the decision-maker. Meanwhile, they go mad because they are not able to do anything about the disease. And eventually, the carer starts to feel nothing but guilt . . . because really they are waiting for death.

So that's when I told her that Dad had just received his date from Dignitas.

And she turned to face me cross-legged.

'So it's decided?' she asked.

'If he wants to go through with it: yes. Although . . . he's being weird.'

'What's he saying?'

'Well, when he told me, he said "for this relief much thanks" – which I guess is something from Shakespeare. I don't know. I mean . . . he *says* it is great. He says it is "the winning ticket".'

She widened her eyes.

'He *says* that it's the security of knowing that there's another option – that Dignitas feels like hope. Like he's back in control. But then . . . then he's also acting odd. I don't know . . . Maybe it's something to do with my brothers.'

'What do you mean?'

I winced. 'They're going to want to kill him when they find out.'

'They're going to be *angry*?'

'Yes.'

'Wait. What? I don't get it.'

'Well – you know – what I call the bad side of Dad?' I put my phone down and turned to face her. 'I think when he was younger, he did a lot of shitty selfish stuff that got to my brothers when they were kids. And he *definitely* did some bad things which drove their mum crazy . . . properly bat-shit crazy.'

'Did they tell you about it?'

'Some of it. But . . . it was kind of . . . taboo. Because of my mum.'

'Right.'

'And he was different with me. New marriage. More money. And he was just – you know – older. It's almost like I had a different mother *and* a different father – and like my brothers were trying not to ruin that for me. Which is one of the reasons I've got so much time for them.'

'I see that.'

'They're over it now . . . But not really. Who ever gets over anything?'

She half smiled.

'I don't know how they're going to take him actually having a date for Dignitas. It will hit them hard in the obvious way. But also . . . they're not . . . I don't know . . . nothing has really been sorted out – on some deep level. And now there's suddenly a timetable.'

'Which they will see as forcing them back into dealing with their shit – right?'

'Exactly. Like everything is on Dad's terms again.' I saw her for a moment as if I were a stranger looking down: her presence, her engagement. 'But the thing is – whatever they say and do – the disease is real. And they're going to have to face up to that.'

'And you?' She reached her hand to the side of my face. 'How are you about him having the date?'

'I'm OK . . . because I'm here with you.'

She leant over and kissed me lightly.

'I always hoped my frog would turn into a database manager,' she said.

'I promise you we can do ten years on your issues after this.'

'Won't be long enough.'

The evening becomes the night and the light from the candles swims and glimmers in the room. My father leads our ill-gathered party away from the shallow choppy little inlets of conversation, in which we've all been bobbing about and crashing into one other, and out to deeper waters where the world is more interesting and we can see for miles and set our course by the heavens. This is for my benefit – because he thinks I'm losing it, or that I'm tired from the driving; but it is also because he flourishes in company. When I was little, it was always Mum for the first half of the evening and then Dad for the second. When he's just the right drunk, all the irritation and frustration and dissatisfaction leave him and it's like his intelligence can stand up straight and breathe and stretch. And now I'm thinking about how we learn a lot by seeing the people we love through strangers' eyes – as if you might fall in love with someone all over again when they are talking to somebody else. So nobody wants to go to bed. We want more wine. Because now is the moment, and now we are here, and now we are all alive without distraction. We want more and more. Longer. Longer. We don't want it to end.

I am standing in the darkness outside. I am exhausted. I smoke. The silent moon is staring open-mouthed at the Earth. There's no wind, no sigh, no whisper; fields deep in shadow and the dark shape of the treetops; nothing stirring.

And suddenly, I know I can't do it. It's an intuition. Something spiritual. I just *know* I can't do it: I cannot drive my father to his death.

You don't simply give up.

So that's OK, I'm thinking. I know. I know. At *last* I know. I'm going to tell Dad: we're going home.

He will ask if I am sure. But I will say that I am. I really am. And so he will say – OK. That's decided, then. And we'll turn around and go home. And he'll make the best of it. I know he will. Because it's the one unshakeable thing between us. That he will do what I ask. That he'll carry on living.

I smoke afresh with thirsty lungs. We'll make it to Christmas. Together. However bad he gets.

I have to go back in there and tell him we're going home.

No . . . I'll tell him tomorrow. In the morning. Let him have the night. Let him hold the table. That's the kinder thing. Yes, I'll tell him in the morning. But I am decided. We're not doing this. We're not doing this. And it's a great all-encompassing relief that lets me breathe again and balm my soul in the merciful light of the ancient stars.

—

Dad asks each of us to tell a story from our own lives. And when we do, he makes us all feel like we're talking about something more than what we're merely saying; that our flimsy tales, badly told, resonate beyond themselves; that in talking about ourselves, we are really talking about desire and love and human nature, the most interesting things in the world. And the candles are three-quarters burned when we say that he must tell us a story, too. And his midnight voice reminds me of when I was a boy and he read to me by the side of my bed; a voice that poured magic and dreams into my pillow.

PART TWO

TWO RIDERS WERE APPROACHING

THE LIBERATOR OF THE LAKE

Outside, in the distance, there's an extremely tall man walking down the long tree-lined avenue towards us, the morning sun at his back. I'm waiting for the moment to tell Dad that I've changed my mind. Meanwhile, we're all dying amidst the exquisite agony of a guesthouse breakfast: muted propriety, furtive greed, napkins and frippery.

Except Dad. My father is enjoying himself. He's got three different artisanal jams on the go with his second croissant and, unusually, he's ordered coffee, not tea. He pours himself another cup – meaning that there's no more left for me.

'Only the French really know how to make coffee, Lou.'

'Apart from the Italians,' I say.

'Apart from the Italians. Granted.'

'And the whole of southern Europe.'

He scoops the darkest jam so that it rests in the hollow cone where he has bitten off the end. I can't think of a time when we have hung out with a hangover together like this; and I'm half glad of its communality and the way it obscures reality, like a big fat sheltering eclipse.

The room has been rearranged since dinner – instead of one long table, we're seated at four separates in a loose semi-circle around the French windows. Dad and I at one end and Beth-Marie and Neil at the other, the latter busily taking pictures of the former as she pugnaciously breastfeeds.

Christopher and Leah are in the middle, positioned on the same side so as neither loses out on greeting the sun. In the centre of our semicircle is another table on which a buffet breakfast has been arranged in front of the patio doors. A bottle of champagne on ice has been placed carefully at an angle as some kind of centrepiece or challenge or rebuke. Nobody knows what to do about it. I keep thinking about going up there and popping the cork, swigging some down myself and spraying the crowd like I won the Monte Carlo GP. There's a weird atmosphere in the room – as if last night was all *way* too revealing and traumatic and now everyone wants it to be known that we are not friends after all. Ralph says the English are the only nation in the world that like to retreat after intimacy.

'Where are we tonight, Lou?'

'I've got it written down.'

'On paper?'

'In my phone.'

There's a pause as if that doesn't count as written down. I start scrolling through the screens.

'Do you know what I reckon, Lou? I think we should camp tonight.'

I look up at him. 'Camp at a campsite in the van?'

He looks back with a where-else face. 'Like we used to,' he says. But the past tense is our enemy. 'Like we always have, I mean.'

I can hear Leah asking for low-fat yogurts and filtered water. Christopher is talking about carbs. Neil and Beth-Marie are discussing 'their eldest', who recently went off on his scooter on account of his adventurous nature, his intelligence, his likely being the next president but two.

'What do you reckon?' Dad asks.

I lay down my phone and flatten my hands on the table.

Softer, he adds: 'Are you OK, Lou?'

I can't believe that he thinks I am hurting about the itinerary change. I need to say it but instead I just come out with some of his phrases for no reason: 'The triumph of triviality, Dad. The championing of the charlatan. The much-trumpeted return of the third-rate.'

His face cracks with amusement and he grips the table with one hand and raises his croissant with the other as if it were the sceptre of freedom. I can tell Leah and Christopher have stopped talking. But after last night, everybody thinks we're nutters anyway. And Dad doesn't care. He lets go of the table and reaches across with his spare hand and then he does something I can't remember him doing for at least fifteen years: he spiders his big palm wide and lays it over the crown of my head and messes with my hair.

'If this is a champagne hangover, Lou, I'd hate to spend whiskey time with you.'

I can feel the effort on his arms that this lean is costing him. And that he's loose and uncoordinated; physically, emotionally, cognitively; labile.

I remember seeing this fox once in broad daylight in London, walking down the street towards me at a slight angle, and not running away or hiding, and I didn't know what the hell was going on and I thought maybe it was aggressive or some new urban strain of day-fox, but then, when it got close, I could see it was really weak and sick and that it could barely walk at all, and that it was dying, and that it was frightened and confused and disorientated, and yet that it knew enough to know it shouldn't be here; but, all the same, here it found itself, veering slightly always to its right; and I swear that as it came past it was kind of smiling – smiling madly, tight with fear – and I stepped out of its path across the street because it scared the hell out of me, even though I could see that it had only hours to live, because that face was the face of death.

Dad withdraws his hand and now we're on the edge of a precipice. If we fall, we fall for ever.

But maybe he's still of agile mind because he settles back and the sceptre becomes a croissant again: 'One thing I will say, Lou, is that these croissants are superb. I can't remember better.'

'That's the Alzheimer's kicking in, Dad.'

'You should eat. And if there are any left we should take them for the van.'

'I'll cancel the next place.'

'Will there be a cancellation fee?'

'Does it really matter?'

He blinks then he offers me his sagging salivary grin and we regard each other from inside the ruins of our mortar-shelled minds – two rebel fighters sharing a joke amidst the casual atrocity.

'I know a great campsite,' he says. 'It's in the forests – near Belfort. It's only about fifty miles from Basle and the border. We've been there before. Next to a river. More or less in the right direction. We can look up the address on your phone. Program the satnav.'

My father puts down the croissant, picks up his napkin and starts to nod, slowly but with his whole upper body.

But I'm thinking maybe the hangover is going to make me weep and maybe I should find me some more coffee and come back and just *say* it. Just say it, Lou: I can't do this any more. Just say it: we're going home.

'Dad—'

But suddenly the French windows are pulled open. And the tall man is standing there with the sun at his back.

He is not eight foot after all. Rather, he has a child on his shoulders and a scooter in his fist. His clothes are dripping wet, his boots and his pale trousers are slathered in mud. He is wiry-thin with luxurious medium-length auburn hair and a widow's peak and he has the demeanour of a wartime airman shot down over marshlands who has nonetheless enjoyed the walk home.

Without stepping into the room, he addresses our break-fasting semicircle from the French windows: 'Ladies and gentlemen, may I present young Felix. He was scootering his way through life – and with admirable conviction – but he has been the victim of an unexpected precipice. Witness knee.'

With his free hand he raises the child's leg from where it dangles. At chest-height, inside his light summer sports jacket (spattered and filthy), the man's white T-shirt has a darker and wetter stain – blood from the boy's injury. But the child, who is also soaking wet, is eagerly jockeying up and down on the madman's shoulders and smiling.

Beth-Marie has risen, indignant infant still affixed to abundant breast.

The man turns a quarter left and a quarter right. He says: 'Except for the knee and some grazes to the left hand, Felix seems clear of all ancillary injuries but he wishes it to be known that he would now like to pass some quality time in the close company of his maternal progenitor . . . Madame, you, I presume.'

'Oh my God . . . Felix!'

The man sets down the scooter and raises the grinning child from his shoulders so as to place him carefully on his feet. Then he bends down to offer his fist. The boy makes a reciprocal gesture. They knock together. Some sweet and secret knowledge of what is funny in the world passes between them. Then the man gently ushers the child towards pale-lipped Beth-Marie, who has dropped to her knees to greet him, the infant as before but suckling all the harder by way of an attention-gathering counter-offensive.

'Felix,' she scolds, 'you must not go so far without Mummy!'

The man stands up and in so doing scatters the spell he has created. 'Hello, Lou. Hello, Dad. You look well – given the *circumstances*. I am fine, thank you for asking. Although my luggage has been detained in Oschersleben. An unforeseen separation of carriages. Which is irritating – especially since I am now covered in mud and child's blood. This all seems very pleasant. Why has nobody opened that bottle of champagne?'

Beth-Marie now sunders infant from breast and passes him to Neil, who hastily puts down his phone. The breast is re-housed and Felix is clasped to the self-same bosom his younger brother has just vacated.

Immediately, the infant starts to fret. Neil has no idea what to do and so he backs away towards the door, seeking mutely to suggest that his experience best advises absence.

'Did you see what actually happened?' Beth-Marie demands as she fusses with Felix.

Ralph bows. 'Witnessed the entirety, madame. As I was walking in.'

She dips a serviette in a glass of water and wipes at his knee. But she has reversed all Ralph's good work and now the boy subsides into tears and the room is rendered awkward and immobile. I feel for the kid.

'Where did he fall? *Where?*'

'In the lake.' Ralph indicates the path beyond the windows with a thumb over his shoulder. He's no longer concentrating, though, because he's craning in through the French windows and trying to read the label on the champagne upside down.

'Demi-sec,' he murmurs to himself from the threshold and begins rather half-heartedly to brush drips from his clothes.

'There's a *lake?*'

Ralph realizes his mistake a fraction too late.

'Why did nobody tell me before that there is a lake?'

Collective uncertainty. Felix starts to cry more vehemently by way of doing justice to his mother's outrage.

'The lake is round to the side over the slight rise,' my father says, gently. 'It's not very big.'

Leah says: 'You can see it from the first floor – if you have one of the big rooms.'

'I think it's artificial,' Christopher adds, both softening and strengthening his wife.

'Well what happened?' Beth-Marie demands. 'I want to know *exactly*. I'm going to—'

'There's a step down at the end of the path just before the . . . before the *minuscule* lake.' Ralph is seeking to meet the boy's eye and convey cheer. 'Our adventurous hero must have plunged headlong to his gravelly fate and then fallen forward into the water. But—'

'Holy Mary, Mother of God.'

'But I was there instantaneously,' Ralph affirms. 'I leapt in after him. I became a sea horse. Then a land horse. He has ridden me all the way here. As you see – all is well.'

Beth-Marie raises her voice against the crying of her infant and the sobbing of her son: 'He fell into the *lake*?'

'Waist-deep, madame. Waist-deep only. To my knees. His waist.' Ralph, too, has to raise his voice. 'Only a drunken midget who had never learnt to swim would run the risk of drowning.'

But Beth-Marie isn't listening. 'Oh my God. Felix. You have to be more *careful*. Oh my God. Oh my God. Neil – *Neil!* – this is *not* acceptable.'

The boy is now desolate – wailing, convulsing. Neil glowers from the corner where he is wrestling with the infant as if forced to share a tumble dryer with a rabid mongoose.

Beth-Marie shouts above the racket. 'Can you just go and *get* the manager.'

'On it!' Neil yells back: 'On it. On it.'

But now something magical happens that holds Neil from leaving the room . . . The madman of the lake steps muddy-booted and sodden through the patio doors and reaches out to an empty chair beside Beth-Marie where he picks up a blue cuddly toy horse about the size of a lapdog. He returns behind the central table so that he is once again framed in the doorway and clears his throat loudly against the yowling and the keening and the fury. Then he stands quite still. Preternaturally still. And then, somehow begins, gradually . . . to disappear.

The crying falters.

And suddenly, we all are staring at this toy horse as it

begins to wake up. We watch it – slowly – taking in its surrounds. The crying stops. The horse acquaints itself with croissants and with cutlery, considers the fruit and the pots, the wide omelette platter, stops here, beckons us there, seems to smile and delight in its new-found consciousness.

Our attention is intently focused. There is nothing else in the room. The puppeteer has vanished. We feel only for the horse. He canters and dances. A gentle tune is humming. And now this horse is not so much animate as appealing to us; in its every movement – real, alive – as if throughout its existence it has been waiting for this moment to perform, to reach out, to declare itself. Oh, did we not know of what a story it had to tell?

And thus, quite naturally, the horse comes forward and begins to sing in a sweet tenor voice:

'I am the lonely horsey, ma'am, that leapt into a lake
To save my young friend Felix, sir, from his big mistake.'

This is what Ralph used to do for me when I was a young boy; these mesmerizing little shows with these terrible-but-somehow-still-amazing songs that he made up on the spot. The horse pauses, looking out at the audience – sadness, he seems to say, sadness, peril, but not without hope.

'His little hand was ouchy, ma'am, his little knee was scraped
But bravely did he ride me, sir; and thus we did escape.'

He takes the centre of the stage now. This is his moment. One front leg rises.

'At our tail – a thousand ogres, ma'am, with very stinky
toes . . .'

He sings of trials, of destiny and overcoming.

'. . . And a big fat troll with problems, sir, and a finger up his
nose.'

Galloping.

'There were witches in the ditches, ma'am, and goblins in the trees,

But Little Felix Rascal, sir, he didn't even sneeze.'

Back and forth, back and forth – a spoon a lance; toast racks the lists.

'He cared not he was wet, my friends, he cared not he was cold.

He fought off all these idiots, ma'am, and fast away he rode.

The monsters and the stinkies, sir, they never had a chance

Because Little Felix Rascal, friends, is the coolest boy in France.'

The horse bows and rears and bows again and then leaps towards Felix, who catches him. And in that instant, as if by magic, Ralph reappears.

Leah is clapping and whooping. Christopher, too. I catch my father's eye. Everybody is smiling. Felix is clutching the horse and his face is suffused in that kind of delight that only kids can know. And that I remember as Ralph's gift to me.

'Holy Mary,' Beth-Marie says again. And then, as if seeing Ralph for the first time: 'You're soaking.'

'Madame, the lake was wet.'

'Do you have any spare clothes?'

Ralph grimaces. 'Oschersleben.'

'Do you want to borrow some of my husband's?'

'That's very kind. I'd be honoured.'

'Neil, have you got a spare shirt and some trousers?'

'No rush, Neil, no rush,' says Ralph. 'I think I am going to have some breakfast now. My trip has not been without its own peculiar trauma. Couchettes. Taxis. Lack of adequate funding.'

Neil finds his voice: 'Can you do that again? I'd love to film it.'

'No, Neil – alas, I can never do it again.' He picks up the champagne, which drips from the melting ice. He reaches out a cigarette from the inner pocket of his battered jacket. 'Lou, Dad, I think *petit déjeuner* out here on the terrace for me – since I am covered in shit. At least until I am bit drier ... Luckily the sun is with us. Can I have your croissant, Lou, and can you bring me a glass or some kind of vessel? I want to explore the world of demi-sec.'

My heart has lightened.

'He's my brother,' I say.

I'm not sure Tolstoy had it right. All families, happy or sad, conceal a great deal of dark matter, something greater than the known physics and chemistry, something that must create the dark energy that holds them together or pushes them apart, something unseen and unknowable that just has to be written into the equations in order to make sense of what we understand and feel and discover about one another. Who knows what this dark matter is or how it creates so much dark energy? Something to do with all that living together, I guess: the getting up every day, the going to bed every night, the bathroom, the brushing of teeth with the wrong toothbrush, the unexpected naked encounters on the stairs, the distinctive sound of water running in particular pipes, the hasty breakfasts, the laborious dinners, the likes and dislikes of every diet, the fact that the oven door swings open and the fridge door sticks shut, the box in the hall that nobody claims, the silent moods, the covert negotiations, the cyclical anxieties, all those matters dealt with, all those matters pending, the ignoring, the badgering, the endless money trouble, the successes and the failures, the summer nights when the light lingers later than everyone remembers, the dark January cold when everything feels a little hunched and in retreat, the fights, the furies, the feuds, everything said, everything unsaid, everything unsayable; the secret understandings of love.

But what, I want to know, is the best way for a family to behave? To drag the dark matter out into the light? To be honest? I feel like that word – 'honest' – I feel like it's blurring or migrating or drifting. Or that its meaning now has a contraband freight of selfishness somewhere hidden below the waterline. Or maybe the word is slipping away from us into the mist like some old idea from the last century. And is it not at odds with love? Doesn't love necessarily require some kind of delusional state? After all, surely only a monster incapable of love would tell a child the truth of the world?

PÉAGE

'So,' Ralph says, as if summing up the entirety of existence thus far, 'the good thing about this trip is that nobody can object if I smoke. I mean – you're going to die any minute, Dad. So passive smoking is hardly a worry for you. And you – Lou – you secretly smoke anyway. I assume you haven't told Dad – since in your case the habit is peculiarly untactful.'

I look across at Dad. He is leaning on his pillow with the map spread on his brand-new summer-holiday slacks, which are the colour of rubber bands, and which he has unreservedly teamed with his sky-blue tunic-fleece. He is happy – there's no other word for it – but he makes a rueful face and shakes his head slowly as if to say we're going to have to retune to radio Ralph. In the rear-view, I can see my brother standing up, falling over, engaging epileptically with the stove.

'Did Lou mention it, Dad?' Ralph asks, loudly.

'He tells me nothing.'

'Well, Lou is a ten-a-day man now, Dad. Swaggers around the office half-arseholed most of the time, I bet, trousers roped low round scrotum and cleft, blowing smoke into the face of every fucker he fancies. Which, I bet, is not that many – is it, Lou? Not in database management.' There comes the attenuated rasp of one of Ralph's slow match strikes. He has found the cooks' matches. 'Don't worry, I *am* opening the window.' He succeeds in unsticking the catch and then sits down in the centre of the bench seat so that he can see out of the front window between Dad and me.

I ease my window down a fraction to let out the dancing horseflies. We're going to buy baguettes later, and soft cheese, and ripe tomatoes, and wine the like of which we've never before dared to look upon. We're going to camp like the old days and fuck this chateau bullshit. Maybe we are falling under a spell that has been cast by France itself – the fine weather, the steady ranks of the vines marching up and down the hills, the faded ochre houses of a blue-shuttered village in the near distance, the white-arrowed sign ahead that tells us '*Toutes Directions*' as if there were indeed no choice. And Ralph: the fact that he is here; the surprise of it; the joy of it; the fresh air of it. Dad says that the greatest pleasure is to meet again with someone you love after a time apart and I'm with him on that.

'Can you use the side seat?' I ask. 'It's depressing looking at you every time I have to use the mirror.'

'Nope. I am going to sit here and enjoy my holiday. Every mile.' Ralph is wearing his own boots and jacket with the clothes he's borrowed from Neil: a pair of pale-grey jogging bottoms and a repulsive green T-shirt that says 'Daddy Day Care'. He's holding a little saucer that he must have taken from the chateau and into which he studiously taps his ash. 'Comfort is the enemy, Lou. Isn't that right, Dad? Or is it death that is the enemy? I forget. Who said that?'

Even though he never concedes a single thing to my father, Ralph still expects him to know everything. And yet, at the same time, he has a way of turning Dad's knowledge into further evidence against him. But if Ralph has been caught off guard by the reality of Dad's decline, then he's hiding it; or maybe this is his way of being obliging. I fix on his eyes for a moment in the rear-view again; they are considering and undecided and they belie the playfulness of his voice.

'That's Corinthians.' Dad is winding madly at the half-broken window handle; sometimes it turns without result; other times the window goes down. '"The last enemy to be destroyed is death."'

'St Paul. I should have known.' Ralph exhales. 'History's least welcome correspondent.'

'Then used by Donne, of course, for the big one,' Dad says.

'The big what?' I ask.

'Holy Sonnet.'

I had forgotten that this is what it's like with these two; it must be years since we three have been alone together.

'You know . . .' Ralph begins, as if reading my mind in real time. 'You know, it's good to see you both after so long.'

Dad has his window down all the way. The country lane ends. I know the answer but I ask just the same to give him the pleasure of responding: 'Which way is it here, Dad?'

'South,' Ralph says, leaning forward again. 'It's south and then a bit east.'

'The satnav says left – do you want to check it on the map, Dad?'

'Already have.' Dad breathes the fresh air from his window as if his lungs were tasting it the same way his mouth tastes wine. He points at the sign: 'Left. Sommepy-Tahure, Suippes, then *direction* Bouzy. Stay Bouzy.'

I ease the van onto the main road. I *like* the driving. I like that my family give the youngest this honour – even though one is unable and the other is already over the limit.

'So how are you, Lou?'

'Fine.'

'Have you got a girlfriend?'

'What the fuck?'

Ralph smiles.

'Stop swearing.' Dad sighs.

'Please tell me that you've got a girlfriend, Lou. People need to be making urgent love all over the world or I start to feel uneasy. Like maybe the other team is winning.'

'I'm fine,' I say.

'You're fine?'

'Is the E50 the same as the A4, Dad?'

'Yes. Bouzy. Stay with Bouzy.'

'Bouzy.'

'Come on, Lou.' Ralph leans forward and pats my side: 'How *are* you? Let's get down to it. I want to hear your news. How is it all going? Spare me the tiresome virtue. Talk to me. I'm utterly sick of myself.'

I glance back at him. 'Apart from this?'

'Apart from this.' He winks. 'Or including this, if you prefer.'

'I'm fine.'

'You're fine? That's it?' He strikes another match.

'Totally fine.'

'You don't *seem* fine.'

'Ralph, seriously: fuck off.'

'Oh. *Oh.* It's "fuck off" now, is it?' I can tell he is smiling without looking. 'Unbelievable,' he says. 'For the last six months I have had nothing from you except "Please fly to

London, please fly to Paris, please fly to Frankfurt, please fly to Zurich." It's been "Oh oh oh, Dad this, me that, Jack the other. You need to be here, Ralph. You need to be there, Ralph. We're all dying, Ralph, we all don't want to die, we all *do* want to die. Please call, please Skype, please teleport. Please come. Please stay. Please go." And now – now that I have interrupted rehearsals to clang and thump across Europe on minor overnight trains – now all you can say is "fuck off".'

'Fuck off.'

Dad cuts in: '*Please* stop swearing, the pair of you.'

'Not possible.' Ralph tips his saucer into the plastic bag we are using as a bin and then shakes it for no reason. 'But we're getting off the point. Have you got a girlfriend?'

'I actually feel sorry for you.'

The sun seems to be climbing higher in the sky today and there are people working in the fields as if the Earth was indeed created for the well-being of human kind after all.

'Eva,' Dad says, disloyally, shifting allegiance.

'Eva.' Ralph says her name almost as slowly as he strikes his matches. 'How old is she? Nineteen, I hope? What did you go for, Lou, looks or personality?'

'Jesus. I didn't "go" for anything.'

'You must have gone for *something*, Lou. We all go for something.'

'A person.'

'Oh, please. We're driving to Dignitas not some hipster festival for total fucking dick-weasels who want to look like D. H. Lawrence. You should come to Berlin, Lou. They have both there – all rolled into one: intelligent, charismatic, witty women who also know what they are doing in the sack. I mean it. *Experts.* None of the bewildered ironing-board routine you get in the Home Counties. It must be their fathers, don't you think, Dad? Teachers. That's what fathers need to be: teachers.'

For reasons I don't fully understand, only Jack can take Ralph on. Or only Jack can do so effectively. I look across at my father as if to say, who is this nutter? But he's looking back at him like, who are *these* nutters? Nobody really understands anybody else; this may be an insurmountable problem for humanity.

The road widens and I steer us into the overtaking lane.

'I wish I had a sister,' I say.

'I wish I had alternative trouser-wear and the prospect of a pork pie,' Ralph says.

I glance in the mirror. 'What about you?' I ask. 'Who are you with?'

'Anyone. Everyone. No one.'

'How does that feel?'

'Sexually very satisfying. Intellectually preoccupying. Spiritually lonely.'

'Maybe you're a frustrated monogamist.'

'Tried it. Feels like death without the mercy of death.' He exhales. 'Not that I would know how death feels. How does death feel, Dad?'

Dad blinks. 'Do you think there will be oysters in Troyes?'

'It's not a very coastal town,' I reply.

'There will be oysters,' Ralph offers, confidently. His smoke rings somehow drift forward despite the air from my window rushing the other way. 'And there will surely be a pork pie. Does anyone have any paracetamol or aspirin or ibuprofen or just something to take away this ceaseless *pain*?'

'They're in the old ice-cream tub,' I say, 'under your seat.'

'Of course. The magic mint-choc-chip box.' Ralph gets up and starts rolling around in the back again, shouting forward: 'Do painkillers have a best-before date, I wonder? After which time the pain can't be killed? Or is there always a solution? What do we think? Dad? Where's Jack, by the way? In Jakarta enslaving a new generation with insurance?' He laughs at his own bad joke.

'He's coming,' I say, deliberately casual.

'He's *coming*?' Ralph noses forward again suddenly interested and hovers with his cigarette in the corner of his mouth. 'I thought he was implacably against? Drawbridge up. Fuck-you flags a-flutter on the battlements.'

'He was,' Dad says.

'He *is*,' I say.

'Do we know why?'

'Siobhan,' Dad says.

'That's not true, Dad.'

Dad raises a shoulder and looks away.

There are untroubled cows crossing a bridge over our heads. If I was a farmer, I'd grow tobacco.

'I was meaning.' Ralph sits back down with the ice-cream tub. 'Do we know why he's suddenly coming? Are we to assume we're now being taken seriously?'

'He can't get a flight at the moment,' I say.

'Late for death. Who would have thought it possible?'

'Is he meeting us in Zurich?'

'I don't know, Dad. It's wherever he can fly to. He doesn't want us to go to Zurich.'

'*Are* we going to Zurich?

'I don't—'

'*Bouzy!*' Dad grabs at the wheel. '*Bouzy, Lou!*'

I swerve us across the road and just make the exit. A horn blasts behind us.

It's true: my brothers were brought up by a different, younger man; one of the prophets of the new literary theory then at the height of his grandiloquence, loudly punishing himself and his people out there in the desert where he also liked to call himself king. He who they knew would allow no false idols but insisted on worship of the one true Marx. Pompous, vain, conceited. So Ralph treats Dad with a kind of unengaged humour you reserve for a drunken bum with good patter begging carriage-to-carriage on the tube whereas Jack treats him with that simmering moral repugnance you reserve for those fat white men who incinerated America's moral authority in the deserts of Iraq.

Meanwhile, the deeper emotional calculus goes something like this. For Ralph: 'Listen, Dad, I find you to be such a staggering hypocrite betrayer that in the face of all your public appearances as the upholder of this and the defender of that I am left no choice but to approach your every decision, action and utterance with the arched eyebrows of amused indifference or disdain.' Whereas for Jack it runs in the opposite direction, more like: 'Listen, Dad, given what you have done to my mother and what you have put me through – you leave me no choice but to live my life as a reproach to you and all that you are; either that, or my interaction with you might be mistaken for forgiveness, which cannot be.'

I'm exaggerating but the point is that the default setting

on Ralph's hard drive is to withhold engagement while the default setting on Jack's is to withhold consent. Ralph feels that to engage is to take Dad seriously. Jack feels that if he endorses one thing, he endorses everything. Dad used to say that when they were on the attack, it was like dealing with Nixon and Kennedy at the same time but not knowing which was which. I sometimes think they're straight-up cruel. But who was their teacher in that?

Ralph once told me that when he and Jack were around nine, my father took them to Keswick in the Lake District to 'climb their first mountain'. Carol didn't enjoy tramping around in bogs and so this was going to be some kind of father–son bonding weekend. A rite of passage; so my father billed it.

In the weeks leading up to the trip, Ralph remembers that Dad duly made a big deal of the gear they would need – buying second-hand walking boots for them both, balaclavas, waterproof trousers and Ordnance Survey maps; ostentatiously teaching them how to orientate a compass over the breakfast table.

Unusually, Dad took the Friday off work. And so they loaded up all the camping and walking equipment into the old van and left London – bright if not early – for the six-hour drive north. Ralph also remembers that the weather was exceptionally good and that he and Jack felt happy on the drive; that they shared a rare father-and-son 'camaraderie' – Ralph's word. They stopped en route and reheated the campfire stew that Carol had made for them on the little stove in the back. The traffic thinned after Manchester and so, sometime in the middle afternoon, they were driving through the shadowed valleys of England's only real mountains.

But when they got to Keswick itself, the boys were surprised to hear that they weren't going to be staying at a campsite after all. Instead, Dad had booked them into a hotel: a vast Lakeland grey-stone house with peacocks in the garden and a view of Skiddaw – the mountain they were to climb in the morning. Money being in much-cited shortage back then, this was the first time my brothers had ever stayed in such a place. But Dad reckoned that rain was now forecast for the next day and that they would need a roof over their heads following the rough weather. Ralph remembers in particular how struck he was by this because it undermined and contradicted Dad's often-professed love of camping come hell or high water (of which both there was usually plenty) whenever they went anywhere in the UK. So why balk this time?

In any case, from the moment they parked the van in the walled garden, Ralph says that they were thrown into a fresh and febrile excitement – pretending to be much older than they were and yet taking a childish delight in everything. There was a dining room with white tablecloths and a menu to read at a lectern; there was a billiard room with a massive table and balls to roll too fast at the pockets; there was a stag's head hanging in the hall above the reception desk and a wide polished wood staircase with banisters that begged to be climbed; there were corridors to be explored and gardens and attics and bowls of nuts free on the tables in the bar. Which is where, also unusually, Dad then said that they were going to have their dinner – and pretty much straight away.

And so my brothers sat in the bay window like twin

princes on a progress – Ralph's phrase – while Dad ordered sandwiches and crisps and – unbelievably – Coca-Cola. Three hundred miles north and this was a new man. His generosity, his ease, his bonhomie. Ralph remembers that he didn't even force them through the agony of eating their salad garnishes. But it was important that they get an early night, Dad insisted. The walk was long and steep. And the weather . . .

Maybe the most surprising thing, though, was that Dad had booked them a separate room – down the other end of a creaky corridor. My brothers were delighted. Their own kettle. Their own TV. A bathroom across the hall with a shower and wrapped-up mini-soaps. Everything.

Ralph remembers that Dad sat with them while they washed and talked about what happened if they got caught in a 'white out' and how to 'save' the balaclavas in their backpacks so that they had something more to put on if it got 'serious'. He read to them about Skiddaw. And when he got up to say good night, he said that they could read too, as long as they promised to be sure to be asleep when he checked on them at nine.

And so the *third* time Dad opened his own bedroom door to their knock – at almost ten o'clock – he was a man in the vice of fury.

Ralph remembers that Dad blocked the entrance again, his bare foot propping the door open a fraction as he stepped out, his right hand holding the white cord of his untied pyjama trousers. So Ralph stood back, caught out by this new register of his father's rage, and tried to speak, gabbling about how the picture had 'just fallen' off the wall and how the frame had splintered and knocked over the glass of water between their beds . . .

But the threshold had been crossed: they had disturbed Dad once too often and now he was in the burning draught of an anger that sought furious vent. He let the door shut behind him with no regard for being locked out and pursued Ralph down the corridor, speaking in a furious whisper that rose as he went.

Ralph says that he saw Jack leaning out of their room at the end of the corridor and he remembers his brother's terrified-but-determined expression when he broke through the fire-door and came towards him with Dad bare-chested and red-faced at his heels – still in his thirties then, at the height of his manly noon.

All in a second, Ralph ran past where Jack was standing and leapt onto the far bed to cower in whatever wrap of the duvet he could twist around himself.

But Ralph says that Jack did not realize the magnitude of Dad's anger. Instead, he assumed that Ralph had blamed everything on him, Jack, and so wanted urgently to set the record straight. In reality, the picture was a cheap print but – in his nine-year-old mind – Jack probably feared it might be as valuable as the paintings he had seen in galleries. And so, when Dad got to their doorway, spitting curses, Jack was still standing there, Ralph says, within easy reach, pleading tremulously in his unbroken voice that this was not his fault, that they were *both* dancing on the beds when it fell and the frame split and the water spilt.

Standing his ground was Jack's big mistake, according to Ralph. Because now Dad did not pause in his momentum and – in one movement – he picked Jack up, strode into the room and threw him back onto the nearer mattress – all with such force that Jack landed on his back and bounced up again, slamming his nose on the side-table as he fell into the gap between the beds.

Ralph remembers his brother's cry and thud – and then twisting round to see his father half-naked and physically shaking as he turned his bare back and took the key out of the lock of their door. Ralph remembers Jack's wail break; remembers Dad turning back again and advancing on them both, arm raised and shouting at them to shut up; remembers kicking himself off his bed and down into the gap beside his brother; remembers knowing with a child's clarity – innocent and experienced – that Dad would find it harder to hit them both together down there; remembers his father lean down over the bed; remembers the taut contorted fury of his face as he brought up his pointed finger and hissed: '*Not another word!*'

They heard him leave. They heard him lock the door behind him.

They didn't move for what seemed like ages.

When they dared to untangle themselves, Jack wasn't exactly crying but he was convulsing with something past tears, holding his nose in the cup of his hand.

And Ralph remembers looking at his brother in horror – looking at his own face reflected – and seeing the red line of blood from his brother's nose to his lips; sometimes Jack sucking it in and sometimes smearing it across his cheek where it streaked and mingled with his tears.

I think of the two of them. The last of the summer dusk at their attic window. The hotel tray and the kettle with the too-short cord. Sachets of sugar and instant coffee. The old television. The beds a mess. The fallen picture – still broken on the floor by their upturned glass. The pillows wet from the water spill. The silence of that room. The two of them sitting on the bed. Jack crying. Ralph – now a child-adult – doing and saying everything he had ever seen a grown-up do at the scene of an injury. His face grave and comforting and sympathetic. A knot in his boyish brow. A hunch in his narrow shoulders. Willing his brother to be OK as he looked across. Holding the bedside tissues. Jack's blood soaking red-brown through them one after another. Head back. Head forward. Still the blood. Then Ralph trying the door. Scared to bang on it and shout for his father – for anyone. What would they say? Ralph pulling the chair to the window. Because if it gets worse, he told Jack, he would smash the pane and shout for help.

The two of them.

Scared that Jack was going to die. No one in their world. And nobody ever coming to their rescue.

Ralph remembers that when Jack fell asleep with stiff-caked tissues stuffed up his nose, he climbed into his bed and lay beside him because his own bed was wet from the spill and he was afraid to sleep alone.

And, in the clear light of the morning, when they woke, Jack's pillow and his sheets were everywhere smeared in blood. There were tissues all over the floor. There were streaks of blood on both of their pyjamas. Jack's nose was swollen and his lip fat. Scared and ruined and sure that they would be further blamed for the mess, Ralph says they had no idea what time it was and so they sat and waited for their unknowable father to unlock the door and take them up the mountain.

Outside, Ralph remembers, the sun was shining as strong and sure as the day before. And the peacock was crowing.

'What are you doing, Dad?' Ralph leans forward like a cartoon burglar poking his head in through an open window.

'Finding some euros,' my father says, scrabbling, sausage-fingered.

'Yeah – but why?'

'To pay the toll.'

'The toll?'

'Yes.'

'But how can we ever pay that?'

'Where's all the change gone?' Dad asks.

Not yet lunchtime and we've recently stopped for gas and what Ralph calls a few 'errands'. We're eighty kilometres outside of Troyes. I don't know why but I've had my foot down. We've been making up time. Which is a dumb idea and a dumb expression because it's the one thing we cannot do. Ralph has started drinking something from an opaque plastic cup. He says it's an 'isotonic' vitamin replenishment drink recommended by his 'personal physician'.

'There's no change,' Dad says. 'It's gone. Do you have any money, Louis?'

'Of course he doesn't. Look at him.'

'Ralph?'

'Offshore.'

'I'm sure I put some change in here. There was at least twenty.'

A vast blue sign frames the road ahead. It stretches across all four lanes saying 'Péage Péage Péage Péage'. We've been getting these signs all the way down from the coast, of course, but the word is just getting nastier and nastier.

'Surely, Dad,' Ralph says, 'now is the time for a credit-card spunkathon – the like of which the world has never before seen?'

I glance in the rear-view.

'I mean shouldn't we be *flying* there,' he continues. 'Private jet. Load up with beautiful girls and designer drugs. You should buy a gun – shoot a Serbian hooker in the ass at thirty thousand feet because she disrespected your pamphlet on W. B. Yeats. Go out in style.'

'You're a maniac,' I say. I'm thinking that I need to text Jack and see if he has booked a flight yet. You spend time with Ralph, you need Jack. You spend time with Jack, you need Ralph.

'Spunk it, Dad,' Ralph says. 'Spunk whatever you've got left. Now's the time to get right down to it. Come on. What do you really want to eat? What do you really want to drink? Imbibe? Inhale? Inject? Who do you really want to sleep with? This is your one shot at consequence-free living. There's no collateral damage any more. A few days where you can finally *let go*. If you're going to be dead, you might as well be alive.' He sips his plastic cup and aerates the drink in a parody of how Dad tastes his wine.

I look across at my father; he's fiddling in the door.

'I think Ralph means we can put the toll charge on your credit card, Dad?'

'Hell, yeah; that is exactly what I mean. All seven euros of it.'

Dad's phrase for credit cards is 'the never-never'. He considers them the embodiment of all that is wrong with capitalism and the West. Even at the best of times, Dad is stressed by transactions: tolls, tickets, bills. When he's in America, he dreads going out because he can't get his head around the tip – the whole idea of tipping and 'the falseness' it engenders 'in society'. Maybe it's because he has never had quite enough money or maybe it's something to do with the shadow of the war and austerity or 'making do', as he calls it? I fix my eyes on the traffic ahead and change down a gear. Péage. Péage. Péage. Péage.

'Pills, that's what we need,' Ralph says. 'We could use your card for that too, Dad. MDMA and some kind of definitive sexual extravagance.'

Thick-fingered, Dad rummages on the dash. I have to choose one of the queues to join.

'I could bust through the barriers,' I suggest.

Ralph shakes his head. 'Not possible, Baby Lou. You're going to have five hundred randy French cops all firing their weapons from behind their vehicle doors. Either that or they'll vaporize your cousin's grocery store from thirty thousand feet.'

'Asymmetry,' Dad mutters.

'I was just—'

'And if they don't shoot you,' Ralph says, 'you're not going to be able to get them to chalk you down with Camus and Sartre and the gang – "it's existence that I'm trying to break here, officer, not the law" – no, sir – you're going to be a *terrorist*, Lou.'

'I don't have any cousins,' I say.

Dad has given up the search and he's struggling like a man pretending he's not in a straitjacket – merely to get his wallet out from under him. I can sense that Ralph is quietly

processing Dad's state in a different jurisdiction of his intelligence. I go for the pay-with-card line because it's shorter.
As if we are in a rush. 'Who inherits credit-card debts?' I ask.

'Who inherits what. That's a good question,' Ralph says.
'They can't transfer debt. Not if the card is in one name and
that person doesn't exist any more.'

'You're shitting me?'

'We need to stop talking like this,' Dad says. He has his
wallet out – no mean feat.

'Jack will know about debt,' Ralph says, leaning back.
'He's an expert on personal finance now. Has anyone tackled
him on life insurance, by the way? How do you *want* us to
talk, Dad? Would you prefer—'

'Can we stop . . .' I interrupt. 'Can we all stop having a go
at Jack.'

The van comes to halt in the queue.

Dad looks over at me. 'Have you definitely not taken any
money out of here, Lou?'

'No. Ask Ralph.'

'Ralph?'

But Ralph has the fingers of his spare hand pressed to his
head as though he's thinking that maybe the Higgs boson
isn't the last word after all and existence has somewhere
smaller to go. 'Seriously, Lou, do you think Siobhan has
taken over Jack's mind?'

'No.'

'Is the Pope living in there?'

'No.'

'Does he tell stories like, "Oh, I saw a tramp on the tube
and he reminded me of the risen Lord"?'

'No.'

'What's he like now? Conspicuously platitudinous?'

'He's distant,' Dad says. 'Unengaged.'

'He's *not* distant. That's not true. Why can't we stay with what is true and real? OK – pass me the card.'

'We're not putting it on the card,' my father says.

'We have to, Dad.'

'We are not putting it on the card. I have cash – here.'

'We have to. We're in the card queue.'

'For God's sake: *why* are we in the card queue?'

Ralph leans forward again, smiling and pretending puzzlement: 'Why are we in the card queue, Lou?'

'Dad. Card. Come on. We're holding people up.'

Dad hands me his card. His irritation fighting the slackness in his face so that for a moment he actually looks disfigured. I have the feeling of being seven again and having just knocked over my expensive orange juice in a restaurant.

I turn away and push the card in the slot beyond my window. There's a guy in the booth whose job is . . . to do nothing since there's no money to take. He looks at me. His eyes are grey and depthless but they glint madly at certain angles – like tarmac. He's wearing his headphones and shaking his head and singing along in that closed-off way people do when they think they are in the band, wrote the song, and nobody feels it more than they do. For a second, I believe that I know everything about him and that we're somehow the same. I want him to take off his headphones so I can whisper 'me too' and let him see the solidarity in my face. I want to call Eva. If I could live in a faded old room with high ceilings, tall windows and a view of an Italian lake and write poems for Eva, then I'd be happy. Is that too much to ask?

I engage first gear. I pull away until the engine's grumble

rises to grievance. I leave it a fraction too long before I change into second – merely to annoy Dad. I don't know why.

'Back to Jack,' Ralph says. 'Has something happened to him?'

'Well, he's got married, had three children and he bought a house. And I think he's trying to live as an ordinary citizen in London amidst the Oligarchs and the Oil Sheiks and the Fund Managers who serve them. He needs—'

'*That* is a whole other issue,' Dad cuts in, his irritation about the card, about money, now channelling into this deeper swell. 'Why – *why* – why does the British government feel the need to open its legs to the world's most morally disgusting wealth?'

'Does it?' I accelerate harder than need be – third, fourth.

'Yes it bloody well does. The message we send out is crystal clear. As soon as you've stolen your nation's resources or otherwise sullied the world, let us know, sir, and we'll find you a big house so that you can use our courts and our best schools and have our police protect you. And no, don't worry, we won't ask you to pay tax. Would you like a newspaper, or a football club? Or just a property portfolio? *That's* the real immigration problem, let's not—'

'So nothing has happened to Jack?' Ralph asks, cutting Dad off. 'He's the same Jack as before. Dad, what are you moaning about?'

'Well, *something* has happened,' Dad returns with sarcasm enough to power a dynasty of dark-hearted generations. 'He used to be a serious political journalist. He used to be an atheist. Now he is peddling sinister insurance scams in the Third World and inviting Father Patrick over for carrot cake and kiddie-fiddling.'

'Damascus,' Ralph says.

'He's got to get the boys through school,' I say. 'It's free if you go Catholic.'

'That's the *excuse*, Lou,' Dad says, his vehemence quickening. 'But he doesn't need to do that. He's earning vast amounts of money from the insurance racket. Why does he need to be fawning over clerics? Why does he need to be perverting the minds of his own children?'

'Maybe it's *because* of what happened with the boys,' I say.

Jack's boys had some near disaster in the womb. If they'd been anywhere else in the world but down the road from the only professor who could perform the operation, they'd both have been dead: no Billy, no Jim.

'So because your children are the lucky beneficiaries of science and medicine, you submit yourself to the world's most insane – not to say disgusting – power structure?'

'Not *most* insane, not most disgusting, Dad. I mean—'

'Up there, Lou. Up there. You thank the doctors in the morning – the people who did the *actual* work – and then you're on your knees in front of the priests in the afternoon – who did not a single thing. You're telling your children they are born brim-full of original sin – whatever *that* is – and that only the man in the black dress up at the front can save them – assuming you let him touch your testicles whenever you get changed at the schools he's so kindly opened to foster grooming opportunities. That the state then *subsidizes*. Leaving aside the misogyny and the paedophilia and the imaginary friends, wouldn't that make you feel bad?'

Ralph strikes a match. He knows, because I've told him, that for whatever reason – the medicine or the disease – Dad is more easily slipping from reason to rant these days.

('Mirroring the modernity he claims to dislike, Lou,' Ralph says.) But here's the thing: Ralph seems actually to relax the more Dad gets riled. He blows a smoke ring and says: 'It's like you always say, Dad. The Enlightenment seems to have passed a great number of people by.'

'It's *got* to change, Lou. Something has got to give. Mark my words.'

I don't know what Dad means or why. What is 'it'?

'Maybe Jack has a predilection for ideology,' Ralph says. 'Millions do. Is this not the same Jack who used to peddle the *Socialist Worker*?' Ralph is Jack's most lethal enemy and his most loyal defender; the precision and cruelty of his attacks are perverse evidence of some kind of love that undermines even its own undermining. 'A lot of religious people – they like rules and punishment. They find it reassuring. They *want* the imaginary strictures. They *like* feeling that they have this private God who redeems their anxieties and connects them to a power structure that has secret dominion over others. Am I right, Dad?'

Dad snaps: 'Jack is *not* like that. You know it. I know it.'

Troyes: forty kilometres. I'm speeding.

'What *is* Jack like? Christ, I would *love* a pork pie.'

'Maybe it's nothing to do with all of that.' I try to keep my voice level. 'Maybe he just doesn't want you to do this.'

'Then why not *say* that?'

I look across. 'That *is* what he says, Dad. He says exactly that.'

'Then why all the . . . why all the "you can't come and see Billy and Jim and Percy. You can't be friends with them. You can't get to know them." It's manipulation.'

'Manipulation,' Ralph repeats, egging him on. 'Manipulation and . . . control. Dad! You might be on to something! But why? *Why*, I wonder?'

I say: 'Maybe he doesn't want his children to get to know their grandfather and then the grandfather just . . . just to *die*.'

Dad looks across. His voice quietens. 'Every grandfather dies.'

'Who was Jesus's grandfather, I wonder?' Ralph asks. 'And did he die? We must ask Jack.'

A flock of birds swirl into the air like a monseigneur's cloak.

'Why do you want to stop in Troyes, Dad?' I ask.

'Oysters,' Ralph says. 'Pork pie.'

'Because I want to visit the cathedral again.'

'Jesus,' I say and look across. Dad's eyes are opaque with their anger for a moment and then they soften as he realizes and he sees me again. I shake my head. Ralph is laughing. Dad laughs. We let the hypocrisy and contradiction permeate and settle for a spell. Then Ralph leans forward, suddenly serious.

'Hang on a minute,' he says.

'What?' I ask.

'What?' Dad echoes.

'Why aren't we listening to any music?'

'We can't,' I say, sadly.

'Why?'

'Because.'

'Because it means too much to us,' Dad says.

'Fuck that,' Ralph says. 'Have you got your phone converter?'

'Yes.'

'Pass it here then?'

'What are you thinking?'
'Let's get this trip started.'
'What are you going to put on?' I ask.
Ralph takes a considered breath. 'Tombstone Blues.'

The second tape begins with about twenty minutes of inaudible talking. Then it stops. When it comes back on, you can hear everything that is being said quite clearly. Either the recording device has moved or the people. The first voice is vehement and repetitive but querulous – listing angry consequences and intentions and threats. The second speaks seldom but the tone is composed. Deliberately so. Little by little the first voice is provoked. The second voice starts asking questions in a flatter tone. Why would you do that? And you think this is a good idea? What is that going to achieve? Each question incites a more fervent avowal. It's hard to be sure but there is a persistence to the second voice that seems false to the moment – as if the second voice is not thinking about what is being said or even what is happening but some other agenda that the first voice – swept along in the rising tide of its emotion – does not heed. The tape cuts out again when the first voice begins to cry – these desolate empty jagged sobs cut ruthlessly short by the click of a button.

THE EARTH'S BRIGHT EDGE

Inside, the cathedral is as cool as the worn flagstones and everything smells of stone and wood infused with a thousand years of incense. We walk slowly up the aisle. Our footfalls echo. Whispers chase one another through the shadows and up the high walls and sound again where they were not. We stop at the crossing.

My father is at my right shoulder, my brother at my left. Above us, the sun is thrown and split by the vast stained-glass windows. Higher than seems possible, the vaulted ceiling appears alive with the play of lapis-lazuli blues, emeralds, ambers, burgundy reds. Great shafts of light fall here and there on the dwarfed human chairs, on the tall pale columns that arch and soar, left and right, forward towards the altar, on the statues of the saints, on the stations of the cross.

I know he wants me to ask so I do: 'How old, Dad?'

Dad speaks softly: 'There's been an oratory here since the fourth century. The place got burned in 1188 and they began building the version that we're looking at in 1200. It took five hundred years and they still haven't finished.'

I imagine men hauling stone towards heaven on spindly wooden ladders – brittle-fingered in the winter. I imagine their 'belief in an idea' – one of Dad's phrases that he uses not that covertly to attack me, or my 'generation', because he thinks we don't believe in any ideas. Which maybe we don't.

Because maybe they all turned out to be so staggeringly bad. Dad is heavy where he leans on me. We walk forward again.

'In 1420, Henry the Fifth came here to do his deal with Burgundy and the wife of Mad Charles the Beloved of France: to ensure that the French throne would pass to him and not the Dauphin – on Mad Charles the Beloved's death.'

'I love the word "*dauphin*",' Ralph says.

'Mad *and* Beloved?' I ask.

'One and the same,' Dad says. 'Which tells us something.'

'Although,' Ralph says, 'I think I love the word "*dauphinoise*" even more. It's a shame that the British only manage to use it in connection with potatoes. Which also tells us something.'

We stop before the altar. There's a full-stretch human effort at eternity here, something colossal and awe-inspiring and monumental and yet something monstrously deluded. And there is eternity's other name – Death – everywhere – in the tombs, in the statues, in the flicker of the candles, in the dying bloodstained body hanging in near-naked agony from the great crucifix ahead of us.

Dad turns on his stick and extends his arm, suddenly animated, alive, spending his energy fast. 'But Troyes,' he pronounces the name with the flat French 'r' but without self-consciousness, 'Troyes is *most* famous for the age and volume of its stained glass. The earliest visible part is the thirteenth-century choir, just up there. My favourite window is that one – "The Wise and Foolish Virgins" – partly because of the name, but also because there's a panel devoted to the Devil. Can you see it – right there?'

We look where he shows us. There's a stunted red figure in armour – visor down but beaked and horned and spurred.

'The interesting thing is that the Devil is everywhere in these windows.' Dad leans on his stick and points again and again. 'Up there, being chained to a mountain by Raphael. Up there, being invited into a convent. And up there, being chased out again by the Virgin. Look how much life and movement the artists give him. It's as though he, not Christ, were the animating spirit.'

Ralph and I turn and turn again as my father speaks, following where he points. I'm dizzy, looking up and thinking about how much my father knows – how much he carries in his mind – not only about the cathedral, the history and the glass, but also the stories that lie behind, the reference of one thing to another, the architecture of ideas and thought. His knowledge is so real and present to him. It is as if he somehow partakes in these stories simply by knowing them. Once, when someone had used the word 'outsource' at the clinic, he said to me: 'Be careful not to outsource your mind, Lou.'

'Give me a hand, boys. Let's sit down there at the front.'

My dad leans on me. We settle into the pew. I am on one side and Ralph the other. We stare up at the cross for a while. Dad is resting. Time slows. Then Ralph clears his throat.

'"Good afternoon, Herr Jesu,"' he says with his comic Sigmund Freud accent. '"Well, how was your week? We were talking about your mother, I think. Yes? The *Virgin*? Tell me – this virginity – do you remember your mother as affectionate or cold, distant?"'

'Ralph—'

'"It's not me, Herr Freud, who calls her the Virgin. My followers give her that name." "Your followers? On Instagram? One moment, one moment, let me consult my notes . . . Ah, yes, these are the people whom you call your sheep, correct? They worship you – is that right?"'

'Ralph—'

'"Yes, my flock." "But tell me, Herr Jesu, *how* do your flock worship you? What happens?" "Most of the time they kneel before—" "The sheep kneel?" "They are sheep only in metaphor." "I see. And the Virgin – a metaphor?" "No." "I see . . . Sorry, you were saying, the sheep kneel?" "My sheep kneel before a statue of me being crucified." "Ah, yes, I remember from last week – this also is to do with the thorns and the lashes, yes?"'

'Ralph—'

'"I know what you are going to say, Herr Freud . . . narcissism." "Narcissism, Herr Jesu, certainly. But also I think we must now accept . . . sadomasochism." "Then I have my followers eat my body." "In metaphor?" "No, here I must be adamant: in reality." "Ah, so. Cannibalism." "And I invite them to drink my blood." "There's a vampiric element?" "This is because I am the lamb of God." "You, also, are a sheep, Herr Jesu? Ah. So. This is most interesting—"'

'*Ralph.*' My father holds up his hand and commands him to stop but he's not angry, he's nervous of being overheard. And I can tell that he is smiling. Though it's the cold war between the two of them, I had forgotten all the backchannel alliances and diplomatic understandings they have. I'd forgotten, too, how much my father dotes on Ralph.

We are shuffling around the stations of the cross when Dad says: 'You've been here before – when you were a baby, Lou. The first trip we all made after you were born.'

'Blocked it out,' I say.

'Me, too,' Ralph nods.

'You and Jack were bickering all the time, Ralph,' Dad continues. 'And Julia was finding it miserable – no sleep and the *screaming* you used to do, Lou.'

'I feared abandonment.'

'She probably had post-natal depression,' Dad says.

'So did I.'

'We all did,' Ralph adds.

We stop before the painting with the number eight in Roman numerals above it.

'I still thought I might actually have to go to court to fight Carol,' Dad says. 'And Julia kept asking me why I was trying so hard to keep you and Jack when you were both being such bastards all the time.' He winces. 'Everything was so tense and fraught.'

I don't like it when my father uses my mother's name in the same breath as Carol's. I don't like to hear him say Carol's name at all, the name itself.

'I don't know why,' Dad says, 'but I knew I was doing the right thing back then. I had this sustaining surety about the divorce.'

'Don't,' Ralph says.

'Even when everyone was screaming in the back of the van and I knew Julia was looking out of her window so that she could cry without me seeing her.'

A rack of candles is lit in one of the alcoves and their flames dance, the spirits of the dead. For the first time since Ralph arrived, I feel the surge of emotions rising again – but deeper, darker, some weird and mingled turbulence of resentment. I want Dad to stop talking.

'I remember driving to this cathedral,' Dad continues. 'The way we have just come. From Reims. In the rain. I remember dreading going back to the campsite afterwards. But, still, I knew I was doing the right thing. I knew I had made the right decisions, even though all the people that I loved were crying or shouting at me.'

I can feel the Devil's redness rising in my face.

'And the thing is . . .' Dad turns away from me and towards Ralph. 'I don't have the certainty now. Not like I felt it then.'

Ralph is standing dead still; a white statue keenly chiselled.

And then it hits me. Dad is not sure.

All of this, the last eighteen months, the trips to the shrinks, to the doctors, the discussions, this journey itself – all of this is because I thought my father was *determined*. But it's a lie. A deception. A performance. My brothers are right. And suddenly, I can't stand to be there. I have to leave. Now that he's decided to show up at long last, Ralph can walk the old bastard down the aisle.

Outside, in the square, men and women I will never know are eating and drinking, oblivious, talking about nothing that will ever matter, breathing in, breathing out. There are restaurants beneath top-heavy wooden-beamed medieval houses with boards advertising '*prix fixe*' in the side streets.

Jack texts. He hasn't got a flight but he's going to the airport on standby.

A white Citroën van is loading brown boxes. As the girl in the boulangerie turns the sign to shut, light flashes in the glass from a sun I cannot see.

I call Eva.

'Are you OK? Where are you?'

'I'm in the square – outside Troyes Cathedral.'

'What's wrong? Shall I come?'

'Dad just told Ralph that he wasn't sure.'

'About the whole thing?'

'About the whole thing.'

'And what did Ralph say?'

'Fuck knows.'

'. . . But that's OK? Isn't it?'

'Why is he asking Ralph? He already decided. Twelve months ago. It's not got anything to do with Ralph.'

'It's—'

'It was all bullshit. The last year. Everything we said.'

'No, no . . . that's not right, Lou. Think about—'

'He isn't sure.'

'No, listen, Lou. You can't—'

'He isn't sure. Now Ralph's here.'

'Lou, he's going to want to talk with all his sons. You have to expect that.'

'Yes – he is *now*. He used the whole threat of this trip – just to get them here. That's what he has been doing.'

Silence bounces off some satellite somewhere above our lonely blue ball. I can't speak.

'Lou?'

'I hate this. I hate what it is doing to me.'

'Shall I come?'

'What's the point? I'll probably be home tomorrow night.'

'You think?'

'He's changing his mind and I don't even know why this is making me so angry. Last night I was . . . Jesus, I'm so fucked.'

'Take time out, Lou. Go somewhere on your own for a

bit. Sit down. Write something. Write something for *me*. Take an hour away from them. Find your way back.'

I owe thirty thousand pounds. What's a little more debt on top of that? So fuck this, fuck it all, is what I am thinking. I can get on a train right now and go to Paris – and check in somewhere with a balcony and a view of the Seine. And I can sit there smoking and drinking and waiting for Eva to arrive. And when she comes through the door, we won't speak, we'll just stand in the middle of the room, facing one another, between the windows and the bed, and we'll keep our eyes wide open and I'll look into those dark irises of hers as if I'm disappearing into some dream about the beginning of men and the beginning of women, and I'll sense the shape of her, of her body, where it comes towards me, where it dips away; and then, slowly, we'll raise our hands and touch each other with the fingertips of our fingertips, so that we can almost feel where our prints pattern into one another, and we'll move closer, but by less than any measurement so that it all slows slows slows right down . . . until at last there comes a moment when we're kissing – kissing – and suddenly we'll be doing the mad ragtime dance of taking off our clothes (the first beat of every bar another kiss) and I'll know her then, not only with my eyes, but with my hands and with my soul, and she'll know me, and we'll fall on the bed, but still we won't speak because we will *be* everything we might ever want to say to one another, we will *be* what we most mean, and we will have become what creation first meant to say when it whispered itself into existence from that bitter bitter nothing all those billions of years ago.

That's what I want.

And after that, we will drink cold white wine together in a big hot bath in a room of pale mirrors and dark marble. We will dress one other and I'll breathe the scent of her perfume and warm-bathed skin. And then we will walk out to some underground place down steep iron basement stairs where we will drink and talk and drink and talk about how people really are. About the masks. And behind the masks, yet more masks, and yet more, and yet more . . . And then, when we're both messed up, we will walk home on those slippery Parisian cobbles that fan out in the rain. And then we'll make love some more until it hurts too much to carry on and we can't come or cry or care about anything else – and then we'll open the window and sit on that balcony wrapped in the same sheet with a bottle of something that it doesn't burn to drink and just watch the night turning from sapphire to blue on those steep French roofs until the dawn slips under the east and the air smells of rain recently passed and we get that feeling that we are new again – a new man and a new woman living where the sun is rising on the bright edge of the turning Earth.

'Do you speak English?'

'I am Canadian, sir.'

'Is this a French-Canadian restaurant?'

'French-Canadian owned.'

'Interesting . . . OK, well, we'd like the oysters on your board, please, and champagne of which no greater can be conceived. No short cuts. My brother is sulking and we're worried he might take his own life. We are a very suicidal family.'

'Shall I get the sommelier?'

'Will he help?'

'She.'

'In that case – as soon as possible.'

Now the light catches in the leaded attic window of an old half-timbered medieval house across the square.

'And to eat?'

The waiter is looking at me. I am trying to respond. But my appetite has vanished; eating is some kind of endorsement that I cannot tender.

'Yes,' Ralph says. 'More oysters. And some fresh bread.'

'Another six?'

'Yes . . . And the paella.'

'We don't serve paella, sir. I'm sorry.'

'That's all we eat. That and oysters.'

Confusion from the waiter. 'Is paella on the menu, sir?'

'How should I know? You tell me.'

'I don't think it is.' The waiter regards the unopened menu in front of my brother.

'We also eat pork pies . . .' Ralph offers. 'If that helps.'

'Ah! Ah! Yes. We do have a *tourtière*, sir.'

'A pork pie?'

'A pork pie.'

'I *knew* it.'

Pride from the waiter. 'Originating from . . . Quebec.'

'*Québécois!* Superb. And another beautiful word. One of those for me, please.'

'Certainly.'

'Is it on the menu?'

'No.'

'You see the problem with going by the menu?'

'*Je voudrais le carré d'agneau, s'il vous plaît,*' my father says.

'Of course . . .' A moment as the waiter looks round. 'And will that be all?'

My father's eyes are shiny, my brother's a *danse macabre*, mine I know are zinc-blue and everything slides off them like those Parisian roofs.

'A green salad for my brother . . . No, please, don't fall into his trap. He likes to punish himself as a means of punishing others. To project his suffering onto the world. It's a trait he has inherited from his father.'

'OK . . . So . . .' The waiter hesitates and then decides his best course is simply to reprise the order. 'And that will be all?'

'Just the sommelier.'

'But here she comes.'

'Mademoiselle.'

'*Bonjour.*'

'Are you married?'

'*Excusez-moi?*'

'You speak English?'

'Yes.'

'Are you married?'

'Yes.'

'So Madame not Mademoiselle. I apologize. An easy mistake to make.'

A smile.

'We need to rescue my brother,' Ralph says. 'Which is your finest champagne?'

'*C'est une bonne question.*'

'*Les plus bonnes,*' Ralph returns. 'Forgive me, my French is terrible.'

'It depends . . . it depends on so many things.' She extends her lower lip and opens her palms. 'It's very difficult to say.'

'As so much in life. But still . . . we persevere.'

A second smile. 'Well, we have the 1996 Gosset. They are the oldest *maison* in the world.'

'And? I sense an "and"?'

'And also . . .' She speaks the name as if a prayer: 'Also the Philipponnat 1990 Clos des Goisses.'

'Which do you recommend?'

A deep sigh. 'Before 1996, I was confident that 1990 was the greatest vintage of the last century. Now . . .' she shrugs as only French women can shrug '. . . now I am not so sure. But . . .'

'But?'

'These are very exact wines, Monsieur. Beyond famous. The—'

'Money is no object. Ignore my trousers. They belong to another woman's husband. Our only concern today is to promote our immediate happiness. We have very little time. My father a few days. My brother perhaps only a few hours.'

'Well, it's a very difficult choice, sir.'

'An impossible choice?'

'Yes.'

'Ah, this so often seems to be the way . . . but perhaps it is only the illusion of choice and perhaps we must have courage.'

'*Courage.*'

'So I think . . .'

'Yes?'

'I think we'll have the '96 first. And *then* the 1990.'

THE HARD PROBLEM

'Is this a one-way street, do you think?' Ralph asks. 'Did you see any signs? Was the wine shop you saw definitely down here, Lou?'

'Yes. I think so.'

'These bastards don't like me driving against the flow. I might need to be more aggressive. Hang on back there.'

He switches on the hazards. This is an emergency. There's a belligerent-looking van up ahead. A Mercedes. The driver is gesticulating behind the wheel like he's a one-man custodian of world righteousness. But he's never dealt with my brother before.

Ralph is half on the pavement. 'Fucking kerbs,' he says.

The Mercedes is in reverse.

Dad inhales slowly. '*The Canterbury Tales*. You should read them. The pilgrimage of life. It's all there – 1392. How to live, given this. How to love, given that.'

'Dad, nobody is taking any fucking notice,' Ralph says. 'I doubt they even gave the slightest of shits at the time; why—'

'Bike! Watch that bike!'

'He's seen me.'

'Great. But let's get off the pavement,' I say.

'Not possible. Not if we're going to get where we want to go.'

'There,' I say. '*Aux Crieurs de Vin*.'

'The wine criers,' Ralph says. 'That's got to be us. OK, Lou, let's get in there and get ourselves a case of something unequivocal.' Ralph clicks the handbrake but doesn't turn off the ignition. 'Dad, you stay here. If anyone comes, explain that you're drunk and dying and tell them to take it up with your sons. Lou, bring the credit card. It's time for some monsoon drinking.'

Eva dislikes some aspects of her job. But she believes in it. She believes in justice. I admire her for that. I can't say I feel the same about database management. Maybe it's the future – and that's what my company believe – but the only people who count there are the algorithm designers. They're like gods or oracles or something. They see into the future. They design the future. They even *summon* the future. The problem is that I want to be a poet. Or a writer of some sort. But, if such a thing had ever been possible, it definitely isn't possible now. By possible, I mean: financially possible. I think when people ask if things are possible, that's what they usually mean: is it financially possible?

My family are kind enough not to bring all this up too often. But I know what they all think because – even though they seldom talk to each other – they all talk to me. As if I am the conversational catalyst. As if I'm the only one who will actually listen. As if I am a proxy for them talking to each other. As if they are all trying to advise me. Or trying to correct their own lives through me.

But life is un-correctable.

So I write everything down.

Dad says, for example, the world has been atomized by the unchecked ascendency of capitalism and 'the great meta-urging to acquire' and that the world is desperate for a new idea.

Jack says look at all the good capitalism has done.

Ralph says he has no problem with the status quo, but let's not pretend it's good news for more than fifteen per cent of the global population.

Dad says the post-war period only recently came to an end – somewhere between September 11th and the 2008 crash.

Jack says that's a little off – that actually the post-war period ends when the last of the war babies dies; by that he means Dad but doesn't admit to it. Jack thinks all the memory of empire and the colonies and the Battle of Britain is what is holding the country back; he says you cannot set a nation against modernity and globalization and hope to thrive.

Ralph says that history will see his as the digitally transitional generation; the world before and the world after; no two more different.

Dad says 'it' is all about ideas.

Ralph says 'it' is all about energy.

Jack says 'it' is all about economics.

They mean it, but they don't mean it.

Ralph says everyone is responsible for their own orgasm.

Jack says whatever any paid-for public communication claims, the exact opposite is likely to be the case.

Dad calls the magazine racks at newsagents 'wailing walls'.

Ralph says regrets rush in where once there were dreams.

Jack says it is impossible to live in London as a normal person any more.

Dad says the world contains everything – the birth of every possibility, the death of every dream, every conceivable cruelty, every conceivable kindness – all in a moment.

And I listen. I listen in ways I don't think other people do. And I write it all down. Because I want somehow to capture it, to seal it, to nail it to the wall. I want something I can point to and say, 'That was me, that was us, that was then, this is what we did and this is who we were.'

My mother says this is the writer's desire.

I won a poetry competition before she died; it was in the summer and it was such a happy day – not only for me. But I've struggled to write much of cogency or worth ever since; it's the lack of ideas, the energy costs, the bad economics. The strangest thing: I have to try not to be angry with Eva for encouraging me. Why is *that*?

My mother never once drove the van. She had a crappy little car. And I remember once when her old CD player broke and suddenly there was silence and we still had miles to go, I remember that she told me that she would have liked to have written not just poetry, but a book: a grown-up love story. Not in the traditional way, though, but between a son and his father.

We drive. We talk. Dad is asleep behind us. After we bought the wine, we flattened the seats and made the bed in the back; it seemed sensible and more comfortable. But also – now that Ralph is here – it seemed OK. Dad and I could never have made the bed in the day on our own because it would have felt too decadent, or somehow *morally* unacceptable, indicative of a wider capitulation, the 'slippery slope, Lou'. Now that Ralph is with us though, we can simply do whatever we like without all these thoughts in our heads that come from I don't know where; we're free; it's like some kind of a miracle; my brother is like some kind of an inverse redeemer.

'. . . your anger is natural,' Ralph is saying.

'Is it though?' I ask. 'Is it natural?'

'Yes. But everything that angers you about other people should lead you to a better understanding of yourself. Think about that for a second.'

I do. I'm still drunk. Conversely, wine seems to have sobered Ralph up. He's driving – responsibly, respectfully, five thousand units over the limit. Slow lane. Lots of etiquette. Mirror, signal, manoeuvre. I'm thinking that maybe we *are* doing this. That – subtly, subtly – Ralph is going to let Dad die just as surely as if he were killing him.

'Basically, Lou, human beings need meaning in their lives. They look for it in all the wrong places and don't realize until too late.'

'Cue puppetry.'

He looks over and his face softens and his eyes smile. 'There are a billion reasons not to put on a puppetry show, Lou. Sure there are. Or not to write your book. Or not to sing the song. Or not to paint the sky. That's not the point.'

'What *is* the point?'

'The point is . . . Can you overcome all of these billion reasons *not* to try to make something worthwhile with a single human act of will and do it anyway? Most people cannot. Think about that.'

I do. I think about everything.

Ralph suddenly looks over and frowns: 'Hang on a sec, Lou. Are we following the satnav?'

'Religiously.'

'You realize the fucker is now luring us in the direction of *Lure*?'

'Obey,' I say. 'Question not . . .'

We drive. Our father sleeps. There are silver trees on the verge growing at wizened angles as if we are passing through some kingdom of the old and wise – men and women who were long ago defeated and could leave no legacy but this.

The conversation becomes about parents in general. Covertly, I watch Ralph at the wheel. Like Dad, he seems happiest when he's talking about ideas but I see that his physicality is very different. The way he flicks the indicator on and off to change lanes is absurdly mannered. An elegant gesture such as a pianist might make to introduce an exceptionally beautiful passage of music. But he's not doing it for me; he's doing it for himself.

He says that the human relationship between child and parents is the most important of all, the most intimate.

'What do you mean – most intimate?' I ask.

'I mean dealing with parental death is the most private thing we ever do,' he says. 'Because the relationship goes right back to when you were a child. Your memories of that.'

'Yeah.'

'And those childhood memories are so private. All those moments – just you and your dad or just you and your mum. Nobody can share them. Your mind goes back to them. Mine does, anyway. Compared to your childhood, everything else feels constructed.'

'Does it?'

'The other kinds of love . . . With your woman, there was a decision. But with your parents, there's no choice. It's in the nature. It's in the nurture. I sometimes think that all our lives we are bracing ourselves for our parents' death.'

'You can always hate them.'

'It's actually the same thing as loving them. Read Freud. Read Jung. Read Melanie Klein. I think the satnav is taking us back onto the N19.'

'Yeah, it keeps changing its mind.'

'Or it likes detours.'

'Or hates destinations.'

The D4 becomes the D12 without telling anyone. We're silent for a while. But I need to press my brother. I need him to come into the moment. The darker side of his dignity is his distance. But I need very much to know what he really thinks.

The grey areas. That's where most people like to live.

Mum and I went to see a human brain once when I was about ten, I think. It was at this exhibition that came to London. Some mad professor had peeled a human body so that you could see everything – muscles, organs, bones, ligaments. Christ only knows how he had made a show out of this. But he had done so and hundreds of thousands went to see it.

He had put one of the organs in a special transparent display case: the brain. A brain. Straight out of some poor bastard's head.

And the thing that stayed with me is how grey it looked.

I miss my mother so very much.

Because of the 'failure' of her poetry, as she said, she retrained as a shrink. She started studying tentatively – as if unable to admit to herself she no longer wrote – but gradually she became more and more committed. She qualified as a therapist but she wished to become a full-blown psychoanalyst. She would seek out exams and attend lectures hungrily. She began to build up a small counselling practice. I didn't realize it at the time but it was a kind of renaissance for her.

A few months before she was diagnosed, she had started to read about 'the hard problem' as part of a course she was doing. That day of the exhibition, I remember asking her about it – as we were walking past a peeled human face with another uncovered brain exposed behind it: no ears, no skull. And I remember listening to her but also being powerfully aware of her spirit as she spoke, her presence. A spirit on the rise. The hard problem, Lou, she said, is to do with our thoughts. How is it that the physical processes of certain atoms assembled as they are in the human brain give rise to consciousness? Whereas the same atoms otherwise assembled everywhere else do not? Or do they? How does self-awareness emerge from the material world of molecules and matter? And what is this thing we call experience? It's funny, isn't it, how the human factor is missing despite all these body parts? I was too old to do so in public but I wanted to lean my head on her hip in order to connect with her. I wanted to ward off the oafish exhibition with her figurative sensibility.

I think my mother could have made it all the way back from her self-described failures and outrun or outflanked Dad in her later years – if she had been given the time.

The engine sound of our van is hypnotic. We talk some more and then I come out with it: 'I'm serious, Ralph,' I say.

'I'm serious, too.'

This is the word; the word we all have to play with, confront; eventually.

'Because – wait a minute – let me speak – Dad will listen to you.'

'This is about him. Not me.'

'What do *you* say though?'

'I say we are what we choose to become.'

'Wrong. He didn't choose the disease.'

'No, but he chooses how to deal with it.'

'So what do you think? Admit it: you're shocked by the state he's in.'

'I think the best thing we can do is withdraw the projection of our shadow onto others. I'm here to accompany not to discuss.'

We enter a forest of some kind. Like we're in a fairy tale all of a sudden. The darkening gloom between the trees. Pine and silence. A glimpse of something: deer, boar, goblins, nothing.

At some point, Ralph uses the word 'manipulative' about Dad again – and it manipulates me. I can feel myself becoming rebarbative but there is nothing I can do.

'. . . What do you mean?'

'I mean, the self-dramatization, Lou.'

'What the fuck?'

'Think about it, Lou. Think about it.'

'You—'

'No, wait. Think about how this is being played out.'

'How can you even say that, Ralph? How can you say "played" out? How can you turn up and just say these things?'

'All his life—'

'What do you know about *all his life*?'

'Uh-oh. Here comes the anger again. I've been – OK – OK – interrupt since—'

'I'm not interrupting. I'm asking you to . . . to . . . to . . .'

'To what, Lou?'

'To *engage*.'

PUPPETS & PROPHETS

We're calm. We're cool. We're camping.

The orange and white barrier at the entrance to the site lifts in the manner of all such campsite barriers the world over – jerkily. It's making me think about limbo. Not the dancing, but the region on the borders of hell reserved for those who died before Christ's coming. Tacitly, we three have somehow agreed: there will be no more ravening today.

'Do you remember being here before?' Dad turns back to me.

I've been asleep on the bed. The rest has done me good. We stopped off for petrol and Dad woke up – so we swapped him into the front seat since it seemed undignified for him to lie down when he was awake. But we couldn't face reassembling the back so I lay down and I have been drifting in and out of consciousness for a while listening to Dad beguile the miles by interrogating Ralph on German politics.

'I remember only trauma,' I say.

'I hear you,' Ralph chimes in from behind the wheel.

'Well, you both seemed very happy last time we were here. We stayed for five days. You and Jack – you used to go and hang around the bar and play table football and try to steal whatever drinks people left behind. And then come back thinking that I wouldn't notice the smell of dregs on your breath.'

'Maybe that's why you've become a tramp, Ralph,' I say.

'And you used to play on your bike until it went dark, Lou. And then I'd find you crouching in a bush with this Dutch boy – Jan, I think his name was – pretending to be a commando.'

'There's still time to find him, Lou,' Ralph says. 'Come out together. Big wedding in Brighton.'

The barrier has hauled itself vertical but now it seems to sway and judder as if daring us to drive beneath.

'Let's see if they've got a spot down that way,' Dad says, pointing away to the left. 'We definitely want to be by the river. Away from the *noise*.'

He starts sawing away with his arm trying to get the window down again.

'Look at that,' Ralph says, pointing up through the windscreen.

We're on a slight rise. The campsite lies in the valley below. Above the trees, the clouds are massed, bruised and purple and pregnant with a coming storm; but the sun has fallen so low in the west that one quarter of the sky is smeared in crimson and gold as if someone has turned up the page of an unimaginably beautiful tomorrow.

'We're going to be grateful we're in a van and not a tent when that shit hits,' Ralph says.

'Always,' Dad says.

'Just imagine what it must be like to holiday in a house,' I say. 'The weather must almost cease to matter.'

I must have been to about three hundred campsites in my life. And they are all subtly different – in design, in clientele, in atmosphere. But one thing they all have in common is the sense of human beings making the best of it. Why is this? If I were being cruel, I'd say it's because nobody *really* wants to be there. Not deep down. Sure, there's some people doing a good job of pretending – bikes, barbecues, badminton – but wouldn't they rather be kicking it with some hot-assed Spanish señorita in a bougainvillea-scented villa with the sea whispering at the bedroom window and the promise of cocktails on the beach at sunset with their pals? They would. Of course they would. But they have to put aside the suspicion that some more fortunate people are doing exactly that – bury it deep – and get on with loving camping.

There are exceptions: my father, for example. He chooses to camp. Loves it. In later years, he's had the money to do otherwise; but no, sir, he'd rather van his way round the Vendée – in his own time, at his own pace, a medieval church here, a Neolithic cave there, a vineyard where possible. I have never known him more relaxed than sitting at sundown in the corner of some foreign field in his big chair with some clever book, the corner of a baguette, his wine in his glass amidst the evening expirations of the warm goodwill of the Earth at the end of the day.

'Nothing has changed,' Dad says, as if this were the apogee of all accolades he might bestow.

There are tents of all shapes and colours – little grey pop-ups and huge red permanent pitches with great square plastic see-though windows. Washing lines of multi-coloured clothes are strung between the trees. There are parked cars and every kind of motorhome. Men in sensible camping clogs carry basins full of pans and cutlery towards one of the sandy-coloured washing blocks. Women are talking across the low-lying hedges that divide the sites. Boys and girls on bikes race to and from invisible appointments. Elderly couples sit side-on to watch us ease over the speed humps. We draw up slowly by the office with its familiar sign – *'l'acceuil'*.

Beyond, there is a strip where families are playing boules – or pétanque, I've never known the difference. We can hear the shouts and laughter. There's bad French pop music coming from the bar. Two overweight middle-aged men walk by on their way to what must be a pool somewhere; they are both wearing tight black trunks with matching turquoise trim. Ralph pulls up the handbrake with melodramatic emphasis.

'Behold the pastoral idyll,' he says and kills the engine.

'Look.' Dad indicates the chalk board. He's excited like a kid checking out the holiday let. 'They still do sausage and *frites*. Do you think they'll let us bring our own wine?'

'I think you're going to have to get a bit more rebellious, Dad, given that you've only got three more days or whatever,' Ralph says. 'If you want to do something . . . just do it. As they say.'

'Who says?'

'Never mind.' Ralph shakes out a cigarette.

'Why isn't the ruddy window working?' Dad asks.

'It's been broken for ages,' I say.

Ralph passes me a cigarette and the cooks' matches. 'Just say *fucking*, Dad. Why isn't the fucking window working? And then when you want to emphasize a point say . . . say "cunting". Like you used to.'

Dad looks at Ralph like he is going to say something but stops himself.

'Sound advice, Dad,' I say. 'No one says "ruddy".' I slide open the side door of the van and let in the evening air to ward off the immediate cancer.

A woman appears in the office.

'Shall I go and see if they've got a place, then?'

'*Not* in the main circle,' Dad says. 'Down by the river.'

'Pass me the credit card,' I say to Ralph, who has taken full possession.

He obliges before my father can object: 'Knock yourself out, Lou. Get all the extras. I want some of those tight trunks that those two guys were wearing. The paedo-chic Speedos.'

Dad looks round at me. His eyes are smiling. He looks almost young. This is some kind of homecoming for him.

I check my phone. The bastard is almost out of battery again.

I text Jack where we are. I text Eva: 'feeling better'.

One time back in May, Eva and I went go-karting with some of our friends. (She beat me in the race but I had the faster lap.) In the pub afterwards we had to share this awkward little table in an alcove because the place was full and the others had got there before us. There were these mock-Tudor windows and we were eating terrible fake homemade chips and scampi with those sachets of thinned-out tomato ketchup that you can't open except with your teeth and that somehow always squirt when you do – even though there is never enough actual sauce in them to warrant so outraged an initial splurge.

And she started telling me about her parents' divorce and how she thought it had made her shy and awkward except with people she knew really well. About how she felt un-comfortable a lot of the time at college and this came out as not-exactly-rudeness, but a kind of unfriendliness and abruptness, which she never meant; but that then she'd got a reputation with a few of the girls for 'taking no shit', which she had cultivated – because they'd praised her for it and had mistaken it for strength and because this persona seemed like an easier way to be when they all hung out since it saved her from explaining herself. And that this feisty persona had started to be her 'character'; but that actually it wasn't her character at all. And wasn't it strange that she'd never felt the need to twist through all these loops of defence and attack and mediation with me; that she could just be.

And that got us on to how hard it is to get a handle on your own situation and how odd it is that other people – even strangers – can sometimes see everything that you can't, or won't. And I didn't think about it then . . . but maybe this is what it means to be in love. You have to feel known. Or maybe known *and* forgiven. Which is how my mother made my father feel, I realize now. Whereas Carol did not. And all of a sudden, my mother is gone and he doesn't feel forgiven any more. And so he's trying to atone in some way.

The rain drums and flutters on the van roof. The windows are steamed up except where I have swiped a spot to try to look out at the trees and down towards the river. But I can hardly see anything – it's as if some kind of veil has been thrown over us – and all that happens is that I soak my sleeve. By way of counter-strike, we have the heater turned on all the way up, and it is whirring strenuously, but it's not really having any effect on the damp. Only in an old camper van in the rain in Europe can you ever feel too hot and too cold at the same time.

Ralph and I are sitting in the two front seats, which we have turned around. Dad is facing us across the table, settled on his pillows without being at all settled, lying side-on in the bed. I'm thinking that there's a big issue we're going to have to confront pretty soon: that either all three of us are going to have to sleep in that same bed or we're going to have to pop up the one in the roof, which we haven't done for a long time, and which (though nobody is saying it) may well cause leaks.

We've only got one cabin light on and we've lit a candle in the lantern like we're smugglers. We are studiously drinking a bottle from the case we bought in Troyes, which Ralph and Dad are talking about as if it were the second messiah. Apparently, I should have a major hard-on about it, but it tastes to me like licking jam off an old church pew. I am a little drunk again, though, and it feels good – like the rats in my stomach have stopped their gnawing and gnashing. But there's no way we can talk about the wine any more so when they shut up for a second, I interrupt. I am a master at changing the subject; another of my skills.

'So what's your new show about, Ralph?'

He sucks his teeth and sends the wine around his gums again. 'What is it about, Lou? Or what is it *about*?'

'Both,' I say to keep us moving and away from wine.

'It is about the life of Moses, a bunraku puppet, who lives on a table.'

'Right.'

'Bunraku?' Dad asks, making a face intended to convey the intense concentration of veteran taste buds.

'Japanese,' Ralph says, 'three-person operated. Cardboard.'

'And what's it about *about*?' I ask.

'God and Man,' Ralph says, matter-of-fact, but meaning it. 'The theatre of religion. The theatre of existence.'

'Right,' I say. 'Great.'

We watch Dad put his glass down with painful care.

'Why Moses?' I ask.

'Because he looked upon the face of God.'

Wine spills on Dad's bedclothes. He winces and then irritably motions with his other hand as if to say that it is the last thing in the world that matters. But I can tell he's also cross about the waste. He cannot help but count the cost. He has been deliberately asking for half measures, pretending it's about the alcohol; but really it's about his fear of not being able to control the glass.

'And what does God look like?' I ask.

'In this case,' Ralph inclines his head, 'he looks like me.'

'Of course.'

Dad hoists himself up a little with his arms and says: 'Moses probably didn't exist.'

'Correct,' Ralph says. 'Correct. And isn't *that* the point?'

I sip the sour-bench jam. 'Isn't what the point?'

'Moses is an invention of his writer,' Dad says. 'People are apt to forget that the Bible – like all the holy books – is *written*. And the one thing we know about writers is they make shit up – as you would say, Lou.'

'I don't say that.'

'Which is why,' Ralph says, gargling wine, 'Moses is perfect puppet territory.'

'Go on,' Dad says.

'Because . . . because my Moses exists only when I – the puppet master – bring him to life. But even then – only in the minds of the audience.'

'Go on,' Dad says again.

I fake a long slow-tasting sip. And it suddenly strikes me on the swallow that Dad is – has always been – desperately interested in Ralph in a way he is not interested in me; that he wants to know again and again what Ralph is thinking and what he feels; and then what he *really* thinks, what he *really* feels. He wants to understand his son and he absolutely does not do so. And he wants to know – after a lifetime – how can this be, how can this be, how can this be?

'You're right, Dad,' Ralph says. 'The Moses of the Bible probably didn't exist and yet everything about his story is so—'

'Irrelevant,' I offer.

'Substantial,' Dad says.

'— yeah, exactly, substantial. Moses writes on stone, for fuck's sake. His eyebrows get singed by the burning bush. He's probably got a cock the size of the Gherkin.'

'He is a commander of plague,' Dad adds. 'And a violent murderer of women and children.'

'Whole tribes.' Ralph leans forward a little. 'He kills and he drinks and he eats and he fucks. He's vain and conceited. He fights war after war after war.'

'And thus he dares to go up the mountain to remonstrate with God,' Dad says.

'We'd all love some face time with Mr Motherfucker,' I say.

'Louis.'

'But God is also angry with Moses,' Ralph continues.

'Of course.' Dad smiles his lopsided smile. 'Whether the Jewish God is good or bad is open to the comments section. But one thing nobody can dispute is that he is mighty – *mighty*.'

They're telling the story for my benefit, I realize. All I have to do is keep the questions coming: 'OK – so why is the Almighty so pissed off with Moses?'

'Because,' Ralph says, 'God tells Moses to go speak to a rock in order to get some water to flow out of it. But Moses is—'

'Consumed by existential incandescence,' Dad interrupts. 'He is bloody furious . . . furious that even the sheer lunatic nonsense of being alive is so glibly mocked by the total obliteration of death.'

'And so Moses thinks, bollocks to it,' Ralph continues. 'And goes beyond what God actually asks him to do; he starts having a go at everyone gathered around, putting himself centre stage, and then he strikes the rock with his staff—'

'In *direct* contravention of God's orders,' Dad adds.

'As if,' Ralph says, 'he did not believe that the mere word of God was sufficient to produce the water. As if he were God himself.'

'Hubris,' Dad nods slowly. 'Hubris. Again and again and again.'

'Right.'

'So,' Ralph sucks his lips, 'God says to Moses: OK, Plague-Boy, you can *see* the Promised Land, but there ain't no way you're going there yourself. So have a good look, breathe it in . . . And then get ready to die and don't be thinking—'

'But but but . . .' Dad is as captivated as I have seen him since we left. Ralph makes my father *live* like no one else can. 'God also says: I will bury you myself.'

'Exactly so. Right there is the deal, Lou. God buries Moses himself – personally – in an unmarked grave.' Ralph reaches for his cigarettes, hesitates, decides not to. We all fall silent and look into the vastness of whatever there is behind our eyes. When the wind gusts, the rain sounds like tarantula armies massing. I feel like some great point has been clinched but that I have no idea what it is.

'So . . . Anyway . . .' I say slowly. 'What is the show about, Ralph?'

Now Dad and Ralph look at each other and shake their heads slowly in the manner of long-suffering veterans the world over.

'Sorry,' I say. 'I need everything spelled out.'

'Lou.' Ralph turns to me. 'Lou. Think about it.'

'I am.'

'Moses exists but he does not exist. Like a puppet.'

'Right.'

'His backstory is . . . is nothing. He was cardboard, wood, glue. But in the theatre he is alive. He is wholly alive. You can't help but believe that the puppet is really there. But you know – you absolutely know – that he really isn't there, too.'

'See how the metaphors accrete,' Dad murmurs.

'Right.'

'To stay in the theatre you have to understand and believe two separate and contradictory things,' Ralph continues, 'that what you are watching is not true but also that it is true.'

'Which is religion,' Dad says, 'if only they'd admit the *not* true bit first.'

'And since Moses is not really alive, he cannot really die,' Ralph says.

I feel like I want to ask questions for ever just to make them talk.

'Do you have subtitles or somebody at the side of the show explaining all this shit to the audience?'

Ralph shakes his head wearily. 'Everything is real and unreal, Lou, true and not true, extant and not. The audience are the people. The puppet is the prophet. I am God.'

'I get that bit.'

'But the prophet doesn't exist without the God and vice versa,' Ralph says. 'And yet the audience don't want to be left on their own in the theatre. That's not what they paid for. Nope. That would be intolerable to them. There would be mayhem. They require that the puppet and I to go to work on stage. Go to work entertaining them.'

'*Distracting* them,' Dad says.

'And that is what we do . . . until, eventually, we pass through yet another wall – yet another illusion.'

'Which is?' I ask.

'Well, midway through the show, Moses turns on me – the puppet master – with a series of demands.'

'He insists on explanations,' Dad says, now speaking as if the show were as much his creation as his son's.

'Precisely. And suddenly the audience see me. They realize I have been there all along. Manipulating things. They knew this but they didn't apprehend it. Now they do. I become an actor in the drama.'

Dad exhales slowly: 'So God is only real when the puppet – the prophet – turns on him.'

'You should have been a critic, Dad.' Ralph is straight-forwardly smiling for the first time since he arrived. 'But how can my Moses live without my hand? My breath? He can't. He's made by me. He's animated by me. I am his prime and only mover. He is not alive. He doesn't exist.'

Dad points his finger. 'And how dare the prophets make demands of their God?'

'How fucking dare they,' I say.

'Louis.'

'And yet,' Ralph says, 'each night we see, we feel, how the audience urges Moses on to insurrection. The moment I reveal myself, they are with him. And they turn on me.'

'But it's an insurrection that you have created yourself,' Dad says.

'Yes.' Ralph is actually grinning. 'Yes. It is.'

'How does it end?' my father asks.

'Little by little,' Ralph says. 'I concede ground. I back up the mountain. I let the puppet come at me.'

'But how does it end?' Dad's eyes are sparkling. 'How does it end?'

Ralph raises his puppeteer's wrists, his fingers extended downward, long and tense. 'I cause my Moses to come after me. He comes after me . . . after me . . . after me. Up the mountain.'

'Then what?' Dad asks.

'I promise him a life without me. I show him the Prom-ised Land.'

'And then?'

Ralph pauses a second. Then his wrists snap down and his fingers flash apart. 'Then I give the signal and we drop the little fucker right where we are standing, centre stage, in the spotlight. And we walk away. And suddenly he is nothing. Nothing. Cardboard and glue. No thing.'

'It's perfect,' Dad breathes.

'And you know the best bit of all: that the audience clap. They clap like crazy. Every night. And what are they clapping, I ask myself.'

'What *are* they clapping?' I prompt.

'They are clapping the summary death of their prophet – killed by a mighty and disdainful God. Again. Every fucking night.'

'Amazing,' I say.

'But there's another level,' Ralph says, 'because now they know – or now they *remember* – as I take my bow – that I am, in fact, human.'

'Surely not.'

'A puppeteer – yes – but one of them. A human being. And so they are also clapping because they are elated and happy and deeply *impressed* that I made the whole thing up. A show. A fiction. About Gods and Prophets. Art. Magic. Religion. Made up by a human being just like them.'

For a moment I think Ralph is going to bow and I feel the strange urge to clap myself.

'I wish . . .' Dad lies back against his pillows. 'I wish that I had seen it, Ralph.'

The rain is falling harder now. And the mist seems to have closed us off from the world. But it's less damp at last and my shirt is drying. The candlelight dilates in the lantern.

'I'm opening another bottle.' Ralph starts fidgeting about under the table where we have stored the case.

'Not for me,' Dad says. He's leaning on the side of the van where he's re-set his pillows. His face is sagging a little more. He's suddenly tired. He's spent his energy too fast in the conversation. He asks: 'What are you going to do next?'

Ralph has the bottle out and is admiring the label as if it were hand-written Tolstoy. 'The Life of Abraham,' he says.

'How long . . .' Dad asks. 'How long does it take to get another show up and running?'

'Six months . . . six months minimum.'

Dad is silent.

'What did Abraham do?' I ask.

'God asked him to kill his son.'

'And what did Abraham say?'

Ralph's eyes flick up as he winds in the corkscrew. 'He said – yes.'

'Jesus.' I let out a low breath.

'Took his only son, Isaac, up the mountain early one morning, built an altar out of firewood, tied his boy to it, got out his sharpest camping knife and was all set to plunge it into the boy's little heart when God announced that he was "just kidding".'

'This is the father of all the major religions?' I ask.

'One and the same.'

'And how did the son – Isaac – how did he feel about his dad and God and everything when he got up off that altar?'

'The Bible doesn't record, Lou. Only mentions the village where they stayed that night.'

'Jesus.'

'Jesus – exactly.' Dad is slurring a little now. 'And – lest we forget, Jesus is supposed to be God's *actual* son. Remember.

He loved the world so much that he gave his only son. Thus trumping the other prophets by actually conceiving his only child on Earth solely for the purpose of killing him. In full public view, of course.'

The cork pops. Ralph holds it to his nose. 'What other conclusion can we come to, Lou, but that in all the major Abrahamic religions you prove love by death? Specifically, if you can, by killing your children with maximum publicity. That's the winner. Though martyrdom is a close second.'

'You should let it breathe, Ralph,' Dad murmurs.

'Death cults,' Ralph says. 'Me, I prefer the Epicureans. Lou – pass your glass.'

'You should let it breathe, Ralph.' Dad lies down. He is deeply tired. 'Let it breathe.'

'No time,' Ralph says. 'No time for that.'

I watch Ralph pour. His pale-blue eyes are so very full of intelligence and life. I wonder if he will ever stop drinking and smoking and what he would be like without the intoxication. Suddenly, I have the thought that he, too, is killing himself. Only a little slower. He watches the wine like Faustus watches the clock.

'Or you might say,' he says, 'you *might* say that Jesus was an elective suicide. Since he knew exactly what he was doing when he rode into Jerusalem on the back of that poor little donkey. Or so we're led to believe . . .'

Dad settles his head; his eyes are closing. We drink in silence. But there's some kind of horrible slow-motion prefiguration in witnessing Dad fall asleep. And I'm thinking that maybe Ralph and I should go out into the rain and smoke one last cigarette. But it has been getting windier and more stormy.

Ralph is slumped back. 'Don't you see what he's doing?' he whispers.

'What? What are you talking about?'

'Come on, Lou.' Ralph picks up his glass. 'What do you *think* he is doing?'

I try to keep my voice low. 'Dying slowly from a horrific and debilitating disease that . . . that . . .'

'Yes. But.'

'But *what*, Ralph?' I hiss.

My brother looks at me directly. 'He's putting it all on to you, Lou.'

Our living father is just there in front of us – his breath noisy where it fights its way in and noisy where it fights its way out.

'What do you mean?'

'He's putting it all on to you, Lou.'

The rats are alive again and afloat in the wine.

'What do you mean by that?'

'Don't get shirty.'

I'm trying not to raise my voice. 'Well fuck off then.'

'I mean he's putting it all on you. He keeps saying you can stop it any time you want to, right? And that's he's fine with that. That's what he keeps saying. Like it's *your* decision.'

I am staring at Ralph. He meets me with steady eyes.

'It's like *you* have got the disease, Lou. It's like you have got to decide. He's been abdicating responsibility for all of this and putting it on to you. No. Don't make that face. That's why you were so cross in Troyes. And that's why you're angry now.'

'No, I'm angry with *you*.'

'Think about it for one second – no, wait – effectively,

he's saying that you have to decide. Is his life worth living? Are you going to make it so? Is there any reason for him to carry on?' Ralph's voice is low and conspiratorial. 'Because he hasn't really decided at all. Instead, he's given you the choice of being either his torturer if you say "no – stay in London until the end"; or his executioner if you say "yes – Switzerland". And actually – actually what this is really doing is . . . is . . . is killing you. His son. This is all killing you.'

'No.' I'm hissing because I'm after the bastard now. 'You can't rock up here and just . . . say shit like you know shit. You haven't seen him for three months! While you've been cocking around with your fucking puppets, I've had to look after him.' My voice is rising but I can't stop it. 'You weren't there. You have not been there for *any* of this. We've seen the psychologists and doctors and the people who actually have this terrible dis—'

'You're angry because it's true.'

I am almost shouting. 'You were *not there*. Do you know what one of the poor fuckers in the home said to us?'

'Not relevant.'

'Get me out of this box. That's what he said, Ralph – lying in a bed with shit dribbling out his fucking backside unable to' – the rain is banging loudly now – 'unable to feed himself. And it's going to be *me* who looks after Dad. Me. I am the one who is going to be at that fucking home every fucking day until the terrible fucking end. Not you. Not Jack. Me. And I am not going to—'

Dad is suddenly shouting above me: 'I think there's some-one out there.' He's trying to raise himself. 'There's someone out there.' For a second, he looks bewildered, frightened. 'There's somebody knocking on the door.'

I'm looking right into Ralph's eyes and he's holding my gaze like he'll never look away.

'You're right, Dad,' he says, quietly, and without breaking. 'There's a madman on the loose.'

I turn, full of fury, and in a second I yank the handle and slam open the slide door and the night comes rushing in like we're sure to be shipwrecked for ever. And standing there in the rain with cabin baggage only is Jack.

My father has tears leaking down his face, from the disease, from the emotions, I don't know. He's drunk and exhausted and all he is saying is: 'Jack, my Jack, my little Jack.' And Jack, my brother, leans into the tight steamed-up space that we're down to as a family, his jacket shrunken and soaking, his auburn hair streaming wet, blinking back the rain while his eyes go out to us one by one. And on his face there breaks the widest grin.

'My Jack. You made it. My little Jack. You made it. We're all here.'

Jack reaches in to return our father's embrace and the trees behind him sway, frightening and mighty, as water is thrown down from the pressuring sky.

'We're all here,' Dad says, 'we're all here.'

'Some parties you just have to get to,' Jack says, 'no matter what.' He straightens up and stuffs his ludicrous cabin bag under the table because there's nowhere else to put it and takes off his muddy shoes and tries to stash them too – all in a second – before he clambers up onto the bed beside Dad because there's nowhere else to go and I grab the door handle behind him and slide it shut with a slam-clunk.

'Hi, Dad,' Jack says. He is grave and warm and funny and serious, as only he can be. 'Great spot. Great weather. Great accommodation. Surprised it's not busier.'

'Don't mind me,' Dad says, indicating his tears. 'It's the bloody disease.' He shakes his head. 'That – and because I'm so bloody glad to see you.'

'Wow. What's with the language? What's happening here?'

'Don't panic,' Ralph says. 'The ladies haven't arrived yet. We're expecting considerable numbers. And we saved you a big bucket of cocaine. Lou's made some nibbles. We've got handcuffs, candles, blindfolds, everything. We're only getting started. All will be well.'

'Hello, mate.' Jack's smile is like everything that you'd hope for in two boys who shared a placenta and he reaches all the way across the table with his arm and pulls Ralph towards him and their foreheads touch and they hold it there and I am thinking that there's nobody on the whole planet who can cross the barbed-wire no-man's-land that surrounds Ralph like that.

'Lou. I made it.' Jack turns to me. 'You, my bro, are the bollocks of the dog.' He takes me by both shoulders and kisses me on the nose and I feel the rain on the bristles of his chin where it touches my lips. 'I'm so sorry I'm late. I don't know what I was thinking. But I'm here now.'

'Well, thank fuck,' I say.

Jack's eyebrows go up. 'Seriously, what has happened to this family's language?'

'We are all here,' Dad says. 'That's the main thing.'

'We've joined the Devil's party, brother,' Ralph says. 'We're on the other side, now. We've had enough of God.

We've decided he's an infantile civil servant and that he doesn't deserve any more time or attention.'

Dad is using his duvet to wipe his tears. 'We've got wine open,' he says. 'Château Pichon-Longueville Comtesse de Lalande.'

'I've got some champagne,' Ralph says. 'We could open that. Thierry Rodez – it's the little-known first choice of all the other houses. A thing of great beauty.'

'Boys, if it's alcoholic, then I'm going to drink it,' Jack says. 'Oh man, I am so tired. I am so tired. I could sleep for nine days.'

He takes off his disfigured jacket and Ralph reaches for it. 'Let me hang it on the back of my chair,' he says, 'the heater will dry it.'

We watch Jack push the water from his forehead with his palm. His shirt is soaked in dark v-shaped patches, and clings to his torso. He's come straight from work.

'So, Dad,' he says, 'what are we doing here?'

Dad shakes his head. 'Tomorrow, tomorrow. Let's talk tomorrow tomorrow. Here, have my glass.'

'What about you?'

'No, no. I have had plenty.'

Ralph pours Jack some wine.

'No children.' Jack grins and raises a toast. 'That's the main thing. No children tomorrow morning.' He takes a long sip and then he just nods. 'You know I'd sleep in an Albanian shittery if you could promise me that there won't be any children for a few hours in the morning.'

'The finish. Wait for the finish,' Ralph urges.

'We're all here,' Dad says, again. His eyes are shining and he's sitting up and leaning forward.

'Tastes like wine,' Jack says, then concedes, but more to Dad than to Ralph. 'Fine wine. Which I love.' Then he grins again.

My dad's face is a smile and a collapse and a recovery. 'I remember when you two boys were two or three – you would race every morning to get dressed and whoever won would come bursting into my room at six in the morning – every bloody morning – and start shouting, "beat", "beat", "beat". And it would take me thirty minutes to stop you fighting.'

'Jesus,' Jack says. 'Not sure I can get used to you swearing again, Dad.'

Dad hesitates then he raises a fist like this is a fight or a revolution. 'Existential outrage,' he says. 'Existential incandescence.'

We hit the sweet spot. We talk for an hour. The rain softens until it whispers and flutters like bats trapped in a coffin.

'And so what is the plan?' Jack asks.

'Switzerland then home,' Ralph says. 'That's the itinerary as it stands. But we're open to fresh input.'

'Jesus,' I say.

'That's not happening,' Jack says, firm, calm, cool, sure.

So now we all drink. Dad reaches out his hand. I pass him my glass. He drinks, too. We're probably alcoholics as well as hypocrites and liars and all the rest.

Jack breathes in the quiet. His eyes go round again – Dad, then Ralph, and then settling on me. 'I meant,' he says quietly, 'what is the plan sleeping-wise? What is happening sleeping-wise?'

'Oh. Oh. *Sleeping*-wise,' Ralph says. 'Well, Dad is in the bed. Me and you in the roof. Lou's going to sleep under the van and get up early to make our breakfast. He's promised St Jacques wrapped in bacon. He's going to set out in a minute to source them.'

'Don't use "source" as a verb,' Dad murmurs.

'Actually, I'm going to find a hotel,' I say. 'And in the morning I'm going to fly to San Francisco to live with a woman who really understands me. And then I might paint portraits of men in the Meatpacking District who look like Old Testament prophets.'

'What's happened to your hair, Lou?' Jack asks.

'Fuck you.'

'The Meatpacking District is in New York, Lou,' Ralph says. 'You mean the Tenderloin. The Tenderloin is San Francisco.'

'And fuck you.'

'I'm afraid fornication is off the menu tonight, boys,' Dad says.

'Which realization . . .' Ralph upends his glass and sets it down on the table '. . . is always the most disappointing moment at any party.'

'We're simply all going to sleep here,' Dad says. 'We're going to sleep right here – in this van – together.'

'I want to sleep so long that I wake up in another season,' Jack says.

'Just so you know, Lou and Jack,' Ralph says, 'I'd like my last few nights on Earth to be exactly like this: an unfashionable van, intensifying mud, and the unspoken promise of incest.'

'Don't worry,' I say, 'I've got condoms.'

'Good,' Jack says. 'Because I definitely do not want to get anyone pregnant. The consequences . . . you would not believe the *consequences* of pregnancy.'

'Oh, I would,' Ralph says.

'Let's do this,' I say.

I stand with my brothers in the cramped space so as to loosen the catches that raise the roof.

'Anti-clockwise to undo,' Dad says.

PART THREE

PORTRAIT OF HIS SONS

MONSTERS OF THE DEEP

The grass is wet through my toes and the trees are dripping heavily with the echo of the rain and the morning air is fresh and tastes of the low cloud that has passed through the woods and valleys of all those Puss-in-boots kingdoms of central Europe. I put on my flip-flops and stand a while looking down towards the river where the mist is still curling gentle-fingered through the trees. After the storm, the morning's stillness has a near-mystical quality of intensity.

The van door slides noisily open behind me. Jack steps stolidly out in his pale striped pyjamas and brown brogues. He has a clean towel over his shoulder and a drawstring bag of fresh clothes. I can tell from the way he is looking about himself that the careless beauty of our morning glade strikes him, too. There's a turquoise Frisbee lying in the longer grass by the hedge that separates one camping plot from another. I walk over and pick it up for no reason.

'When we wipe ourselves out,' I say, 'this is the kind of shit that they'll find. Like we find dinosaur bones. Assuming life ever starts again.'

'Too big a universe to be just us, Baby Lou.' Jack raises his eyebrows and we're standing there for a moment as though actually it *is* just us. Birds swoop and dart and flit from tree to tree, staying low as if confused by the fallen sky.

'Have the boys got a Frisbee?'

225

'No.' He parts finger and thumb to massage his hairline.

'I'll put it in the van for them.' I lean it against the back tyre. Something feels different. Then I realize that this is my first future thought since I left London. Now that Jack is here, some kind of energy has changed direction because it feels as though we definitely can't be driving to Zurich; something new is being incubated.

I walk over to the trees where he is standing and say: 'If you want him to change his mind, you're gonna have to leave the religious stuff out of it.'

'You sound like you think he's changing his mind?'

I can't help but come across angry-defeated. 'I don't know. Ralph . . .'

'Ralph changed his mind for him?'

'Dad started talking to Ralph like he hadn't made up his mind at all. Ralph's refusing to engage. I don't know.'

'You don't *have* to know, Baby Lou.' Jack smiles. 'All for one and one for all. The three of us. Remember we used to say that when you were little? We'll sort this out.'

A scarlet butterfly hovers undecided in a bed of ivory flowers that somebody must have planted with the last of the summer in mind since they're blooming crazy only now in September.

'So what are you going to do?'

'Talk to him.'

The van door is sliding again. I'm wondering if Ralph is actually helping Dad in there.

'He thinks you've gone Catholic.'

'I haven't. I'm a secret druid. But all this bluff-calling is not—'

'It's not bluff-calling. He's dying, Jack.'

'Good morning, soldiers!' Ralph hails us, bent-backed in the frame of the doorway which cannot contain him. He jumps down as if to parachute the eighteen inches to the ground and lands on both feet, standing square in his boots, his borrowed jogging bottoms and Dad's epic shirt, which is long, un-tucked and without cuff-links so that only the fingertips are visible beneath the ends of his sleeves.

He calls across: 'The long march starts today.'

'The long march was a retreat,' Jack calls back.

'Precisely.' Ralph comes over, inhaling the world and smiling like a spy at the gladdening innocence of civilians. 'What other course do we have, comrades? Are we not incalculably defeated?'

'Interesting shirt,' Jack says.

'Interesting pyjamas,' Ralph returns. 'Morning, Lou – want to go find a lap-dancing club and drop some acid? Take the day by surprise?'

I shake my head slowly and walk back to the van. Dad is sitting on the edge of the bed, looking out at the trees. He needs my help to climb down off the back bed. I gather our wash things, give him his stick and stand still as he sits on the step and hauls himself to his feet.

'It's like the beginning of the world here, Lou,' he says.

The others walk back. I slam the van door shut, too violently. Water sprays in a dying arc. As one, my family look at me like I'm precisely the kind of prick they have devoted their lives to not getting to know.

Ralph shakes out a cigarette. 'I think Lou's trying to tell us something. The van doesn't matter – is that what you're trying to tell us, Lou?'

'Do they have personality transplants in Berlin yet?'

'They have everything.'

'Book yourself in. Ask for the opposite.'

'I'm just saying: without that door, Dad might fall out and die.'

'Don't "just say".'

'Not that we're going anywhere *near* Dignitas,' Jack says, smiling. 'Are we, people?'

Silence.

'We'll talk after.' Dad grimaces.

'After what?' Ralph asks.

'Jesus,' I say again.

'After we're washed and dressed and we've had some breakfast. They sell croissants at the shop – superb ones if I remember rightly. The boulanger comes every morning. What's the jam situation, Lou?'

'We're good.' I offer Dad my shoulder. 'I bought Morello cherry backup.'

Ralph is suddenly concerned: 'No damson?'

Dad holds up a don't-panic hand: 'The damson is already open.'

Ralph relaxes. 'What tea are we on?'

'Darjeeling,' I say. 'Jungpana. First Flush.'

'Been keeping Lou and me going,' Dad says. 'They also do *pain aux raisins*.'

'What about *pain aux raison d'être*?' Ralph asks. 'I think that's what we need.'

Jack is standing, looking from one to another of us as if he simply cannot believe what kind of delusional assholes he's got to deal with. 'Just so we're all clear,' he says. 'We *are* going to talk about this – and properly. I have not lied to my employers and paid Lufthansa three million pounds to watch you three coax your minimal genitalia through a tepid shower and then ram yourselves with croissants.'

'Shall we make a start?' Dad says. 'The sooner we get there, the better the chance we have of hot water.'

'It's what our genitals would want,' Ralph says.

I offer Dad my shoulder. We shuffle forward.

'I've got hot-water tokens,' I say. 'The showers are token-operated. So at least the hotness is guaranteed.'

'Genital delirium.' Ralph sighs.

'Good name for a band,' I say.

Jack shakes his head and exhales slowly.

We fall into slow raggle-taggle step together – Ralph on our right, Jack on our left. I'm thinking that Dad won't be able to walk at all within the next few weeks. Maybe less. I have the feeling that the disease is accelerating. (Fits and starts – so our consultant said.) Or it might be that because this bit is so physically noticeable, it *feels* like it is accelerating. Either way, I'm thinking that this walk to the showers is a long way for Dad now and it's going to cost him.

I slow it up and struggle a fraction more, as if I want to make some kind of a point; like now that Jack is finally here, he can *face the fuck up*. I get the vague feeling this is what Dad is doing, too, but it could be just my imagination. I can feel that the MND is registering, though, and that my brothers are backing up or off or down or something; that they are now having to take account of this disease, however they feel about everything else.

Meanwhile, all around, people are making chatty virtue of their necessary morning camp tasks. A young boy and a girl are riding the speed bumps on their bikes and doing wheelies – the boy's front wheel veering wildly as he holds it up off the tarmac in a deliberate display of casual mastery. I'm worried that if he loses control Dad won't be able to get out of the way fast enough. So we stop and let him by – so much motion and energy and boisterous, carefree risk.

We struggle on.

On Dad's instructions, we have camped at the furthest remove. The thing is that Dad loves to be with the real people, but he also wants to be away from them, on the edges. Sure, he wants to be hailing his fellow man in the bakery queue every morning; and sure, he wants to be jauntily joining the tables at the camp bar in the evening; but always after having walked in from the furthest field, which is where he wants to sleep, to work, to rest, to be. Now, of course, it's madness to be this far out.

Close by the washing block, an elderly man and a woman are conspicuously partaking of an immaculately prepared breakfast on newly varnished decking beneath a taut canvas awning. They watch us go by, unashamedly staring. Dad stops, grateful of the rest, waves his stick and asks them if the boulanger is 'on site' – like it's the big event of the day – and like this is a great holiday we're all having here together – but they're unable or unwilling to hear the humour in his tone. Ralph asks them in German if they know where he might pick up some caviar for his blini. Jack tries French. But either they are deaf to all languages save one that we don't know or they're simply unprepared to deal any longer with the world as it presents itself.

We're on the steps up to the block when we see the bird.

It's some kind of pigeon and it's just lying there to one side; grey-to-charcoal tail feathers fanned out, white back, mottled wings folded in, black neck, head turned flat against the concrete so that its slightly parted beak is somehow smiling while its yellow-ringed eye stares black and empty at our feet; dead.

We've all stopped. I have the urge to kick it away. I can tell Dad is looking at it too. It doesn't seem to have been injured or wounded – simply dropped down dead. And the more unmoving it is, the more we're thinking about how much it must have moved every second of its life – bobbing, pecking, flying, flapping, squabbling, hopping.

But not now.

Now, it is so very dead; and there's nothing moving at all save for where a very slight wind disturbs the feathers and a drip of rain from the trees above runs off its head in a gross parody of a tear. I start to imagine the flavour of death in my mouth – as if I have to eat the corrupting flesh; I can taste slimy cold rotten meat churning with dirty feather. I'm going to be sick.

Jack speaks softly: 'Let me help you up the step, Dad, and let's go and have a hot shower. We'll all feel better and then we can sit in the van and have some decent tea.'

I leave them on the steps and run to the furthest cubicle and smash open the door and retch. But nothing comes up.

'I would say . . .' Ralph begins to unbutton his dress shirt. 'I would say that the decision has already been made.' He gestures to the room, the company. 'I think it's . . . I think it's Zurich here we come.'

I have Dad's Crocs off and I'm helping him hold his legs up so that he doesn't get his socks wet. I have to fight the urge to look away. His feet smell strongly of a long day and a long night. We're in the communal showers. There are three big old-fashioned rose-heads down either side with plastic chairs at the end and one of those pale tiled floors with little raised square bumps that remind me of the public baths where Dad took me to learn to swim after school one bleak midwinter when England was perpetually dark and the wind like a pumice stone.

'I don't think that a *serious* decision has been made yet,' Jack says.

I have to consciously unclench my teeth. The word 'serious' makes me want to join Ralph in his mutiny or refusal or whatever it is. I'm furious with Jack, the same as I was furious with Ralph – for his turning up like this and having opinions. But now I notice I'm feeling this new extra thing: somewhere between afraid and *embarrassed*. Because, in a way, Jack is worse than Ralph. He won't back down or let up. Or he's the opposite of Ralph: once he's engaged, then he's *all* engagement and there's no obliqueness or subtlety. For Ralph the world is a joke; for Jack it is a test. The problem is that if one thing starts for us, then everything starts and then we're going to be falling and we won't be able to stop – all the way down to why Jack is like he is, and why Ralph is like he is, and their mother, and my mother, and Dad and the whole unholy shit storm.

'I don't think we know what this really means.' Jack says, evenly. 'The implications – for all of us. But – like I say – we can talk in the van. And we *are* going to talk, Dad, or else you're going to be on your own.'

And that's when Dad just comes out with it – loud and

spitting – as if he's angry with not only us, but with every-thing that has happened in the world since the Berlin Wall came down: 'I am happy to talk, Jack. I want to talk. Believe me. But, Jack: we *are* going to Zurich. I have an appointment – a *consultation* – tomorrow afternoon at two. The doctor sees me – assesses me. I get the prescription. And if—'

'Dad,' Jack cuts in.

'Believe me, Jack, I don't want to be a bloody burden to you now any more than I want to be a bloody burden to you in London. But I—'

'Dad—'

'Burden!' Dad raises his voice: 'Burden. Burden! Burden! I even hate the bloody awful clichéd vocabulary.'

'You don't—'

'*Burden!*' He shouts the word loud so that it echoes off the tiles and ricochets around the room.

I don't know where to look. I've not witnessed his fury – or not his fury loud and overt – not once in eighteen months. Is this what Jack summons up? Nobody speaks. I can feel my brothers' anger contending with their reason.

Dad pulls himself back. 'But I'm too much of a coward to . . . to stage an amateur suicide and so—'

'Dad,' Jack interrupts again.

'The law being the ass it is, I have to do it with one of you.'

'I'm not—'

'*Has* to be family, Jack.' Dad cuts the air with his hand. 'Bloody has to be.' The effort again – to control himself; his face slack and then tense, slack and then tense; the struggle. 'Or the carer faces prosecution. Stupid bloody law. Of course, I could have asked just Lou. But that didn't seem fair or right either. If it's one of you, it's got to be all of you.' His voice becomes embittered with sarcasm: 'Or those of you who *wanted* to come.'

'Dad—'

'I'm bloody dying.' The echoes are like bars that imprison us. 'I'm bloody dying!'

'Dad—'

'I'm bloody dying. And let me tell you boys: it's as real and as shitty as it comes.'

'Nobody is saying—'

'I realize I'm not the first. And I certainly won't be the last.' Dad tries to smile but it comes off as a leer. 'I don't *want* to die. Of course I bloody don't. But that's not how death works, boys – is it?' The cheap plastic chair legs scrape on the little bumps of the tiles as he shifts his weight. 'The main thing is I'm not in any pain. And believe me – that is great news. Great news. Tomorrow, we'll be in—'

'But—' Jack tries to come in again.

'What I want . . .' Dad cuts him off regardless, 'what I want, Jack – is that we stay like this together and we carry on talking about whatever we're talking about. Silly, serious – it doesn't matter.' Drool spools from my father's lips. 'When you're . . . When you're *ill* like this . . . You realize that being human is a physical thing. All the other stuff is on top or beside the point. You're my bloody sons. So what matters now, boys, is your physical company. Being together. Let's do some things together. Together. We're all here. But mark these words: we *are* going to get to Zurich.'

He looks round at us with eyes that you'd be mad to doubt.

Nobody can speak or move.

I'm thinking Jack is going to leave – for ever maybe – but just then some poor half-Chinese kid sticks his head through the swing doors and sees an old man (semi-naked) sat on a plastic throne with a young man (semi-naked) on his knees in front of him while two middle-aged men (semi-naked) look on from either side – all four persons are gooseflesh-cold and yet seemingly without any plans to go, stay or even shower. The kid takes this in, thinks better of it, then ducks away to some other future where none of these people will ever matter. I want to go with him.

Jack hangs up his towel and balances his wash bag pre-cariously on the same peg. Then he asks: 'Can you stand up to wash, Dad?'

I feel I must intercede on my father's behalf: 'He can stand if he holds on . . . One of the main dangers with MND is actually from falls. Especially at the transitional stage – which is pretty much now.'

'Transitional?' Jack asks.

The sickest shit is rising in my mind: that – yes – I want it to be only me and Dad again. Like it was before – when we were on the ferry or tasting that wine. Everything is twisted and cauterized inside of me now. But somehow I glance around with this serenely earnest face, like I'm Student Carer of the Year, and say: 'A lot of people with the disease divide their remaining time up into three sections: walking, wheel-chair, bedbound. Transitions are the cusp periods in between. Dad is at the cusp between one and two.'

'I can still stand,' Dad says. 'As long as I can hold on to something.'

'Tokens, Louis, tokens,' Ralph says. 'Or we shall soon be a genitalia-free family.'

I reach up and put my hand into the baggy pockets of my shorts where they are hanging on my peg behind. But somehow, when I pull out the fiddly little ridged bronze discs, one of them slips through my fingers, drops to the floor and then rolls away with a tinny tinkle – in slow motion – down the slight slope of the floor straight into the wide vents of the drain.

I am down on my knees and fiddling with the grille, my fingers unable quite to pinch back the bronze disc that I can see glinting in the narrow channel of grey murk.

'You can share my shower,' Dad offers.

'Or mine,' Ralph says.

'I might be able to get it back,' I say over my shoulder.

'Lou,' Jack says. 'Don't worry about it, I'll get you another one.'

My knees hurt from the ridges in the tiles. I am cold and naked and shivery and I can feel hot tears rising inside me and I know I have less than two breaths to stop them.

'I can't get it,' I say, 'I can't get it.'

'Pass me my wash bag,' Dad says, softly.

He's giving me something to do, I realize; a distraction; like you distract a child. I stand up and turn to him.

'Open it up.'

'Why?'

And now he's smiling like we're all set, like we're all totally fine and he is all kindness and no gnarl, no wrath.

'Because there are some tokens in the bottom, Lou.'

'You're kidding?'

'No.'

I rummage through the crap in the ancient black wash

bag. Ralph and Jack are watching like this is a magic trick decades in the execution.

'I'm not sure if they are from this exact campsite,' Dad says. 'But they might be. They all use more or less the same system. I've had them for twenty years in there – just waiting for the moment.'

My fingers find the little discs down in the corner at the bottom amidst dried toothpaste and unknown pills burst from forgotten blister packs. I hold them up like miniature gold medals. 'Here we go – two more.'

Dad looks from one to other of us and does this big stage wink. 'Because ye know neither the hour nor the day,' he says.

And it's some kind of supreme triumph. And fuck knows why but we're all grinning. Because everything is somehow trumped by this. Like these tokens are tokens of our communal story and Dad has been keeping them – all but forgotten – until now.

I hand them out and Ralph slides his into the slot and hits the push tap and immediately a geyser of hot water gushes down. He tilts back his head.

I haul Dad to his feet. I get this sense that everything inside me has realigned again – as if around some new magnetic force – and that force is to do with my dad's bravery, his courage, the way he has not once pitied himself.

'Let's get your trousers off, Dad,' I say.

Dad holds my shoulder as he steps out of his paisley specials.

'I'll do it,' I say to Jack. 'You go and have your shower. Dad can hold on to the pipes . . . or me.'

Jack nods like he's honouring that I'm the one who has been looking after Dad. He stands beside Ralph and inserts his token and a second geyser begins.

And suddenly the cold echo-chamber is gone and now the place feels alive with rising steam and falling water like a room in one of those grand old neo-classical bath houses that Dad used to take us to sometimes when we were in Germany. Already it feels warmer: warm mists billow and curl out of the long narrow windows at the top and it's soothing and delicious and like we're meant to be here. And something else: the fury is draining away because Dad says we're going to Zurich. Which makes me feel better; *happier*.

But I underestimate Jack.

Or I don't understand what kindness is.

Or I forget that he is my father's son.

Or maybe we've been baptized and born again.

Because now in all the warmth and soap and spray, Jack starts up and his voice is somehow loud and clear enough to cut through the patter and gush.

'Dad, I know you think that the religious stuff with the boys' school has changed me,' he says, the shower streaming off him. 'But I want you to know that it definitely hasn't. It's just . . . I see all this in a different way.'

'Go on,' Dad says – like now he's vented his fury, everyone can say what they want and you never saw a more reasonable and open family.

Jack has this mini Mint Source shampoo which he's tipping into the palm of his hand.

'Do you remember when the boys got twin-to-twin syndrome?'

'Yes,' Dad says. 'Of course I do.' His grip on my shoulder

tightens and I can tell he's greedy now for Jack in the way he was greedy for Ralph – as though he's suddenly realized he doesn't understand Jack either and he wants urgently to hear him speak.

'Well, we were at St Thomas's for the twenty-week scan and the doctor says, "Go now – straight away – to King's Hospital. The foetuses are going to die in the womb." And so we get in a cab and go straight to the wrong hospital because we are so freaked out.'

'I remember,' Dad says.

I glance at Ralph. He is lolling his head from side to side as if he's listening to music only he can hear, all the while his eyes fixed on Jack.

'So then we get to the right hospital three hours later and this professor takes us into this tiny room and she says, "OK, Mr and Mrs Lasker, this is a seriously complicated pregnancy. Unfortunately, you have what we call twin-to-twin transfusion syndrome. It's quite common when the placenta is shared. But, basically, they are both likely to die in the next two or three days."'

Jack is massaging his hair. Half the time he's got his eyes closed as he speaks.

'The professor says, "I am the only person in the country that can do the operation to save them. We pioneered the treatment at this hospital. But I have to tell you there's only a thirty per cent chance of both surviving and they definitely won't go to term. So your choices are – one – to let nature run its course and maybe – just maybe – one will survive. Or – two – to terminate the pregnancy. Or – three – I go into the womb with a laser gun and try and ablate the connecting vessels in the placenta that are causing the problem. The chances of both dying are about a third, the chances of one dying are about a third, the chances of them both living are also about a third."'

Jack stands on one leg to wash his foot. 'The professor says that as well as that, there are several risks involved in performing such an operation *in utero* – for the mother and for both foetuses. "I can't tell you what damage has already been done," she says.' Jack switches legs. 'You'd be completely within the normal parameters of what we deal with here if you decide the risks are too great and you want to terminate. The risks *are* too great. But if you do want to go ahead, we'll do the operation tomorrow. Have a think and then tell me what you want to do. I'll wait out here for your decision.'

Ralph's token has run out. Jack is letting the water rinse his body free of soap. His stomach is convex where Ralph's is concave.

'So . . . so we said . . . We said we would risk it. We had to choose and we chose a shot at life – life for both of them. Why?'

Jack's water stops. Ralph is covered in un-rinsed soap. Dad and I are side by side. Our shower turns itself off as abruptly as it started. So now we're all four of us standing there in the echoing silence again.

'Why?' Jack asks again, his voice suddenly quiet and intimate.

'Go on,' Ralph says.

'Because . . . because life is a miracle. A totally inexplicable miracle. Not in a religious sense. No. But in the sense of how the fuck did it get started at all? In the womb. On Earth. In the sense of it might not be happening anywhere else in the universe. We don't know and we don't understand. In fact . . . I don't have to tell you this . . . but . . . but life might be the only true miracle, the greatest mystery. And so . . . you know what? Even if you've only got ten more breaths left to draw, you should . . . you should suck in every single one of them. Because *not* to do so is an insult. Against life itself. Which is the greatest privilege. This miracle. This . . . This all we have.'

'Go on,' Ralph says, again.

'And – what you're doing now, Dad . . . This is turning yourself against creation . . . You're not like that. You're not. We are optimists in this family. We're curious. We're engaged. We choose life. Don't we?'

Jacks looks from one to other of us.

All my hostility has been washed away and I'm lost with these people.

'We're going to need more tokens,' Ralph says, quietly.

THE FACE OF A GHOST

The broken arch of the branches still drip the storm. Jack is helping Dad walk back to the van. On either side of the track, the organized and the determined are making their plans for the day. I have to wait and halt myself continually. I hadn't realized how slow it felt when out from under my father's shoulder. Ralph walks ahead, turns, smokes, looks at the sky, watches us, falls back into step. I stand sideways on, waiting. I catch Jack's eyes but they flick away as if he is not concerned to deal with me any more. Abruptly, I feel as though I've been helping Dad to his death – physically helping him – and that Jack has stepped in to take him in the opposite direction. I feel that I am wrong or worse than wrong, and that my brother – my persistent, noble, undauntable brother – is right and his rightness and his character is a mercy to us all.

'You used to say . . .' Jack speaks softly and then stops as they ease across a speed bump. Neither can talk directly to the other because they are shoulder to shoulder and Jack must instead address the road ahead. It strikes me that Jack is *making* Dad walk just as I did on the ferry; and that Dad is obliging him – just as he did for me.

'You *used* to say,' Jack continues, 'that our relationships are a big part of who and what we are. More than half our identity. That we're about the love we give, receive, withhold, venture.'

'I still stay that. Of course I do.'

Dad is irritable again – despite himself. The fatigue; the alcohol; the night.

But Jack is outwardly patient: 'I suppose I'm asking you to consider your relationships . . . What this means for those relationships. Actually, not only for us but—'

'Please, Jack.' My father raises his head. 'Don't make this sound like . . . like some kind of *bribe* involving my grandchildren.'

'Let him speak, Dad,' Ralph says, clear and sharp where he stands ahead of us, looking back. 'Go on, Jack.'

'All I'm saying is that with you gone, Dad . . .' Jack's voice is plain-chant empty. 'With you gone . . . There's no centre.'

Dad stops walking. He is wearing his dressing gown and little else. Anywhere but on a campsite, he would be stopped and taken to a police station or a homeless shelter.

'Jack, I am going to go,' he says. He stops and leans on his stick. 'We're all going to go. Even you.'

They set off again. I want to step in beside my father but it feels wrong – to interrupt, to divert, to steal back the burden. The burden. I can hardly bear to watch. Is this how Jack feels when I walk Dad? Excluded? Debarred?

There is a family packing a people-carrier – nappies, fold-up chairs, a sports bag labelled 'swimming things'.

'Siobhan . . . Siobhan *and* I . . . We both thought . . .' Jack uses his free arm to press his palm against his chest. 'We both thought we didn't want the boys and Percy getting to know you because of this . . . because of the MND. And maybe that was wrong. I don't know. Siobhan felt it strongly. And it didn't feel like a fight I had to fight. But now . . .'

He tails off. And again it is Ralph who speaks: 'Go on, Jack.'

'Now what I've realized is . . . That people need to know where they are from. The boys and Percy . . . they want to know who they are. And that means knowing you.'

Dad stops again. 'What do we have in common, Jack? You and I, specifically.'

We all wait.

'What do we share?' Dad persists.

We are still six hundred metres from the van, which is around a corner. Dad's eyes are watery.

'What do you mean, Dad?'

'Let me tell you.' Dad half turns. 'We're both fathers.'

Now it is Jack who hesitates.

'And if you were terminally ill, what would you hope for from your boys – from Billy and Jim? From Baby Percy? When they are a bit older, I mean. What would you hope for?'

Jack doesn't speak.

'Let me tell you: you'd hope for understanding.'

Before I met Eva, half-drunk and alone, one night I pulled down the paperback copy of my mother's poetry – the only collection she ever published – the one in which I knew my dad had made his notes. I wanted to read some of the poems again, but I also wanted to read the margins where my father had written with his pencil. I sat down and turned the pages. And it started to affect me badly – pretty much tore up my heart – just seeing the two of them there – the *attention* he was paying her, the concentration, the devotion, how seriously he was taking her . . . I couldn't handle it and I wanted to tell somebody – look, look, look at this. But where do you go and whom do you tell?

We want to eat breakfast outside so we are putting up the awning by the side of the van because the trees keep causing these mini-squalls of residual rain from the wet leaves whenever the wind gusts. I am standing on these little fold-away steps in order to reach up to the roof of the van. Behind me, Jack is holding one supporting pole, Ralph the other; they're silently urging me to hurry up by deliberately not moving. They look like two soldiers either side of a decrepit earl. Dad is sitting in his dressing gown on his camp chair watching me. He is utterly exhausted. He can't walk any more. That's the truth. Not any kind of distance. We're at the end of his walking days. Even two hundred metres is killing him. He's hungover and ratty and admitting to neither. He still hasn't changed into his fresh clothes because they are in the cupboards under the seats which make up the bed. But there's an irascible energy to him and he wants us to get set up. By this he means disassemble the bed in the back, fetch out the other chairs, put up the outside table, get 'the bloody tea' on and send me to fetch the croissants from the bakery. We should have flown. Airports, hotels, two clean and civilized days in clean and civilized Zurich. A clean and civilized ending.

'Come on, Lou,' Dad says. 'We need tea.'

'I'm *doing* it.'

Dad modified the awning twenty years ago to replace the prissy little one that was supplied as standard. He cut and sewed and folded some kind of canvas to enlarge the thing so that we could all five of us get round the table comfortably and sit outside in the rain. Completely sheltered, Lou; everyone able to eat, drink, play cards, talk. But the modification is thicker and so tight and tricky to unwind from the VW housing since Dad has origami-doubled the material and the bastard thing now takes three people to extend and erect.

'I should take the Littles camping,' Jack says from his pole station.

'I can't believe you haven't,' Dad replies, aggressively. 'It's the only way . . . I can't understand these *idiots* who want to lie on the beach.'

The awning is jammed. But I don't want to say so because that will be a criticism of Dad's workmanship and therefore Dad. I climb down to move the steps so I can free the other side. The air smells of wet leaves and pine like it must have done before there were humans. We need to get breakfast. We need to eat.

'They've heard about the van,' Jack says, like maybe this idea *is* a bribe. 'They want to go camping in the van.'

Dad is brusque: 'Siobhan would never let them.'

And for the first time Jack is brusque in return: 'That's only because she doesn't want them forming a relationship that's going to end in certain grief.'

'Everyone dies, Jack. Can you not grasp that?'

'Not on a given day and at a given hour.'

I free the awning.

'Oh, so it's the *date* that is the problem.' Dad is openly derisive. 'Think of it as the opposite of a C-section.'

'What is—'

'If you make the decision relatively early . . .' I interrupt. I have to stop them. I can't take Dad pushing them. Like he wants to . . . to salve himself in their wrath. But if they turn on him, I don't know what will happen or what we'll do.

'If you make the decision early,' I continue, 'the shrinks say that everyone finds it harder to accept. They call it pre-grieving.' I start rolling out the awning over Dad's head like a shroud. But I keep on talking loudly like a tour guide: 'It's like you're grieving for the death of a person still alive. The same five stages: anger, denial, bargaining, depression, acceptance. It's the most emotionally toxic state possible.'

'Sounds about right, Lou,' Ralph says. 'You're still at anger. I'm at depression. Jack's at bargaining. Dad's at acceptance. Maybe we should all get back to denial.'

I hook the eye over the spike of his pole as he leans it towards me. Ralph is trying to help me, I realize. Like he's been helping Jack speak. Like he's been helping all of us. In his way. I cross to hook over Jack's so that now Dad is the only one under the awning and we are looking at each other over the top. Ralph holds up a hand to Jack to stop him from responding.

Dad's voice comes from beneath: 'You know, I would have liked to die in Britain,' he says. 'But I don't recognize my country any more so . . . so what does it matter.'

I fix the peg into the wet earth so that I can create the required tension on the guy rope to pull on the pole and hitch the awning taut. I peg Ralph's guy rope. I peg Jack's.

I tighten them and the awning rises and straightens, square and true.

When I see Dad's face again, it is white and drained and hollow; the face of a ghost.

There was an email on my father's computer that he didn't know I saw. Something he was drafting about two weeks after he had found out about the MND. Addressed to Doug. I don't know if he ever sent it; I copied it and sent it to myself then deleted it from his sent file. He wrote:

My own father was terrified at the end. Crying and begging me. Racist about the nurses in the hospice I had found for him. Even though he knew better. The worst of his personality – Doug – and let me say that, despite his relative prosperity, he was a small-minded and nasty man, full of vindictiveness and resentments and umbrage – the very worst of him had risen to the surface and come pouring out of his mouth. Bigotry, misogyny, racism. Drains backed up in a flood. All the litter and scum afloat. Devoid of any grace or dignity. Forgotten whatever education he once had. Mind like that of an overfed donkey left too long braying to itself in the stall.

He was trying to make these little gestures of what he thought was reconciliation – me and him in it together – having a chat at last. And I couldn't stand it. Couldn't look at him. I wanted to leave the minute I arrived. I had to fight every second not to transmit my desire to go. My father and I in a small room on the outskirts of Bradford.

He . . . he wanted us to be friends. Friends! After all the years so replete with his many rages. Still called it 'that' London. If he hadn't been my father, I might have laughed. A child at the age of seventy-nine. An infant.

Ah, but you can't do it, Doug. As you said about yours. You can't turn on a tuppence and race back across the six decades of distance you put between yourself and your children. Too late, old man, too late. The walls were all built long ago and fortified – too well, too well.

Even so, even so, he should have performed better. Of course it is terrifying. Of course it's horrible. Of course it's keen and fell and lonely and the world just drops away – no longer interested in you, no longer even pretending. And the speed of it. You lose your friends, you stop your work and – guess what? Nobody is in the slightest bit interested. The speed of it. You get to forty-five and you realize everyone is either busy with the wrong thing or dying – and you're in the lucky ten per cent of the world population where they have good health and hospitals! Any minute you might get cancer, you might get a heart attack, you're swept off your brand-new bike by a bus driver who didn't even see you. The whole thing is dark and uncertain and constantly on the threshold of total catastrophe or, worse, pointlessness – the years spinning faster than on one of those Italian lira petrol pumps. (Remember them?)

So you have to perform. Like you say. If you can't be close to your children, then perform for them. Act. Put on a show. Give them something to believe in. Smile in the photographs. Turn up and look like you might at least know something about wisdom. I think that is why I'm

writing to you, Doug. Can't write to them. Not about this.
I envy you your daughters. Lucky fellow.

Thanks for the stuff on Happisburgh by the way:
reassuring to know that our ancestors braved the bitter
conditions 850,000 years ago to settle in . . . Norwich.
Norwich! Didn't realize that was then the Thames estuary.
I bet they lived on shells. (The aquatic ape theory – that's
what my money is on.) Let's get back out there. I've got
some good months yet. I want to discover my own flint.
Just one. I'd love to find just one treasure. I'm going to do
something that

But he stopped there. What does he want to do? I don't
know. I won't ever know. And I can't ask because I shouldn't
have been reading his private email. Pity the relationship
where understanding is gained through spying.

No blood for oil. Not in my name. Saturday, February 15th,
2003. London skies of seal-belly grey. A marrow-creeping
cold. Human breath hanging visible in the air. And all day
we marched. Me and Dad. Hand in hand. And it was a grand
and mighty day of cold fingers and hot cups of tea and the
close comradeship of those we met and the deep solidarity
of millions of people across the world who were doing the
same. The world belongs to its people. Surely. Surely. Surely.
'Stop the war'.

I remember I carried a banner for a while – 'Blair's
Achilles' heel is the way we feel'. And what we were doing
felt important, significant. And Dad seemed to know all the
important and significant people. And when we got to Hyde

Park he said, 'Hang on to me, Lou, let's see if we can go back-stage'; and so I held on to his hand and we squeezed and slipped through the press of the people like were crossing the busiest dance-floor in the world. And on the loudspeakers, some politician was saying . . . 'Friends, we are here today . . . to found a new political movement . . . This is the biggest demonstration ever in Britain and its first cause is to prevent a war against Iraq.' And Dad nodded at someone here, and raised his fist at someone there, and on we went, and on we went until we were standing right at the side of the stage. And the politician was saying that the world in which we live is dominated by the military, the media and the multi-nationals. And then Harold Pinter came past and Dad says, 'Hello,' and of course I didn't know who the hell Pinter was but Pinter said, 'Hello there, Professor, good to see you. And who've we got here?' And my dad, who isn't a professor, said: 'This is Lou. He's with us. Aren't you, Lou?' And I nodded and Pinter nodded back. And Dad said, 'Let's wait here and see if we can catch the mayor,' and he looked around to see who else he knew.

And three hours after all of *that*, we walked home back across the Thames because – I don't know – we wanted to keep on walking, to stay in the streets and because we were high, I think, on the whole day. Tripping. Elated. Like what we were doing really mattered. And that's when we stopped in at Jack's old flat near the Oval for a cup of tea.

He had just started going out with Siobhan back then – and she was somewhere in the bedroom or something and he had been writing about the march for the paper and so he was residually stressed from the deadline – as he always was on Saturdays. And right there in the kitchen, Dad started to have a go at Jack for not being out there on the march. How could you write about something if you didn't take part and get among the people? So Jack said that he had been there all morning. And Dad said it didn't get going until the afternoon – with the speeches and everything. So Jack said he watched it on TV because he had to be at his desk to write because the newspaper needed him to file by six. And Dad scoffed. And that really got to Jack and he started asking did Dad see all the pro-Palestinian groups? And was Dad still pals with Hamas and Hezbollah and what about the IRA? And why don't you grow up, Dad, and stop with the posturing bollocks? Which wasn't what Jack thought, I knew, but it was what Dad goaded him to say. So Dad said, look who has changed his tune since he got a new paymaster – and did Jack think it was a *good* idea going into Iraq? Had Jack any idea of what a shit storm the war would unleash and he hoped that the *consequences* would make an appearance in Jack's article. And Jack said – so what? – you're pro-Saddam: you think he's the good guy here? You think America is the bad guy where people get to vote and there's the rule of law and freedom of expression and nobody gets tortured or goes hungry? And Dad became all incredulous – what nobody gets *tortured*? What about people being executed? What about the bloody *death* penalty? And Jack said, hang on a minute – didn't you have dinner with Blair six months ago? And weren't you telling us all about *that* – what an impressive guy he was and how *competent* he seemed. And Dad said, there were fifty people at that dinner and *of course* he went – you'd have to be truly incurious not to go to the dinner with the Prime Minister and that doesn't mean I support him or this idiotic war. And Jack said, then why did you go on the radio then – why did you go on the radio and tell the nation you hated every minute of the dinner because all you could think about was the poor Iraqi families?

And neither of them meant what they were saying – but they were saying it because something enraged them about each other, which was nothing to do with the Middle East or any of the world leaders or Hezbollah or Tony Blair. Which they also knew. But couldn't admit. Because of something about honesty and deception; about the *necessity* of this deceit which they saw through and despised and which infuriated them even as they could not abandon it. Because of something about honesty and deception that was deep-deep down wholly impossible to confront. Because humankind cannot bear too much reality. Which is why it had to be Hamas and Bush and Blair and Iraq – their own proxy war instead of the real thing.

And that's when Dad said, we saw Evelyn backstage, by the way, and *she* hadn't given up her principles. And Jack said, if Lou wasn't here, Dad, I'd tell you to fuck off out of my flat right now. And I asked, who is Evelyn? Because I'm standing there and I've got to say something. Which was when Siobhan came into the kitchen and Dad said loud and clear that Evelyn was one of Jack's girlfriends from his *Socialist Worker* days, Lou, and hello Siobhan, it is lovely to see you, we're just having a discussion about Iraq.

And I was pretty sure of one thing: whoever Evelyn was, we didn't see her. But I couldn't say this to Jack. Or Siobhan. Or Dad. So whom do you tell?

ALL FOR ONE

My brothers are exactly the kind of people you would have wanted on one of those pilgrimages way back whenever Dad was saying they were. The two of them have so much going on that you just know the conversation would be interesting all the way to Canterbury – or Jerusalem or Babylon or Gomorrah or the Celestial City or wherever the hell we were going. They want to open you up not shut you down. And at the camp shop, without Dad, I feel this sense anew in my heart . . . that the world is sunnier and restored and open-ended. And I'm suddenly glad they're here again – unequivocally and without the cross-currents of whatever else I felt.

'Four of every kind of croissant you have, please,' Jack says in French.

'Especially almond,' Ralph says in English.

The shop assistant is wearing a short-sleeved blue polka-dot blouse and she smiles a smile that speaks of the certainty of fresh French bread every morning and a world untroubled – untouchable – by anything else.

'OK, yes. Sixteen in total,' Jack says in French. 'Thank you.'

'Thank you,' Ralph says in English.

We watch the back of her caramel-blonde ponytail dancing – three stupefied aliens – as she cheerfully tongs the croissants into the sleeves of her paper bags. The smell of fresh bread mingles with the faint scent of the sugared fruit in the pastries. The radio is tuned to something classical that sounds pretty as a river running on polished pebbles in spring's first thaw. I'm thinking that if we never find a way out of here, it won't be so bad.

'We have to go deeper, Jack. The problem is . . .' Ralph tails off.

He is continuing the conversation from before we came in. We didn't exactly plan it, or say anything, but we wanted to come to the shop together. Without Dad, we can breathe, we can talk, we can be. We left him sitting down, resting under his awning.

'Maybe the problem is that you can't distinguish between your support and your agreement,' Ralph says.

One by one, the woman flips the paper bags and twizzles the corners so that they are twisted shut. She is thirty-two at a guess and has lightly tanned arms from the many seductions of the French sun.

'You can *not* agree with something that somebody is doing, but you can support them in their decision.'

'Can you though?' Jack asks.

'We do it all the time.'

'Do we?'

'Marriages. Divorces.'

'We should get some bread in case they run out,' I say. 'Make baguette sandwiches.' Outside, a frenzy of kids chase white ducks through the railings of the pool. 'Maybe some of the apple tarts that Dad likes, too,' I say. 'And – fuck it – some custard slices.'

'*Millefeuille*,' Ralph says, slowly.

The woman's arms stop their croissant-wrapping roll. I think she's cross about my bad language, which I am instantly ashamed of. But actually she is waiting for confirmation. This seems to have to come from Jack. I'm thinking that Jack is like Dad in this: wherever we go and whatever we do together, everyone assumes he's the authority. Maybe he is. He reiterates our requirements in French. The problem is that I can tell that Jack is going to ignore Dad and start over at some point when we get back. Whatever the Latin rhetorical term is for the force of cumulative argument, that's what Jack is going to do. Part of me thinks we're heading for a physical fight – some of us battering the others to force a way into that suicide room for Dad, some of us battering the others to force a way out for him; none of us sure which side we're on or why.

'You can support without endorsing,' Ralph says.

'So,' Jack says, 'somewhere on a campsite in France – Christ knows where – you are telling me that I can – no – that I *should* – support my Dad's suicide but—'

'Assisted death,' I say, quietly.

'—but not agree with it? That's what you're truly saying?'

Ralph is equanimious: 'I'm saying that there is a difference between support and agreement.'

'And I am saying that this is all way too late from both of you.'

The more time we spend away from Dad, the easier it is to talk theoretically; but then another thing I've noticed: the theory of something is much easier to discuss than the doing of the something itself. The door tinkles like an altar bell. A family enters behind us.

Ralph ignores me and says: 'Maybe the problem is that Dad is after your approval not just your consent.'

The woman finger-punches the numbers into the till – impervious as happiness itself.

Ralph takes the paper bags, piling them up against his chest with exaggerated exuberance. 'Can you pay this nice lady? I can't reach my wallet.'

Jack pays with a fifty euro which looks as though it has actually been ironed. I take the patisserie box. Jack tucks the baguettes under his arm. Ralph indicates with his head for us to go first. The father and his young children behind us meet our eyes with the kind of expressions that look like they've never had a better holiday in their lives. And I have the bad thought that we are being decimated as a family, that this is the end whatever happens, that we don't exist any more except within the narrow parameters of this single conversation. Maybe that's why Dad wants us to talk about . . . about ourselves, about our work, our relationships. He realizes this. Of course he does. (Maybe he realizes everything.) Anything but him and his disease. And surely we have a duty to make these days good for him? Do my brothers understand this? Outside, the children have chased the fat French ducks into the water, which seems to be where they least want to go.

'Think about it, Jack,' Ralph continues. 'There are only three things Dad can do. One: do it – like it or not. Two: do it – with you on his side. Three: don't do it and get worse and worse and have you as witness to that – as helper, aider, abetter.'

Jack half turns. 'And what about you?'

'I am here,' Ralph says.

'Meaning?'

'Just that.'

'You approve? Or you approve *and* you consent?' A jibing tone of enters Jack's voice. 'You support? Or you support *and* you agree?'

Ralph ignores the aggression. 'Meaning that Dad has to decide for himself.' He pauses. 'Meaning . . . that he has decided. Or so he says. Meaning I refuse to be embroiled in the drama if he hasn't. Meaning that I myself have only two choices: to be here or not to be here. And – since that is the only real question for me – because I've no moral objections – here I am.'

Ralph says the word 'moral' like it's code for 'primitive'. Awkwardly, I have to carry the patisserie box flat in front of me like an offering through the congregation of the campsite because I don't want it to tip and squash the *millefeuilles*.

'And yet . . .' Jack says. 'And yet we are being *invited* to have an opinion. You, me, Lou. And we have been – all along.'

'Jesus,' I say.

'We are the ones who must live with the consequences,' Jack says. 'In one way, it is a decision that *only* affects us. Which he knows. And which is why he covertly solicits our opinions.'

'And yet we can't let ourselves be implicated,' Ralph says. 'Or we will be implicated all our lives. Because this is nothing to do with us – these are his decisions – unless you let the manipulative bastard drag you in. Which is my point. And which he also knows.'

'For Christ's sake,' I say. 'Dad has got nobody else to talk to. Who the fuck else is he going to ask?'

'Maybe we have to go deeper,' Ralph says, ignoring me again. 'Maybe we have to find where compassion lies.'

'So fucking late in the day,' I mutter. 'So fucking late in the day.'

'I think it's wrong,' Jack says. 'I think it is wrong for all the reasons I have said.'

'But this big rebarbative "no" of yours,' Ralph counters, 'maybe it's solidified into a position rather than a reason. Wait—'

'It's not a big—'

'And there's guilt – your wife, your children – which is harder to rationalize – but maybe the truthful reaction is fear. Fear.'

'Why don't—'

'I'm not attacking you, Jack. Maybe you just don't want to lose him. And maybe if you said that.'

'I don't want to lose him.'

'Say that.'

'Say that,' I mutter.

'I *have* been saying that – for a whole fucking year.'

'Not quite, Jack,' Ralph says. 'You've been saying things around it.'

'While you say nothing? And you feel nothing? Because it doesn't affect you – the great puppeteer?'

'Of course. But . . . For me . . . For me, this is Dad's decision. I'll go along with whatever he decides. I'm not participating in the self-dramatization – that's all.'

'You keep saying that. But maybe you're hiding behind your show of indifference. Maybe—'

'I'm—'

'I'm not attacking *you*, Ralph. I'm just saying that—'

'Don't "just say",' I say.

'—that maybe Dad desperately wants to hear from you. But you don't want to make yourself . . . vulnerable. That's it . . . that's *it*. You don't want to be emotionally vulnerable. You'd rather blank him. Why is that, Ralph?'

'What I want is impossible,' Ralph says. 'I want Dad to be well.'

'But this is happening now,' Jack says. 'We have to deal with it. This is now. You can't be absent from everything.'

Ralph is clear-voiced: 'I support Dad's decision – whatever that is. I'm not in the persuasion business. I'm just saying that—'

'Don't fucking "just say".'

'—that you have a view – a strong one, Jack – but that maybe the most powerful thing to say is that you're afraid and you don't want to lose him.'

'I don't want to lose him. I have no problem saying that.'

'But you *will* lose him, Jack,' I say. 'Because he *is* dying. And do you know what: actually, he doesn't want to talk about it any more. He wants us to tell him about our lives. He wants us to *distract* him. That is what he wants.'

'Christ, this whole fucking thing is some kind of . . .' Jack tails off and sighs.

'We have to go deeper,' Ralph says again. 'All for one and one for all. Compassion is not something you have or don't have like . . . like red hair; it's something you choose to practise. That's what we all need to do: practise compassion. And—'

'Maybe he *wants* to be talked out of it,' Jack says. 'Maybe this is his way – as shitty as it is – as shitty as he has always been – maybe we have to be big enough to let him do that to us. Maybe he wants to be talked out of it, Lou.'

'Maybe the compassionate thing is . . .' Ralph stops short. 'Oh shit! What the *fuck*?'

Up ahead, there is a car on our plot – twelve feet behind the back of the van. The wheels are skidding on the wet grass. The driver is over-revving the engine in neutral, then sliding forward again, the car skewing a little, then stopping two inches closer, digging in, creating ruts of mud. The noise is terrible, trapped and echoing in the trees. But what pulls us up short like we've run into a wall of invisible daggers is the sight of Dad staggering along the side of the van without his stick . . . He's doing this weird, flailing, hip-dipped walk and he's waving and motioning at the driver who obviously can't hear him even though he's shouting pretty loud. He's still in his gaping dressing gown. When the engine noise drops we can hear his voice.

'No. No! Round the bloody side. Round the bloody side!' He has picked up two long wires with crocodile-clipped ends. He's waving them madly and shouting. 'Round *this* way. This side. I can't reach you there.' He gestures at the car furiously like a man shooing a hated neighbour's dog – and then he does these massive exaggerated repeat sweeps with his arms to indicate that the driver come around the other side of the van from where we've erected the awning. 'Take her back and start again. Take her back. Start again. Back. Back! *This* side.'

The noise of the revving engine is somehow trapped in our shallow wooded valley so that it sounds like some kind of deafening insult against nature.

'Jump leads,' Jack says.

'Flat battery,' Ralph says.

'The heater,' Jack says. 'I bet you had the heater on for hours last night.'

'Fuck,' Ralph says.

The driver is in reverse and yet the wheels are spinning. He's got this sick rocking motion of the car going – in and out of the muddy ruts, which it can't now escape and which the wheels are making deeper with each revolution. We're all running now. But before we're seen or heard or can actually do anything, Dad places his hands on the bonnet and dips to push like he's twenty-five years old and I can tell just from the angle of his body that he's in the grip of all his fury and why-the-bloody-hell-do-you-have-to-do-*everything*-yourself?

And now Ralph and Jack have dropped their brown baker's bags and we're all running as fast as we can and shouting. But the engine revs and the wheels spin faster and Dad can't hear us. And for a slow-motion moment we watch him try physically to push the car back onto the tarmac – 'Go on! Go on!' he's shouting . . . Then his legs do this horrible flailing-crumple under him and he collapses down beneath the front of the car so that the mud from the still-spinning wheels is spattering him; and now the driver stops trying to reverse because he can see what has happened so that the energy changes and the car lurches forward again back down into the ruts; and I'm thinking Dad's legs are going to be run over because he's fallen right in front of the car's bumper, his feet all twisted over like they're broken and they'll go under the car, they'll go under the car.

But Ralph is there and grabbing him and yanking and sliding him away.

And then Jack.

And I'm the last one because I'm still carrying the pastry box which I don't want to drop or tilt.

And we don't know how to be with each other or how to live with what is happening to us and Dad is on the ground and his dressing gown is gaping open and he's got mud on his face and he's crying.

I also found this essay by Seneca in my dad's library. It's called 'On the Shortness of Life'. It is written to Seneca's friend Paulinus. He says a lot of stuff. And you can see what the appeal is to my father. I picked out a few quotations that he underlined.

On time:

The life we receive is not short but we make it so; we are not ill-provided but use what we have wastefully.

On reading:

[Those who read] not only keep a good watch over their own lifetimes, but they annex every age to theirs. All the years that have passed before them are added to their own . . . We are excluded from no age, but we have access to them all . . . why not turn from this brief and transient spell of time and give ourselves wholeheartedly to the past, which is limitless and eternal and can be shared with better men than we?

On life:

The greatest obstacle to living is expectancy, which hangs upon tomorrow and loses today. You are arranging what lies in Fortune's control, and abandoning what lies in yours. What are you looking at? To what goal are you straining? The whole future lies in uncertainty: live immediately.

—

We haul my father up. We sit him down in the passenger seat. He will not look up. He keeps his hands over his face. He mutters. We stand around at the door like we are waiting for someone else to arrive. His cheeks are wet – from the tears, from the spittle, the dew of the world. Mud is streaked in his beard.

I can feel that Jack wants to leave him alone – like he thinks Dad needs to regain his dignity. But – I don't know – maybe Jack is using this as an excuse for something else – an excuse to absent himself. And I can feel that Ralph is moving into some sort of overt anger for the first time. Most of all, I can feel that my father just wants to die. That's all. And so I'm suddenly sure that I have to do something – anything – to get us out from under this or else we'll all be crushed; it's like time is a massive triangle in the sky and the whole weight of the sharp end is on us here, right now. And I can see some wet wipes in Jack's open bag, so I step over to the sliding door, past my brothers, and reach down and pull them out without asking Jack – like I'm going to start cleaning Dad up, like that's what we do next, like there's always a next.

This works because now Ralph walks over to talk to the driver of the car and persuades him to let him drive the thing out and into position. So then Jack goes to help and the two of them are pushing and revving the engine and shouting instructions. Meanwhile, I don't know if I should touch Dad or not – so I am just standing there beside him – ready, not ready, with the wet wipes. And I can hear the birds all jittery in the trees.

Dad is sitting with his hand still on his face like I've never seen him. We're being crushed.

And then Jack's back – suddenly Mr Total Competence –

with the jump leads. And he's opening the driver's door and hauling the seat forward and swivelling it round because that's where the battery is stowed on our van. Meanwhile, Ralph is nosing the other car up sideways-on to the driver's side so that Jack can reach the leads in. Which was what Dad was yelling about. And I'm still standing there under the awning, leaning on the passenger door next to Dad, trying to think of something, anything, to say. And still the world turns.

'Is there a negative connection?' Jack is asking.

But nobody is answering.

'I'll go straight on the chassis,' he shouts to Ralph as if Ralph needs to know.

And I can hear Ralph shouting back: 'Are we on?'

So Jack yells: 'We're on. They're on. Give it some welly.'

And Ralph is revving some stranger's engine. And I'm thinking that this is Dad's domain. That he loves all this stuff. That he should be issuing instructions, overseeing. But he isn't moving.

Jack climbs into the driver's seat across from Dad. He ignores us. Ignores Dad. Ignores me. Like *this* is the task in hand and we'll get to Dad in a bit. And I am still standing there with the wet wipes trying to live through the seconds that keep on coming while Jack tries the ignition of the van. But the engine doesn't quite turn.

'Dad?' I say, soft as I can. 'Are you OK?'

But Dad doesn't speak and he won't lower his hands from his face. I don't know if he's crying in there or if it's shame, or pain, or what.

'Dad?'

But there's no point me shouting over the racket Ralph is making revving the other engine and I'm thinking maybe we've drained the battery so far that it's never going to start again because it's totally fucking dead.

The noise is *too loud* for the clearing and everything smells of petrol. I don't want the memory that is being formed in my head. I don't want to see this or hear it or smell it or feel it. I don't know what we're going to do. I have the sudden clear thought that I can't go into that room and watch my father die because then I'll see it and know that I was there – for ever.

'Leave her alone. Just give her a minute,' Dad says, quietly. 'Tell Ralph he doesn't have to rev so hard.'

Seneca also wrote: *Learning how to live takes a whole life, and, which may surprise you more, it takes a whole life to learn how to die.* He committed suicide. Tacitus gives us the story. Seneca was ordered to kill himself by Nero, who falsely accused him of plotting assassination. So Seneca duly severed some veins. But the blood loss was slow and the pain an extended agony. So he took poison. But that didn't do it either. So he dictated his last words and surrounded by his pals he was carried into a hot bath in the hope that this would speed the blood loss. He died in the steam.

Below, through the trees, the river is the colour of empty wine bottles. The engine is running but we're going nowhere. We're afraid to turn it off in case we can never get it started again. We sit beneath the makeshift awning. Dad is on his chair; his face of tears and mud half-cleaned. Ralph is opposite, smoking. His jogging bottoms also spattered from mud. Jack squats on the van steps. We're drinking tea. But we're all broken down. The breakfast is untouched, muddy bags piled on the table like a parody of the future. And nobody can speak. Which feels like the end. Because we always talk. We always find a way to speak of things. We always find the words. That's what we do. We keep talking. We enquire and we explain and we listen. We share our souls as best we can. And if not that?

I remember standing in a courtyard at night with an old house behind me, probably from six hundred years ago or more, and the hulk of a barn close by, and somewhere an owl hooting, and the dark shapes of creaking trees, their branches like the fingers of grasping witches from one of my childhood picture books. I remember looking up at the sky with my father. I remember my father holding my hand and there being so many stars that the dim are not so much scattered as smudged between the bright. This is what it is like in the countryside, my father says. You can really get a good look. The problem with the city is that there's so much light that you can't really see.

I remember the cold and the murmur of the wind. The hope of snow. The excited talk with my mother of being snowed in. I remember that I had come out in my pyjamas with my coat thrown over and my wellington boots, which felt too small even though they were new. I remember that I didn't want to let go of my father's hand. I remember that my father somehow understood this and bent down and pointed with his other hand so that we wouldn't have to part, even though it was awkward.

'OK, so that's Venus,' my father said, 'and that's Jupiter.'

'Those ones?'

'The bright ones – low down.'

I didn't know what the word planet really meant. I didn't know why planets were different from stars. But I wanted my father to know how much I listened to him. And, above all, I wanted to be good at learning – at remembering – because I knew this pleased him.

'Is that Mars?'

'I think that one is Mars higher up.'

'So that's all three,' I said. Even at the age of four, I knew my father liked it when we completed a task.

'No – you remember. We're supposed to be able to see four tonight. You're forgetting Saturn.'

'Oh yeah.'

'Tell me about Saturn, Lou.'

I knew the answer and it filled me with happiness to tell my father what I knew: 'It's got rings.'

'That's right,' he said. And I asked him if we could see the rings and he said not from down here but that we'd have to go into space. And I asked him how would we get into space. And he told me that humans had already been there. And I asked him – 'Are we humans right now?' And he said: 'We are, Lou, we are.'

I remember how my father leant down to pick me up and how my father's beard felt scratchy to kiss, but how I put my arms around my father's neck, determined to press our cheeks together despite.

There was light in the kitchen window.

I remember that I was on my father's shoulders as we crossed the courtyard and that I was taller than the rest of the world up there and closer to the stars and the planets and the moon which was so much bigger than I have ever seen. And I remember that I had to duck down so as not to bang my head on the low lintel of the door so that when we stepped inside my head was resting tight beside his.

My father is the one who saves us. Somehow, despite everything, he has his fingers still on the ledge and he is prepared to attempt to haul his sons back up to the cliff top one last time.

He takes a croissant and holds it aloft. 'There was something I was planning on going to see, boys,' he says. 'It's on the way. I want to . . . I want to . . . I want to just go and—'

'Yes, Dad,' I say. 'Let's keep going.'

'My legs are killing me,' he winces. 'I need lots more painkillers. And my feet.' He looks round. 'Come on, boys, let's pack up and get out of here.'

DENIAL

We chuck everything in the van. We drive to the office and the wash-house. This time all three of us carry him up the stairs. The pigeon has gone. We sit Dad down on the chair in the showers. He is full of purpose and chatter. He wants to tell us about the Upper Palaeolithic. All his life, he says, he's wanted to visit this particular prehistoric cave and now he's going with all three of us.

Ralph takes the credit card to settle the bill and 'see what else they've got'. Jack goes to tidy up the van – he's going to change the bed, wash the utensils, re-pack.

I help Dad. I dress him in clean clothes. He has purple bruises on his ankles. They look terrible. He says more ibuprofen will do it; he has hundreds of pills in his wash bag. He says he was expecting a lot of pain. He's already taken three. He's never taken more than one at a time in his life before. Of anything. He swallows two more. I am silent.

The others come back in and we haul him out and sit him on a bench. Jack is actually doing the whole dustpan and brush thing inside the van. He's using his baby wipes on the 'upholstery'. Ralph comes out of the shop. He's bought salami, cheese and tomatoes to go with our bread and the remaining four million croissants. Jars of artichokes. Cigarettes from hell, he says, it's all they had. He sits next to Dad and smokes and watches Jack while making cheery sarcastic comments. But there's something about Jack that is impervious or unreachable – like he knows for certain that the secret to human happiness lies snugly curled up inside a life devoted to minor sacrifice.

I text Eva. She's with her phone and free and we do some back and forth. I tell her we're on the move and that's somehow good.

Jack is ready. We all climb in. Ralph takes the wheel. I slam the door too hard. I help Dad arrange himself. He's pleased to be clean and in fresh clothes. He's lying down with his feet towards the back and his head at the front so he can 'join in'. His shampoo smells of apples like we're straight from some gently billowing summer orchard in Normandy. He wants his pillows piled so he can swivel his head and see forward. I sit up beside him, also leaning forward onto the back of Jack's seat. The engine starts OK but the dashboard is beeping and clacking as if something is urgently wrong. Many things.

'Low fuel?' Jack suggests, in a mock-helpful voice. 'Lights? Oil pressure? HIV?'

I poke my head between my brothers' seats into the cabin. 'Are the hazards on?' I ask.

'No, Louis,' Ralph says. 'Thank you. The hazards are not on.'

'Bloody hell.' Dad is shaking his head and frowning with the pleasure of puzzlement. 'I don't understand it. Must be something to do with the jump leads. Or fuses. But it doesn't make any sense though. How can the jump leads affect the circuit board?'

'The van is going insane,' I say.

Dad and I are both leaning into the cabin now; it's like we all want to be in the front, like suddenly we all want to drive.

The clicking noise won't stop. Ralph raises his hands above the steering wheel as if to surrender.

'I think it's because you haven't got your seat belt on, Jack,' I say.

'Somehow all the defunct alarms have been reactivated,' Dad says, shaking his head. 'The dash used to beep when you didn't buckle up in the front. But I don't really see how—'

'No,' Jack says, fastening his belt. 'Not insane. The van is coming back to life.'

The clicking stops.

'It *is* the fucking seat belts.' Ralph exhales like the world is entirely new to him. 'Amazing.' He revs the engine unnecessarily. 'OK. Stand by.'

He stalls.

Silence.

'I just don't think we're going to make it, Dad,' I say.

'The gods are against us,' Ralph says.

'Or the gods are for us,' Jack says.

'It's always been so hard to tell,' Dad says, lying back down into his pillows with a sigh. 'I told you, Louis.'

'What? What did you tell me? Why does everyone keep telling me things?'

'That a man meets his destiny on the path he took to avoid his destiny.'

After an hour or so, the road becomes narrow and more dramatic. This is mountain country. Dad wakes up and lies on his pillow looking backwards out of his window. I do the same. Up front, my brothers are talking about Siobhan's Monday-night yoga. We pass along a deep gorge. Then we begin to loop precariously this way and that up the steep-shouldered valley. Now and then, there is a short tunnel cut through the tawny overhanging rock. A river runs swift below us – turbid, opaque, the colour of Oxford stone. I have a new game that I am playing with myself. I imagine that I am seeing the world with my father's eyes. It doesn't work at first – I'm *telling* myself things about the beauty of the landscape, but I'm not experiencing it; I'm too self-consciously aware of what I'm doing. But then the thoughts that notice the thoughts I think about what I'm thinking start to quieten or drop away and the trick begins to work . . . And gradually everything *does* seem miraculous and inexplicable to me: the fact that I am here with Dad and my brothers – on this day in all of history, on this planet in all the universe. And that's when I get the thought that if there's one thing – and maybe it's the only thing – that is good about what we're doing, about this journey, then it has to be that we're getting to feel what it means to be alive together. Truly alive. Truly together.

I breathe the air coming in through Dad's window. I look out at the world. I listen to my brothers. Their talk is a comfort to me. We've always talked in the van. Dad and Mum and Ralph and Jack. I used to lie half-sleeping in the back when I was little – listening to my family taking everything apart and putting it back together again; and then dreaming of the world.

Jack is saying: '. . . All I am suggesting is that *maybe* you should take up meditation. Give it a try. Lots of troubled people swear by it. It teaches you mindfulness.'

'You mean mind*less*ness?'

'I don't think that's what they say. I think—'

'Well, doesn't it teach you – specifically – to think about nothing? Isn't that meditation?'

'That's one aspect of it.'

'And isn't the essence of your humanity to do with your reason and your ability to think?'

I glance across at Dad. He half turns and he shakes his head a little on his pillow. But he's listening, too. He is greedy greedy greedy to listen to Ralph and Jack regardless of the conversation – can't help himself – like they're two of his pupils who have become famous but whose essays he never bothered to read at the time.

'I love my thoughts.' Ralph lifts one hand from the wheel. 'They are the only thing that is the slightest bit interesting to me. Imagine if I had to rely on yours.'

'And yet you're a physical creature. You have a body.'

'And it's in much better shape than yours. Thin, for example.'

'Troubled.'

'Free.'

'Not so. Your mind is tyrannical, Ralph.'

'Not so. You hear tyranny because you've enslaved yourself.'

'By enslaved, I take it that you mean that I'm married.'

'Your word-association.'

'And what about *your* heart?'

'My heart is like a blister.'

'And this is a good thing?'

'I believe in love. I believe in death. I'm trying to experi-ence as much of the former given the latter. But we're talking about you. What do you believe in? Life *insurance*?'

The further up the gorge we climb, the more swiftly and turbulent flows the river. The boulders by the side of the road are a sandy colour now and look like the illustrations in children's books about the 'Holy Land'.

'I believe in constancy,' Jack says.

Ralph clicks his tongue and glances in the mirror. He shakes his head slowly but his eyes are smiling at me. 'I refuse to accept,' he scoffs, 'that you are the kind of man, Jack, who says to himself: "Let there be no more love affairs." How can you say that? This is my last experience of women. *Are* you that kind of a man? Should we drop you off somewhere punishing and abstemious?' He indicates the landscape. 'You could live in a cave. Eat rocks. Fight with the devil for forty days and nights. Although I bet he'd be bored to tears with you after an hour.'

'Marriage isn't the end of the love,' Jack says. 'Watch out for that goat.'

Ralph slows. The goat frisks nervously into the road.

'No, but it's the end of all the other forms of love.'

'Again: no. Love evolves.'

'Subsides.'

'Wrong. For many people – marriage is a beginning.'

'But you—'

'In my case . . . If we're talking about my case.'

'We are.'

'In my case . . . *despite* all my stupidity and immaturity and being a dick, guess what?' The goat hesitates, uncertain.

'It turns out my younger self arranged a good marriage for me. Yep – I know – it's staggering. Given me, given us. But each year that passes, I am more and more grateful to him for his wisdom. Each year that passes, I fall further in love with my wife.'

'Then you are almost unique in the world, Jack. And your marriage a shining beacon for the rest of humanity. No doubt it is visible from space.'

'Thank you.'

'There are probably foggy-visored astronauts weeping silently into their helmets as we speak.'

'Love is not what you think it is. That is all I am saying.'

The goat scrambles away up the rocks to where we now see others are waiting. We start off again. The road straightens and Ralph changes up through the gears.

'Tell me, how does this overwhelming love manifest? A mutual interest in TV dramas? Fashionable shades of paint? Fresh herbs?'

'You underestimate people. You underestimate everything. Except yourself.'

'Not so. I'm at the bottom of all my own estimations. There's no man alive who can estimate me lower than I estimate myself. I merely disguise this in order to appear convincing and self-assured. Just like everybody else. Though, in my case, with the additional disability – and honesty – of knowing what I'm up to.'

'Maybe lots of married people are *happy*. Have you ever considered that?'

'Oh, please. Come *on*. Look around you, Jack: all these oafish husbands discussing the missus this, or the kids that. Alternative routes through upcoming roadworks. Business-class breakthroughs. Market capitalizations of taxi companies. For ninety per cent of women, marriage is the opposite of fulfilment.'

'Are you a feminist now, Ralph?' I ask.

'No, but I am an *expert* on married women.'

'Lucky them.'

'Most of these wives, Jack, they're sitting around reading *The World of Interiors* while the world of their interiors falls into shrunken ruin. Not a single appeal to their imaginative faculties in *years*. Unless we count imagining other men in the sack. So I say . . . I say how about at least one of us falls in love with your wife, *mate*, and we see how that goes? Why the sanctimoniousness? Why the—'

'Decency.'

'Our love affairs define us.'

Jack is exquisitely breezy: 'You don't really understand the family until you have got a family, Ralph. Nor the real relationship between men and women. Go and watch a woman giving birth to a few of your children sometime. I promise you: it changes everything. I'm afraid this inner-humanity stuff is inconsequential once you've been through the other end of sex.'

'The other end of sex,' Ralph repeats the phrase. 'I like that. But answer me this: when you die, what are you going to remember? What are you going to look back on? I'll tell you: the times you lay beside a woman in the warm after-noon and made love and talked and ate and talked and made love and drank and made love and talked about this and that and her and you and everything good and bad and lost and found until the world stopped its mattering and the evening sun fell across the bed – where you then made love again, the deeper this time for your communion and the coming of the dusk. What beats that? What the fuck beats that? What else is there?'

Jack turns in his seat: '*Is* that what you think about, Dad.'

'Among other things,' Dad says to the roof.

'Such as?'

'Your children. What a mess you made of that.'

Up ahead, above the road, something strange is going on with the weather: the sky is surreptitiously tearing itself apart so that the grey is revealed to have been hiding torn sheets of white which in turn have been concealing secret robes of blue.

'I think that love turns out to be the opposite of what you describe.' Jack is more engaged than he's pretending. 'In fact, love *is* the procedures, the practicality. Making sure there's milk for your coffee. Changing the bulbs. Picking the wet towels off the floor so that they dry.'

'For Christ's *sake* – if love turns out to be picking up the towels, then haven't you got to ask yourself who – or what – you've fallen in love with?'

'I'm saying these things are totems of love.'

'And I'm saying they're not.'

'I'm saying that after all the melodrama and madness has subsided, what you are left with . . . is life itself, Ralph. The reality. You really have to give reality a try one day.'

'The superficial.'

'Look to what a person does, not what they say.'

'Pick up towels.'

'Consider the million *actual* sacrifices and daily kindnesses. Look to the acts not the words. Who prepared the food you are eating? Who changed the interest rate on your mortgage so that you had money for your holiday? Who organized the plumber? Who found your door keys?'

'And why would I want to make love to this person? Because of their steady determination over the towels or their quiet proficiency when it comes to mortgages?'

'This is what life is made of.'

'It's not what *my* life is made of.'

'And so you are lonely.'

'Free.'

'Sad.'

'Truthful.'

As if to make his point, Ralph accelerates and we overtake a labouring old Renault. It's not the best place to be making such a move, though, and he has to brake severely for a hairpin, which we then swing round a little too fast. There's a dent in the barrier on the outer edge beyond which you fall down the mountain, maybe for ever. We need another driver. Someone with a different surname. Dad has rolled into me. I help set him back on his pillow.

'You're being dishonest, Jack.'

'No: *you're* the dishonest one.'

'Don't you walk out into your day and ache for some escape from your prison?'

'Your word.'

'The unspoken implication.'

'Of course.' Jack puffs out his cheeks, conceding a little without conceding anything. 'I see women all the time and I want . . . I want what you say you chase: an intimate and enlightening conversation that is physical as well as everything else.'

'There you go. *That's* what I'm talking about.'

'But I choose not to.'

'You choose imprisonment.'

'Because actually those choices damage me. I choose—'

My father interrupts in his lecture-hall voice: 'I'll no more dote and run to pursue things which had endamaged me.'

'Who's that?' I ask.

'John Donne,' he says. '"Farewell to Love".'

'Donne thinks love is *damage*?' I ask.

Dad looks at me without raising his head. 'Long answer or short?'

'Short. Always short. This is the twenty-first century, Dad. We all have attention deficit disorder.'

'If we take love here to mean sexual desire—'

'We do,' Ralph says, vehemently addressing the landscape. 'We must. We can. And we do. Without desire the world withers.'

'Then, yes, in this one instance – amidst dozens of poems with different points of view – love is damage.'

Ralph glances in the mirror and I can see his eyes are bright. He's not had a drink yet, I'm thinking. He's not even thought about it.

'Keep arguing with each other,' I say. 'It's making me and Dad feel better about our personalities.'

'And how do your choices – the ones you have made – how do they leave you, Jack?'

'Happier than you, Ralph.'

'Dreaming of a mistress who you could trust.'

'Living with a wife who I already do.'

'Dying inside.'

'Living . . . and not in some fantasy.'

'Constrained and compromised.'

'In some ways, yes, but not everything about relationships is physical.'

Ralph laughs out loud like Jack has just lost everything with a single catastrophic move on the chessboard. 'For fuck's *sake*.' He lifts his hand from the wheel and gestures at the world. 'Sexual chemistry, sexual *charisma*, is what we're all about here on planet Earth. Take a look around, Jack. Watch some nature documentaries. Every gene in every life form is going absolutely mental trying to attract someone, something, anything in order to make as much love as physically possible. In order not to be lonely, in order to pass itself on . . . Every gene in the world wants to fuck *like there's no tomorrow*. And you want to know why? Because there *isn't* any tomorrow. As soon as the fucking stops, we're all dead for eternity. You, me, Dad, the planet. Even Louis.'

'I don't know what to tell you,' Jack says. 'I love my wife dearly and I'd hate to be without her.'

'Maybe this is why we could use some sisters,' I say. 'Get a fresh perspective.'

'It's not too late, Dad,' Jack says. 'Maybe you're going to meet some hot Neanderthal ass in this cave. The sort of prehistoric señorita that you never could say no to.'

'I'd love a sister,' I say. 'I'd really love a sister.'

'It's not a Neanderthal site,' Dad says. 'It's Upper Palaeolithic. *Homo sapiens*.'

'Pleasure is not the same as happiness,' Jack says. 'You should remember that, Ralph.'

'Contentment is a form of boredom,' Ralph says. 'You should remember that, Jack.'

'It's really not boring. Children are . . . children are the opposite of boring.'

'Oh, oh, oh,' Ralph is mocking. 'Here we go: the fatherhood defence.'

'It's not a defence.'

'A compensation.'

'Wrong again. Fatherhood is a unique relationship. I love my children in a way that is entirely free from the tangle of Eros you describe. And that *is* a kind of freedom, Ralph, a kind of love that you don't get to experience otherwise. And – yeah – an experience that trumps all others.' Jack breathes in as if the temptations of this mountain wilderness had been dismissed long ago. 'You need a family to understand the family. You need children to understand yourself and the women you are with. Childbirth. Motherhood. Daughters. If you don't see any of that, you only get half the picture. I promise you, bro. Hate me. Hate what I'm telling you. But it's true.'

'Except not true at all. What about all the gay artists *in the history of the universe*? From Virgil and Plato . . . via Michelangelo and Marlowe . . . to . . . to . . . Auden.'

'None of whom understood the first thing about women.'

'Henry James,' Ralph says. 'Shakespeare. Flaubert probably. Gay, gay, gay. The list is endless. Pretty much everyone who is good at anything to do with deep human understanding is gay.'

'Did the Neanderthals fuck *Homo sapiens*, Dad?' I ask. 'Or just the gay ones?'

'Louis, there's no need for that language.'

'Did early humans make heterosexual cross-species love?'

'We now know they did.' Dad sighs. 'Not in any great number but to some extent. We all carry a small percentage of Neanderthal DNA.'

'There you go,' Ralph says.

'There you go *what*?' Jack says. 'That doesn't prove anything. What the fuck?'

THE UNDERWORLD

We climb out of the van.

The sun is bright and strong and fierce when it rides out from what remains of the cloud so I reach back inside into the little docket on the back of the driver's seat where I keep the dark black sunglasses that Eva bought me. We are high on the side of a mountain where the road has been widened to allow maybe a hundred cars to park obliquely. But there isn't another vehicle in sight. And it feels like we are entirely alone in the world: the precipice before us, the cliffs behind. All about our feet lie jagged rocks as if lately discarded by rampaging giants. From this vantage, the valley below is like some fevered imagining of the approach to hell: the twisting snake of the road, the sheer plunges, the violent outcrops, the overhanging escarpments, the serrated columns that march madly downward into the throat of the gorge itself.

My brothers come round and we ease Dad out. Ralph has Aviators; Jack has Wayfarers and my Dad has these vintage flip-downs which are the only cool thing he possesses; he bought them in 1969 and every few years he clears his writing desk to mend them himself with a tiny screwdriver and this old-school jeweller's magnifying glass stuck in front of his eye.

He swallows some more pills and then throws his now-familiar arm around me. But we take one step across the dusty ground towards the entrance and then we stop. Dad is going nowhere fast. His legs are weak and his ankles sore and tender notwithstanding the painkillers. Jack stands in and supports the other shoulder. Ralph waits. We move forward again – limping, super-slow and tender. We are lined up like Mafiosi bringing in the Godfather after a shooting; and maybe he's gonna die, maybe he isn't. We're more or less carrying him. There's no way, I'm thinking, we're even going to make the entrance . . .

Then we see them: adjacent to the ticket office, there is a row of state-of-the-art mobility chairs – 'fauteuils roulants électriques' – all lined up like the start of Le Mans. Wheel-chairs. Better than wheelchairs.

Given the remoteness of the location, the worldwide lack of interest in human history, plus the time and money and engineering that must have gone into creating a smooth track through what must be the boulder-strewn darkness of the cave, this eventuality strikes all of us as something close to a miracle. Because only now have we realized that Dad could never have walked all the way to the paintings. What were we thinking? We stop still and stare. The sun surges out from behind another cloud. The mobility carts glint. They are pristine, hitherto unused and look like the sort of vehicles NASA might have designed for an ostentatious assault on one of Neptune's moons.

'Socialism,' Dad says, his weight heavy on our shoulders.

'Yeah,' Jack says, 'you have to hand it to the French – they can't run their own economy but they do great prehistoric cave-access.'

'Best food. Respectful of artists. World ambassadors for

adultery and champagne.' Ralph lights a cigarette. 'What's not to love?'

'Is this the right place, Dad?' I ask. 'I mean where is everybody?'

'It's hardly ever open,' Dad says.

'How come?' I ask.

'They only open a very few days of the year, Lou. Because of . . .' he winces, 'because of the air.'

'Because of the *air*?' I ask.

'Because of the breath of the tourists. It creates fungus and mould. On the cave paintings.'

'Well, lucky it's open today,' I say.

Dad leans harder on me.

'Why the facilities?' Jack asks.

'Because they had to pretend that they wanted to welcome the whole of France. Even though they can't, and don't, and never have.'

'Socialism,' Jack says.

So I just come out with it: 'Dad, do you want to go round in a wheelchair?'

And Dad does not hesitate: 'Would seem stupid not to.'

Wheelchairs: you think they're a huge psychological problem, you think they're the end; then, one day, they're the solution, they're the beginning. We move forward again while Ralph walks over to inspect the beautiful machines.

'They've got wine-glass holders,' he says.

'Coffee-cup holders,' Jack says.

Ralph straightens. 'We could open the Thierry Rodez early and drink-drive our way round in the darkness. Get rid of our headaches. It's what the Neanderthals would have wanted.'

'Maybe some of the fuckers are still hiding in there,' Jack says. 'Waiting for things to die down a bit. Did Neanderthals drink, Dad?'

'Not Neanderthals,' Dad says, wearily. 'How many times? *Homo sapiens*. This is a Palaeolithic site.'

'How old?' I ask.

'Between thirty-two and thirty-five thousand years old. Aurignacian.'

Dad hates standing in the direct sunlight; he *wants* to be underground. We are all fair but Ralph and I seem to handle the sun better. We hobble Dad over to the shade by the ticket office and sit him down on a bench. Ralph goes to the booth and leans in to the glass and starts speaking loudly with the man inside – English, then German, then Russian while Jack and I look at the mobility carts.

After a few seconds, Ralph calls over to us as though such a thing were inexplicable: 'The man speaks French. Can you talk to him, Jack?'

'What would you like me to say?'

'Explain our mission.'

Jack and I walk to the booth.

'What mission?'

Ralph stands aside and gestures Jack towards the window. 'I may have confused him. He thinks we are all trying to kill ourselves. Tell him that we're not.'

'We are not all trying to kill ourselves,' Jack says in French.

'Explain the concept,' Ralph urges.

Jack looks round. 'What concept? What the fuck are you talking about?'

'That we are doing everything together. That therefore

we'd like to book *four* disability buggies. In concert. In sympathy.'

Jack sighs and then says some of this to the man, who is now hunching forward so that he can peer up – grimacing and narrow-eyed through the gap where the money and tickets pass back and forth beneath all the stickers advertising other, more attractive, attractions.

'Tell him,' Ralph says, 'that we have agreed to be together in all things. Until we part ways.' Ralph grinds out his cigarette. 'On the sad shore of the River Styx.'

'Until we part ways,' Jack says in French.

Nothing happens.

We are at an impasse. We three stand in a fraternal horseshoe while the man looks back at us, his face like a washing machine mid-cycle.

'Maybe he is deaf,' I say, quietly. 'Or maybe it's the altitude.'

'Tell him we will pay him two hundred euros,' Ralph says, 'And no questions asked.'

Jack does so. Instantly, the man disappears.

Again, we stand with no purpose.

'How is it going?' Dad shouts over from the bench – not without sarcasm.

A door opens somewhere round the side and the old man comes out, hurrying towards us, his back bent, his arm on his hip, wizened and worn down, his life spent at the entrance to a cave. He clasps each of us by the hand but then crosses over to the bench and reaches down for Dad so that the two embrace – not heartily, but with the delicacy of age.

The man speaks in French as thick and jagged as the rocks on which he stands: 'I have wanted for so long to end my own vigil, sir. But I do not have the courage. You are a hero to me. I salute you.'

Dad is taken aback but he is smiling. He flips up his shades. 'It's my children,' he says also in French. 'They're driving me to it.'

The man clasps his elbow.

'Your children?' The old man gestures at us enquiringly.

'Yes,' Dad says, smiling. 'I thought when they were little that one day . . . one day they would cease to be a burden to me. But it just gets worse with each passing year. You think your parents are a nightmare all your life until you have your own children and then you realize it was the children who were the problem all along.'

'Can we take the wheelchairs?' Ralph asks.

'Armand Pujol,' the man says. He stands upright away from Dad, spreads his fingers to his chest as though preparing to self-administer his weary heart's restart without quite knowing which side to press. 'Of course. *Les fauteuils roulants électriques*. Yes, come. Come. Let me guide you.'

There is a wide roadway cut smooth into the rock that bends this way and that down towards the entrance – as if they were expecting the entire disabled population of Europe to stage a marathon through the cave. Armand seems to have shut up shop for the day as part of his bribe. He drives ahead. He tells us that our mobility cars can get up to twenty kilometres an hour. But he is strict that we mustn't go ahead of him. So we follow him down, weaving and bunching like racing drivers behind the safety car. And thus we enter the underworld.

The cave smells of wet stone, cool and damp and earthy, like it must have done for every single one of those thirty-five thousand years. The original entrance – higher up the gorge – was sealed off millennia ago by a rock collapse and so now we must take the same long route inside that the explorers took when they accidentally discovered the paintings. Sometimes we are able to drive two or three abreast. Sometimes we must drive line astern. One joystick controls the angle of our forward spotlights, the other our direction and speed of travel. Either side of our pathway, the walls are lit in eerie lights: yellow, white, reddish, pale blue. Many of the lamps are hidden and angled so that features of the rock are shadowed or illuminated, creating vast imaginary shapes and silhouettes; the suggestion of human intentions, imaginations, intuitions. Everywhere we hear the drip and seep of water.

Armand has some kind of speaker on his cart and he tells us what we are supposed to be seeing in an amplified voice that is eerie, then muffled, then echoic by turn; a voice that comes at us – now as if rising up out of the earth and now as if crawling across the walls. Dad translates after each pronouncement with a sardonic inflection that Armand cannot guess. 'Here is the Emerald City, high up there on your left. And there's the Devil's Tongue . . . right down low on your right. If you look back, you can see the Hags' Fingers above us. When we stop, just up ahead, please look over the ledge: you will be able to see the Organ of Persephone – beside the shore of the Stygian Falls.'

'Did Armand say Persephone's organ?' Ralph asks, loudly, from the back. 'Or was that you, Dad?'

'Armand,' Jack says.

We are side by side, paused on a wide turning area, our carts stopped at odd angles like dodgems at a circus awaiting the music that signals the power being switched on and the next session.

'But the organ was invented in . . .' Ralph hesitates. 'Dad, when was the organ invented?'

'Thirteen-nineties – more or less.'

'Maybe he meant Persephone's organ – as in her urethra,' I say, helpfully.

Ralph leans over towards the rail. 'Do you see a goddess's urethra down there?'

There are two eerily still pools of water illuminated from within by a tiger-eye light. The lower one is filled by a single stream of water that falls in a constant stream – quietly, solidly, without splashing – from the upper.

'Looks pretty urethral,' I say.

'Is the urethra an organ, though?' Jack asks.

'Was Persephone a goddess?' Ralph asks.

'Your phones don't work down here, so I guess you'll never know,' Dad says as if he (and his new pal, Armand) are determined to teach us a lesson and serve us right.

'If that's the Styx,' I say, 'then we're not going to need much of a ferryman to get you across, Dad.'

'Not big enough for the Styx, Baby Lou,' Jack says.

'There were five underworld rivers,' Dad says.

'Styx, Acheron, Lethe . . .' Ralph says. 'Go on, Dad.'

'Phlegethon and Cocytus,' Dad says. 'The rivers of hatred, pain, oblivion, fire and wailing respectively.'

'*Now* we're talking,' I say. 'This is much more like my kind of holiday.'

'Should have bought sandwiches,' Jack says. 'We could have had a picnic where the five rivers meet.'

Armand calls to us from the next bend in the track.

We move off again. Our electric engines humming quietly. We file by some jellyfish fossils from three billion years ago and then, for a while, there are no 'features' and Armand is silent as we go.

The path has little cat's-eye lights that bead the edges. The darkness beyond the pools of the lamps above us is an absolute black that contains everything, nothing.

My mind moves away from itself. I start thinking that this is probably what Dad most wants in the world; that this is precisely how he'd like to enter eternity. And that gets me on to thinking about why he likes these places. Which I'm slowly realizing is to do with time . . . and perspective. The setting of his life in a great context; the relief and easing that such a context brings . . .

And it works. Because now we're all thinking about thousands of years – instead of the next few hours, days, weeks. We're no longer trapped in the present. Instead of myself and instead of tomorrow, I'm thinking about all my ancestors and all of my pasts, I'm thinking about all of those people I can never know – my father's father's father a thousand times over, who maybe looked a bit like me and who was himself a son. I'm thinking about how he must have thought and wondered as I think and wonder. A mind exactly the same in biology and in capacity. About how, after he had eaten, he must have sat beside a fire in the shelter of the caves and looked out over gorges like these and seen the moon and stars and talked and talked and talked with his kin. In what language? And what must they have said? My father was a great hero to me. My father was a great coward. My father was weak. My father was brave. And I'm thinking about how the Earth is so ancient. And the dignity of that. The dignity of age. Even though dignity is only a human word and doesn't describe it. And I'm thinking about how an alien-god might stop by as it passes through the cave of the universe and look down upon our blue globe of beautiful light and how it might hear all the millions of human voices in what might be the equivalent of less than a second for such a being – since it will surely have conquered death – and how this alien-god would be amazed at our confusion, at how we swaggered and worried and mistook what matters again and again and again and again in the brief match-flare of our own lives and in the repetitive failure to see what our species might best be and yet become. And it would sigh to itself and shake its head and say, 'Well, OK, fuck up then, so-called *sapiens*, but don't lose it, guys, don't totally lose it, whatever you do, do *not* totally lose it' – and then it would reboot its satnav and get back on track for some distant star system where they'd long ago got the hang of how to live well, intelligently and for ever.

Armand has slowed us and we concertina again. We are driving onto a long and wide viewing gallery, two or three feet above the floor of the cave. And here we stop. He tells us to park against the rail and look over it into the darkness. He asks us to put the brake on and to turn our lights out. We do so. He must have stopped himself somewhere near a master switch behind us because suddenly the lights go out completely.

We can see nothing – absolutely nothing. So black is the darkness that I swear I can hear the shape of the walls, taste the stone, smell the water that has passed through from the Earth from above.

'Now,' he says. 'Now look with your eyes. Friends, look!'

Gradually, gradually, a light grows. Like a hallucination. Like a red shape behind our eyelids. So that we think we're mad. Or reborn from the womb. But it widens and it spreads so that the opposite wall starts to shape itself, the light growing sharper and brighter, sharper and brighter. We see ochre hand prints; the human mark. We see strange red patterns and dots; human signs. We begin to see the outlines of animals – the beasts. The human mind, the human imagination, the human signature. And now the light starts to flood the wall and we see that these animals crouch and creep and crawl this way and that all around us – lions, hyenas, panthers, cave bears. The light brightens still further. There is an owl daubed in white paint. We sense the finger that smeared the surface of the wall on that day thirty thousand years ago. There is a rhino notched and scored in black. We see the artist has chosen a certain place on the wall where the shape of the rock serves his purposes. We see a heavy-haunched bison painted in sweeping flowing lines. We sense the human being standing back and admiring his artistry in the flicker of his torchlight. We see the curved flourish of the antlers of a reindeer. We see head after head of black-drawn horses, each on the other's shoulder, as if caught in the instant of the herd's fierce gallop, their black eyes somehow still alive.

We are silent.

Dad's voice is full of wonder: 'I've wanted to see this all my life,' he says.

I get this feeling like the opposite of sickness – the feeling that these paintings are being sucked inside me and that they will somehow live there for ever and ornament my soul.

'This is it,' Dad says. 'The *beginning*.' His voice has the hushed tone of long yearning met – as though he has been trying to get to this moment ever since he was born. As though now that he apprehends the beginning, he might understand the ending. 'This is it as best we can know it, boys. The dawn of a distinctly human kind of consciousness.'

And then another thing hits me: that whatever happens to Dad, we will remember this always. Yes, when I am old, I'll think of this . . . of Ralph and Jack and me and Dad on our carts. And if this was my father's intention, then he's achieved it. Because this journey – Dad's journey – has its sacrament now. A moment, a monument, made in our memories that will stand outside of time.

My father's voice is still quiet but he sounds strong and unfaltering in the silence: 'Can you see how the shadows fall to create the illusion of movement? You can tell that the artist understands the drama of space. And can you feel it? That we understand that he understands. And that this understanding connects us to him. The human conversation not bound by time or space.' He's talking to us now like he did when I was little and he was teaching us. 'Testimony to the inner life, boys. The life of thought and feeling. That which makes us what we are. That which separates us from these beasts we draw.'

Jack speaks softly: 'Did you know this place was open today, Dad?'

'I did. I did.'

'You planned this?' Jack asks.

'When I got my date, I had the idea. Then I – just – I just looked on the internet and it was too much of a coincidence. I was going to come along on my own with Doug – you know, Doug – because I didn't know if you'd be free . . .'

The word seems so inexplicable now – 'free' – but this is how we were; so bound in by our lives that we were unable to see life itself.

'I didn't know if you'd . . .' And now Dad wavers. 'I didn't know if you'd be with me.' His voice thickens. 'But . . . you are. You are all here.'

The wall is alive. We don't die. Or, if we do, we die all together – every human being that has ever lived.

'And I'm so glad,' Dad says. 'So happy that you all made it.'

'Well, you'd never have got us all here without promising you were going to kill yourself,' Ralph says.

'The truth,' I say. 'And isn't that something?'

My father says the most staggering thing about human beings is not the tools – it's the art, it's the language. Because art and language allow us to consider and talk about things that don't exist. Other animals communicate, he says. But they are bound in by the physical world – where the food is, where the predators are, the cold of the winter and the return of the sun. Only we create art and fictions. Only we deliberate over things that do not exist: our gods, our nation states, our money and our laws. Only we design an imaginary architecture of ideas and then persuade one another of its reality. This is what art and language have given us. The ability to share these great games and structures of our imaginations and to persuade one another to live by their strictures. We are absurdly successful because of our fictions. Truly, this is the theatre of the imagination.

The race for the finish is like the last three laps at the Brazilian GP at the end of the season when the championship is yet to be decided. The (unknowing) safety car – Armand – peels off and we're released. Basically, it's an uphill drag out of the mouth of the cave towards the first left hairpin and then a short uphill sprint into a sixty-degree right and so back up the gentler incline to the finish by the ticket booth.

Dad goes left for the inside and Jack goes right, quicker to react to the restart than me and Ralph. I tuck in behind Dad and Ralph veers even wider than Jack, planning for the cut back.

Dad is hogging the racing line and leaning a little on Jack, forcing him out wider. There's a gap opening up in the inside therefore. And so I'm right there. It's all going to be about the brakes.

Dad leaves it too late in an effort to hold Jack off and keep him wide around the left-hand hairpin. And so I'm suddenly right up his inside trying to keep as tight a line as possible. But I'm also too fast and deep into the bend and I can't slow my cart down enough. I T-bone Dad, who, in turn, has now wedged into Jack. And so we three are unable to straighten up and get back on the gas up the hill for the right-hander and – unbelievably – Ralph has come sneaking through on *my* inside. The fucker must have braked early, swept it out wide and turned in sharp so as to slip through the gap as it opened up.

'It's all about corner exit speed,' he shouts.

He's away and in the lead. But I'm after him. Only a cart-length behind. I guess it's a fifty-metre sprint to the right-hander. And we're both at max speed. The question is, therefore, who has the nerve to take the last corner flat. I hang out wide to sweep in. I can watch Ralph, I'm thinking, and see if his trajectory takes him into trouble. There's no way he's going to back off. He's too insane. I watch him swing in for the racing line but – halfway round the corner – it becomes clear that he's definitely not going to make it. I slow myself down. But it's not enough. Ralph is scraping along the outer wall, effectively narrowing the corner exit by a cart's width, and I therefore need to get even tighter to miss him which I cannot do. I bump into his back wheel and come to a head-jerking stop. At the same time I feel a thump up my backside. It's Jack, who is doing to me precisely what I have done to Ralph. We're rammed nose to tail. All three trying to free our front ends. Ralph deliberately blocking me. Me deliberately blocking Jack. And that's how Dad comes bowling by at half speed and takes it through the gap before accelerating up and away for the chequered flag that is already waving in his mind.

We drive up slowly. Jack and Ralph are laughing. But a child's joy is dancing in the blue of Dad's eyes. Gone the furrowed brow, the drooping eyelids, the horizontal lips, instead his face is an adolescent grin radiant with excitement and with being one of the boys – one of us – but one of the boys *and the winner*.

'Fair and square, Lou,' he says, as I come to help him up. 'Fair and square.'

'Hamilton-esque,' I say.

'Schumi,' Ralph says as he pulls into *parc fermé*.

'Prost,' Jack says.

'Lauda,' Dad says. 'Lauda.'

He's still got his hands on the controls. And it's like he doesn't want to get out of his cart ever. He thinks he's on the start–finish at Monaco and all the world's most beautiful people are cheering as he takes off his helmet and ruffles his hand through his sweat-soaked hair. And he just can't help his gloating and his pleasure.

This is it, people, I'm thinking; this is happiness.

THE WHEELCHAIR

'You shouldn't spend his money without asking him,' Jack says, eyeing the fifty-euro notes that Ralph fans with clever thumbs. 'Did you just take those?'

'If I asked him, he would never spend it on anything except fucking croissants. And there are only so many croissants you can buy . . .'

'It's not your money, Ralph.'

'Thank you, Jack. I realize that. Which is why I'm buying things *for* him. I myself do not require a wheelchair. Yet.' He strikes a match. 'And when I do, boys, please don't hesitate.' He has a way of shifting his cigarette to the very lowest angle in the corner of his mouth. 'And it's not *just* the wheelchair, is it? Actually, I am buying Dad experiences, comfort, happiness. More than this: *possibility.*'

Jack is quiet – like maybe he shouldn't block this gesture towards the future – and Ralph sees this as he squints against the smoke. So he presses home his advantage: 'You should be delighted. This is what he is incapable of doing for himself. What else are we going to do with the money? Or – don't tell me – he was keeping cash for the boys at the clinic.'

'It's not a clinic,' I say.

'Do they do cash discount?' Ralph exhales through his nose.

But Jack is dogged. 'It's not your money and it's not your decision what to do with it.'

'It will be soon. How about this? I'm spending my third.'

'Oh, Jesus,' I say.

'Do we even know it is going to be thirds?' Jack asks.

'Oh, Jesus,' I say.

'Well, I'm going to put it back,' Jack persists. 'How much have you taken?'

'Two hundred for the grand prix event. And a hundred for this.'

The door starts to jiggle; someone or something is trying to enter the store-room backwards with his arms full.

Ralph affects to relent: 'Maybe you're right. Maybe extending your life is even more expensive than a funeral. At what stage does the cost of living outweigh the cost of death? *There's* a question for your new actuarial pals, Jack. Thank you, Armand.'

With much clatter and awkwardness and grimacing, Armand has finally arrived in the room; he turns and puts down what must be the wheelchair that he has agreed to sell us. Last-generation, he avows, never been used. They shipped him fifty from Paris. Before they'd even opened the cave. Then they sent *les fauteuils roulants électriques*. He has never been to Paris but, clearly, he thinks of it as some kind of El Dorado where an endlessly prodigal elite lie around half-naked frittering the national wealth and idly cycling though vice. He's going to put the rest of his stock on eBay one at a time when 'things' 'die down'. He's not clear what things or why they need to die down.

With several sweeps of his arms and kicks of his feet, Armand clears a space amidst the stacks of leaflet-guides to the cave – Polish, Flemish, Portuguese – and begins to demonstrate how the wheelchair unfolds and how to slot in the wheels. I was expecting something from a First World War mental asylum but this is sleek, cool, useable. Ralph smokes. Jack and I pay attention to the various demonstrations. No tools needed. Quick-release wheels, like so. Anti-tip stabilizers here and here. Cup-holder. Brake. Armand starts to show us how to pack it away again. Ralph re-counts the money in bad French. Armand joins in. He is a paragon of enthusiastic corruption; the sight of cash being offered to him for stealing or re-selling his nation's assets strikes him as nothing less than long-awaited justice, vindication and due. He takes the banknotes with a nod that says – 'Finally, recompense.'

A bell sounds.

Jack speaks in French. 'I think someone else is trying to see the cave, maybe. We should let you go.'

'No, it's fine,' Armand says. 'We shut at two, today.'

Outside, the sun is searing the red lands as though we're in a movie about the first epoch of Martian terra-forming. The van seems to shimmer in the heat haze. Dad is sitting on his bench in the shade looking out across the gorge.

'Bad luck,' Ralph says in a voice of commiseration to the two gap-year students standing earnestly at the ticket booth looking at Armand's improbable *'ferme'* sign. 'If it's any consolation, these particular cavemen were terrible at drawing.' He indicates over his shoulder with his thumb. 'The buffalo look nothing like buffalo; and the horses – really infantile. Scribbles, to be honest.' He makes a flailing gesture. 'No hand-to-eye coordination.'

Another difference between Jack and Ralph is that Ralph doesn't give a fuck what is in Dad's will. But it now occurs to me that Jack does. He's anxious Dad is going to have done something he finds dumb or divisive. So he wants to know. He wants to talk to Dad about it. And maybe that is part of why he wants to keep him alive.

Dad is still sitting on his bench half-swivelled round as we walk up with the wheelchair. 'Look at the view,' he says, 'it's beautiful, boys.'

My mother had this way of beckoning you over to sit beside her, too; but not to look at the external view; rather, to talk as if in deepest confidence. Like you were great friends, intimate friends; and only you two together were really able to see and judge things as they truly were. She did it with men and women the same – but, if it was a trick, then it worked. Because you felt special beside her – simply because that come-over-here-and-sit-beside-me-because-I-need-to-talk-to-only-you-in-all-the-world conferred something unavailable from anywhere else. She liked to sit on our ragged old purple sofa and watch the sceptical London birds in our tiny garden.

She liked to say that 'her predecessor' had 'given birth' to 'two archetypes of masculinity'. She tabled this as a joke, I suppose. But who is happier, Lou? she would ask – not rhetorically. And what is happiness? Is it contentment, ease, dependability? Or is it elation, excitement, exultation? Or does it turn out that the consolation prize for never having the elation is contentment? And the consolation prize for never having experienced any contentment is elation? Can the one turn into the other? She used to ask me these things straight out and it made me feel grown up and embarrassed at the same time. I don't know why. But I told my father some of this after my mother died. And he said something which I will never forget: 'Don't make the picture too narrow, Lou, because there's nobility on both sides.'

Another time, she told me that she believed the boys' 'basic issue' was not that they didn't feel any love from Dad, but rather that they felt that for a long time Dad had thought of their existence as a problem. They thought that if they hadn't been there, the divorce would have been cleaner, the new life easier. Everything. They were the problem. Or they were the manifestation of all the problems. And because they were children and dealt with all the stress, they internalized it. That's what children do, she said to me. And probably your father gave them that impression at times because he's so bad at hiding his feelings . . . and so bad at expressing them. And so now we must work hard to counter this stuff. We have to help your dad and your brothers. Our job is to make Ralph and Jack realize that your dad never stopped loving them – realize it in their hearts, I mean. My mum was always placing her palm softly against my heart to make her points. Like she was sealing in secrets. Like maybe she always knew she was going to be gone.

One of the last thing she said to me: now the Mighty River flows through you a while.

'Where next?' I ask.

'Lunch,' Ralph says.

'Lunch on the road,' Jack asks, 'or lunch in a restaurant?'

'I'm starving,' I say. 'Lunch quickly.'

'That's the hangover, Lou,' Ralph says.

'If you don't want to wait,' Jack says, 'then we'll have to drive and eat. We're miles from anywhere.'

'Yeah, but drive where?' I ask.

'We don't have to go to Zurich *tonight*,' Dad says.

'Dad,' I say.

'We're not going to Zurich,' Jack says.

'Jack,' Ralph says.

'For fuck's sake,' I say.

'So let's just . . .' Ralph shrugs. 'Let's just drive.'

'*You* drive,' Jack says.

'I drove us here. Now I want to drink. You're the one who's going to start moaning if I do both.'

Dad inhales deeply. 'Open the champagne then, why not? I think it is time for Thierry. Will you *look* at that view, boys.'

The sun sears the cliffs, ignites the gorge, pours molten light towards us – as if all the world were but a narrow cast for the forging of mighty swords.

'OK,' Jack says, 'I'll drive. But just to be clear I am not driving to Zurich.'

'Please, Jack,' I say, 'don't—'

'I'm not. But I'm just saying—'

'—don't "just say"—'

'—that I'm not driving this van anywhere near Switzerland. Apart from anything else, we've just bought you a state-of-the-art wheelchair, Dad.'

'Which *is* awesome,' I say.

Ralph winces: 'Don't say awesome.'

'Awesome.'

'OK,' Jack offers, 'so where would you like me to drive?'

'London,' I say.

'How about a strip club in Barcelona? I hear they're the best. Or it might be Bucharest. I never get definitive information. Anyone?'

'Dad?' Jack asks.

'I'd like to go somewhere good for dinner. Michelin stars. Actually . . . you know what? Truffles. I really want truffles. Is that possible?'

Ralph nods slowly. 'Two days to go and at last – *at last* – you're starting to talk like a serious human being.'

'I'd also love a concert,' Dad says. 'To hear some music. Bach. Mozart. Chopin.'

'OK,' Ralph says. 'Concert. Truffles. Armageddon. This has got to be possible somewhere in Europe. We need a city. Where is the nearest city? Where are we?'

'No idea,' Jack says. 'You were driving.'

'Try to be more helpful,' Ralph says. 'You can be very negative at times, Jack.'

'Dad?' Jack asks.

'I tell you what . . .'

'Speak, Baby Lou,' Ralph says. 'I like that look on your face. Speak to us.'

'Well . . . I'm just saying: you remember Malte and Dean, Dad? The Debussy and whatever festival. We could go and see that. Where did they say it was? I looked at it before. It's on my phone. I don't think it is miles off track. It's a food festival, too.'

'I take it all back, Lou,' Ralph says. 'Only now am I beginning to understand the subtle complexion of your genius.'

'I need to be in Zurich tomorrow by noon.'

'Dad, stop being ridiculous.'

Ralph holds up a hand. 'No no no . . . Jack, listen: if we

agree it is Dad's last night on Earth, then we are truly free to go anywhere and do anything. We can—'

'Here it is,' I say. 'Denzlingen. Yep. We just have to cross the Rhine.'

'Beautiful,' Ralph says. 'How do we know these people?'

'Me and Dad met them in this car park near the Somme. Changed their tyre.'

'Is that some kind of code?' Jack asks.

Ralph nods slowly. 'You were dogging again, Lou, weren't you? But . . . that's OK. No judgement. No judgement here.' He holds up his hands. 'We all need to relax from time to time.'

'Let's just say they owe us.'

'Great,' Ralph says. 'Well, then, get us guest-listed for everything. Explain that we'd also like some kind of return-the-favour sexual encounter. Rhine-maidens, wheelchair-friendly dwarves, that kind of thing. Whatever they've got.'

One of the things that Dad blames 'it' on is the sudden acceleration of human 'progress'. Think about it, he used to say, invitingly, calmly: in ancient Mesopotamia 7,000 years ago – rough figures, rough figures – the fastest human communication could move was the speed of a horse, pigeon or sail; in the England of the 1820s, the situation was much the same – horses, pigeons, sails. All right: throw in smoke signals and the odd semaphore station. That's 6,800 years (or three hundred-odd generations) of the same pace for everything. No change. (Not to mention *Homo sapiens'* one hundred and ninety-five thousand pre-civilization years.) And then (here he used to become more animated), in the withering flash of two hundred years, or a mere eight generations, we get . . . we get *this*. All of it. Modern Life. And then – around 1989 – it *really* started to speed up. Just around when you were born, Lou. Unbelievable. Staggering. Instant. A billion tentacles. Imagine the rate-of-change graph – imagine where we stand – now – at this moment in human history – how steep it suddenly rises. The technological revolution – in terms of how our computers actually work – is already utterly beyond the comprehension of all but – say – a few thousand people. No wonder our psychology and our belief systems have not had time to adjust. We are editing the genome. No wonder there are side effects. We should not be surprised, Lou. Indeed, it is amazing that *everything* in the twenty-first century isn't a side effect. Maybe it is. Maybe that's the problem. Maybe this is the first generation to be entirely consumed and preoccupied by side effects. Maybe your mother was right. Things *have* fallen apart. We *are* distracted from distraction by distraction. We *are* filled with fancies and empty of meaning. It *is* all tumid apathy with no concentration. I'm glad it's not my problem any more. Over to you, Lou. The slouching beast is in downtown Bethlehem.

Dad calls my brothers 'The Transitional Generation'. He says he is fine and I am fine but the technological revolution hit my brothers like a tsunami in the 1990s when they were too old and too young. He says it's left them stranded some-where between the Old World and the New.

SHOOTING THE RAPIDS

The good mood of Dad's victory plays through the afternoon like a soundtrack we all love. Jack is driving. Ralph is in the passenger seat. Dad and I are seated in the back. Dad has been napping again. He's eaten another fistful of ibuprofen. We've cut loose from the law. So we are driving table-down and I am not even wearing a seat belt. Instead, I'm trying to make salami, artichoke and tomato baguettes on a plastic plate. Dad only ever travels with one prep knife, but it was made by Bronze Age warriors or something, and it's so sharp that you could slice clean through your finger and not feel the pain until you trod on the severed end. I have a jar of mustard from the kitchen cupboard and these little packets of salt and pepper in my pockets, which I stole some-place back along the line at a service station. We have just turned left, north, on the E35. The signs says Fessenheim, Bad Krozingen, Freiburg. We have crossed the Rhine.

I made the calls. Malte almost died with unexpected delight. Leave it all to me, he said, everything is going to be perfect; he will talk to the sponsors, pull strings, move mountains; there's this castle-restaurant we just have to see, he said, overlooking the river where they serve the Feinsch-mecker Hochgenuss. I asked him if he'd be OK to agent the rest of our lives. He said he would – gladly – and he'd even drop to ten per cent if we did the maintenance on his van.

Meanwhile, here on the autobahn, the traffic is thickening and we seem to have moved on to Ralph. His life. His situation.

'You did what?' Jack asks.

'I said . . . I said I offered to help edit her novel.'

Jack is incredulous; this is not the brother he dined in utero with. 'You offered to read her book?'

Ralph sighs without irony. 'Every word, every line – with a pen in my hand for almost three weeks.'

'Big mistake,' I say. 'Big mistake.'

'Was it any good?' Dad asks.

'No – it was terrible.'

'So why did you do it?' Jack asks.

'Does this lighter still not work?' Ralph asks.

'Because he wanted to sleep with her,' I say. 'Why does Ralph do anything?'

'Wrong. I'd already slept with her.'

'Must be the sadomasochism then,' I say.

'It's possible, Lou. Humankind is addicted to agony.' Ralph presses the broken lighter as if a little patience might be all that is required to coax it back from its long decease. 'Isn't that so, Jack?'

'Nope.' Jack slows gently for the traffic, which is backing up ahead of us, one set of brake lights after another. 'And anyway – we're done with me, Ralph. It's agreed: I'm the embarrassingly defeated husband of bourgeois society. We are on to you. Don't deflect.'

'That's all he does,' I say. 'His whole life is a massive deflection. You start off trying to guess who he is from the angle of the deflections. Then you realize that if he doesn't deflect, he won't exist at all.'

'Thank you, Louis. Can you pass me those matches from the kitchen?'

The smell of the mustard is making me want to stage an Edwardian picnic. The baguettes are something beautiful. And we're drinking the kind of champagne that only champagne-makers know to drink.

Dad says: '*Please* be careful with that knife.'

'Don't – whatever you do – accidentally stab anyone under-braking, Lou,' Ralph says.

'This traffic is getting worse,' Jack says.

Ralph undoes his seat belt and half turns around. 'Maybe the whole of Europe intends to ram themselves with the mighty Feinschmecker Hochgenuss and then commit suicide. Can't say I blame them. We seem to be in a deterioration phase. The new Dark Ages are coming. Ignorance will not only be bliss, but power. Matches, Lou?'

I pass them forward.

Dad says. 'Can I have a cigarette?'

'Make that two,' I say, 'I've run out.'

Ralph shakes out two more cigarettes.

I light up. They are horrible – like smoking the exhaust of a Russian tank. Dad does the same from my match. We're crawling now – and the traffic is queuing for miles ahead of us.

'There must have been an accident,' Jack says. He looks back into the dense fug. 'Oh, for fuck's *sake*. Cover the food up.'

'Doing it.'

'No. No!' Jack glances back angrily from watching the traffic. 'No. Lou – don't just put the newspaper over it. Do it properly. Dad, tell him. What is *wrong* with you people?' He winds down his window to let in some German diesel fumes to go with the sliced salami and cigarette smoke.

'You might as well join in, Jack,' Ralph says. 'Then your sandwiches will taste better. Evens things out.'

'Jack likes his smoking like he likes his aggression,' I say, 'passive.'

'Louis,' Ralph says, 'try not to be mean about your brothers all the time. Tell him, Dad. He's being really horrible to us.'

I put the food in a plastic bag and lay the newspaper on top. I get the feeling that we were getting into something with Ralph. Something almost genuine. So I press him: 'Why did you read her book?'

Ralph strikes his match as slowly as it is possible for a human being to do while still achieving ignition. 'I read it, Lou, because I was falling in love with her.'

We're inching forward and then stopping again. Jack looks over. 'You don't use that word very often, if I may so, brother Ralph.'

'I read it because it was a way of seeing her more often. And because when I began reading it . . .' Ralph reaches forward to place the matches on the table. 'When I began reading it, I would come across these lost, lonely, isolated passages that were full of a kind of beauty and humanity.'

'You wanted to save her?' Jack asks, warily.

'Uh-oh,' I say. 'This is going to end badly.'

'I saw that behind the lazy fakery, she had real talent – an imagination – something rare and worth attending to. I don't know. I wanted to pay her my full attention. I wanted to encourage her. I still do.'

'This was the woman who . . . who . . . This was the last

serious woman?' Dad asks – almost as if of himself. 'I didn't know. I didn't know anything about this.'

'The last serious woman on Earth,' I say.

'You're saying the book wasn't the start of it?' Jack asks.

'No. We met at a screening, we talked . . . Mostly about music. We had lunch and planned our future. We had dinner.'

'She eat a lot?'

'Yes – as it happens, Lou, she did.'

Jack says, 'You're sure that this was love? I—'

'As soon as we knew one another, we were amazed that we had not known each other before. Within a week, all previous relationships seemed juvenile – anaemic, paltry.'

Jack turns his head from the road to look directly at his twin. 'I know who this was. You never said it was serious. At the time.'

'Oh, it was serious.'

'What was she like?' I ask.

'For fuck's sake, Lou – I don't know. That's a silly question even by your standards. What is anyone *like*?'

'What was she like?' I ask again.

'I have no idea . . . Christ.'

'What did she eat, then? When she was doing all the eating?'

'She didn't much like fruit cake. She liked her bacon undercooked. She ate a lot of garlic and a lot of butter. She used the word "deliquesce" on the westbound platform at Royal Oak. What can I say?'

There are trees beside the carriageway. A glimpse of the mighty river beyond. Other cars. Other lives. Mostly single people staring forward in consternation and anger at the blocked road ahead. And nobody talking. Nobody except us.

Jack edges forward.

'What was she like in the sack?' I ask.

'Louis,' Dad winces.

But Ralph doesn't flinch: 'She would put her hand on her stomach and she would say, "I'm greedy for it all." Which she was. Is. Greedy for all of it – all the time. And then she would go to pieces all over my head.'

Dad says softly: 'Tell us why you loved her, Ralph.'

'I don't know, Dad. Her dark brown eyes. I loved her face of enquiry. I loved her face of fright. I loved her confusion. Her beauty. Her cheekbones. I loved her endless hurry . . . mainly to get away from all these fantasy versions of herself that she had constructed, but which never quite rang true. I even loved the fact that she was such a liar. Christ, I don't know . . . I'm a sucker for a good-looking girl with an imagination and real intelligence.'

We're at a total standstill on the road. Sun stark and certain in the sky. Cars all around. Heat-shimmer from the engines. The river just out of sight. I'm thinking that there's no place like a traffic jam to give you the feeling that humanity has somehow taken a wrong turn.

But wherever we're going, I want us never to get there.

Dad speaks softly again: 'When you were together . . . what was it like?'

Jack half turns back from the wheel the better to attend to what his brother is saying. Ralph opens his palm slowly and we're all watching him – his puppeteer's fingers; he makes the gesture of reaching out, of connection.

'I would hold out my hand – and she was there. We were wed. In thought, in feeling. In desire.'

'How did her love declare itself?' Dad asks, almost tenderly. 'How did she—'

'Music,' Ralph says immediately. 'She bought me music. She sent me music. I did the same. Duets. We would meet in town and say nothing – simply swap our headphones so she could listen to whatever I was listening to and vice versa. And then we'd walk beside each other.'

My father nods slowly.

Ralph exhales. 'The world was reconfigured in front of my eyes. We were remade in one another's company.'

He douses his cigarette in our ashtray and immediately fingers another from his pack.

'Love remakes us,' Dad says. His face is full of feeling and his eyes are shining. 'That's it: that's what love does. Love remakes us.'

The traffic is still. I can feel that my father wants to reach out for Ralph like he would to me. But that he can't. They cannot touch.

'And the book?' Jack asks, quietly. 'What became of the book?'

'Oh, this book became our joint project. Line by line, minute by minute, I went through it. In hotels, cafes, kitchens, bedrooms, train carriages. I sat with her and together we dragged this limp and bogus thing back to life. Scene after scene. All this ersatz shit she'd written.' He sparks his match.

'She let you do that to her work?'

'Yes, Dad, she did. Because . . . like all the other stuff in her life, she was absent from it. It wasn't really her. She'd managed to write an entire book without putting in more than five lines that she actually meant. It was breathtaking.

She'd chase me and hound me to work on it. Not that it was saveable.'

Dad asks, 'What was it about?'

'Nothing.'

'Even in a gestural work, there must have been an ostensible subject?'

'I don't know. It was full of stuff that she was pretending to herself to be writing about. I don't know. I didn't care after a while. We would work. Then we would climb into bed and make love. I cared about that.'

'But you persevered with the work?' Dad asks.

'I gave her everything I could give.' He winces as if there's a nerve which gets trapped in his heart whenever it pulls in a certain direction.

The traffic inches forward. Jack turns back to move us along. I put out my cigarette, which has burnt to the filter. Dad does the same. I pour more champagne. We stop again. Jack pulls the handbrake and swings an arm over the back of his chair so that we make a broken circle around our plastic table.

'But why?' he asks. 'Why did you care about her? If you say she was such a—'

'I don't know. Why do we do fall in love? It's a dream, it's a fantasy, it's real, it's everything. I just felt received and understood. But also because she was – she *is* – so clever and capable – and yet so ensnared and muted and bound in – all at the same time. Vulnerable. Invulnerable. It's hard to describe.' Ralph's eyes seek the window and the world beyond for what he is trying to say. 'It was like being with a creature hell bent on doing this mad dance of self-concealment and showing off all at the same time.'

'Go on,' Jack says. He helps Ralph speak, I'm thinking, just like Ralph helps Jack speak. Despite everything, he's the only one who can climb in there with his brother, take the other paddle and shoot the rapids; these boys, they'd die for each other in a heartbeat.

'There was none of that shit you normally get, the slow traipse through the foothills,' Ralph continues. 'She was quicksilver smart. She was able to slalom from one thing to another without self-consciousness.' He exhales. 'When we were doing the book . . . something strange happened: I realized she wanted *me* to tell her what she meant. She didn't know. Because nobody else . . . nobody else had ever talked with her about her inner life.'

'Go on.'

'Her mother worked every hour because her father was absent – he had another family. Her mother had another family, too, really. She had a step-dad. She lived in the gap between the two families. So basically she had to make herself up to herself.'

'Absent father,' Jack says.

'Absence was her thing. And she'd had no companion. Or not the kind of companion she needed. I honestly think she was . . . she was estranged from herself. Not in a surface way – but inside. She was acting.'

'No companion but married?' This from Jack.

'Married.' Dad breathes in slowly.

'She was *married*?' I ask.

'Married,' Ralph says again.

'Married,' Jack says, quietly. He turns back and loosens the brake. We crawl forward a few metres.

'Jesus Christ.'

Ralph smiles, but wearily.

'Married to whom?' Dad asks.

'Precisely the wrong person – psychologically. Married to the embodiment of her own deepest and most secret fears. Not that he could know any of this. He had no time for psychology.'

'A good man though?' Dad asks.

'Yes. Of course. A superb, wonderful, kind, generous, man. Helpful. Decent. Dependable.'

'I like him,' Jack says to the Mercedes brake lights ahead.

'Me too,' I say.

'A man who stands up straight and makes a point of doing so,' Ralph continues. 'Not exactly handsome. Not exactly not. Well travelled. Says "don't hold back" like such phrases are in and of themselves funny. Doing well at work. How could he not be? Likes his films. Likes his music. Grooms but not gay. Favourite sunglasses. Favourite T-shirts. Ostensibly considerate, reasonable, steady, proud . . . but, oh, these dull and dreary people neck-deep in the platitudes of life. A professional fetcher and carrier. The kind of brittle, enervating masculinity that makes you wish for death. Sorry, Dad.'

'Don't hold back,' I say.

'And underneath?' Jack asks, sarcastically.

'Oh, underneath.' Ralph ignores his tone. 'Under*neath*. A wounded child. Not his fault. Some kind of trauma back there that took away his certitude. So he, too, had been required to make things certain for himself. You know the routine: I am unable to deal with the truth of human exist-ence – and thus I must erect a grand architecture of right and wrong, a series of ingeniously idiotic totems purporting to delineate reality – this decent, this not; this fair, this not; this good, this bad. Surround yourself with titles and uniforms and clerical collars and hope that everybody will agree to forget that we're all born mammal-naked and none of it matters a shit one second after you're dead.'

Jack: 'You met him?'

'No.'

'So how do you know all this?'

'She talked about him. He spoke to me through her. I listened carefully because I listen carefully and because it is interesting to hear another human being talk about love – especially if you're in love with her.'

'I feel for him,' Jack says.

'I did too. In a way . . . In a way, they had the same problems. Or cousin problems. Which is a disaster. First rule of a successful marriage: have different problems.'

'Why was she with him?'

'Why is anybody with anybody they only half want to be with? Accidents of timing. A certain non-specific thirst and a few self-welcomed delusions. Followed up by some subtle bullying, cajolery and entrapment from the other side. But it was worse than that.'

'Worse than *that*?' I ask.

'He's Christian,' Ralph says. 'A quiet faith. Except of course not quiet at all: it was all moral imperatives and social orders – the whole grand suite of commands supposedly given unto humankind by fuck knows who to enthrone the status quo and have us all skivvying for our betters. Oh, it was all masters and servants and the class system with him. Abasement. Humiliation. Worship. Your mother would have had a field day with him, Lou. Issues galore.'

'I'm getting a lot of anger,' I say.

'Anger is how we cauterize the wounds of love,' Dad says. Then gently: 'He can't have had an easy time of it with you in the picture, Ralph.'

'He sluiced shame and guilt upon her head until her only duty was to sacrifice herself hourly at the altar of his rectitude, of his so-called love, which was actually *possession*. But what can anyone do? We all live at cross-purposes to one another. The misunderstandings are exponential.'

Dad asks, 'You feel no guilt?'

'Yes, I feel guilty that I only made love to her about twenty times. I feel guilty that I was cautious – out of a respect.'

The traffic edges forward again.

Jack asks: 'What did she do for *you*, Ralph?'

'She bought me gifts. A CD of Gesualdo – the composer who murdered his wife – and a dictionary of what actors do when they want to fake emotions.'

Jack glances towards Dad and clicks his tongue: 'Would you say this was . . . a drama?'

'Oh yes. Plenty. It was a drama as much as it was a reality. We were like two Oscar-nominees slugging it out at the Dionysian. And – believe me – reality went down and took several counts. But at the end, it was reality still standing there with one punch more to throw.'

'What do you mean?'

'I mean reality defeated us. I mean pragmatism and convention triumphed. As they must. As they must.'

'And you're sure her feelings were real? How do you know she wasn't fucking with you?'

'Oh, she *was* fucking with me. She was definitely fucking with me. About fifty per cent of the time. She lied to everyone – mother, father, husband. I was there. I heard her. I have no illusions. I was way down the line in terms of important people to lie to.'

'So there you are.' Jack ratchets the handbrake.

'But she also *wasn't* fucking with me.'

'How do you know?'

'The things she did. The things she said. You have to look at the behaviour. Certain calls. Certain texts wanting me. Others declaring love. As real and as heartfelt as anything I've ever known. She took risks all the time to be with me. She called me back once – after a long conversation – and she just came out and said it: "I love you." You have to respect another human being when they say that. It may be the *only* thing we have to respect.

'How did it end?'

'Pregnancy.'

'Whose baby?'

'Hers.'

Softly, Dad asks: 'How did it end for you?'

'Agony. Amazement. I drank and smoked and cried for nine days. I wrote her letters that I could not send. Then I moved to Berlin and became the greatest puppeteer the world has ever known.'

Jack meets Ralph's eye: 'Are you not better off without her?'

'Profoundly so. Unquestionably. But she is the most interesting woman I have ever met.'

'And . . .'

'And I was so in love with her.'

'Sounds like your pride was hurt,' Jack says.

'Oh, don't think I haven't been through all of *that*. But,

after the mutual exploitation and the drama and the narcissism and the sheer fucking misery for everyone, I find myself three years later unequivocally in love with her the same as I was before.' He shrugs. 'Love is what is left after every other motive, emotion, reason has fallen away. I strip my existence of all the darkness and self-deceit. I go at it with acid and a blowtorch. And when at last I stop . . . love remains, still standing there, quiet and true.'

'When did you see her last?' Dad asks.

'Three years ago. We met up in this cafe – for coffee – Christ, it was the most disingenuous hour I have ever sat through. I tried to keep it real but she was gone . . . gone.'

'What did she say?'

'She said we were never going to agree but she wished that we had never been lovers. Because then we could have been friends and talked every day.'

'And what did you say?' I ask.

'Had to agree.'

'Had to?'

'Well, I couldn't say that when her body was shuddering to a climax on the tip of my tongue, that she didn't *seem* to be wishing it wasn't sexual.'

'No.'

'And I couldn't say that when she lay beside me with her eyes beaming her deepest existence into mine and me pouring mine right back, saying that she loved me and that this was how the world was meant to be, I couldn't say that she didn't *seem* to want it not to be physical.'

'So that was it?'

'I asked her to sign her book.'

'And?'

'She couldn't do it.'

'Right.'

'So . . . so I got ready to leave and I asked her if she had ever loved me.'

'And what?'

'She said, "I believe so."'

Jack is quiet: 'She was just protecting herself.'

'And so what's left?' I ask.

'Sorrow. Grief. Sadness. Emptiness. Loss. The memory of happiness. The memory of love. Affection.'

'Affection?' my father asks.

'Yes, deep and timeless affection that beams out into the universe like those hopeless radio signals they send in the search for extra-terrestrial life.'

Jack comes in softly: 'Any lessons?'

'None. Not a single one.'

Dad says: 'You'll find someone, Ralph.'

'No.' Ralph is sharp. 'I don't need someone. Women are particular, Dad. Not general. You know that. And I'm OK. It's just . . . sad. But this whole thing.' He drains his glass. 'This whole thing is good for me – your suicide, I mean. It's really helpful, actually. The perspective. More champagne, Lou, come on. And what about the sandwiches?'

'It's moving again,' Jack says, 'up ahead.'

PART FOUR

LET US NOT TALK
FALSELY NOW

FOR WHOM THE BELL TOLLS

We are sitting in the small Hansel-and-Gretel square of a hilltop German village.

'Only the Germans really know how to make beer, Lou.'

'Apart from the Belgians, Dad,' I say. 'And the Italians and the British and . . . pretty much everyone who tries. The Indonesians.'

'And you have to hand it to the Germans: they love real concerts. None of the struggle or shame that there is about classical music in Britain. There are Debussy posters everywhere.' He indicates the village noticeboard. 'What d'you put it down to?'

'Could be that Dean is big in Denzlingen.'

'You mean it is more Dean than Debussy?'

'Let's not rule it out.'

'Dean Swallow?'

'Dean Swallow,' Dad affirms. 'You said yourself he was talented.'

'Oh bloody hell.' Dad's brow furrows deeper. 'We never listened to his CD.'

'We've other things on our minds, Dad.'

'It's unforgivable though.'

'And we don't have a CD player.'

Directly across the flattened grey cobblestones of the square, there's an old hotel with a big wooden door beneath a pointed arch; dark beams rise and cross in crooked rectangles across its facade like bones – all the way up to its steeply raked roof from which elvish garrets protrude. On our left is the pale-pink Rathaus with turquoise-grey shutters and flower boxes beneath every window with just about every colour of petal you can imagine – velvety-violet through to blanched almond. On our right is an immaculate pale-yellow church with a simple bell tower, a witch's hat steeple, a white clock, a neat belfry with two self-restrained arched windows. Behind us is another row of wooden-beamed buildings – each with those vast triangular roofs that sweep down almost to the ground in which the upper floors are contained. The evening smells warmly of the green of the vines in the valleys all around – and somehow, faintly, of basil or cloves.

We are sitting outside at the only bar, waiting for Ralph and Jack who have gone with Malte to fix a table for the Feinschmecker Hochgenuss. Malte met us here forty-five minutes ago. He turned up in a copious double sweat of delight to see us and pre-concert distraction about the piano, the audience, the programme, classical music in general. The festival always took place in several of the surrounding villages as well as Denzlingen itself, he explained, and there were constant transportation and smaller-venue issues. But he suggested we come with him super-quick in person to the nearby castle where the food events were centred – and there he would introduce us to the maître d' of the restaurant as 'friends and family of the artist' and see if he could get us a table. He had some traction, he reckoned, since everyone knew Dean in Denzlingen. Still, it would be better to go and pretend to be Dean's family and guests of the sponsors . . . And so, rather than load Dad back into the van, Malte shot off with Jack and Ralph, our van chasing his van in odd communion down into the valley below.

I say Dad and I 'are sitting' as if I mean the word casually . . . But the thing is that my father is sitting in his *wheelchair*.

That we have adjusted to be just the right height.

That we have fixed with a brake.

Dad reaches for his beer. I affect not to notice the care that he puts into the action. He is sideways on to the table because he cannot get his legs under in the chair. Which does not help – because his left arm has a new tremor. We are pretending that none of this is happening. That much I get. But this extra bit – this pretending he is *not* now in a wheelchair . . . I should be all for it, of course. I should be delighted. But what I want – what I *want* – Yahweh, Jesus, Mohammed, Zeus, Brahma – is my father as he was. I want my father healthy, robust, independent, funny. Cooking, talking, eating, joking, walking, swimming, teaching. And I want his fucking face to work. Normally.

And I don't want to push him around.

And I definitely don't want anyone else to push him around.

And if I can't have that, if I can't have that, you idle fucking gods, then maybe I don't want my father at all. Maybe I don't want my father at all. Something cold strikes my soul as Dad reaches for his glass again: that without my brothers, all of a sudden, we are back to it: the reality. And actually . . . they are the ones . . . they are the ones casting spells . . . taking us away from the truth. The truth which is the same question it has always been: to be or not to be.

'The problem in Britain . . .' Dad takes an ostentatious sip for my benefit – to show me he can do it – but some of the beer spills as he sets down the glass. 'The problem is that knowledge has been confused with snobbery.'

'Go on,' I say.

But I'm not listening. Because this is not the problem. I'm thinking that the problem is that Ralph and Jack have never even exposed themselves to the basics: like going online and reading the MND message boards and forums. All the pain, and loss, and courage, and trauma, and fear, and heartbreak. It's like some kind of post-terrorist-strike chat room – except worse because it redraws itself hourly – new outrage, new anguish – wider, bigger, spooling down every screen that seeks it out. This – *this* – is the problem.

'Well, expertise is to do with the assiduous collection and assimilation of knowledge – right?'

'If you say so.'

So many real people posting in real time from all over the real world. Disaster detonating in lives here, there, north, south, one after another. 'Angry and Bewildered.' 'Crying while I type.' 'Exhausted – just got hubby home from the hospital.' 'Be kind to yourself, Sam, you have courage and reserves that you don't yet know.' 'Biting the Inside of My Mouth.' 'Michael began with walking more slowly – catching his feet only now and then. It progressed to his legs giving way. After a while he was unable to get up without assistance. Then he couldn't stand. This was over eight months to September. Now he has no arm movement and the start of choking and speech changes.'

'But snobbery is nothing to do with expertise,' Dad says.

'What?'

'Snobbery is essentially an emotional manoeuvre that goes something like, I know – or pretend to know – a certain thing – which I use – *emotionally* – to make myself feel better about myself for knowing it – usually by way of making you feel worse about yourself for not knowing it.'

The truth is that Dad loathes sitting sideways on, too. The effort of twisting his body to talk to me is irritating, tiring, exasperating. But it's too late for me to move round and sit somewhere easier for him in the direct line of his sight. That would be to acknowledge the problem. That would be to stop the pretence. This pretending . . . this *pretending* is extra-ridiculous given that before this trip we both faced and understood and dealt with the physical actuality – every morning, every night, every minute, for months. Until my brothers arrived, in fact, and bought this wheelchair. Now we're pretending there are options. I hate the word options. I hate the way it, too, pretends . . . the way it pretends to agency and power and doesn't notice the vast black universe laughing its massive black hole of a heart out at such a fleeting creature on such a fragile planet.

My father is waiting for me to respond. But I can't remember what we are talking about. So I say: 'Remind me why this is an issue, Dad?'

'Because, Lou,' he replies, agitated, 'people are now using the two terms interchangeably. People call experts snobs. And it's a disaster for the culture.'

Maybe only my father is left in the world to say things like 'a disaster for the culture'.

'Now the emotional transaction goes the other way, Lou. Because you do *not* know about subject "a" or "b" – you bring balm to your emotional anxieties and insecurities with the diversion of a simple catch-all attack – you ascribe snobbery to me. This makes you feel better about your lack of knowledge.'

'Can we leave me out of it?'

Maybe what sort of person you are comes down to how much truth you can table and how much truth you can take.

'Rather than make the effort,' Dad presses, 'the effort to learn or admit that there *are* things to learn . . . And rather than respect the fact that someone else has taken the time and trouble to learn them, you negate my learning and soothe your ignorance by calling me a snob. In this way, ignorance becomes some sort of a *vindication*. You feel better. I feel worse.'

'I don't feel better. I never feel better.'

'But the subject in question – music, trainers, coffee, art, beer, sunglasses, telephones, computer games – remember we are all experts in something, Lou – the subject in question is not engaged with at all. It's not even being *discussed*.'

Birds that I'm guessing are swallows dart and circle the steeple of the church – maddened with life – like they've only just realized that the day is nearly done and so they must seize and swoop and binge upon the evening.

'So you see what I mean?'

'Not really.'

'When we use the word snob we have been talking about our feelings for ourselves and for each other. We haven't really been disputing the subject in hand *or* the relative levels of our expertise.'

'Dad?'

'In fact, Lou, the truth about most experts is that they are the opposite of snobs: they like nothing better than to share their knowledge, to teach . . .' My father is raving and burning now. 'Most of the time they're *desperate* to do so – all they want to do is share and explain and demonstrate and pass their passions on. But instead . . . they're made to feel guilty – *guilty* about knowing things! That is the modern world in a nutshell. And it's a—'

'Dad.'

He's gesturing like we're at a political rally. 'The right to an opinion does *not* extend to the right to having your opinion taken seriously – unless you can—'

'Dad.'

'I mean – you sign up to Twitter and away you go. Away you go, Lou.'

'What—'

'But tell me this. How do you make sense of suffering on Twitter? Tell me. It's knee-jerk and skin-deep and awash with idiocy and sentiment. All this *opining*. There's no moral virtue in anything. The world is gone for me. Gone. I don't understand what is happening any more. I don't understand. You know all my—'

'Dad! Stop. You—'

'—all my study and effort is rendered meaningless, Lou.' He's holding his glass so tight I think it might shatter. 'Meaningless and dismissible. There's no respect. Nothing you can *measure* any more.'

And then the fucking bell tolls.

Just like that – as blithe as it is solemn: the church bell just starts sounding out the hour. Toll. Toll. Toll. Knell. Knell. Knell. And the sound rings across our little square and down into the valley and there's nothing we can do about it. And the moment seems like it will stop us here for ever.

Trapped in time. And I'm thinking – this is it; finally, we're down to it; at last, the hour when we speak our hearts. My father and I – we can do it. We can speak to one another without falsity. Yes. Because the bell tolls for thee.

But then there comes a second sound of an engine straining up the nearby hill. And slowly Dad sits back in the wheelchair and eases his grip on his glass.

'Ralph treats that van like he's flogging a dog,' he says quietly.

'How do you know it's him?' I ask, like anything matters.

'Unmistakeable sewing-machine sound of a VW engine, Lou.'

'No, I mean how do you know it's Ralph? Could be Jack.'

'No sympathy in that right foot.'

The van appears across the other side of the square. Ralph is at the wheel. He drives not-quite-slowly-enough into the pedestrian zone and parks up boldly in front of the hotel. The side door slides open.

'Come on,' Jack shouts across, 'we're really late.'

I put down some money for the drinks that neither of us have had time to finish and I push my father across the cobbled square beneath the bell tower, which is silent again – totally silent – as if nothing has happened.

The third tape is the worst. The first voice is screaming and the violence is immediate. A glass smashes really close by the machine and then something else is thrown. People are moving around the room fast. You can hear bangs and crashes and furniture either falling or being pushed aside. There's swearing from the second voice. Then you hear a kind of wet thud or thwack. What sounds like a heavy fall. And the second voice cries out from what must be the floor in what is obviously real pain. Then more swearing and the second voice saying: 'There's glass – it's in my eye – my eyes – there's blood in my eyes – I can't see. There's blood in my eyes.'

And then – right up close – the sound of the first voice breathing . . . shallow breathing . . . in and out . . . right by the microphone . . . in and out. And then in a hissed whisper: 'I hope you're fucking blinded.'

I wheel Dad up to the van door.

'We have a table.' Ralph says from where he is half-turned in the driver's seat. 'Dad, it is your birthday – and you are Dean Swallow's uncle for the night. Lou, you are Dean's cousin.'

'Who are you?'

'Dean's boyfriend.'

Jack helps Dad in. I try to collapse the frame of the wheelchair. I don't quite have the knack yet.

Ralph continues: 'Malte says it's fine since Dean never has a girlfriend anyway. Jack is my brother.'

'Which is an honour,' Jack says, leaning out again to help lift up the wheelchair. 'Dean Swallow's boyfriend's brother.'

I get the thing folded and offer it up and Jack catches my eye like this is the future and it's amazing how things work out.

'I don't know what you guys did for Malte,' Ralph clicks his tongue, 'but he loves you like you're best friends for ever.'

'We saved his considerable bacon,' Dad says.

I slide the door shut – too hard.

Jack slots back into the passenger seat, and swivels round as he pulls on his seat belt. 'The concert is about ten minutes from here.'

'Where?' Dad asks.

'A church in a little town on the way.' Ralph lets down the handbrake.

'And the restaurant is in this castle overlooking the Rhine,' Jack says 'On the battlements. We're in business, Dad. They're world class.'

'What are we doing?' I ask. 'I mean . . . where are we even going to sleep. I don't—'

'*Wohnmobilstellplatz*,' Jack says.

'Worry not, Lou,' Ralph says. 'There's a mobile-home park on a nearby hill. We can bathe our wounds in the gentle light of their Michelin star and stagger home. Only one, I'm afraid, but that's all the three wise men had and look what they found.'

The pews are filled with the faithful who all believe in music. Late arrivals, we stand at the back behind our father; his sons, a trio. There must be two hundred pilgrims here tonight – all clapping in concert. Dean comes back on for his encore – Chopin – and bows, embarrassed in the piano's crook; he flicks out his tails, fine-tunes the stool, and thus begins once more to conjure harmony and dissonance from the empty evening air.

Above the dais, three windows arch. They must look over the valley and into the west because the light lingers there, in dying orange, ochre and blood-red; and there, too, the dusk's long shadows point and steal and swear that the day is not done, the chance not yet gone. And, fleetingly, all the beauty in the world is gathered up in human notes. One last time. And the music is a yearning and a requiem and a prayer.

I can tell that my father is weeping. I cannot lean forward. I do not know if my brothers have noticed. I grip the handles of the wheelchair.

The programme says Chopin died at the age of thirty-nine. Tuberculosis. I think he must have known for quite a while. I'm sure of it. He must have foreseen his own death a few bars ahead. For – yes – the music is a yearning and a requiem, a mystery and a declaration, a heart-song for the people whom he loved, a prayer that the moment can be stayed, a concession that it cannot, a defiance, a defeat, an exultation.

The day my father told me that he had motor neurone disease, I had left work to go to the house to borrow the van to help one of my friends move flats. I was on the top deck of the bus, listening to some music that I didn't know in the hope of hearing something that I liked, looking down at the variously bunched resentments of London's yellow-vested cyclists. And I was hoping that my father would be out so that I could get into the house, grab the keys and raid the kitchen cupboards, and then leave without having to talk to him.

He was upstairs. He called down – 'That you, Lou?' Like if it wasn't, what then? And I shouted back: 'Hello, just stopping by.' He said he'd been planning to phone me. So I asked why. He said 'news'. And I went straight on into the kitchen to steal some stuff – tea, batteries, anything – before he came down.

He walked in. He told me. And then we both went crazy. But not in a crazy way. In the way of going crazy when two people know that they've gone crazy, but they're pretending not to go crazy, because if they admitted, for even a second, how crazy they were going then they'd have to start screaming and never stop.

Two hours later, we were sat in the library, a bottle of wine more than half gone and he was talking – crazily – and I was writing it down – crazily – and he didn't mind. As if this – this *writing* – was now OK. As if this was now urgently what I had to do. As if his imminent death OK'd or unlocked or sanctioned me as a writer. As if, even if this aspiration of mine was total fiction, then suddenly, it was a fiction we could both converge upon. Or accept. Or promulgate. Or indulge. I don't know. As if here was a way to be his son. As if here was a way for him – pristinely – to be my father.

He was saying, 'But everyone is insane, Lou, insane and half-wrecked . . .'

And I was writing it down, which was itself insane and half-wrecked, as if it was his last will and testament.

And he was saying: '. . . I'm telling you: you spend your thirties thinking that it's only you and that they're all doing fine – maybe a little rude at parties, a little tense, a little cold, odd, oblique – but they've arrived on the scene feeling totally together and you're the only one packing the panic and the anxiety. But then it hits you – in your forties – it hits you that most people are going quietly mad inside themselves. And they're all self-medicating – not just the alcohol or the yoga or the children or the vocation or – heaven forbid

338

– the hobbies, but everything. Everything. Every single thing they say to you is more self-medication. I'm not this, I'm that; that's what they want to tell you. I'm better at this than you think. I'm deeper, wider, more than I appear. I'm not at all "x". I'm more "y". And then it dawns on you. You are not alone. They're all hurting like hell. They *all* wanted something else. A bit more of this. A lot less of that. They're all trying to block out the missed opportunities and the wrong turns. They want to know how-the-hell-did-this-happen and is-this-good-enough? Am I too late? And they all want to be understood in a different way. They're all being tormented by different versions of their own stories that they never got the chance to tell. Seriously. Even the President of the United States wants you to rethink your view of him. Reconsider. Remember this. Forget that. I know about the whole Iraq thing, but . . . Sure, there was semen on the dress but what about . . . ? And so then – when you realize that this is everyone – the panic, I mean, the anxiety – you know what happens? You start to relax again. You do. You start to think: well, if everyone is insane and panic-stricken, then that's OK. That's a big relief. That's much easier to live with. Why didn't they tell me? The bastards. And you know what that is? That's your fifties, Lou. That's your fifties when you suddenly get everything back again because you . . . you ease up, you *understand.* Of course everybody is doolally because that is the nature of being a human on a planet that has no interest in humans. Has to be. The way out of the mid-life crisis turns out to be the realization that life is one long crisis. For everyone. So – yes – you ease up. The crisis passes. You start to enjoy things again. You don't have to prove yourself to yourself so much. And then what happens? I'll tell you what. I'll tell you what happens . . . Just as you've worked out how best to live, you are betrayed by your own bloody body. Just as you've got the hang of how to go about your own bloody life with a modicum of wisdom and relaxation. Just as the money worries recede, your body starts packing up. And so then you realize yet another thing, Lou: that you were an animal all along. A mammal. Blood and tissue. Organs and limbs. With an embarrassing and pathetic best-before date. And you can't do all those things you realized you should have done – let alone enjoy your own thoughts and feelings – because it's all about your body from now on. In fact, it has been all about your body all along – if only you had noticed. Because if your lungs don't work, or your heart, or your legs – then everything else is totally beside the point. And that's your sixties – right there. The realization that you have about twenty minutes left to live in the way that you've finally – *finally* – understood is right. But with gathering disability and the certainty that something is going to hurt more and more in your body until – agony of agonies – you'll wind up *hoping* for death. Begging for it. I'm not joking. Lou. Seriously. What kind of a life is this?'

FEINSCHMECKER HOCHGENUSS

We follow Malte. His stock is high in Oberotweil. Now that the concert has been deemed such a success (and there's every chance of a rebooking next year), he is all bad jokes and bonhomie again. He waddles up to the desk to greet the maître d' – a thin and wiry man with an inclined head and eyes that glance sideways every few seconds as if to intimate that, yes, he is peripherally aware that the world is a conspiracy. They seem to be friends – or, at least, familiar collaborators of recent days; and so this, we quickly understand, is the fluid colloquy of equals. Nods and checks-of-the-system ensue. Mute re-agreements are remade. And then the maître d' looks past Malte at us four with the brief concern of a man with many wider worries; he sees my father's over-worn black corduroy blazer, Jack's over-smart dad-casual jacket, Ralph's over-battered boots, my too-skinny drainpipe jeans. And there is a moment when he might object – rightly, rightly – but Malte's presence and the need to get *on* with it prevail.

'This way,' he says, the menus in his arms like scrolls of law or worship.

The restaurant is not on the battlements but rather on a terrace in front of the castle overlooking the Rhine. We pass through high doors and outside into the warmish evening air. I am at the back, pushing Dad, glad of the thoughtful German access ramps and the flatness of the tiles and the generous space between the lamps and tables.

'Is good, *ja?*' Malte asks over his shoulder.

'Sensational.' Ralph is additionally delighted that he will be able to smoke because our table is outside.

The castle must have been medieval originally – rebuilt when Germany felt romantic – and it rears up in the glow of soft architectural lighting beside us. There are square battlements. High round and narrow towers with tight conical roofs. A yellow banner, suspended between two windows far above, announces to the river-valley below (and the world beyond) in black Gothic writing: *'Das Gourmet-Festival Denzlingen: die Feinschmeckermesse am Rhein.'*

Dad twists in the wheelchair. I lean in to hear him as all such carers do.

'Find a world,' he says, inclining his head after Malte, 'and rise therein to greatness.'

'That's what I'm doing, Dad,' I say. 'But in database management.'

The place is full. The other diners are a mixture: fellow concert-goers still carrying their programmes; one or two families with teenagers; two bigger tables of more elderly couples, stiffly dressed and falsely good-humoured (as if meshed together on some atrocious 'Romantic Rhine' cruise); and several undeniably heavy-weight tables where an atmosphere of great gastronomic seriousness is evinced in the care with which forks are raised to mouths and eyes are closed and grimaces of delight or disappointment disport themselves across the kind of faces that start revolutions. We've been told that the castle is very popular and used throughout the year by everyone from bat-watchers to medieval re-enactment specialists. We are lucky. Some terrifying and irresistible psychological pincer-movement perpetrated by Ralph and Malte has ensured that we have a special table at the far corner of the terrace. This turns out to be situated on its own – on a round area that juts out a little as if the base of an un-built hexagonal tower planned to give the best possible view up and down the river. And, here, the maître d' stops, turns, smiles, inclines his head.

'Your table, Herr Lasker,' he says in English. His eyes travel briefly sideways and back again. 'If there is anything we can do for you, then let it be done. And may I say, Happy *Birthday*, Herr Lasker. We are honoured to have the family and friends of Herr Swallow for this occasion.' He indicates the expensive linen with a magician's flourish. There are candles in teardrop glass to thwart the non-existent wind and I can smell the scent of the roses that climb the old walls around.

He lays out the menus. 'I will send someone over to begin . . . the process,' he says and backs away as if from the Holy Roman Emperor.

Malte comes forward – his head trampolining in the mattress of his neck.

Ralph pauses in the lighting of his cigarette and makes a gesture of appreciation with his hand. 'Thank you, Malte.'

'You must have a drink with us,' Jack says, 'and Dean.'

'Amaretto and lime,' I say.

'Where *is* Dean?' Dad asks. 'His Chopin was . . . I don't know. Transportative.'

'He is with Rheinmetall. He must eat with them,' says Malte.

'Who are they? A rock band?' This from Jack.

Malte demurs: 'No – the sponsors.'

'Rheinmetall sponsor the Debussy festival?' Ralph's brows rise.

Malte nods. 'Yes, we are all grateful to Rheinmetall.'

None of us knows what to do with this information; it seems to mean something about the universe that can't be tackled in a single night.

'Well, thank you, Malte,' Dad says. 'I, for one, am having a wonderful evening.'

Malte bows. 'No, thank you, Herr Lasker. We would not be here without you guys. They say one good efforts deserves another and so this is my pleasure to help. I know nothing about the vans. But music and eating – I am the man.' He clasps his white hands together so that they rest over the gelatinous dome of his white stomach. 'Well, we see us in a while, crocodiles.'

'Come and have a drink with us,' Dad says again. 'And bring Dean. We thought his Chopin was . . . sublime. Truly. Tell him. Tell him.'

'For sure. Yes. I will try to come back with Dean . . . But if you have finished before I find you – then there is a jazz bar in the castle – on the other side. Sometimes Dean plays. I will be there, myself, later on. They serve the excellent – how do you say? – snacks.'

'We'll be there, Malte,' Ralph says.

Malte smiles his curling-bacon-on-the-grill smile and backs away with a waddle and a wave looking like that rarest thing – a happy man in a world more or less to his liking.

I park Dad up next to the stone wall and put on the brakes so that we can look out across the valley. The Rhine is wide and oily-black tonight. Long shimmering poles of reflected light from the villages opposite reach out across the surface – crimson, yellow, pale green. The vine-terraced hills beyond are massed shadows save for another old fortress opposite that is likewise under-lit in amber and set forward on an outcrop-vantage overlooking a distant bend. The darker shape of a night barge is passing by with its forward light – like a long diamond-studded tongue lapping through the water without a mouth.

We eat and drink as if Valhalla will indeed be destroyed in the morning. Course after course; little portions but lots of them; stuff on strings, see-through soups, stuff made of seeds, stuff made of skins, some little lobster tails with some kind of lime-frost, bits of pigs with figs, and then some kind of pasta with truffles, which has my father more or less singing, but smells to me like socks and tastes like sodden mushrooms.

I have never seen Dad so happy, though. He's having the time of his life. The liquid light of the candles a-swim in his eyes. The castle, the river. The mighty night behind him. Talking about the Valkyries. Talking about Volkswagens. Ralph on one side, Jack on the other.

But maybe the three bottles of wine are the problem because, sometime around about dessert, this dark vapour starts to permeate our talk – something clammy, cold and noxious that has slipped from the water, slouched up the banks, climbed the walls below and now comes creeping and curling into our conversation. Maybe it started with what my father was saying about my mother and a camping trip from fifteen years ago because that's when Jack suddenly jolts forward.

'. . . But I don't think that's right,' he says. 'How *can* Lou really understand? He wasn't there.' He pauses a moment. 'And then you lied to him.'

My father's face flinches but sluggishly like everything is running slow because he desperately needs to clear out the cache on his hard drive but hasn't got the time to shut down properly and reboot. 'That wasn't important, Jack. It was the past. It didn't matter. Not as far as Lou and—'

'Not true.' Jack stops him, sharply. 'I'd say concealing things from your children hinders them in their effort to understand who and what and *how* they are. I'd say it really sets them back, Dad. I'd say it's damaging.'

I put down my glass. 'What are we talking about?'

Jack continues: 'I'd say it is something you—'

'Dramatized,' Ralph cut in. 'Yet again.'

'Oh, come on,' Dad retorts. 'People conceal things from their children all the time. For their own good.'

The night vapour is a spirit that is more than noxious, I'm thinking, something toxic – insinuating its way within.

'That's how families work,' Dad says. 'Have to work.'

'What are we *talking* about?' I ask.

'I wanted to protect you and Ralph from th—'

'Not true.' Jack interrupts. 'In fact, now I have my own children, I can't believe y—'

'I wanted to make a clean start, Jack.' My father makes a swatting motion with his hand. 'I wanted to make a clean start.'

I bang the table, half-meaning it. 'What are we talking about?'

Everyone goes cold-silent. Maybe it's me. Maybe it has been me all along. Maybe I was just waiting for the right moment to grab the wheel and lurch us across the road into the oncoming traffic. Because now we're going to crash. At last.

Ralph reaches forward for the wine. 'I would say now is a pretty good time to tell him, Dad.'

'Tell me *what*?'

My father's eyes are tired but there's something else I've not seen before – something wan and weak that has hidden itself from sight; shame.

'I didn't meet your mother in New York, Lou,' he says, slowly. 'I met her in Russia – about eighteen months before you think.'

Ralph's voice is equanimous: 'Taking the total amount of time you behaved like a fuck-pig to around three years.'

'Your mother lived in London, Lou, before she went back to New York.'

Jack interjects: 'Dad liked to pop round and see your mother once or twice a week and then come home and scream and shout with ours.'

'We tried to stop, Lou. She went back to America. To stop.'

'Ralph and I used to lie awake listening to Mum and Dad fighting while all this was going on,' Jack says.

Ralph smiles, cold as cracked china. 'It was *very* soothing.'

'We were upset for the first six months,' Jack says, 'but then we got into this game where we'd count the swear words.'

'Dad used to swear a lot back then, Lou.' Ralph sucks his teeth. 'Lots of cunt and fuck.'

'I was . . . I was *trying* to talk to Carol. I never stopped trying to—'

'Not really,' Jack interrupts again. 'Dad thought the best approach was to lie, Lou, and then – when Mum found out – as she was *bound* to do – he thought the next best plan was to move from coward to bully.'

Ralph does this swimming fish gesture with his hand. 'From lies to torture and back again. Isn't that right, Dad?'

'It went on for a long time, Lou,' Jack says. 'A long, long time.'

My father looks at me as if for mercy. 'I didn't know what to do,' he says.

There's a black hole burning inside of me; I'm dark, invisible and I have no centre but I'm dragging everything in.

'So you went for the option which created maximum suffering for everybody.' Jack shakes his head.

'You don't "go" for "options", Jack.' My father's derision is weak and shabby and ugly. 'It's not that simple.'

'Isn't it?'

'There was dignity in leaving. There was dignity in staying—'

'For fuck's *sake*.' Ralph laughs dismissively.

'There was zero dignity.' Jack speaks almost as though he is the father and Dad the disappointing son.

'There was *cowardice* in leaving,' Ralph says. 'There was cowardice in staying. I think that's what you mean, Dad.'

'I was going mad.' Now my father is wheedling. 'You have no idea. I was afraid of my own mind.'

'Wrong people to ask for sympathy, Dad,' Jack says.

'I'm not asking for sympathy.'

'You're asking for *something*, though,' Ralph says. 'Aren't you?'

'I could not talk straight to Carol. I could not talk straight to Julia. They . . .' Anger enters my father's voice – a vehemence part alcohol and part rebarbative. 'There was so much drama in it . . . I was being fucked over by both of them.'

'Don't speak like that about my mother,' I say, quietly. But my own voice is strange to me. I want to go. But I can't. I have no other family.

'How would you *like* me to speak? I thought you three were all big on reality.' Dad expels that last word like it's the bone that has been stuck in his throat all these long years.

'But the thing is, Lou . . .' Ralph is composed by way of counter. 'My mum still let him in. She still let him come in and sleep in the spare room. Can you imagine what that was doing to her? Night after night. Week after week. Even after she found out.'

'Every morning,' Jack says, 'every morning we used to have these horrible little breakfasts . . . Mum all tense and red-eyed with controlled hysteria trying to make our toast and ask us about our school work and then kiss us on the way out.'

'The best bit,' Ralph says, 'was when Dad promised to stop – swore blind that he had. And then—'

'Carried on.' Jack shakes his head disgusted.

'I didn't carry on.'

'Sorry. Started again,' Jack scoffs. 'In secret.'

'I had to go to New York—'

'Ah, this bit is true, Lou,' Ralph says. 'Important conference on Emily Brontë's misuse of layered narrative.'

'I thought I was having a bloody breakdown, boys.'

'No; a breakdown was what you caused Mum to have,' Jack says. 'She was a steady woman before. Naive maybe –

but with her own life and plans. You – you created her suffering.'

'I . . . I was falling apart. My mind was a hall of broken mirrors. You don't know.' Dad is leaning forward, his eyes burning – muscles twitching unbidden in his furrowed brow. 'You try . . . you try to sort out the love from the desire, the desire from the madness, the madness from the meaning, the meaning from what the hell you are supposed to do. But you are on your own – on your bloody own – with no experience and no counsel. On your own. With your children in revolt and your wife hating you and a job which eats your waking existence and the shit-spray of everyday life in your eyes all the time. So, yes, I go to New York and suddenly . . . suddenly it stopped. On the plane. Over the Atlantic. Everything cleared and eased. I *felt* better.'

'Fine,' Jack says, derisively. 'Fine, Dad. Glad you felt better. But instead of never coming back. You went for the other *option*. You came back for . . . what? For *more* cheating, more lies. Another eighteen months of torture.'

'Of staggering self-indulgence.' Ralph pours himself more wine. 'You have to admire the commitment. The narcissism. However malignant.'

'I don't presume to judge you, Ralph.'

Ralph's eyes are mica. 'No children, Dad.'

'I—'

'Big difference, Laurence.' Ralph places the wine down with slow deliberation. 'What I do is between consenting adults. We all agree to the agony. We don't enlist child soldiers.'

'I didn't—'

'Of course you did.' Jack's drunkenness is like some sort

of super-sobriety. 'How could we not be involved? Dragged into the psycho-drama. All children are half their mother and half their father. You divided us against ourselves in the worst possible way at the worst possible moment.'

Ralph exhales. 'But even forget that. Forget us. It's just that you behaved like *such* a cunt for so long. Didn't you? Such a total cunt.'

Dad's face is tight and he's not moving. They're going to tear him apart in front of me, I'm thinking, and hang him from the battlements. And I don't know whether to save him or join in.

'The *second* discovery is what sent my mother properly crazy, Lou,' Ralph says. 'Dad lied. Dad was found out. Dad swore he would stop. Dad lied again – deeper and with more duplicity. And Dad was found out a second time. Good old Dad.'

'There are as many kinds of love as there are people in the world, Ralph.' My father gestures wildly. 'We love one way here. We love another way there. Of course we do. You know that. I . . . I was the one trying to get reality into both pictures. I was—'

'After being found out *again*.' Jack's disgust is written in the lines of his face. 'These were not pictures, Dad, these were lives. Listen to yourself.'

'First rule of any affair,' Ralph says, 'is that you protect the people you *know* you love over and above whoever it is you *think* you might love.'

'The only explanation is that you wanted to be caught,' Jack says. 'You wanted us all to know.'

'You wanted the drama,' Ralph adds.

'You wanted all four of us to see . . . to see how much we

needed you. You know what I think?' Jack pauses. 'I think you were preening yourself in the reflection of the suffering you were creating.'

Ralph takes over: 'You seek conflict, damage – you drag everyone else in – down to your level – and it's all the classic stuff a cunt needs to make himself feel better about his miserable soul. But what's really depressing,' Ralph says, 'what is *really* fucking depressing, Dad, is the idea that you haven't grown up at all. Because here we are again. It's all about you. It's all about you.'

'I tried . . .' My father's face is pale and his hands are tight to the arms of the wheelchair. I can tell he's being annihilated not just by what they're saying, but by the cool fervour with which they are saying it. 'I tried . . . I tried to drain the thing of all the drama. I sat with your mother . . . And then I sat with *your* mother . . .' He points at me with a stabbing finger. 'And I said . . . I said . . . But there was no reasoning with anyone.' Anger notches his brow again. 'There's no bloody reason to it – to any of it. She became a monster. You don't know.'

The four eyes of my brothers are as one creature.

'You don't know,' Dad says, his voice rising. 'Some nights I sat in the van on my own hating myself. Knowing how much you hated me. Knowing that. Can you imagine? And that you were *right* to hate me. And—'

'We didn't hate you, we just thought you were a total cunt.' Jack saying it – Jack saying the word rips into my father the deeper. 'We couldn't understand why you didn't just fuck off.'

'A coward and a cunt,' Ralph says. 'You were the monster. Whatever she became, you turned her into.'

My father recoils. All the light goes out of his eyes. He cannot take much more. But I am not the referee and I'm holding the sponge in both corners.

'There was no escaping . . . the situation . . . because you can't stop loving your family and the mother of your children. I loved—'

'Don't pretend—'

'No, Jack, no. No.' My father is shaking as he leans forward in his wheelchair – and now I can see the ghost of his former violence stirring in him – as though he would rise and beat his sons if only his body were still able to do so. Beat them into tears and submission. 'I did *not* get married lightly. I loved your mother. I loved Carol. Do not . . . do *not* . . . do not tell me who I loved and who I didn't. Never tell me that. Never. Never. Never. Never. Never. She was my north star, my guide, my safety. I loved your mother dearly before it was all so . . . so *incinerated*. You two . . . you two . . . you don't know—'

'You could have made a decision and stopped – *stopped* – involving the rest of us,' Jack says. 'One way or the other.'

'Everything was self-created,' Ralph says, 'self-inflicted, self-designed, self-centred, self—'

'You two know *nothing* of what I did—'

'We know enough.'

'—or what was done for you. For you!' My father rises from the chair and stands, shaking, swaying, one hand on the table, one hand on the armrest of his wheelchair, fury coursing through him. He reaches for a knife and tries to bang it down. But he has no control and it flails wildly into his wine glass which spills, expensively, rolls in a half-circle and smashes onto the floor. He cannot stand but sways a moment, the stars stealthy in the sky behind him, his face cracked by feeling and smeared with its flood, before he falls back heavily into the wheelchair that jolts and bucks – held only by the brake that I set.

'What was done for *us*, Dad?' Ralph asks in a voice of deadly calm as he lights a cigarette from the candle. 'Are you talking about that weekend when we drove across Wales in the van with Mum chasing us in her car? Or what about Keswick when you smashed up Jack's face and then locked us in that room. Can you imagine what that felt like for us? I thought he was going to die. He was fucking bleeding everywhere. And it wouldn't stop. I thought Jack was going to die from having no blood. I was *nine*, Dad. Meanwhile you were down the corridor busy in bed with Julia. Christ, the deceit of it. The lies. I mean what the fuck were you doing? What the fuck were you *thinking*? Beating us up. Taking all your shit out on us.'

'Or what about Devon when you left us in that shitty hostel?' Jack asks. 'No food. No call. No money. No idea if you'd had an accident or something. Was that done for us, too?'

'I'm sorry, boys.' My father's voice is hollowed out. 'I'm sorry.'

'Why didn't you just go?' Jack asks.

'Carol was drinking. She was hitting me. And it became – it was violent. Terrible.'

'You made her that way.'

'Maybe I did. But I saw that she was . . . she was becoming unstable. And I was worried what would happen to you.' His voice has no tone of combat left. 'And in those days the court always decided in favour of leaving the children with the woman. I was told that she'd get custody of you. Unless I had overwhelming evidence. And I thought . . . I thought she would take it to court. I wanted to be with you, boys. I wanted to be with you two.'

Ralph is looking directly at Dad – his eyes the world's most powerful and precise tunnelling apparatus. 'You're saying you stayed to collect evidence?'

'I felt I had a duty to look after you . . . both. I didn't want to lose you.' Now the emotional lability takes him. Tears leak from the side of his face. 'You two – my boys. Christ.'

But Ralph is relentless. 'You stayed to collect *evidence*? This is your defence?'

'Sorry, this is the disease—'

'Forget the fucking disease,' Ralph says.

'I stayed so I could take you with me. I didn't want to be without you. I thought she'd stop me seeing you ever again. Not everything I did was bad. I loved you.'

Jack's voice is identical to Ralph's: 'So what? So that's why you deliberately tape-recorded her screaming and crying?'

This is the creature that crawled out of the river. Two heads, one voice.

'That's why you did it?' Jack presses. 'That was your solution?'

'Yes.' My father's is quiet now – as if it is a relief to give it all up and lie down and die. He closes his eyes. 'Yes. That's why I recorded her.'

But the creature isn't done.

'And did you let it all happen naturally, Dad?' Jack mocks.

'Or did you goad her to get the good stuff on tape?' Ralph asks. 'Did you set the whole thing up?'

My father is silent.

The creature's voice is two vicious whispers.

'You deliberately *staged* it, didn't you, Dad?'

'You deliberately provoked her pain and suffering to get it on tape.'

'I didn't know what to do,' he breathes.

'Can you imagine – can you imagine – after all that had happened – can you imagine how Mum felt when she found out – from her solicitor – about those tapes? About what you'd done?'

'Did you know that she asked to listen to them? So she could prepare a defence. But they wouldn't give them to her. They said no because they were too harrowing and there was no point.'

'But even then . . . Even after she knew she would lose, she *still* wanted to hear them.'

'You know why?'

My father is silent.

'Because she wanted to make herself confront what you were capable of so that she could hate you instead of loving you.'

'She wanted to listen to the sound of love being pissed on.'

'That's what she said. To us.'

'Those exact words.'

'She told us she remembered the nights you did it. *How* you did it.'

'What you contrived. To make her attack you.'

'She told us about the faces you made that the tape would not pick up.'

'Your mother was—'

'Those tapes. Her whole life.'

'You – *you* were the sick one.'

'I had to make a judgement . . .' My father's eyes seek mine but I can't look at him. 'I've been happy for the last twenty-seven years. Really. And I think you've been . . . I think you've been better off, too. I think—'

'Fuck it.' Ralph suddenly scrapes back on his chair to stand. The creature is gone. They are two – my brothers again. 'It doesn't matter. We got over all this a long time ago. You did what you wanted to do. We're through it, past it; you're the one with all the shit to carry, not us.'

Jack rises slowly and speaks as if to himself. 'As a child you trust the relationship of your parents. As an adult you realize that this is an unreasonable expectation.'

'Yes. Who gives a fuck? Not us.' Ralph throws down his napkin. 'Much worse going on right now in some Cambodian lithium mine. Besides, there'd be no Louis otherwise. Let's go and see Malte and listen to some more music. I'm fucking starving.'

Jack is swaying. 'Come and find us, Lou, if you want to.'

'Thanks for dinner, Dad,' Ralph says. 'Lou, be sure to use his fucking credit card. Least the cunt can do.'

Eva's beautiful face fills my phone. She is telling me that she has a flight for the day after tomorrow. She is going to fly to Zurich whether we are there or not. She has booked a tiny Airbnb apartment – in the centre near the lake. I can come and get her or she can come and get me. Whatever is happening. I say I will see her the day after tomorrow. I'm not driving back with these bastards. And I kiss the screen goodbye. Then I look at myself in the bathroom mirror. I don't really know who I am; but I know that with this woman's love, I can do whatever it takes. I can outlast. And I can endure.

REQUIEM

A gibbous moon is rising fast in the westward sky as if late to its command. The air is good to breathe and clears my head. The path back to where we had parked the van forms a shallow saddle – down from the castle and then back up along a paved escarpment to the mobile-home parking place. The valley of the river is on our left. We can see a cruise ship lit up with a daisy-chain of lights hung high from stern to bow and the water has changed from oily black to a dark and glassy blue in which the moonlight now pools and polishes its silver.

There are couples stopped here and there to look down at the view – most of them older, but two that I guess must be my age and who walk ahead of us, stopping playfully and lightly to kiss, like it's their little joke; save that it's not a joke and it's really all they want to do. Kiss. Stop. Kiss. Walk. Kiss. Stop. Kiss. I have to hold the wheelchair hard and lean backwards to prevent Dad running away down the slope ahead of me. His hands are folded in his lap and I know he won't get anywhere near the brake if I let him go.

'. . . before that,' he is saying, 'we met at this conference at Yasnaya Polyana,' he says. 'You know – Tolstoy's country house.'

'Go on,' I say. We are together again. Just me and him. He's sobered slightly and he is desperate to talk – to pour himself out to me. And I'm too tired and unable to do anything but listen and prompt and let him be. And it's like when we were on the ferry; except that it feels as though we've survived a shipwreck since then.

'She was there as a poet, of course. But she ended up being an interpreter. She interpreted everything for everyone.' He shakes his head. 'So we went round Tolstoy's house together. This is the black couch on which he was born, she would say; this is the chair with the sawn-off legs on which he wrote *Anna Karenina*; this is his treasured picture of Dickens. Later on, when there were lectures, we played truant and she came and sat in my room and we talked for five hours straight.'

'There was a connection?'

'*Connection*. Oh, much, much, much more than that, Louis. Whoever loved that loved not at first sight? It was like meeting—'

'The exact shape of the hole you did not know you had in your heart.'

My father twists around, his eyes wild and full of feeling. '*Yes*. How did—'

'You wrote it in your sonnet book – the copy you gave to Mum.'

He turns his head back but raises his right hand to the side. I let go one handle and offer mine forward. He grips it and we shake our common fist a moment.

'There was a dinner at a long table in the woods, Lou. We sat beside one another. She was still interpreting. She was such a good dining-companion to everyone. I don't know . . . We ended up holding hands under the table. I was so . . . so *wired* to her touch. I'd never felt anything like that before.'

We draw level with the kissing couple who are taking

turns at looking through one of those heavy metallic coin-operated binoculars that they place around the world so we can all bend down and pay to look into the distance for half a minute.

'We went back to my room. She left. She came back. Then she left again. Four in the morning. I slept for two hours then something made me get up . . . I sensed she was leaving. I remember dressing quickly and I remember running outside. I was right.'

'She was leaving?'

'Yes, she was already on the early bus that was taking half the guests back to Moscow. So I just stood there in the trees and she looked back at me out of the misted window. I was doing this begging thing, saying – please, please, please come down. I was pretending to be funny about it but – you know – really – really, I *was* begging. Until, eventually, she got off the bus. She was so reluctant. She said she knew she had to go because otherwise we would be in deep trouble. I gotta get out of here, she was saying, I gotta get out of here. I couldn't tell if she was crying or if it was just the rain . . . I had to implore her for a number, an address. Anything.'

'She knew you were married?'

'Yes.'

'The whole truth?'

'She had already guessed it. I didn't lie.'

Behind us, I can hear the kissing couple; the view through the binoculars is black, says the man. *Schwarz*. And the woman laughs.

'It felt like fate, Lou. And all the things I'd taught myself not to believe in. We were just standing there in the yellow mud and silver birch of Yasnaya Polyana. And then the bus started to get ready to go. And only then – only *then* – did she step down for a minute and let it slip that she was going back to Moscow for the night and that she wasn't flying until late the next day. So I made her tell me where she was staying.'

'You went after her?'

'I was supposed to remain for a few days longer at Yasnaya. I had a hell of a time trying to organize a Moscow hotel and get a train out of there. I had to involve the entire Tolstoy family. Endless phone calls and admin with my passport. But I did it. And that night, I called where she was staying – left a silly cryptic message for her to meet me at this other hotel I had managed to book – and then I left early the next morning . . . hoping, just hoping. It was so different in those days. No mobiles, nothing. You just said a time and a place and you had to be there and hope the other person felt the same.'

'And she was?'

'I couldn't believe it, Lou. She was standing in the foyer at two p.m. sharp. Waiting for me. For *me*. I couldn't believe it. She looked so beautiful and so everything. She looked so everything-despite-herself.'

'How long did you have together?'

'We had three hours because she had to go back to her place and meet the other Americans to get to the airport.' He breathes deep the cool of the midnight air. 'Christ, Lou, your mother and I – we always really lived – really *lived*. Every day felt like another chance to me.' I'm thinking that his favourite subject is my mother and that in speaking of her he is most eloquent of all. 'Then she had to go. She had to hurry. She was worried that her boyfriend had been calling her hotel phone . . . It wasn't just me, Lou.'

We're at the bottom of the saddle, the place where the

path turns upwards. We stop to look over the Rhine. All the while, since the dinner went bad, I have had to resist the urge to say, 'I know.' I have had to resist the urge to say, 'I know, I know, I know,' for so long . . . Because, of course, my mother told me all this when she must have known she was dying and we were walking by another river. And because of course my mother swore me to secrecy that day. She let me link arms and said, don't tell you father, Louis. Don't ever say. Promise me. As long as he lives. Because he is ashamed of what went on and he wanted to start clean again. That was his phrase. He feels that he sacrificed his integrity for us. And it's not true, of course – this stuff goes down all the time – *all the time* – all over the planet – but he's from another world. We have to remember that. He was a child of the 1950s. The North of England. And it's in the bones. The libraries. The deference. All the old stuff. Britain before – it was like a whole other country and he's the last of it. But what makes him strong also causes him a lot of pain. You can't just ditch the values that made you – no matter what you try. Because they're in *everything* you do and feel – so you go against yourself in one thing and it feels like you're going against yourself in everything.

Yes, although Mum didn't know what exactly went on in the old house with Jack and Ralph, she told me what she'd gathered – so I could understand 'the deal' – and she told me everything about Russia and what followed. But I never said a word to anyone, not even my brothers – not then and not now – because somehow that would be to betray my mother and she and I . . . she and I, we are separate to all this. No matter Ralph and Jack. And, anyway, I want to hear my father speak. I want to hear it all again. But from him. Hear it renewed. Like their vows or something.

So I put my back into pushing him up the incline and I say: 'Three hours was never going to be enough for you and Mum.'

'There was no time even to wash. So we dressed in a rush and we went out into the Moscow evening. I remember the cars and the lights and the rain. The Soviet Union falling apart. And this terrible sadness. Swelling up like a flood, Lou. I remember thinking that the rest of the world was empty – loveless. And that they were all driving in circles to fill the emptiness. And that this was going to be me again. We stood on the corner at Pushkinskaya metro station, the rain coming down. And these endless rivers of headlights. And we did not know if we would ever see each other again. She was saying no, no, no – the rain plastering her hair to her forehead. I remember there were two old women selling flowers, stood there – like sentries of the heart at the top of the stairs down to the trains. I kept saying yes, yes, we must. We held each other. What else could we do? Me saying I want you to come to London, I want you to come to London. Or let me go to New York. She saying she couldn't. We couldn't. That it was impossible. Me saying when – when – when can I see you again? She saying never. Never. And then we kissed. We kissed. Since our lips wanted to go on saying something other than these useless *useless* words.'

'And you thought that was it?'

'Honestly, I thought that this was the defining moment of my life. Then she just ran down the stairs into the underground. Into the Earth. And straight away – straight away – this wild regret rose inside me and possessed me.'

A horn sounds on one of the barges and echoes in the valley. I never told my mother about the audio tapes, though. I don't think she knew. And I never told my father that I found them. Or that I listened to them on his old Walkman cassette player all the way through. Or my brothers. Whom do you tell? Whom do you tell?

Some bird of the night is flying in from the further shore, its wings outstretched like it's looking for somewhere to rest.

'The saddest thing, the saddest thing, Lou, was when I got back to my room. Chopin playing on the radio. The ashtray with our dead cigarettes. Two glasses half-empty where her lips had been only twenty minutes before. And the bed . . . the bed all in disarray. Pillows turned this way and that. Duvet strewn. You never saw a more heartbreaking sight. Such *life* – only just there – and now . . . gone.'

My father's head is down. But I don't want him to stop here. So I push on up the hill. The night is colder now. Behind us the castle glows. The river runs below.

'Tell me about London.'

His voice is full of feeling and he has to let himself breathe consciously. 'There was nothing for three months. I wrote to her. I called her. This was before email and all of that rubbish. I thought she was gone and I convinced myself to go on . . . to love where I'd loved before . . . all these things you say to yourself, Lou.'

'What? What did you say to yourself?'

'Oh . . . I convinced myself that the reality – the *task* – of manhood is to learn to live with inappropriate feelings – inappropriate everything – lobotomize yourself and live in the family.' He raises his hands. 'Or else I'd tell myself a different story: that all that had happened was that I had built a chrysalis out of lust and trapped myself inside it.'

'But you didn't believe yourself?'

'I don't know how anyone believes themselves about anything. When I woke up, I thought of her; when I slept, I dreamt of her. And what was this thing inside me trying to get out and flutter into the light?'

The hill steepens.

'Sometimes I would tell myself that my duty was to the institution, to marriage, to my wife. Other times I would say that I had a duty to myself . . . Because we have one life, Lou. And it's fleeing. Fleeting. Flown. If we don't seize the day, then . . .'

'How did Mum come back?'

'She made it happen. It was her initiative. One day, out of the blue she called me at work. She was in London on some spurious summer scholarship, she said. She hadn't meant to call me. She hadn't meant to tell me, but maybe, she thought, we could meet "as friends". And, of course, in one second all the bullshit I'd been telling myself evaporated.'

'You saw her a lot?'

'Not enough. I was so cautious and crabbed. We actually tried to be friends for a while. All this – it was harder for me to deal with in London. I just couldn't find a way to be and I made it all a lot worse. Your brothers are right.'

'What do you mean?'

There are the lights from other mobile homes parked at the edge of *Der Wohnwagenstellplatz*. I push my father on up the last of the hill towards the gate.

'You get to this stage and it's all accounting, Lou. You look at all the things you did and you can't believe you wasted so much time. I don't know now what the hell I was doing. But I was ... I thought ... I made a bugger's muddle of everything. Anybody who thinks that he can reason his way in and out of love understands neither his own humanity nor love itself.'

'How long did it go on for?'

'Too long. We went out together – maybe once every two weeks but it was so . . . so difficult. We went to book events because it was almost OK for us to be there together. But it was torture not to be with her naturally, fully.'

'You couldn't stand being apart?'

'Whenever we were in public, I felt as though every other conversation was a distraction until such a time as I could go and stand close beside her again. I was continually aware of where she was in the room. I could sense every other man's eye upon her. I would strain to hear what she was saying over the babble. My heart paused when she left and beat the faster when she returned. I needed a thousand eyes just to see her. Then – you know – abstinence just melts away. I knew—'

'That you just had to be with her?'

We stop at the top of the hill.

'No. The opposite. I knew . . . I knew that our choices in love bind us, Lou. We must command and enter service. We will require and be required. I knew I had to kill it and honour the vows I had made to Carol.'

'So that's why Mum went back to America?'

'I asked her to do that. And she *wanted* to. She said she should. I had been preventing her. I kept changing my mind. I tortured her, too. You're the only person in my world that I haven't tortured, Lou.'

I say nothing.

We cannot fit the wheelchair through the kissing gate.

So I haul my father up. We're face to face. His hands are cold but he's warm beneath his arms where I hold him a moment before he leans on the wooden fence. Then I half fold the chair to get it through.

'What was it like when she went?'

He looks down over the valley. Clouds are snagged on the moon. 'That last day, my heart felt like it was withering inside me, dying. I saw her reach the door of her room and everything shrank to that moment, her hand on the handle, knowing that she must turn it, her hair still not quite dry from the shower, her smile, as if there might yet be time and space for more madness in our lives. And then she opened the door . . . And I knew she was going to step outside . . . And this terrible feeling of emptiness opened up inside me that I knew I'd never escape . . . And her lips – one more time – wet with her tears and with mine, and still nothing to be done except split up. Nothing to be done.'

I open up the chair again and set the brake then I shoulder my father through the gate, bound together as we were before. His walking seems already to be quitting the memory of his muscles. His eyes are dark to me but I can feel his breath on my cheek.

'Why did you go to America, then? What changed?'

'I didn't go deliberately to see her. Or maybe I did. Subconsciously.'

I smile and say: 'You can't be subconsciously deliberate, Dad.'

'But I just got this sense, Lou, growing inside me with every mile that the aeroplane flew. That this – *this* is where my life must go. That I had to step free of the bondage of . . . of my parents. Their censure. You look all your life for certain things in a woman. You find something here and something there. You treasure this, you treasure that. But then . . .'

'Then?'

'You find everything you have been searching for *in one place*. Everything you ever lacked or wanted – everything met so exactly. Everything reciprocated, everything under-stood. And you have to take that seriously. Like Ralph says: you have to take love seriously. What else can we do? What else is there? The miracle of finding one another through all the noise and distraction and the mess of life. Here she was; and here was I.'

I help him back into his chair. And I get the same sensa-tion that I had on the ferry – that I can see my father clearly. For who he really is. All this that he has been thinking and feeling for so much of his life.

'You mean in New York you were back together?'

'When I got there, we stayed in her place in her tiny walk-up and just listened to music. There seemed to be nothing we could say or do that was sufficient. We couldn't sleep or even make love. We just lay there on the bed holding hands with this music pouring through us staring up at this slow-spinning fan. And I was thinking about all the people who have been in love and how so many of them cannot be together . . . and . . . you know what?'

'Tell me.'

'I began to think I had a duty – not to anyone else, not even to me – but a duty to love itself.'

I slide open the van door and turn to face him. He looks up at me from the wheelchair. 'When I met your mother, Lou, I felt as if I had known her all my life.'

I raise him up.

'I was my truest self with her. The needy rancour inside of me – it just disappeared, evaporated. It was as if I'd been walking the Earth only half of myself like . . . like a shade.'

We swivel round and he sits on the edge of the bed. I take off his jacket. Unbutton his best shirt – blue Oxford weave.

'She was so sharp-witted, Lou, so perceptive, so quick. She could express herself like . . . like no woman that I had ever met before. She was deadly. She was funny. She was serious. She'd do these cartoon faces whenever I was being bearish or earnest – mocking me but so warmly and cheekily that I stopped instantly and just became a better man on the spot. Most of all she had so much *spirit*. She understood people inside out and she could say it so well . . . I don't know . . . I just . . . just . . .'

His bare shoulders are caved forward. The white hair wiry in the shallow cleft of his chest. He shivers. I'm standing there with the cold air behind me. But I don't want to climb in with him and slide the door shut behind because there won't be enough room to undress him. And I want to be alone out here. Maybe the only reason I don't run and keep running is that I know I'll have to come back – because the world is round and your father is always your father.

'When I met her, she was so beautiful – I mean really. She had this *intense* beauty – the real thing, Lou – not made up, or contingent on her haircut, or clothes, or anything. Luminous.' He says my name but he is talking to himself. 'And the closer you got, the more you felt it. You *felt* it. It was that kind of beauty. Whenever she came into a room, it startled me all over again. I never really got over that. I never got over her beauty.'

I bend down: 'Shoes off,' I say.

'I just don't want to do all this . . . all this decaying . . . now that she has gone.'

'Give me your arm. Up. So. Can you feel your legs? There you go – you're standing.'

'It's cold, Lou. Stars are out.'

'We have to take your trousers off. Lean on me. Two seconds and we'll be done.'

When I look up again his cheeks are wet. 'Sorry,' he says. 'It's the disease.'

'No it isn't.'

'No it isn't.' He's smiling. 'What can we do, Lou? You meet such a woman – and bang – it's like the Large Hadron Collider – here at last are the true particles of existence – except you've both smashed yourselves to pieces to see them.'

I fish his brown paisley pyjamas out and help him put them on.

I say: 'I'll put up the bed in the roof – for when Ralph and Jack get back.'

'You think they'll come back?'

'Whatever they're going to do, they're going do it together. And since Jack is never going to let himself do anything to hurt Siobhan, they're going to wind up back here.'

I climb on the bed to undo the catches for the roof.

He lies down under the bedclothes – almost like a child. But when he smiles up at me in the feeble cabin light, the triangles of skin at the corner of his eyes are wrinkling like the dog-ears of a book softened from so much reading.

I throw the duvet and pillows into the roof for my brothers.

'Here are the painkillers and a bottle of water,' I say. 'I'm going to smoke outside. Can I borrow your fleece?'

'Yes.' He gulps some water and swallows the pills. 'Take it, Lou, take it.'

I tighten the lid on the bottle of water and prop it beside him.

He settles back into his pillow closes his eyes. I struggle into his fleece. He sleeps in a second – snoring like he's far hungrier for his dreams than for his waking.

I slide shut the door. The window is open an inch for air. My thoughts are swooping crazy all over my kaleidoscope mind like when I try to write. So I sit outside smoking and I look back across at the castle and watch the river flow for what feels like a very long time.

THE PILGRIM'S PROGRESS

In the half-sleep of the powder-blue morning, I think Dad must want to piss and my first pulse is irritation because I know I'll have to go with him. All night I have been near his feet, trying to turn away, trying to breathe. Whenever I wake, which feels like every half-hour, his snoring is so loud that I can't get back to sleep. My brothers, too, have been noisy from their drinking and they stood on me when they came in. The air smells stale and foetid with drunken, sleeping men. My single pillow is old and lumpy and slips away into the well by the side door. The bed is too hot, too cold. I dream I'm sleeping on the edge of a narrow ledge between the cold castle walls and the rising damp of the river.

'Help me up, Lou,' he half whispers. 'Help me up.'

I can feel the difficulty he is having turning. But I know something is odd because he's doing what he does when he wants to wake everyone up without waking them up: not really being quiet. I try to sit in the cramped space. I'm in my clothes more or less except for my trousers. I reach on top of the units for my phone, which I put in their pocket. I have a message from Eva. My heart rises – the thought of another reality. The thought of holding her tomorrow. Her kiss, her body, wrapped around mine in the clean of some strange bed that is nothing to do with any of this. And then the world again – waiting for us; the world undestroyed.

Now from somewhere in the gloom comes this muffled old-school beeping like we're back in 1998 or something. And it takes me a moment to realize it must be an alarm – Dad's alarm – which freaks me out – because I can't believe that Dad even knew his old Nokia had an alarm function, let alone how to set the bastard.

'Help me up, Lou,' he urges. 'Let's get the tea on.'

He is sitting up. His pyjama shirt is open. I'm only just understanding what is happening: that he's deliberately set himself to wake up at – what? I look back at my phone. Six thirty. What the fuck?

Ralph's voice is an angry hiss from above: 'What are you *doing*?'

Dad has thrown back the covers. His pyjama trousers have ridden up in the night so that his legs poke out the end; they look so thin and wan except where they are lividly bruised and swollen and I get a second pulse of aversion which I have to override.

'We must get on the road,' Dad says. 'How many of those croissies have we got left, Lou?'

My brothers are stirring angrily.

I pass my father his fleece and help him get it over his head. He doesn't seem to want to take off his pyjamas. He's in a hurry.

'Five or six hundred,' I say. For a moment, his eyes are alive but somehow focused internally as if possessed. Then he smiles at me like he was doing before my brothers arrived. 'We'll have breakfast on the road. Get through them one by one. Help me up, help me up.'

'The road to where?' Jack asks, his voice rasping from somewhere above.

'Zurich,' my father says.

And it's like with that single word he's taken back all the authority he has ever ceded, like on this new morning, in this steady early light, his life is his own again – for all the good, for all the bad – and whatever we might think, whatever we may feel, however strong my brothers might be, we'll no more deter him than determine him; his will is deeper than ours and his dignity and his suffering and his shame entirely his own.

'I have to be there to meet the doctor,' he says.

'Jesus,' Ralph rasps. 'What time is this appointment?'

'Two,' Dad says. 'And I don't intend to be late.'

'It can't be more than three hours to Zurich,' Ralph says.

'I want to check in to our hotel first and take a shower,' Dad presses. 'Get sorted out for the interview. You can sleep in the back. We'll drive with the back bed down again.'

'I'm not driving to Zurich,' Jack croaks.

'Jack, this is just the appointment to get the prescription – nothing to do with actually *taking* it. I'm not going to miss it. I'm not going to miss it after all this. Lou, can you pass me my pills and the ibuprofen. Let's get that tea on.'

'The prescription,' Ralph says, quietly. 'The prescription.'

'Yes. As I say. I'm going to be assessed by a doctor. Nothing else happens until the next day or the day after that.' My father lifts his own legs with a tremor in his hands. His right ankle is swollen from the fall. His expression takes no notice. He's all business. 'Open up the doors, Lou. Let me get out. We need tea and then we've got to get this show on the road. Help me. Help me.'

I slide open the door and the fresh air is cold and welcome and new. The other motorhomes are all closed up – their windows opaque with human breathing. There is mist on the Rhine below and the pale valley and the pewter-coloured water are so still that they might have been enamelled.

'I'll drive,' I say. 'You sleep. Everyone can sleep.'

I pay with the credit card at the petrol pump. I am deep tired. I keep getting this idea that I need to hide away in some monastery somewhere and eat vegetable broths and rest up for a month. Jack comes out of the shop; he's swigging apple juice. He has bought four cartons. Ralph has walked over to the street where he is standing in the drizzle, smoking. We look like ragged frontiersmen strayed into the suburbs of northern Zurich in search of supplies for the winter – short of cash, clothing and tempers. And everything here is grey. White-grey statues. Slick light-grey paving in the streets. Beige-grey buildings. Grey-brown Alpine water in the little rivers that run by the side of the road.

I feel the heat of the engine and smell the long-journeyed oil as I walk around the van. I want someone else to take over the driving. Doug. Where's Doug when you need the bastard? I open the door. Unbelievably, Dad has swivelled his chair round to face the bed.

'What are you doing?' I climb in.

'Park us over there.' He indicates the tyre-pressure bay.

'What?'

'Just go over there.'

'Are the tyres flat?'

'No. But we're nearly there. The satnav says twenty-eight minutes to the hotel. We're early. We have time.'

I start the van up and point through the window so that

Jack understands what we're doing. He watches me drive slowly across the forecourt with an expression of hungover incomprehension. I stop and pull on the clockwork hand-brake. There's a Michelin man looming over us.

Jack slides open the door and takes his brogues off to climb into the bed.

'Conference,' Dad says.

I twist round in the driver's seat.

Ralph appears in the doorway behind Jack, their twin faces echoes of one another. 'How can the gateway to the Alps be so depressing,' he asks.

'The centre is beautiful,' Dad says. 'The rivers and the lake. Best place in the whole of Europe for city-swimming. The water is exceptionally clean, too.'

My brothers have been sleeping; now they're like drowsy soldiers who have just woken up and who do not yet understand that they have arrived at the front.

'What are we doing in the tyre-pressure bay?' Ralph climbs in after Jack and starts to prise off his boots. He's wearing one of Dad's fleeces and he looks for a second disconcertingly like Dad did in the photographs from when I was born. 'Do we need air? Or is this lunch? Is it even *time* for lunch? I've lost track.'

'Conference,' says Jack, folding pillows behind himself so he can sit up.

Ralph slides the door shut without slamming it and crosses his legs. I turn the driver's seat round and lean forward. Even Jack is looking dishevelled. As a family, we definitely need to clean ourselves up. But at least we never sulk.

Dad looks from one to the other of us and then says, 'You think because I'm your father I know what to do.'

Jack shakes his head.

Ralph asks: 'What's going on, Dad?'

Dad ignores them. He's past listening. 'You do. You think I know what I'm doing. Maybe not in here.' Dad fingers his temple. 'But in your hearts. Inside yourselves.' He makes a spider with his hand and presses it to his heart. 'You believe I have a plan. That I have calibrated intentions.' He pauses. 'We're always children and it takes us a lifetime to get over the fact that our parents don't know what the hell they're doing.'

'Seemed obvious to me,' Ralph says.

'Well, you're lucky,' Dad replies, quickly. 'Because I'm almost dead and I don't understand the first thing about my own father yet.'

I unscrew my carton of juice. Though the others don't see it, I can tell that Dad is on fire. You live with someone long enough and you can divine their mood by the way the smallest muscles are moving beneath their skin; I could sit all day in complete silence with Dad and I could pretty much work out which writer he was reading just by the way he held the book and turned the pages. And I can tell that Dad is getting high on the fumes of this fire – high with this weird excitement and something else, something that might be fear, or relief, or expectation. I don't know. It's like he's freeing up. Like Zurich is suddenly his freedom and his permission, his impetus and his prerogative.

'What I'm trying to say is that I don't know what to do.'

His eyes go round us – deliberate, wounded, commanding.

'I don't know what to do.'

We are sharing too little air. We need to wind the window down further. But the smell of petrol is too strong outside.

He says it again. 'I don't know what to do . . . You're the only people I've got . . . So I talked to you about it. Maybe I should not have done that.' He chews at his lower lip. 'I hoped . . . I don't know what . . . I've been . . . confused. I've been in a terrible state.'

Jack's face wears the tight frown of responsibility – but maybe he's grasping this at last.

'What I'm trying to say is . . . is that you can't see me clearly. Any of you. Because I'm your father. I'm your dad. And because of all that's between us, it's the hardest thing in the world to see you parents and your children clearly.'

Ralph starts slowly undoing the screw top of the carton that rests in the crook of his legs.

'I can't make the things I have done wrong right again in a day or two. Or six months. Or ever. And maybe it doesn't actually matter. Like you say, Ralph, worse happens all the time. And maybe we understand each other a bit better – after this time together. But now – right now – we need to try to put all that to one side. I need you to see where I am – here, today, in this bloody garage. Not so much your dad, but . . . but because I'm a man. Like you.'

Ralph swigs from his carton. 'I don't know why, Dad, but it's so much easier to take you seriously when you swear.'

Jack says: 'Maybe you *can*—'

'Wait, Jack. Hang on. My choices . . . my choices are to go through with this and die before it gets worse. And it *will* get worse. Or not to go through with it – and inflict suffering on me – and on you – and then die anyway.'

'I—'

'No, Jack, listen. When you talked about your boys, about what happened before they were born, you said that you "chose" life. That's—'

'I meant—'

'That's the word you used – when we were in the showers. You said you "chose life". And it was your choice to make. Well, let's not beat about the bloody bush. We choose all the time. It's normal. Go to any hospital. Watch the news. We choose which people live and die – wars, famines, disasters. Who we help. Who we don't.' He smiles his lopsided smile. 'Relativism is the luxury of the ethically decadent. When it comes down to it, we're a very judgemental species living in a life and death world. Have to be. Has to be. Always were.'

'This is so much more like it.' Ralph swigs.

Jack's voice is without combat: 'Listen, Dad . . .' He pauses. 'I'm saying maybe you *can* do this. But n—'

'The illusion, Jack, is that we are in the middle of life. In fact we're in the middle of death. And we're all agreed there is no God. So what can we do?'

'I just think that now is not th—'

'Let him speak, Jack,' Ralph says. 'Let him speak.'

'What can we do?' Dad asks again. 'We just have to find the joy and sing while we can. We have to find the love and celebrate – often. We have to engage with one another.'

My father's brow is deeply furrowed. The PDFs say that ptosis is the name for the drooping of the eyelids and that furrowing is an effort to combat this. He must be fifteen times more tired than we are . . . But he's concentrating like he's going to burn all the energy he's got left in this one big bonfire. Like he's going to ignite the world.

'You get one quick life, boys. That's what I'm trying to tell you. One quick life. And then it's over. It's over *so* bloody quickly. We all know this. But we forget, we forget. It seems like twenty minutes and you're looking back and you're thinking what . . . What was I playing at? What the bloody hell was I thinking?' The words are coming out of him like he's young again. 'I'm not talking about your mothers. Not any more. Forget them. They're not here. I'm talking about me and each of you. The four of us. I'm talking about us, now, together.'

Another VW van pulls out of the garage; it's the new model; two generations later than ours; unaffected.

'What I'm trying to say is . . . Forget the damage and the mess. For a moment. Just for a moment.'

He pauses as if to marshal the warring armies in his mind.

'You know, there were so many days when all I did – all I did – was look after you two – you two strawberry-heads. When you were babies, I bathed you. I dried you. I dressed you. I fed you your milk and later your food – spoon after spoon – the two of you – despite all the moaning and the crying and the turning away. Then, when you were bigger, I sat on the floor and played with you. Lego. Jigsaws. All these endless jigsaws of wild animals. And all that drawing you used to do. Terrible scribbles. I held your seats as you rode your bikes. I watched for dogs from the corner of my eyes in the park. I stood beside you while you learned how to wee. I wiped your bottoms. I must have spent years of my life tending to your bottoms. I carried you out of the car and up the stairs to your beds. I took off your shoes. I slipped you out of your coats. I tucked you in and made sure you had your zebra, Ralph, and you your giraffe, Jack, and, later, that you had your little piglet, Lou.'

'Where *is* my fucking zebra?'

'And I read to you – oh so many books. I must have read you five thousand books. And when I went away, I missed your stupid faces so much. I used to sit with your pictures on my desk and tell myself I was writing my silly books for you. I tried to teach you to love the same things I do. I tried to teach you. I tried to answer every question you asked of me.' He spiders his heart again. 'I want you to know all this. I want you to feel it . . . *in your hearts.* Can you do that for me?'

He looks at Ralph. 'I still have your zebra,' he says. 'It's at home. You used to make it dance.'

Ralph meets his eyes. 'Dad, I don't think you—'

'No, let me speak, Ralph – while it's all here in my mind and before it crumbles.' He raises his finger to his temple again. The PDFs say there is a cognitive dimension to the disease; a strange and subtle elation. 'I can't tell you how this last eighteen months has been for me. I watch a woman walk down the street and the slightest swing of her hips seems miraculous. I listen to a young lad whistling in the car park of the supermarket and I can hear creation whistling. And that's before we get on to the rivers and the mountains and the forests and the coastlines. Or the music we make, the human voice, the dancing human form, the art we paint, the cathedrals we build, the poetry, the bloody *poetry*. The stark beauty of it all. Like you say, Jack: it's all miraculous. Miraculous. Each moment – each and every breath. And you want to know something?'

We are silent.

'I'm almost *grateful* for the illness. For the time it's given me to appreciate my life and to see things in the true light of the real day. Instead of dying unexpectedly, I've been able to think – to consider. I've had time to review. It's yet another privilege I've had. Among the many.'

'Dad?' Ralph asks softly.

'And by the way, death is . . . well, I'm thinking of death as a mighty relief. Not just for me. But for all of us. A positive gift. For the human race. I mean – just imagine if all the shits who ruin the world for the rest of us . . . imagine if they lived for ever. All the angry old men. Imagine if they never ever died – the war-mongers and the people who poison our minds and our societies and our—'

'Dad,' Ralph asks again. 'Are you actually doing this? Because you—'

'I'm happy, Ralph. My ankle bloody hurts. But I am happy. And these last few days . . . I want you to know . . . They've been the best days I've had in a long old time. Even last night was . . . was superb in its own way. Meaningful. Worth it. Important. Transforming.'

Cars are pulling in and filling up with petrol. Driving away again. Like it's the most normal thing in the world. People to meet. Places to go. And I am thinking that this is it: now that we're here, we're all changing our minds. I can feel it: Jack is hearing Dad at last; Ralph is hearing him; I am hearing him. And so we're all changing our minds. One more time. One more time. Those against – now for. Those for – now against.

'I'm not going to say I'm not scared,' Dad continues. 'Of course I am. Only, I'm more scared of carrying on living. So I hope I get this prescription. And that it's all straightforward.

I don't want any snarl-ups because of paperwork. And then we'll see. We'll see what to do after that. Tomorrow.'

He smiles.

'Dad?' Jack asks.

'The sooner we do this, Jack, the sooner you can all live again. We should look at this time as if . . . as if it has been a great chance that most people don't get. A real blessing.'

'Dad.'

'Because, you know, it's not like this for most people – it's not me having a stroke all lonely up in Leeds while you're all at work in London or whatever. Falling down dead on my own. At some point, I'm going to have to go. And this has been great. We have had this chance. To be together. We get this prescription today and we see about tomorrow. Talk some more tonight and tomorrow . . . And we will see.'

Jack says: 'Dad, I can understand why you think that this is a good idea. I can. But I—'

'Sorry, Jack, something else.' He presses tremoring finger-tips to his forehead. 'I keep not saying what I want to say.'

'You—'

'What I want to say is this: that we are what we give. We are what we leave behind. I only realized this yesterday at the cave like it was a blinding flash of insight – which shows you what kind of an idiot I am. Because of course – it's obvious and the poets have been saying it since the dawn of time. All that a human being leaves behind is what he or she has created. Life is all about creation. The *only* meaning is creation.' He manages his slow downward grin again. 'It is not what you have taken but what you have given. Of course it is. Whatever you have given and whatever you have made. So here it is. In this van. Everything important that my life amounts to. And the thing that I'm most proud of. The three of you. The way you are. You three boys. Whom I love. That's what I wanted to say. Just that.'

'Dad,' Jack says. He's leaning forward, holding out his hand.

Dad clasps his wrist, like he does mine, and raises it for a second. Then he does something I have never seen him do: he reaches out his other hand and lays it on Ralph's shoulder.

I lean in so that we form a loose circle.

'When you get to where I am, you see it clearly, boys. Finally, finally. And what is really important to me . . . most important . . . the only thing that I ask . . . is that you go on . . . talking to each other like we've always talked.' His eyes go round us again – Ralph, Jack, me – the circle of father and sons, holding steady for the briefest moment. 'Don't fall out. Don't ever fall out. I want you to promise to stay friends. And to help one another where you can. Because you're very lucky to have each other. I don't know how that happened. It's another miracle.'

'Dad,' I say.

'Let's get weaving, Lou. Let's get checked in and cleaned up and ready for what's next. The readiness is all.'

PART FIVE

PAINTINGS ON THE WALL

THE CELESTIAL CITY

After the van, my room in the Hotel Ambassador is so staggeringly beautiful and spacious and *private* that it feels like I have crossed into another world. As soon as the heavy door is shut, I sit down in the big leather chair amazed by my polished table (on which there is fresh fruit) and stare at the vast bed and the thick cream stripes of the wallpaper. The light is coming in through some kind of diaphanous lace that hangs tall in the windows and seems to make the place luminous with an unvarying daylight that somehow glimmers even in the dark wood of the big desk. At my elbow, there is thick ivory stationery – as though I might be an actual ambassador about to write despatches home. Maybe civilization is a Swiss hotel. I don't know. I never stay in hotels. I have no idea. But Jack is helping Dad. And so I have ninety minutes to rest and the prospect of this bed in which to sleep tonight. And I am so relieved. I could live in this room for ten years. Come out when it's all over – ISIS, the climate-change crisis, the new Dark Ages, my fucking father's happy fucking demise.

Suddenly, I want to be naked and clean again.

I go into the bathroom – my own, my own – with its huge bath and lights that dim and a sink wide and deep enough to bathe twin babies. I take off my clothes – grimy and crumpled from the camping – and run the water, which is copious and hot. There are lots of small bottles that say things like 'balm' and 'soak' and 'infusion'. So I empty them all into the water. Then I fetch my phone and place it on the bath-side table.

I can't believe the size of the towels; or their thickness; or their number.

I ease myself into the bath and close my eyes and sink slowly under the water.

When I come up, I am calm again.

So I dry my hands and pick up my phone and search for where Eva's apartment is located on the other side of the lake; that's where I am going – whatever happens, that's where I am going tomorrow. She lands in the morning. She'll be there by nine, she thinks. The flight was crazy-early and cheap.

But when I climb out of the bath – all warm and serene – I make the mistake of going over to the windows and pulling back the lace so I can take a look at the actual lake – just away to the left of the hotel. I see across to the neighbourhood where Eva will be staying, past the boats and the sun all busy in the water between us. I wonder if I can guess the building. But it's too far. So my eyes travel half-right towards the old town where the shore narrows into the rivers. Then I look back at the Opera House directly opposite the hotel. And then – below, to the right, my attention is taken by a cafe, almost beneath my window but a little way along.

And that is when I start watching this family. Not doing anything much. Five of them. Sitting and fidgeting at this fussy and too-small pavement place. And that's when I see the kid – I don't know how old he is – maybe seven – knock over his father's glass of wine so that it spills in a spreading red spear across the table.

Instantly, his mother jumps up to stop it staining her clothes; and the older kids – a girl and a boy – they jump up, too, because some of it is on their plates. And so I'm watching everyone hammering the kid (while all the cars go by and nobody else notices), like he is the kind of idiot they all wished was nowhere near their family. And he's shrivelling up because he's got nowhere to go; and he's too young to tell them to lay off; and what can he do but sit back in his seat and wish to disappear? Except, now, his father is also up and doing this 'calm down' thing with his hands and moving round and round and in and out like some kind of Morris dancer, mopping up with the napkin. Sorting the mess out. Making it easier on the kid.

The thing is – when we checked in – we discovered that Dad had only booked two rooms. We parked the van and wheeled him in. And he was all super-cheerful and polite and still bonfiring his energy. And straight away in the eyes of the receptionist – surprise: 'Hello, Mr Lasker,' he said, 'good to see you but you have only reserved two rooms. This booking was made in March, I can see. But, listen, we have no problem here, because . . . I think . . . yes . . . we have two more rooms . . . if that is good for you. Lucky for you and lucky for us! Because there are only three left in the whole hotel . . .'

And Dad was fine to pay for the extra two and put them on the card. More than fine. Eager. Of course, he said, of course, handing the card up from the wheelchair. Bloody hell. Yes. Of course.

He had forgotten. But we had all registered it. He had only booked two rooms. Because that's what he was expecting back then: two people. And the second one was reserved in Doug's name.

And suddenly, staring out of the window, it starts to happen. I don't even know what it is at first . . . this weird water brimming and spilling from the corners of my eyes. Because I'm watching the mum go inside the cafe and I'm watching the dad change seats with the daughter so that he can sit next to the kid. And I'm shaking and my face is all scrunched up. And I still don't really know what is going on with my body. But I am sniffing my breath and my voice wants to talk but it has gone hoarse and thin – and something feels trapped in the muscles of my cheeks.

These must be tears, I'm thinking. These must be tears.

And I am not me. But I am me. And I must be crying because these heavy tears are rolling down my face into my mouth like I am dissolving and soon I'll be made of water and nothing else.

And I really want to talk to my brothers. And my dad. I really want to see my dad. Which I can do. Since he is next door and I have his spare room key.

But what about when I can't? Because he isn't next door? Or anywhere?

We are early, of course. So we sit in the doctor's waiting room. We are lined up on three upright chairs, like this is all fine and normal. Dad at the end. Clean, scrupulous, fresh. Like maybe we're enlisting. Like maybe we're waiting to renew our passports. Like maybe we're having our toenails done. There is the smell of carpet-cleaner. Traffic is passing outside where we parked the van. Touched-up photographs of people on the covers of untouched magazines. A woman, a receptionist, is speaking somewhere in hushed German on a telephone. On the wall for no reason, there are pictures of impossible families on impossible holidays with impossible teeth. There's a dot-matrix board which calls patients in for consultations. I watch the names. Traschsel. Fassnacht. Enz.

Lasker.

But there is no way of processing the fact of those English letters – the way they are formed so unconvincingly; then flashed; then dissolved – and so I just stare at them like maybe I'm going to find something meaningful in my own hallucinations. And yet they contain nothing of me, neither identity, nor meaning. I am in space looking down. We are a deluded family in a delusional species. We wait for a magician dressed in white to cast a spell that permits us to die. Yes, from the vantage of the stars, I can see that there is a madness raging through the collective human mind and it won't stop until we have destroyed ourselves and vanished from the world. We have to fight back. We have to face reality and deal with it.

Lasker.

So we stand up. Jack moves in for a moment – almost as if to take the handles – and then steps aside and lets me wheel Dad towards the surgery. Ralph follows, seeming slow and deliberately so.

Lasker.

The door opens and the doctor stands on the threshold. He is tall with delicate rimless glasses and has the rigorously pristine old-but-new look of someone who scrupulously sand-blasts his facade every weekend.

'Thank you all for waiting,' he says, his English as close to perfect as his shave. 'I'm very glad to see the family here.'

We haven't really been waiting. It is precisely two p.m. We are exactly on time.

I can't speak. Only Ralph has managed any politeness with the receptionist.

'So – it's great to see the family here,' the doctor says again. 'Are you all . . . sons?'

Ralph steps forward into our silence. 'As far as we know,' he says.

'Lucky man,' the doctor says. There is a vein that spasms in his temple. 'We have a saying here in Switzerland that red hair is the sign of fire in the spirit.'

Ralph returns the smile with interest but says nothing and we're all stuck in the doorway for a second until the doctor realizes – what? – that time is no longer illusory and insubstantial to us but as real as starvation and thirst.

'OK – so – if you wouldn't mind,' he says. 'I need about fifteen minutes with your father. That would be great. And then we can all have a chat together.'

He offers to take the wheelchair handles from me and I cannot do anything but accede.

'Let's go and have a cigarette,' Ralph says. 'Cheer ourselves up.'

The grey street outside is absurdly normal. The sun is shining in the windows of the office building opposite. Cars are parked down one side. A little boy is scooting past with his mum. A man with a bag of groceries fiddles with the lock of his door. We walk a little way down to near where we left the van.

Ralph shakes out his cigarettes. He looks different now.

Somehow he has bought some thin pale trousers and a fitted jacket and a new shirt – all in less than two hours.

'How did it go washing Dad?' he asks Jack.

'Painful.' Jack sighs deeply, like the whole of his breath has to move through the whole of his stolid body. Conversely, he looks worse in his clean clothes: his jeans and his uneasy polo shirt. He seems somehow thickened by the weight of care and for a second I think he might take one of the cigarettes. He says: 'I'm going to ask the doctor to give him something for his ankle.'

I see now that we are standing by a shop – a chemist: 'Apotheke' – and beside a yellow zebra crossing that feels wrong to our British black-and-white sensibilities.

Ralph shakes out his match to extinguish its fire and squints through his smoke across the narrow distance between us: 'Is he actually doing this?'

'I don't know,' Jack says. 'I don't know.'

'What did he say when you were with him?'

'He says he just wants the prescription. He says that's what he wants. To know that he has the option.'

'Is he just saying that to stop you arguing with him?'

'I don't know.' Jack's whole bearing has changed – as though certainty was the Action Man wire within him and, now that it has gone, he has got nothing with which to set himself upright where he stands. But maybe all it took was an hour alone with Dad – undressing him, washing him – because now I can tell that Jack is *in* it: the life-and-death zone. Which is where we all are.

Jack sighs again and rubs at his stubble which has become a fatherly beard: 'He says it's ironic. He says that it is a pilgrimage.'

'What's ironic?'

'This whole thing. Like a religious pilgrimage . . . but to suicide.'

'Assisted death,' I say.

'So it's *not* just about the prescription?' Ralph presses.

'I don't know,' Jack says. 'I don't know. He says it is. He says he wants to keep going and then decide tomorrow.'

Ralph half turns his face to exhale his smoke but keeps his eyes fixed on me. 'How you doing, Lou?'

'I was fine.'

'Was?'

'Until we got to the hotel. There's something about the hotel. I don't know. It totally fucked me up.'

But the truth is that I think I *do* know. I think that we all know. We all know that Dad wouldn't be so blithely paying for four rooms in a four-star hotel on Lake Zurich unless he'd made up his mind. Because it's the money that talks. Or Dad's attitude to the money that talks. He just wouldn't be doing this otherwise. Unless he meant it. He couldn't stand to . . . to waste thousands of pounds. Or that is what we all suspect. And I think that this suspicion is killing us because – after all – if it is only the money that tells us the truth, then this seems like another something that is insufficient. And there is already so much that is insufficient.

A car comes and hesitates, ludicrously polite – the driver thinks that we are planning to cross on the yellow zebra. Ralph bends to the window to wave the stranger on. He nods from behind the wheel and smiles. He looks sixty. How long does he have? Another fifteen summers. Or thirty more? Two? How many does he want?

'The hotel just fucked me up,' I say again. 'I'm not sure we should ever have got out of the van.'

We all look at the van, which is waiting solidly by; irrefutable. What are we going to do with the van? There is no way we can sell it. There is no way we can keep it.

'All for one,' Ralph says. He's looking back at me like he's my boxing coach.

'I want it over,' I say.

'Yeah,' Ralph says. He puts out his cigarette. 'We're pretty much at the truth now, Lou.'

I feel an arm go round my shoulder, which can only be Jack's.

'I want to say, Lou.' Jack draws himself up. 'I want to say that I'm sorry about last night. It wasn't anything to do with you.'

'I know.'

'Yes . . .' And now Jack pulls me in so we're forehead to forehead. 'But what you don't know is how bloody amazing you have been all your life. With your mum and – now – with Dad.'

That's Dad's word, I'm thinking: bloody. Why is Jack using Dad's words?

'And what you don't know,' Jack continues, 'is how you, me and your annoying other brother are going to stick together whatever happens. Always. Right until we're back here for one of us – probably him first because he is such a penis.' Jack breaks to look at Ralph.

And Ralph reaches out for my other shoulder so we're standing heads down and arms locked like a team before the big game.

'All for one,' Ralph says.
'It's his choice,' I say.

When we get back inside, Dad is sitting opposite the doctor's desk. He turns round – almost spins round – with a smile for me and wink for Ralph and Jack as we come in. He's getting the hang of the wheelchair already. He'll be one of those wheelchair veterans whizzing round town in another week or two, I can see, sharp with knowledge of every ramp and lift.

We don't say anything. Dad's instructions as we drove to the doctor's through Zurich with the satnav were not to fuck anything up. But it's hard to see how things could be more fucked-up than they already are. Still, we sit down to one side on this too-low grey sofa and stay silent as per our father's wishes; three brothers, our knees knocking together.

The doctor starts talking about all this stuff I already know – 'the condition of your father's health and matters we have discussed relating to this'. His tone in English is too breezy. He sounds like he's describing the slightly disappointing failure of a much anticipated aerodynamic upgrade on a high-performance car. There's a clock above the desk that ticks just audibly with a relentless sarcasm.

'Of course, as a doctor my first duty is to save life,' he says, 'but here in Switzerland, I have an extra duty that I can perform. Which I am prepared to do in this case.' He presses his palm down on a slim folder in front of him.

I feel so tired; but were I to sleep, it might be for a season or a century; or for ever.

The doctor smiles. 'Three sons,' he says again. 'A lucky man.'

Ralph says: 'Yeah – and we're only just getting to like him.'

'Doctor, can I ask?' Jack begins. 'How long is the prescription valid for?'

'Well, obviously, it is the decision of your father how he goes from here. That's a matter for him in consultation with our friends from Dignitas. They will be calling on him later this afternoon after I have spoken with them. But the prescription remains live for three months.'

'Live,' Ralph says.

'Good to know,' Jack says.

'Well, you have everything from me.' The doctor stands. There is a note of – not of triumph but of *completion* – in his voice that makes me feel additionally sick. 'We have all the necessary reports and these will go alongside the civil documents should you wish to proceed.'

Ralph speaks in a sudden flow of fluent German.

The doctor is unnerved and his temple spasm gives him away again. He answers something that I don't understand before coming forward and bending down in front of Dad – a little too hammily.

'Might as well get something powerful for your ankle, Dad,' Ralph says. 'Just in case. You never know. Could be miles yet to go. Let the doc have a look.'

Awkwardly, gingerly, the doctor removes my father's shoe and then his sock.

Time stalls. The moment feels like every moment condensed into one. But nobody can object. Nobody can do anything other than what they are doing. Which is thinking about the possibility of everything and nothing; the distillation of time; to be or not to be.

The doctor looks at my father's swollen ankle and nods. He is a doctor again. Uncomplainingly, my father accepts his touch. He is a patient again. The doctor moves the joint tentatively this way and that – his fingers feeling for living sinew and bone. We listen to the diagnosis.

'A bad sprain,' the doctor says. 'No worse.'

Ralph says a few more words in German and the doctor nods and goes back behind the desk to write a second prescription.

'Painkillers and one of those surgical socks,' Ralph says to us, neutrally. 'We can get them at the chemist down the street.'

Without the certainty of his English mask, the doctor's voice sounds very different. Now he stands and gives the second prescription to Ralph and then – with unnecessary exactitude in the gesture – he picks up the main folder to hand it across the desk to my father.

When Dad turns to look at me, he has a soft, calm, near-beatific smile.

'Let's go back to the hotel, boys,' he says, sprightly, holding his folder with both hands. 'I think we should all . . .' He regards us with mock admonition – as if we're children who have stayed up too late, which, of course, we are. 'I think we should all have some of their afternoon tea on the hotel roof. And then lie down and get some rest. They do genuine apple strudels.'

The doctor comes round to take the handles of his wheelchair and turns my father towards the door – deft, comradely, affable. But I am up faster than my brothers because I don't want that bastard pushing my father anywhere.

We stand a moment in the spruce-grey reception and the

world feels woozy to me like we're back on the ferry and we're listing. The doctor nods to each of us. There's no need to make another appointment, I'm thinking, no need for follow-up, no need for him to say come back if it doesn't clear up in a few weeks.

'Thank you,' Dad says.

Then I follow my brothers out of the surgery, pushing my father carefully down the ramp, which I'm thinking they must have put in for all the people who come here in wheel-chairs.

For some reason, the old alarm has gone off on the van again – but there's no noise, just the hazard-warning lights flashing feebly.

Later, not long before dusk, we three brothers leave the hotel without our father. We pause a moment on the pavement outside. The staff on the reception desk say that it was the first Opera House with electric lights. So we look across and think about that – for no reason. Then we turn left towards the lake shore.

There is the smell of cooking – a man selling some kind of caramelized nuts. Couples. Roller skates. Bikes chained to the railings. The air is still warm. The lake is like Lalique glass – so still, amethyst-blue and opalescent. They say you should wear a colourful hat if you're going to swim from one shore to the other so the passing boats don't mow you down.

We walk towards the Old Town. They seem to be digging up the roads everywhere. Sparks from the welders working on the tram tracks flash like lightning in their double-dark visors. They say they have found further evidence of the

Roman settlement here. Maybe a customs post. Before that, there was a Celtic settlement. There are digs all over town. And it's all under the city. Layers. Dad would love this, I'm thinking; but he wants some time alone, he says; to sleep.

We went up on the roof and drank tea and then the people from Dignitas came and Dad talked to them. They'll be back again tomorrow morning for another chat before we go.

So we know now.

As much as it is possible to know.

Because, of course, they offer you every opportunity to change your mind. Encourage you to do so. Right up until the last moment. Even in the little blue house of death.

But we know we're going there, at least.

That's the plan.

To the little blue house of death, I mean.

We will need to leave by 10:00 in the morning.

To make our final appointment.

We don't want to be late.

As we walk, I tell my brothers that it's about twenty-five minutes on the train from the station right by the hotel – Stadelhofen – out the door and one hundred metres to the right. Probably why Dad chose the Hotel Ambassador in the first place. I explain that the little blue house is in a small village called Pfäffikon. Out in the country. But that, yes, you can go direct from our station. 'Our' station, I say. Take a cab at the other end. Five minutes. I measure everything in time not distance.

It's not really a house like you'd think, I say, more like this boxy-square two-storey blue building that looks as if it's made out of very expensive corrugated iron. In the middle of an industrial estate. On a semi-rural road called Barzloostrasse.

A field of maize growing opposite. And behind . . . really *close* behind is this massive white warehouse that's three times as tall and maybe three hundred metres long. Gigantic. Looming. Fuck knows what they make there. But it's such a huge building – and so close up against the back – like it's trying to push the little blue house off its tiny square patch of land.

Incongruous doesn't cover it, I say. Such a weird place. Yes, this blue metal-ish building. Like the temporary on-site head office of a fancy urban regeneration project. But surrounded by concealing bushes. And it's not exactly blue, either. More of a grey-blue; ash-blue.

We walk together along the big Quaibrücke, the road-bridge at the head of the Zurich lake. Trams to our right and the shoreline to our left. There are still pedalos and people enjoying being out on the water. The dusk is rising though, and the light is thickening. We can just about see the Alps to the south, the snow like a white crown on the jagged peaks. Or more like the palest possible violet.

And there's a builders' cafe, I tell them, right there, next to the little blue house, which is where all the guys who work in the warehouses go and eat crap for lunch. Also corrugated. And you know what? If you go to the cafe toilet out back – then you can see right into the shitty garden of the Dignitas house and in through the windows. Where the people are having a chat about dying – yes or no. I say 'garden' but really it is just a plant-pot area and a concrete path with what they call a summerhouse at the end except that it doesn't have a view because . . . well, why would they have a view? Why would they want you to see the mountains and the lakes and the sky? Instead, people go out into the pathetic garden and cross this miniature stream. I don't know why. Like it's supposed to be *symbolic*. Beneath the shadow of the massive warehouse.

How do I know all this, my brothers ask.

Dad and I have met people. I've seen their pictures. I've talked to them. We watched a video on a phone, I admit. What do you think we've been doing all this time?

We turn off by the side of what looks like a little canal but which is prettier and more kempt. We are heading for an open-air bar called Rimini beside one of the bathing areas in one of the rivers that flow out of the lake through the back of the old town – a place called Männerbad Schanzengraben. We're following Google Maps on Jack's phone. This is a special place, they say, with wooden steps down into the water. People swim there. The water is drinking clean, they say; it's like a secret garden or an oasis in the middle of the city. Right near the botanical gardens. Enchanted. Magical.

The twilight slips by us somewhere as we go – a brief sepia shadow – and when eventually we find the place, it is already indigo dark and the reflected colour of the bar lights in the water seems especially beautiful. The yellowy-orange halo lamps are smeared and smudged across the surface while a redder light reaches downward like it's way deeper than you can think – or maybe there's a fire in the depths somehow; and then there is some kind of shimmering pale-blue light under the wooden pontoon that reaches out across the water. Where there is no colour, there's just the viscid glistening blackness.

Opposite, in the botanical gardens, the foreign trees with their fat foliage and tall thin tropical trunks form a soaring wall of shadow and light as if there is nothing beyond. Everything smells fresh and without the taint of city or mammal

– as if the purer air of the mountains has been borne here by the river. And I can hear the sound of the water running when I stoop to listen.

The bar itself is like some old Grimms' fairy-tale tavern. There are upright rustic wooden beams along the bank, a pointed wooden roof and rough tables around the wooden pillars. So we order burgers and sit turtle-backed on our stools peeling the labels from our bottles of beer with our fingernails.

That's when I tell them I'm not going.

That's when Jack says – what?

That's when Ralph says – wait.

That's when Jack says he doesn't want to go either, but he's going. Of course he's going.

That's when Ralph says he wants me to come.

That's when I say again I'm not going.

That's when Jack says that you can be for it or against it, Lou, but you have to be there.

That's when Ralph asks – am I against it?

That's when I say you can be for it or against it and *not* be there.

That's when Ralph says – what about Dad?

That's when Jack says all for one. We were always that. All for one.

And I love my brothers because they are the kind of men you do not meet every day.

But that's when I say – no – I'm not going.

I take out the spare key card and the lock clicks and I quietly push open the door. There is some classical music playing and the room is very softly lit by the desk lamp. I can see my father has been writing with his old ink pen. He's lying on the bed, turned away. I can tell that he's awake.

'Lou?'

'Yeah.'

He half turns onto his back so he can see me. 'OK?'

'I'm not coming.'

'Lou.' He raises himself with an effort.

'I'm not coming tomorrow,' I say.

My eyes grow accustomed to the half-light. The pattern of the dim lamp scatters petal-shadows on the wall.

He props himself up. 'I fell asleep,' he says.

'Have you been writing?'

'To you. To your brothers.'

'I'm not coming with you, Dad.'

'Lou, come in. Come on – sit on the bed.'

He's not quite drawn the heavy curtains. The night outside the window is just a narrow strip of darkness. The milky-cataract moon has probably fallen in the lake – blinder and blinder with age.

He indicates beside him. I walk three steps and his old face is looking at me and there's water in his eyes but they're not leaking. His white hair. His beard. The music is so beautiful. He reaches out his hand to me.

There's something between us which I can feel now – something numinous – something that has always been there – only we had no sense of it before, could not feel it quite so tangibly. But now we could both lean into its presence. Something of me and something of him; something more than us both. Something going back a long way.

'Take your shoes off,' he says. 'And sit down.'

I slip off my boots and sit on the bed beside him.

He winces as he moves his leg as though he's got to make room for me even though there's enough space for an entire family.

'Can you get stories on your phone, Lou?'

'What do you mean?'

'Audiobooks?'

'Yeah. Probably.'

'You know what I think we should do?'

'What?'

'Listen to a story. Talk in the morning.'

I meet his eyes for less than an instant. All his dignity is back; the best of him; his endurance and his stoicism.

'How about . . .' He pauses. 'How about Steinbeck? He's the guy we need. The most human writer in the world after you know who.'

'Which book?'

'*Cannery Row*. See if you can find someone good reading it on your phone.'

I search.

'Got it,' I say.

'That was quick.' My father smiles. 'New world, Lou. Brand-new world.'

And I don't know why but it's in my mind, in the room, in my heart. So I just ask: 'How did your dad die?'

He looks across and says the word quietly. 'Dementia.'

The music is so ethereal – it's like they're playing as close as they can get to not playing at all.

'But you know that, Lou—'

'Were you there?'

I feel the bed move because he's nodding with his whole body. His weight. His presence. He speaks softly: 'It was slow. I was up and down to Leeds for a year. Slow and terrible. Worse every time I went back. I nursed him for two weeks straight towards the end. It was the pneumonia that finished him off . . . He had no idea who I was when he died. We were strangers.'

'Were you ever close to him?'

'No . . . Yes . . . No.' He looks at me – a frown of regret, something long gone. His eyes seem deeper set behind the crag of his white-grey brow like they're retreating further inside. 'We were close in a way . . . in the way that there was an entire history between us. All of those shared days – they create a shared world – unique – inside a family.'

'But you didn't talk to him much – when you grew up?'

'No. Not about the outside world. Not really.'

'Not like us.'

'Not like us.'

He looks at me and I look at him.

'Not like us, Lou,' he says again.

The music is ending. We sit side by side.

'Put the story on,' he says.

I press play on the screen and put the phone on the bedside table. Then I lie down beside my dad. The reader says the title – two words – in a friendly voice but a voice that is also full of wonder and promise – like everything that comes next is going to make you so sad and so happy and all you are going to want to do is laugh and cry.

'Paintings on the wall,' Dad says.

Then he puts his hand across so that it's in my hair like when I was little and I close my eyes.

'Speak tomorrow, Lou,' he says.
'Every day, Dad.'

I leave the hotel at nine in the morning wearing just my flip-flops, some shorts and a shirt that I don't want. Nobody knows where – but they know I've gone. It's sunny outside and I have to squint because I don't have my sunglasses.

They won't find me. I turn left and walk quickly as if I'm being followed. I have to wait at the lights to cross the traffic. I can feel the sun prickling on my bare arms. I cross and walk down to the lakeside – on to the thin strip of park and the promenade. The water is glinting. There are hundreds of boats, some tied up with their blue tarpaulins thrown over them, others putting out. It is going to be a beautiful day. People are walking past me, young and old, children running, someone roller-skating. I go past the cafes. I walk beneath the trees and beside the benches.

He did not know it, but the thing that my father taught me – with his life, with his life – the thing that my father taught me is that sometimes you just have to leave people behind in order to go on living yourself. The shrinks say that the emotional logic you don't *want* to pass on to your children is precisely the emotional logic that you do. So maybe it was cruel to bring us, maybe he's a great man of courage, maybe he's a small man of cowardice. But my father left a woman to be with my mother. And that's where I come from – that decision. And sometimes you have to stand up to people – the ones you love just as much as the ones you don't. And sometimes that means you have to walk out on them. Leave them for dead. My brothers – they're still all tangled up; they *have* to go with him – all the way to the bitter end because they can't get clear, they can't get far enough away; no matter where they go, they can't break the chains, they're bound to him all the way to that little blue house. It was never a question of right or wrong, but the road to Zurich is a tortuous one; with fresh torment at every turn. And my brothers . . . My brothers are still trapped in all of that because of who and what they are, because of how and by whom they were made. But I am running free. Yes, I'm free. I can do it. I can cut the rope.

And I'm lucky because it's such a beautiful day on which to be alive.

And I am biting the inside of my cheek so that it hurts like hell. But I keep on going.

And now – just up ahead is where I am headed: Bad Utoquai. It's some kind of belle époque bathing house on the lake. And I'm thinking – there's something really pretty about the place. This lovely old white-painted wood and this elegant ironwork. A single storey, gleaming in the sun. Graceful balconies up above. Parasols. Wooden decks. Tasteful colonnades. The way it reaches out into the water reminds me of one of those paddle steamers on the Mississippi that you see in Tom Sawyer films.

I pay the money and I walk in. Right is women-only, left is men. In the middle, mixed. There are families, couples, singles. I walk out on the wood-stripped decking where people are already sunbathing and reading and sipping drinks from the restaurant. Out on the lake, there are pontoons. The water is slate-blue and seems to move hardly at all – only faintly side to side – like it's been hypnotized by staring too long at the sun.

I take off my shirt and my flip-flops. I stash them under a chair. I walk along the decking, stepping past people where they lie. I walk down the side beneath the colonnades. One of the vast passenger ferries is putting out from the end of the lake. There are many smaller boats.

I reach the ladder. I think about going off the diving board. But it seems too much and instead I climb down the rungs and I feel the cold of the water but I don't want to break the rhythm of my going or show any pain or shock or anything. So I just ease in like it's no problem and then I let go and the lake envelopes me and – in a moment – the water seems warmer and I move away from the ladder on my back and look up at the sky.

Then I turn and I start to swim, the water arcing off my arms and glittering in the light. And I swim a little harder, out past the pontoon. I don't have a bright-coloured cap. No cap at all. And the passenger ship is coming. Lots of boats passing this way and that. But there's a way across – maybe – if I time it right. And I'm swimming easy now and everything sparkles and dances in the water – the beauty of the day and the blue sky. And I'm swimming forward, kicking my legs. And I can feel the sun and the rhythm of my breathing. And I'm swimming across the lake. I'm just swimming away. I'm just swimming.

EPILOGUE

My dear Louis,

Writing to you is the easiest and the hardest. I saved it to last.

It's easiest because you know me the best. And you know how happy I am and how lucky I feel and all the careful consideration and thinking that has gone into this decision. Which is the right thing to do. So definitely don't feel bad on that score. I know you won't. Give it a year and you'll be like all the others we met: it's a great idea! (BTW: if, in time, you felt able to share our experience as widely with others as they shared with us, then I think that may help lots of people; as with so much these days, Britain seems to be in a strange confusion on the issue . . .)

I want you to know that these last days have been among the happiest in my life – I'm not just saying that. The ferry, the Champagne chateau, the campsite conversations, the cave, taking the chequered flag, our excellent dinner (notwithstanding the deserved denunciations), our midnight walk by the Rhine – and yesterday afternoon eating strudel on the roof-garden looking at the mountains when even R and J stepped at last into reality. (Reality: the hardest thing in the world to deal with.) We're so lucky to get that time and in this warm late summer sun! Makes me want to believe in God. (Kidding.) But what I said in the van is

totally true – I am actually grateful both for the disease
and that this way of ending it is available to me. We all die.
It's not really a problem – not at my age – though of course
there is such a sadness inside me that the great dream
is over. (And it does feel more than ever like a fleeting
dream . . .) And yet I believe I am dying in the best possible
circumstances. This is the truth, I promise, and you can
know it when you feel sad.

But of course I don't want you to think of just these
last few days, Lou. I want you to think of our whole lives
together. Think of when you were little. Think of Mum.
Think of the fun and laughter and the silliness we had.
Think of when we played and ate together and went on
trips. The bathtimes. The bedtimes. Swimming in rivers
and lakes. All that we have been and done together.
All we have said. Whatever moments that have stayed
in your mind. If we live on anywhere, it's in the minds of
those we knew and those we loved most of all. So – actually
– don't feel sad. Or not too often!

Yes, keep the best of me from whatever you remember
of our lives together and take it with you in your heart on
your travels.

I've come to believe that a reliable gauge of a person is
how much soul they put into their lives – their capacity for
offering and responding to the deeper feelings and thoughts
and desires. There's a world of difference between the people
who think and feel and enquire; and the people who set
themselves against enquiry and thought. The people whose
hearts are open and generous and the people whose hearts
are closed and calloused. The richer the interior life, the
more beautiful the exterior life; attend to one and the other

will flourish. Apart from that, Louis, be sure to feast on nature's great beauty and humanity's great genius. Treasure your friends, read as much as you can and take the braver choice when there is one.

Your mother taught me two things which I wanted to pass on. (I know she taught you a million more.) The first is to try and see – as she would say – the person behind the behaviour. Those who understand the architecture of how we come to be as we are experience a great liberation and insight. Your mother taught me psychology late in my life and like everything, so much of it is nonsense – but in amidst the rubbish, I found a lot of wisdom and understanding that I wished I'd known when I was a younger man and 'a prisoner of my own personality'. (Her phrase.) How can you know anything if you don't know yourself? The second is to be strong. I don't mean not to lie down in despair from time to time – no, I think secretly all human beings do this in their lives; we all make a mess of things; we all inflict suffering and suffer in return; and the world is brim-full of tragedy, misery and misfortune. I mean be strong in that – even in your bleakest moments – you should believe that you have the resource within you to go past the test, to out-think, to out-feel, to out-last. Strong in that you should know that you will somehow find this resource again even if it's not obvious how or when. Let no one define you and nothing defeat you. My father and his father were the strongest men I ever met in this way – their resilience and their stamina and their determination. You've got all their strength inside you, I promise you that. Without the bad bits, I hope. Or not too many!

Writing to you is the hardest, too, because I love you so very much and without shadow or complication. So I want to thank you for all you have given me, Louis . . . so much, so much. When you were little, a kiss from you was more than all the joy in the world. We had a game, I don't know if you remember, where I would pick you up and you would take me in your tiny arms and squeeze my face to yours and say daaaa . . . dy. There has been no happiness greater than that for me. It's what I will be thinking about when I drink the cup we must all drink.

More than this though, Lou, you made me a more noble man and restored a lot of dignity that I felt I had lost. You've been the main pleasure and the purpose of my later life. And your company these last years has been my great gladness. Most of all, you have helped to heal the division in our family. Look after your brothers as I have asked them to look after you – but be sure to ignore their advice. I'm half joking.

One more thing – choose your life partner carefully and be sure that you love her – it's the biggest decision we make and love goes a lot further than anything else we humans have yet discovered when it comes to the crunch, which it always does one way or another. No two human beings who lived together yet avoided the crunch unless they avoided themselves.

I need to sleep despite myself.

So just this: to say you should keep writing your secret book if you can. Even if it takes you another ten years!

And also this: to say at the last that you're everything that a father could hope for in a son and more. You are my clever, perceptive, beautiful boy with a musical heart and

a poet's soul. You are my spirit's joy and my heart's pride.
My great companion. And I send you my kisses and
wish you always courage and the tempered surety of
your father's love to travel with you wherever you go and
however you feel.

 I love you, Lou. Always and for ever.

  I love you.

   Dad.

ACKNOWLEDGEMENTS

My thanks are long overdue to the people at the Oxford Motor Neurone Disease Care and Research Centre. The patients who generously took the time to tell me about their experiences with such openness. Professor Kevin Talbot whose expertise and insight was invaluable. And the truly wonderful Rachael Marsden whose compassion and generosity of spirit would surely qualify her for honours if only the world were just. Similarly, I owe an un-payable debt to the people who have shared with me their deeply private experiences of Dignitas, even when my questions were painful; in particular, Lesley, for her dignity and her profound humanity.

In terms of the writing, my thanks to my agent Bill. And to my editors: Kris for his assiduousness and advocacy and Paul for his ticks and Cleaver Square wisdom. Likewise to Lucie and Nicholas and all the brilliant folk at Picador. I am grateful to Rachael and Olivia. And for their thoughts on the early pages – to Leo and Kate. I'm indebted to Mark, my boon companion in the labyrinth. Thanks also to Richard for the various hiding places and for a quarter of a century of enthusiasm and friendship. Thanks and solidarity to those of my long-suffering siblings who read, listen, revolt – Hec, Goose, Hugs, Bebs, Widge and Chubb. My heartfelt gratitude to Elisa, who probably helped more than anyone else in making this book a reality. And, of course, thanks unending to Emma who is the sine qua non of my every day.

Finally, in remembrance of MH, philosopher-poet and on-the-road friend. I still hear your poem, Matt, just the way you read it – that day in Saint-Siffret.